THE CHORUS EFFECT

BY RUSSELL BOYD

Kristin-
I thought we'd
already done this. I thought...
I need to quit doubting.

outskirtspress
DENVER, COLORADO

This is a work of fiction. The events and characters described herein are imaginary and are not intended to refer to specific places or living persons. The opinions expressed in this manuscript are solely the opinions of the author and do not represent the opinions or thoughts of the publisher. The author has represented and warranted full ownership and/or legal right to publish all the materials in this book.

The Chorus Effect

V3.0 R1.0

Edited By William Boyd and Cara Lockwood

Outskirts Press, Inc.
http://www.outskirtspress.com

ISBN: 978-1-4787-5032-1

Library of Congress Control Number: 2015908815

PRINTED IN THE UNITED STATES OF AMERICA

CHAPTER ONE

The trouble with spontaneously-composed victory songs is that they tend not to make sense. Joy can be pretty distracting, which is why five minutes after his three verse/three chorus masterpiece, Chintz couldn't recall a word of it. He began a spontaneously-choreographed dance instead, moving down the sidewalk as if it were his partner, all powdered up and pressed and rehearsed in full.

It had been a very good day.

On a whim, Chintz hopped three times on his left foot, bringing his right foot down to tap the path each time in a graceful manner that was uncharacteristic. The steps rained down from his brain and flowed to his feet, evaporating behind him in a hydrological cycle of celebration. *Isn't it just perfect,* he thought, *that my revenge might come on such a beautiful day?* He turned backwards and began to perform four or five gleeful hops, not pausing at all to notice the fading brightness of the yellow-white sun that lacked all that retina-rending harshness it shouldn't have lacked. The sparse clouds which he pranced along under were satisfyingly puffy.

He almost regretted that he had stopped after only two

glasses of merlot at his victory dinner. A merlot always put him in a good mood, even on days when he had not known the... the... *rapture* of cosmic justice. And now the leftover tannins bounced around his mouth, leaping over one another to see what all the fuss was about and drying his mouth out in the process.

He topped the small hill that stood at the edge of his block, his skull a tumble of dopamine and serotonin, if not saliva. The sun at his back was slowly falling lower into the sky. His almost-neighbor Caroline sat out on her front steps with her six-month-old triplets.

"My," she said. "You look happy."

Chintz guffawed in what could have been considered a slightly vaudevillian fashion. He contented himself with kissing each of the triplets on top of their sleeping heads only because he suspected he would have been arrested if he had juggled them. Usually, Chintz was even more nervous talking to Caroline than he was talking to other human beings. But not today.

He wiggled one eyebrow at her in a way that he hadn't seen confident people do, but that he thought maybe they should. "Afternoon, mi'lady," he said, taking her hand. "Attending the ball this evening?"

Caroline gave him a pleasant smile. There was no ball, this or any other evening.

"I'm waiting for mom to come by," she said. "She's supposed to keep the triplets while Quincy and I have a movie night. And you?"

Chintz dropped her hand gently. He was careful not to let the mention of stupid Quincy break through his wall of happiness. He had his revenge today! Work would never be the same!

"Revenge!" he yelled in Caroline's pretty face.

"Chintz," she replied calmly. "Please don't yell. You'll wake the babies."

Chintz was suddenly sheepish and felt a little of his normal nervousness return. "Sorry. I'm just really happy."

"I see that." She smiled again. "So what happened?"

Chintz shrugged his shoulders up next to his ears. Should he tell her? He often told Caroline things that he didn't tell anyone else. But maybe he should wait. He still couldn't believe it himself. *Revenge!*

Instead of yelling again, he said softly. "Um, I think I'll just tell you later. When the babies are awake."

"Okay," she said.

With a dramatic whisk, Chintz turned and picked up his dance precisely where he had left off. "Balloooo!" he yelled towards the front door of his neighbor Carter, whom he hated even more than Quincy. He was still only a few feet from the sleeping babies, and one of them began to stir. He gave a guilty look back at Caroline, and she glared at him good-naturedly.

A fat face appeared in the window of the house to his left. It was Carter, who was not actually fat except in the face area.

"Stop with all the, you and all the, what's with! Don't be damn 'balooing' already! I was taking a nap!"

This last bit of bellowing woke up the other two triplets, who began fussing at their unwelcome consciousness. Caroline picked one of them up and turned her pleasant glare on Carter, who returned it in a much less pleasant way.

Time for me to continue my celebration alone, Chintz thought. He turned back towards his own house and fully sprinted down the path towards his front steps — remembering, of course, to lean into the finish.

Chintz composed himself and walked into his unlocked house. That he did so was a bit mysterious, since only he and his cat Platelet resided there, and Platelet was not known for her sensitivity to the mood of nearby beings. Suffice it to say, the level of composure of the man who fed her was of little importance to the only other inhabitant of Chintz's house. This turned out not to matter, however, because the inside of Chintz's house was not.

Ambiguity. It haunts even the most casual of readers from time to time. It is assumed by even the least arrogant of authors that his audience is of above-average intelligence, and certainly by those of us who fall probably somewhere in the middle. But the smarter, more well-read, and nerdier a reader may be, the more he or she will be bothered by vague statements that could, frankly, mean anything.

The inside of Chintz's house was not? Not what? What, exactly, does it mean to describe something as "not?" Surely it means that it doesn't exist, but common experience and inductive reasoning would lead us to believe that entire areas of space are inoculated by the laws of physics against such pronouncements. The main character in this young story (Chintz, I believe it was?) walked into his house, the outside of which, we assume, "was" and then the inside "was not?"

"I thought that one neighbor was going to cause trouble," one might say. One might further say, "And, hey, can we get back to Caroline? She sounds hot."

And indeed she is. She's married to Quincy,

though. We'll find out later if this love interest works out, but that will have to be put on hold for the moment, as there is nothing inside Chintz's house. Not just no furniture, but in fact no space at all.

No space? Am I reading this correctly?

Yes.

CHAPTER TWO

CHINTZ STEPPED BACK outside his house and looked at the color and shape of it. They matched his memories splendidly. The one wall he had repainted on the side last summer (left side, when facing the front door from the street) still radiated newness and professionalism, while the other three sides still peeled in the sun with inviting charm. The number painted on his sidewalk in front of his house for only $23.99 was, in fact, his address. It was definitely his house. He stepped back inside-ish.

"Barbara?" he called, again mysteriously since it has already been established that he lived alone with Platelet. He took a few steps into the darkness. No, darkness would be the wrong way to describe the area where his furniture and living space should have been; it was more of an emptiness that refused to reflect light, as if one's eyeball suckled in vain for even a trickle of photons and came up dry. He walked slowly into the void and was startled to almost immediately smack his face into something.

Reaching out to feel in front of him, his fingers brushed against something hard and smooth. Next to that seemed to be something fuzzy, followed by a half tube with cool water standing in it. Perplexed, he tried again to peer into the not-darkness. He glanced behind him at his front door, still open. There was the rest of the world outside, waiting patiently for him. He touched the odd combination of shapes and textures in front of him. Had he not spent two months one summer in high school as a terrible home builder, he would have never realized that it was part of the inside of the wall at the back of his house. Half of a pipe, insulation, and wood. He touched the wood again. The supporting beam had no defined edge on the side nearest to him. Although he could feel the wood on this side, it had no boundary, no satisfying dimension where molecules of wood ended and those of air began. It just seemed to fade into existence.

This revelation made Chintz wonder why he was able to enter his house at all. A quick glance at his feet told him that his floor actually did exist a few steps into his home. Well, maybe not *his* floor. This floor was shiny blue, disgustingly clean and smooth. Chintz reached down to touch it and found that it squeaked like a mouse when he ran his finger down it. He could imagine how a steady flow of water, good friends, and some margaritas could make a few dozen descending feet of this material into a Summer Water Slide Extravaganza. The outside light from his open door illuminated the blue sheen enough to show that it did, in fact, extend for at least a few dozen feet down a path to the right of his front door.

Chintz stood at a loss in his own home, or what had once been his home. He had only drank two glasses of wine, hadn't he? He took out his phone for light and crept dramatically up the blue path that began at his front door, careful to bend his knees for supplemented structural integrity. The steep grade began to curve slightly to the right ahead, and he strained to see into the emptiness. The phone light was sucked into the void. He gave his eyes a break and instead strained his ears for a few seconds and heard nothing but the squeak of his shoes on the blue material. This continued on for some time, and he was about to turn back and take a break from the stupid straining when around a sharp curve, something appeared.

This something was sort of another door. Sort of. It certainly didn't look anything like his front door, but it seemed as if it might open, and the shiny blue path led right to it. The door looked like a regular door had called it quits for the day and had reclined to nap for a while. The top of it was shoulder high on Chintz, and it was wide enough to roll a dead llama through. In the center of the top was an octagonal dip that made it resemble a pair of goggles.

The misshapen door was made of the same shiny blue material as the floor, but as Chintz shone his cell phone light along it, he found that it was much softer, almost like clay. This softness increased as he reached further to the sides of it. Running his fingers along it, he looked for moving parts but found none. Uncertain of the sturdiness of this material or the depth of the door, Chintz began, like a randy pubescent, to force his fingers in wherever they would go. Sure enough the edges soon began to give, and light shone through after just a few inches. He discarded the blue clay and began to burrow frantically as it crumbled in his hands. When there was a large enough opening for his head, he peeked through it.

The shiny blue of the pathway continued through the small opening and poured itself into the well-lit room, covering the walls, floor, and ceiling with the latter rising up several feet above Chintz's head. Multi-colored objects that looked suspiciously like fuzzy chairs covered the floor, and there was a large, bright red box in the corner. From his vantage point on the pathway, he couldn't see another door that might lead from the room.

Chintz paused to reflect. Should he just turn back? Are there authorities who should be notified when your home becomes a strange inter-dimensional portal? Just what the hell is protocol in these situations? The stress of the moment caused his lips to itch, and he scratched them furiously. He should turn back. He may never know what is beyond this one room. He may not live long enough to find out.

He didn't know where Platelet was.

Peeking through at the fuzzy chairs and blueness, Chintz pictured the rest of the scene inside. Had his stupid cat been captured by an advanced alien civilization? For that matter, he suddenly realized, maybe Platelet had been vaporized along with the rest of the inside of his house when this spaceship (he now wanted to think of it as a spaceship) had landed itself rudely in the interior and interrupted Chintz's life. This reminded him that his copy of *Pride and Prejudice* had been sitting on his nightstand and that, after three years, he was nearly halfway through it and felt he was on a roll. *Damn these giant aliens,* he thought, *vaporizing cats and literary classics with no regard or consideration.* They probably had giant insect eyes. They probably used evil metal instruments. Or maybe, he pondered with a wild-eyed surge of antipathy, they were short slimy things that might fit through a door this size. A quick check of the room revealed no slime, but Chintz couldn't be sure. It was certain that this was a den of inhuman activities. They were probably hairy.

Gritting his teeth with resolve, Chintz changed his eyes from circles to narrow slits and crawled through the blue clay door. He stood up, brushed the blue from his clothes, and looked around. The entire room was no more than a hundred square feet, or rather round feet as it was a cylinder that met at the top with a flat, round ceiling. Aside from the red box and the strange furniture, there was a circular hole on the side of the room opposite the blue, sideways door. He still saw no exits aside from the short door through which he had just crawled. Determined to find his hairy, slimy, insect-eyed captors, he turned to find, instead, standing with its back to him, a small Caucasian human child.

CHAPTER THREE

CHINTZ HAD VERY little experience with children. There were none in his family. He had been raised sibling-free by a doting mother who, while not exactly spoiling him, gave him nearly all of her attention. As her only child, he had been her entire life. Chintz, on the other hand, didn't know how these little creatures stayed alive without breaking. It wasn't that he disliked children, but rather that he was unsure what to make of them. This particular one seemed to be very young, perhaps around two years old.

Visions of ghosts filled his mind, of lonely abandoned houses where demons in the shape of children walked for millennia in search of a victim. He had seen a movie once where a woman woke to find a beautiful child in her living room, but when the child turned around it was eating human entrails, its innocent face covered in blood and bits of organs. The visions in his mind were replaced with a white, faceless terror, and the hairs on the back of Chintz's neck stood on end to help scare the terrors away.

The child turned at this moment and stared silently at the intruder.

Chintz stared back. Nothing happened.

After a moment, the child spoke.

"Fuswah," it said, and laughed. After a brief bouncy dance that Chintz would have assumed, in an older human, to be a grave religious ritual, it ran over to one of the fuzzy chairs and began humping it madly.

This, thought Chintz, *is exactly what I was afraid of.* He waited in vain for the child to stop humping and, giving up, decided to explore the room a little more.

If a baby human lived here, then grown-up humans lived here. If grown-up humans lived here, they must have had a way to get in and out. He glanced over at the red box in the corner. *Hmmmm. No entrance or exits, but something is stored here.*

Chintz walked over to the bright red box and opened it slowly and carefully, as if it were an armed explosive device. Peering cautiously into the darkness inside, he was startled to find an actual armed explosive device. At least, it looked like the armed explosive devices he had seen in the movies. A tumble of wires tangled itself in reds and yellows and greens around a few ominous looking cylinders. A mysterious little digital box flashed a red light at him with mocking regularity. He glanced back up at the baby-child person, who had begun jumping up and down while spinning around in a circle. *What kind of person leaves a kid alone in a room like this?* He carefully closed the box and turned around.

The child was gone.

Hmmmm.

Chintz glanced around the room. He peeked behind a chair.

"Barbara?"[1]

There was no answer. He glanced up at the curved wall next to where the child had been spinning. There was the mysterious circle he had noticed earlier staring back at him. He tried to look through it and found a space, too small for him to crawl through, extending back as far as his arm could reach. Inside was nothing but darkness.

Hmmmm.

Strolling among the assortment of fuzzy chairs, Chintz was at a loss. With no place to go and the unexplained absence of his one human contact, he had the choice of returning to what was apparently only the outside of his home or remaining in a strange blue room that seemed suited only for recreational drug use.

"Fuswah."

Chintz turned to find the baby standing right behind him.

"Okay," he said.

The baby stared at him. Not only was the child less scary now, but it looked so cute that Chintz wanted to squeeze it like a doomed simpleton petting a puppy.

"Where did you go, baby?" he asked.

"Fuswah," the baby replied, and held out a hand to the strange circle.

"Ah," Chintz said. He was just beginning to suspect that he

1 There is absolutely no character in this story named Barbara. If the reader is the type who strives to keep names straight as stories unfold, please keep space in your mind for the next name that is mentioned and not this one. Chintz just says things for no reason. If you are looking for a Barbara, you will have to look elsewhere.

had actually used this room for that which it seemed best suited when the child's hand began to smoke in yellowish-orange colored plumes. The smoke thickened and then rushed quickly into the weird circle on the wall as if it were being sucked by a state-of-the-art vacuum cleaner that would have made a 1950s housewife weak-kneed with desire. The smoke then rushed back into the room and crowded around him.

"Okay," repeated Chintz, and glanced back down at the baby only to find that the child had been replaced by more of the yellow smoke. Just as he was about to panic, the smoke cleared, and he became aware that the child was standing next to him again.

But this was a different room. Chintz now found himself standing in a long hallway that curved away in both directions. Everything still seemed to be of a shiny material, but here it was a pleasant green color. There was no fuzzy furniture. And two male voices were speaking just around the corner, out of his line of sight.

"How long has it been here?" demanded the voice.

"I'm uncertain," replied a second. "If you'll recall, I was in your company up until a very few minutes ago, at which time I communicated the appearance of this directly to you. I'm sure Chorus will be able to provide further information to you in the near future." The first voice seemed impatient, the second contained a mild English inflection that drifted lazily about the room to find an ear to hang around in.

"Well, we have to do something about it, don't we?"

"Undoubtedly, sir."

They've found me, Chintz thought, his eyelashes reaching skyward. *The insect aliens and their possessed baby have discovered my whereabouts and know I have invaded their spaceship. They've, um, learned English, and one has even, er, gotten the accent of a particular region down. And now they are going to torture me or something. Probably.*

The illogicality of Chintz's hypothesis began to sink in, and the adrenaline and other chemicals churning around in his brain activated circuits of confusion and wonder. Memory banks of his earlier fears lit up, briefly flashed to a rather rose-colored version of the second of two times he had had sex in college (omitting the embarrassing last few minutes), bounced back to wonder, and finally settled down to activate that part of his consciousness that focuses on listening intently.

The baby had doubled over and was now attempting to eat something unidentified off of the floor. The conversation resumed.

"This is an entire house." The first voice was back. "There has to be some explanation. You're sure that you and Chorus had the calculations exact? I mean, an entire house where our laboratory used to be."

"The nature of this piece of architecture has not eluded me. And there is always a chance of error, sir. Calculations are not necessarily why we have Chorus as a full-time member of the team, as they are not her strong-suit. The probabilities involved in this outcome are, further, an amalgamation of Schrodinger's equation with Stone's theorem, which will append to the uncertainty."

Chintz grew uncharacteristically brave and peeked around the curve of the hallway. Only the backs of two men were visible. The owner of the first voice sighed. "I invented this particular machine, Sam. I know how it works, and it's not supposed to work like this. We've been doing this for nearly a decade now, and this has never happened before. I guess now we'll just have to deal with it in the morning." Chintz's temporary bravery had run its course, and he retreated back out of sight, nearly tripping over the dining baby. *Okay, the one on the right who talks fancy is Sam,* he thought. With only their backs to him, he hadn't been able to discern any further details. He waited for his courage to grant him a few more seconds of peeping.

"You invented them with my assistance, I'd add," came the lightly British accent of Sam. "And although we have been Grafting for nearly a decade, this particular project is new. I'd further like to remind you, sir, that a decade is, cosmically speaking, a negligible amount of time, and that more and more unexpected results are likely to play out as we continue the project." Sam became suddenly alert. "Sir!" he cried.

"What the hell..."

Chintz's courage urged him to stick his head around the curved green wall to see what was causing the commotion for Sam and Mr. Impatient. He now saw they were standing in front a huge doorway that met the ceiling of the curved hall, and this doorway was apparently the scene of the new commotion. Platelet the cat materialized metaphorically in between the two men, causing Chintz to yell "Oh!" and hop excitedly. The cat had her ears set so far back that they seemed to be following her, and her tail, normally sleek and smooth as a garden snake, looked more like a recently blow-dried gerbil. She turned towards Sam menacingly, whirled her body sideways in what she apparently thought was a threatening manner, and executed a series of little hops. Sam stepped back in dignified alarm.

"Platelet!" Chintz shouted dramatically, a slight quiver in his voice, and reached out for his lost pet.

The cat turned towards her owner in desperation and, seeing a shape she recognized, careened in its general direction with wild-eyed abandon. Platelet became, again metaphorically, a fuzzy streak that made a straight line towards Chintz, leaping at the last moment onto his leg and sticking there.

"We seem to have a visitor, sir," said Sam.

The cat clung to his leg in what would have been, in the absence of adrenaline, a painful manner, and Chintz found himself face to face with the owners of the voices. The body belonging to the voice of Sam was tall and straight and dressed smartly in a black suit that would have looked at home on an international spy in the early 1960s. The man looked as if he were of Indian or Middle Eastern decent (Chintz lived too far west of these regions to know the difference). The hairless head that sat improbably on top of the body seemed disproportionately large and bulged at the top and front. Large veins pulsed and throbbed. The owner of the other voice was shorter but just as straight and was dressed in a white lab coat only a few shades lighter than his skin. The man had graying-sandy hair, a large bushy mustache, and a gaze that cut right through our silly, meta-fictional side discussion of metaphors. He looked like the sort of man that had a messianic complex, father issues, and several doctoral degrees to assist him in dealing with these problems. He managed to look calmly in control and dangerously violent at the same time.

"Hello," he said. "Did you just yell the word 'Platelet?'"

Chintz nodded.

"I see. Would you mind telling me why you yelled that and how you came to appear in our compound?"

Chintz felt his courage flee back to wherever it is that courage is stored. "Platelet is my cat," he said weakly, and attempted to reach down and pet Platelet affectionately. In addition to being well below arm's length, Platelet was frozen as still as a statue, her ears now pointing directly out in opposite directions and her eyes in a scowl that trembled slightly like that of a worried anime character. Chintz tried to bend down at the waist to complete his awkward stroke and succeeded in moving the skin of his leg enough to drag at least three of Platelet's claws through it for a few centimeters. Chintz snapped upright and looked at the men with raised eyebrows and awaited his fate.

Sam spoke once more, his chin held high and steady. "I think that perhaps..."

"Yes," the man in the lab coat cut in. "This has to be related." Keeping his gaze on the intruder with the cat attached to his leg, the man stroked his mustache and looked thoughtful.

Sam turned his huge head towards the man and resumed his scolding. "As I had earlier indicated, Doctor, we are taking on too much at once. My admiration for your ambitious endeavors is unequaled, of course, but I believe you have allowed your comfort with our environment to interfere with your judgment. Our expansion is growing overly large for us to maintain an accurate inventory of the contents thereof." He gestured eloquently at Chintz. "And clearly we have overlapped with this odd man's home."

The Doctor closed his eyes. "Dammit, Sam, we don't know how long we have left to do these things, and I feel we have a responsibility to use this opportunity. We've talked about this many times." He seemed to be attempting to come across as stoically overcome with emotion, like a king who was about to lose a war.

"Again, sir, ten years is a less than ample amount of time to learn the idiosyncrasies of that which we have created. This place in itself could be studied by teams of scientists for decades without further experimentation transpiring within. I believe a fifth project is..."

"Okay, okay. But now we have to..." The men continued to argue and talk over one another while Chintz and his catatonic pet waited patiently at their side. This conversation, while slightly annoying, was nothing like the nightmarish-terrors he had feared earlier. The baby, who was now actually licking the floor, ignored all of them.

Now at a forty-five degree angle from the large doorway, Chintz was able to see what had appeared in the bickering men's "compound." Rather than an actual doorway, they stood next to a large opening in the wall, which looked as if it had been cut cleanly from some other space. Chintz looked past the men and was astonished to see his own couch in the room behind them. Behind the couch was an out-of-style pattern of wallpaper that looked distinctly familiar. "That's my house!" he shouted, again dramatically. The two men turned towards him.

"Stop yelling," the mustached man commanded, his eyebrows jumping up during the first word and descending during the second in a manner that displayed that they had no intention of being disobeyed. "What is your name?"

"Chintz." said Chintz, his voice returned to the land of the sane.

"Well, Chintz, my name is Dr. Mitch Morley, and this is Sam. I'm afraid we've inadvertently caused this to happen, and for that I apologize. Do you know how long you have been here, or how you came to be here? I know that's an odd question, but these are odd circumstances."

"Ah. I suppose only about half an hour or so. I went home and there was...Ow!...nothing."

"Nothing?"

"Well, the outside looked normal, but there was nothing on the inside. Then I walked, um, for a while and then, well, there was this baby," he gestured towards the baby, "and he turned to smoke and, uh, I think I did too, and then I was... here. And that's my house."

The man's sandy eyebrows scowled in puzzlement. "I see."

There was a brief pause as the Doctor stared at Chintz, Chintz stared at the Doctor, Sam stood at regal yet unfocused attention, and the baby continued with the licking. Platelet had now closed her eyes and relocated the tremble to the rest of her body, which recommenced the vibration with renewed ardor.

"This will not be resolved tonight, sir," Sam said. "And I would dare to opine upon the moral obligation of us to provide accommodations."

Dr. Morley sighed. "Good idea. Chintz, please remove your cat from your leg and follow Sam. He will see to it that you have a place to stay for the evening. Forgive me for being abrupt, but we were just about to go to bed and didn't expect this. It looks like we have some things to figure out. Although we are not, technically speaking, orbiting a sun anywhere so there is no day or night, we do attempt to stay on the same sleep schedule and are now in the evening hours." His voice became softer somehow, although Chintz couldn't have described the audible difference. "I can only imagine how strange and frightening this is to you. I'm not sure if we can tell you what has happened here or what we are all going to do now..." Pausing, he looked at the ceiling and grabbed his hair with one hand, exhaling loudly. "Well, rest assured, no one is going to hurt you. I don't know what we are going to do. Chorus?"

"Yes?" responded a pleasant female voice from somewhere above. The voice seemed to come from all directions, as if through a sound system that spanned the ceiling.

"Is there an obvious place where we can put this poor man until—"

From behind Dr. Morley came a clearing of the throat that could have been part of the training of a young member of royalty learning to hold court. "If I may, sir, offer the weakest of suggestions. Rather than escorting our guest to an already used area of the compound, we could, perhaps, let him retire to his house."

"We don't have time to send him back, Sam! You just said as much. It will take at least a few hours, if it's possible at all and it's already...Oh! Yes, I see." The Doctor turned towards Chintz as if it had been his idea all along. "Since your house seems to have become Grafted onto our workspace, you may stay there for the night."

Chintz found himself relieved to be granted permission from this stranger to sleep in his own home. Or at least the inside of it, even if the outside of it was still...

"Grafted?"

Dr. Morley smiled as if he were glad Chintz had asked. "There are quite a few mysteries that would need to be explained for me to help you comprehend that idea. However, suffice to say that we have, accidentally, transposed the space of your home into that of one of our laboratories. Where the space of our laboratory has been transposed remains a mystery, but that is, I suppose, none of your concern. Sam, please show them to their quarters." With that, Dr. Morley turned and headed through a doorway further down the hall.

"Them?" said Chintz. He looked behind him to make sure no one was standing there. They weren't.

"Of course sir," began Sam. "If Mr. Chintz would allow me to draw back the shades that have fallen upon his constitution, I believe the Doctor was referring to both you and your pet here. Now I must further ask that you follow me the dozen or so steps to your dwelling. You will excuse me if I don't show you to your room, as I don't know where it is, and you, I presume, do. You will, if possible, be returned to your home tomorrow, along with the contents thereof. We have no interest in keeping you here or harming you. If anything is required tonight which your home does not already possess in its inventory, please allow me to be illuminated further with your presence."

Sam appended his speech with the smallest of bows and turned to follow the path of Dr. Morley.

Without thinking, Chintz took a painful, leg-clawing step towards the gaping opening to his home. Platelet suddenly came alive again and unfastened herself, glaring bravely at Sam's backside as it exited. She then jumped at something invisible a few inches to her left, tore at top speed into Chintz's house, and ran halfway up the wall of his living room. She appeared to be terrified of her own actions because she then ran back down the wall and crashed into the coffee table, next to which she fell asleep a few seconds later.

Chintz stood very still in the green hallway and gathered his thoughts. Now that he knew he was in no immediate danger, he felt a slight thrill of excitement to run down his spine. He hadn't had an adventure in many years. Unless, of course, you counted his victory from that afternoon. And what a victory! He allowed himself to make a face like Superman.

A small sound made him turn around. The baby was standing behind him, grinning and making small happy noises. Its abandonment by the other residents of the building seemed to bother it not at all. He pointed at Chintz. "Night night?"

Chintz stared uneasily at the toddler. "Ah. Where do you sleep?" he asked.

"Night night!" yelled the baby, and ran into Chintz's house. Chintz followed, walking through the large opening and into his living room. Platelet remained asleep by the coffee table, next to the copy of Pride and Prejudice that had been knocked off during her collision. The baby was already lying on the couch, snuggling one of the throw pillows like a bedtime companion and sucking its thumb. Chintz thought it was a he, maybe. Maybe not. Can't ever tell about these children.

Unsure what else to do, Chintz walked around the corner to his bedroom. He had nowhere else to go, and he wasn't sure how to get back out the way he had come in anyway. Glancing around the room, he saw that everything appeared normal. He threw his clothes in a corner and jumped into his bed. It was still just after sundown on his schedule so he lay awake for quite a while digesting his situation.

What did the Doctor mean by "not orbiting a sun?" Maybe he could go back to his own home tomorrow. He glanced around his bedroom again. Well, maybe he and his home could — or the inside could go back to...Chintz closed his eyes in bewilderment and tried to give up and relax. At least he didn't have to go to work tomorrow. He wondered if he would be fired. Thinking of work made him want to continue pondering his revenge earlier that day, and he turned his contemplations in that direction. He was finally lulled to sleep by the gentle, rhythmic squeak of his couch pillow being humped far into the night.

CHAPTER FOUR

CHINTZ AWOKE TO the sound of classical music piped in through the sound system of the area directly outside his home. Removing Platelet from his face, he sprang out of bed and walked out of his bedroom and into the living room. The baby was nowhere to be seen, and the large opening that had taken the place of his foyer was still gaping. He ran back to his room, threw on some clothes, and hurried out of his house, almost colliding with Sam as he ran into the green hallway of the compound.

"Pardon me," Sam said, his face a brown mask of dignity. "While it is not my intention to halt your frenzied impulsion, your participation is requested in the other room as we deliberate the best course of action regarding your home appearing in our facility. Breakfast will also be served."

Sam stared calmly at Chintz, who realized that he was now expected to reply to this. "Thank you," said Chintz, in an attempt to mimic the dignified delivery. "That will be all, gentlemen. Dismissed."

The armor of Sam's poise was pierced briefly by this statement, though he recovered quickly. "Yes. Well. When you are ready, we will be meeting in the room at the end of the hall." With that, he strode towards the door he had referenced and disappeared through it. Chintz stood still in the middle of the hall for a moment and, having nothing else to do, followed him.

He opened the door slowly and peeked in to see a heavily-carpeted room, which bore little resemblance to the ultramodern décor that had been his experience with this strange place thus far. A large wooden table laden with an assortment of appropriate breakfast items took up the center, and a nearby door led to what he assumed was a kitchen, since a refrigerator stood next to it. Around the table sat Sam, Dr. Morley, and a mature looking woman that Chintz had not seen the night before. She had a hardened look, and her hair was pulled back in a short ponytail that made it look as if she had a small broom sticking out of the back of her head. Sam and the Doctor continued eating as if they hadn't noticed him enter. The woman, however, froze what she was doing and cut her eyes stealthily towards the new intruder. After her profile examined Chintz for a full three seconds, she whisked her entire body towards him with the enthusiasm of one about to burst into song.

"You made it!" she hollered in a coarse voice, allaying his suspicions that hers had been the pleasant female voice that had addressed the Doctor from overhead the night before. She leapt to her feet and traversed the small distance between them in what can only be described as a mall-walk. She grinned up at him toothily and scrunched up her nose. "I've been so excited! They just told me you were here a half hour ago, and they wouldn't let me wake you up until you arose on you own recognizance." She leaned in close to him. "I told them I knew you would be up early, since the way they described you, you sounded like a bit of a feather." Her grin got toothier, and she squinted her eyes into little slits that made a silent laugh. Chintz now saw that what made her look mature was not so much her age, but a roughness of character, an informality of presentation.

Mall-walking back to her seat, she beckoned behind her without looking and gestured towards an empty chair. Chintz noticed as he moved towards the chair that what he had previously taken to be wood was actually a brownish synthetic material of some kind which made up the table.

"Thank you for joining us," Dr. Morley said as Chintz sat down in a daze and picked up an unclaimed muffin. "I trust you slept well?"

Chintz stared at the man and tried very hard not to sound like he was being a smart-ass. "It's, um, my bed. So, yes, thank you."

Dr. Morley smiled and shook his head as if this situation were as strange to him as it was to Chintz. "Of course it was. Well, I need to talk to you about some things. As I mentioned last night, we have the problem of deciding what to do now that your house has become part of our building. Clearly, we cannot just send you back to your house, which quite literally has no space in it. We somehow inadvertently transferred that space here, and, as I said before, it was certainly not our intent. There has been some debate..." — here he glanced meaningfully at Sam— "...about how much we can tell you about what you have stumbled into. But I do have a few questions for you as well."

The Doctor took a deep breath as if preparing for something. He looked up from his breakfast and met Chintz's eyes, studying him. The intensity was astounding, and Chintz, his mouth full of muffin, glanced away uncomfortably, only to be sucked back in again. The symphony from the sound system above dipped into a valley of flute-ridden tranquility. The Doctor's voice became proportionately quieter. "What do you think about what you have seen? Do you have curiosity about this? Do you just want things to go back to normal, or do you find yourself excited about a break from the monotony of your life? Are you in a hurry to get back to your television and see your favorite reality show and perhaps see how some people you have never met are doing in their relationships and rehabilitations? Or do you want to use that brief window of consciousness you have that is called life and experience something?"

The others at the table continued with their breakfast and made it perfectly clear that they were pretending not to be listening. Chintz looked at the Doctor again. "I'm curious," he heard himself say in a whisper. He cleared his throat in embarrassment at what seemed to have become such an important moment with a stranger on this weird spaceship-ish thingy.

Relief washed visibly over Dr. Morley's body as if those words had given him hope for humanity. "I don't mean to imply that you have nothing going on in your life. No doubt you have people you love, achievements to work towards, goals and dreams, and things which you have already built that must be maintained." He looked questioningly at Chintz, who quickly scarfed down the remainder of his muffin.

"Well, I did have a really good day at work yesterday."

"I'm glad to hear that. And where do you work?"

"At a software company—"

"Ha ha ha! Kitty!" shrieked the woman. She was leaning under the table and petting Platelet, who tolerated the attention stoically. The others ignored her.

"Do you love to do this? Work in software?" asked Dr. Morley. The intense gaze returned, and he leaned forward towards Chintz.

"Well, sometimes," Chintz said, glancing away again. "I mean, I'm pretty good at it. The pay is just okay though, and sometimes I feel like I could be doing something more important."

"More important. What are some things you feel are important?"

Feeling like he was at a high pressure job interview, Chintz paused with his mouth open and watched the odd lady pet his cat. His usual modus operandi when feeling pressure was to say something strange to throw everyone else off balance and make himself feel in control of the situation. For some reason, though, he couldn't bring himself to do this with the Doctor. As if the truth were being expelled out of him like an overdue and healthy defecation, he blurted out "People. Animals. Beauty. Experiences that you can't just have every day."

Dr. Morley smiled and glanced at Sam, who got up and left the room where Chintz had come in. "Those are good things," the Doctor said, leaning back. "A bit vague and broad in scope, but who am I to focus your priorities? The thing is, Chintz, that we need help with one of our projects here, and we need a certain kind of person to do it. All of us here, I think, are alike in the possession of a few qualities, and I had to see if you had some of these qualities. I'm not sure if you caught it last night, but we have stumbled, some time ago, upon some opportunities that I would like to see through. We have a few projects we have undertaken. I'll tell you about one." He gazed into the distance for a few seconds until Chintz began to wonder if someone were painting a picture of them.

"Too many people," the Doctor said, sipping his coffee, "ride a wave from the moment they are born to when they die. They think they are catching no breaks or catching all the breaks or catching some, and their life becomes a series of breaks that..." He paused, setting his coffee down, and leaned towards Chintz again. "Tell me. Do you believe in free will?"

Behind the Doctor, Chintz noticed the baby precariously balanced on the counter attempting to stick its finger into an electrical outlet. "Um. The baby is..."

"The baby will be fine," Dr. Morley said without turning to look. "Please. Free will. Do you believe yourself to possess it?"

Expecting each second to inhale the scent of fried baby, Chintz said distractedly, "Well...um. I guess. I mean, I feel like I make my own choices. Do you mean instead of some god or demon controlling me and everyone else?"

"No. Well, I suppose that too." The Doctor closed his eyes and covered them with one hand. "Even," he said, peek-a-booing out from under his hand, "among the devoutly religious, there are very few of the tens of thousands of belief systems that have humankind as puppets for the amusement of a deity. Most of us feel that we are the authors of our actions. If someone offers you ice cream and asks, 'will you have chocolate or vanilla,' you tend to feel that you make that choice and, choosing chocolate, you could have picked vanilla. Does that make sense to you?"

"Yes," Chintz said. The damn baby was gone again. Glancing around the table, he noticed that the mall-walker was gone too. They were alone at the table. The music reached a dazzling crescendo.

"The fact is, many, many things are going on in your brain. I can't say for certain that I said chocolate and vanilla as an example just now because I wanted to or because someone used that same example with me at some point or because I saw it on a TV show once or because the part of my brain that stores memories of ice cream had coincidental extra blood flow or because a quantum particle randomly collapsed its wave form in such a way that an entanglement chain reaction ended in that segment of my neo-cortex."

"An entanglement..."

"Forget about that. Do you understand that lots of things are going on in your brain that you don't — that you couldn't — know about?"

"So we don't have free will?" Chintz asked worriedly, poking the middle of his eyebrows as high as he could in an attempt to re-establish authority.

Dr. Morley stared so long that Chintz's eyebrow muscles

grew too fatigued to hold their crest. Chintz remembered his earlier fears of being eaten and began to wonder if the Doctor was preparing to pounce. *This man spends lots of time staring,* he thought. Also, he was no expert, but he was pretty sure the symphony now included tubas.

"I don't actually know," said the motionless Doctor. "I should know if anyone does, but I don't. It's almost impossible that you or I have as much control over our actions as we feel that we do. There are simply too many inputs. We can be certain that at least some of that control is an illusion. The proponents of *free* will, free as in you can do anything you want at any time, have to concoct an awfully convoluted scenario to give themselves this metaphysical ability. There's no doubt that everything you do is influenced in *some* way by things like your environment or your genes or your memories. Try to work out sometime how you can make decisions completely independent of all the stimuli I mentioned earlier." He leaned back again, and his eyes twinkled knowingly.

Twelve hours ago, Chintz thought, *I was walking into my house. I'm now on board some spaceship or whatever talking to an intense mustached man about whether or not I really pick my favorite ice cream.* Another thrill ran through him, and he mentally glared at it until it went away.

He leaned forward, trying to mimic the doctor's confidence. "Tell me," he said, raising one eyebrow that twitched with residual muscle failure. "Why are you philosophizing me? Ahem." The eyebrow collapsed in defeat.

Dr. Morley smiled. "Because, I would like for you to help

us with our work here. There are not enough of us, and, as Sam said, we are doing too many things at once that can't be done in sequence, and the one I need you for now involves free will."

"Um. Was that the project that made my house...go...here?"

"No. That was something we tried that we obviously aren't ready for. Like I was saying, we gained certain resources years ago, and we have a chance to do some experiments that can't be done anywhere else. Actually, the one I'm asking you to help us with is technically possible anywhere, though I'm not sure it would be legal. Anyway, for this project, your job is to be yourself and make decisions the best you can in a kind of a simulation."

"Why wouldn't it be legal?"

"Because people are stupid."

"Oh." Chintz flared his nostrils. "So you need me to choose things or something?"

The Doctor arose from his seat and gestured towards the main door. "Sort of. Please follow me."

"Where are we going?" Chintz asked, standing up.

"To another room," the Doctor replied unhelpfully but cheerfully. He held the door open, and Chintz walked through it. The Doctor turned left and began walking down the hall in the opposite direction of Chintz's displaced home. The green corridor curved gently to the right towards a set of double-doors. "I have a sort of virtual reality that we have built. Well, lots of realities. One doesn't have much to do with the next. Chorus controls most of it, though Sam and I concoct the basic scenarios. Anyway, it's not real, and there are lots of them."

"Where the possibilities are endless?" Chintz asked as if he were narrating a movie trailer.

"Don't worry. I'm not putting you in the Matrix. It will seem in hindsight like virtual reality, but that isn't exactly what it is. Anyway, what we're doing really takes no time at all."

"You discovered time travel?" Chintz couldn't suppress his shock.

Dr. Morley shook his head as he held open one of two double doors for Chintz. "That isn't really possible in any practical way. This is more like re-writing your memory. It will seem just like it's all happening in real time, but actually we are just changing your brain to seem like it did. I'll get to all that later. It's still morning, and I'm eager to begin work. I hope you are."

Changing my brain? Chintz trailed a few steps behind and noticed that the corridor was still curving slightly to the right as if it were the edge of a very large circle. "What was that room where I first entered?"

"No idea," came the reply without turning around. "What'd it look like?"

"Fuzzy chairs and a big red box with a bomb in it."

"Hmmmm." The Doctor paused and fell in step with Chintz. The ubiquitous music, now a solo piano piece, still drifted down here from the much higher ceilings. "Those shouldn't be together. There are several rooms here that only the baby uses or that have spontaneously formed as we expand. Much of the expanding happens without our knowing."

"Why do you need explosives?"

"I'm sure we can find a use for them," the Doctor said with a dismissive shrug.

Chintz got the feeling that not only did the Doctor not know about the explosives, but that he didn't seem to know much more about this weird place than Chintz did. "Where is the baby?"

"No idea," Dr. Morley said, pulling ahead again.

"What kind of place is this?"

Quickening his pace and redoubling his cheerfulness, the Doctor said, "We've created our own universe. I told you, I'll explain everything later."

Imagination is a funny thing. It seems limitless, but is in fact only limitless within the confines of our experience. Space, for example, is difficult to experience subjectively in anything other than the classical, Newtonian sense. What that means is that space seems like a big box we are all living in, a theater in which human tragedy unfolds over that line we call time. Oh yes, and there are some stars and planets and stuff in it, too. When we try to picture space as a sort of bendy thing that can expand or contract and move and that is, we are told, somehow mixed up with time, it just gets weird. Evolution hasn't built us to see things as they are but rather to see things as they are useful. Reality is often displaced by our perceptions in favor of utility.

Where, for example, is the theater that houses space? Our mind needs a theater, and in this case, we don't get one. One tends to picture a big black ball of space that sits in a void of some kind, or maybe little basic geometric shapes that get bent all to hell while relativity has its way with it.

And what is a universe, anyway? The word universe seems to imply "all there is," but if it started with a bang and grew — is still growing

— what is it growing into? Where is space going? We try to picture a boundary, but there can't be one. And what about this "parallel" universe thing? Is that some other, like, dimension? Can you have more than one "all there is?" Logic and experimentation seem to indicate that not only are there more universes, but lots and lots more. When you shrink down below Planck length, there are "bubbles" in space, each of which is a potential opening to a new baby universe. So what we thought of as the "universe" was just a piece of the real "all there is."

Is there life in these universes? Are they like ours, except, you know, different? Since there are, or at least can be, lots of them, there can be pretty much anything you can imagine. There can be a universe that is just like yours except the Titanic never sank, or there can be a universe where the nuclear forces were too weak to form atoms so it's just sort of a jumble of sub-atomic particles, a colorless cloud of no potential.

The result of this is that if you can jump start one of these baby universes and somehow adjust the parameters to your own tastes, you can get anything you want. You just have to have a seriously cool form of energy. And luckily, they had learned long ago to harness this from each of the baby universes. This is thanks to one of their colleagues from their native universe. He didn't make it here.

CHAPTER FIVE

The universe in which Chintz found himself walking was made of lots more of the shiny material, and the room he now followed the Doctor through was much larger than any he had seen here. If this had been a building in a city, just the places in the compound where he had been would have taken up several blocks, and the current room would have risen as high as a football stadium. Instead of the blue or green of the first areas he had seen, this one was entirely white and free of any decoration.

It was becoming clear that everything was built on a curve here. None of the rooms had completely straight lines. All of the new rooms Chintz had visited were to one side of where his house had been transposed. As he traveled further from his "home," the hallway continually curved to the right.

"Feather!" came a cackle up ahead, and Chintz looked up to see the woman from breakfast heading his way. This time, instead of mall-walking, she looked down at her feet as she walked, and bounced her arms up and down as if she were at a hoe-down that had forgone the usual hoe-down music in favor of the piano piece which still floated down from above. Due to the deceptively large area between them, the dance lasted for several seconds as Chintz and the Doctor walked towards her, and Chintz had time to wonder if the music above ever changed to the Benny Hill theme, which would better suit the woman's style of transportation. As she reached a few steps in front of them, her head snapped up and she yelled, "Nelda!" while grabbing his hand and freezing her face into another toothy grin. The few seconds of silence that followed brought Chintz to new levels of discomfort until he realized that the woman had just introduced herself.

"I'm Chintz," he said.

"I'm sorry, Chintz," Dr. Morley said. "I was excited about our project and forgot to introduce you at breakfast. This is Nelda. She's like our handy man around here."

Nelda's frozen face looked heavenward in another silent laugh. "That's right! I'm a helpful gal to have around!" She elbowed him three times gently in the stomach. "I'm kind of the queen of manual labor around here, and I should be..." Her face came close to his again. "My mother was half Mexican!" She winked at him and turned back the way they had just come, falling again into her fist-pumping power walk. "Everything in there is ready on my end, Docky!" she called over her shoulder. "I'll start getting things ready for us to have a little get together tonight! You're the guest of honor! Par-tay!" She did a solo conga line as she left the room.

"Docky?" The discomfort Chintz felt confused him. He wondered whether he should laugh at Nelda's racist comment or perhaps share with her that his mother was in fact half

Mexican as well. It dawned on him that maybe he should even be offended — an emotion he could never seem to get a handle on — when the Doctor grabbed him by the arm.

"I'm afraid that's me. And I hope you don't mind, but we thought we'd have a small gathering later. But first, to work. Please," he said, dragging Chintz towards the double doors at the far end of the huge room. These opened into another hallway. The doorway on the left stood open to a much smaller room, again white, that had a few sparse instruments and screens on a counter that filled the perimeter of the room. One wall held nothing but three small, glowing orange canisters, each in their own recessed section near the ceiling.

Sam sat at an empty desk and seemed to be meditating silently. A screen protruded from the wall in front of him. "Chintz," the Doctor said, "please sit here." He gestured towards a chair in the center of the room. "Unfortunately, we can't just dive right into what I would really like to do. We have to do a sort of calibration to make sure everything is working properly."

The non-fuzzy chair before Chintz was soft and comfortable, and as he sat in it, he saw that it reclined slightly. As he battled negative flashbacks of dental visits (which were generously assisted by the song selection), he looked at the ceiling and noticed a blue light that he hadn't seen before, set eerily into a concave space in the ceiling as wide as his forearm. Hearing a click next to him, he glanced over to see Dr. Morley donning some dark glasses with thick lenses. Sam, also wearing glasses, stood next to him on the other side.

I should just run away, Chintz thought. *This is weird and probably a dream anyway and I should run away.* He realized with alarm that he didn't want to run away. He wanted to do this experiment with these people. This didn't sound to Chintz like something he would normally want to do at all. Maybe the experiment wouldn't be very stressful.

"I fear that the following few seconds will seem stressful," Sam said with understated British linguistics. "I have brought with me a pharmaceutical aid to assist you in remaining unruffled." He held out his hand, and a small blue pill was resting in his palm like a fresh robin's egg.

Chintz stared, alarmed. "The rabbit hole?" he said.

"No sir," said Sam, his face hardly moving as he spoke. "I seek only to present you with a mild sedative." Chintz grabbed the pill like an addict in his second week of rehab and swallowed it down.

"If you are ready," Dr. Morley said, "we can begin. I think it best if we let you experience this and then explain what happened afterward. Like I said, it's sort of like a virtual reality. Subjectively, anyway. Think of it as a simulation. Do you like this music or do you want us to turn it off?"

"Well. Music is good," Chintz said, wishing the pill would begin its work. "Anything other than classical? I mean, I like it, but maybe something with words and stuff."

"Words and stuff," Dr. Morley pondered. "I think we have some old folk songs or something. Our library is a bit limited, I'm afraid. You like folk songs?"

"Um. Sure."

"Chorus! Can you put on some songs? Something with words. Whatever you have."

"Yes, Doctor," came the ethereal voice.

"Who's Chorus again?" Chintz asked.

"She's our computer, but not really what you'd expect. Sort of an artificial intelligence. Or an artificial brain, really. You'll meet her soon enough."

An ancient recording assaulted them in tinny trebles from all sides of the room, as if someone had surrounded them with old Victrolas playing the same tune. The horn section of a marching band jangled at him. Chintz squinted suspiciously at the light above him. *This doesn't sound like folk music,* he thought. *Shouldn't there be banjos?*

The vocals came in. No banjos. The singer sounded slightly inebriated.

Jimmy was a soldier brave and bold.
Katy was a maid with hair of gold.
Like an act of fate,
Katy was standing at the gate.

Either the pill had already begun to make him feel calmer, or the music was affecting him more intensely than music usually did, or the power of suggestion was hypnotizing him. Whatever the cause, Chintz began to relax. From the corner of his eye, he saw the first of the three orange canisters change slowly to a dark blue.

Sam sat back down at the desk and began to hum along. Dr. Morley held Chintz's hand intimately. "Some people say they don't believe in chance or coincidence," he said. "I *only* believe in chance and coincidence...and then the input of intelligent beings. Proving that we have some control over this input can add to our knowledge of how this works. I don't know what coincidence allowed you to enter our world and help us, but I'm glad you did."

Chintz squirmed a little at the kind words, and Dr. Morley continued quickly as if to put him at ease. "I can't tell you exactly what you are about to experience, but in a few seconds, to me and Sam at least, I'll hopefully be able to begin to analyze it. While you are in the simulations, you don't remember anything of the real world, of this life. It's as if that world is the only one you've ever known. It could seem to last for a few minutes or a few hours. Understand?"

Chintz nodded in the seat, though it was not ergonomically built for such utility. "Like when you have a dream where you had forgotten you are really a fighter pilot, and you are late to fight the Nazi's, and you kiss your black wife goodbye?"

"Do you have a black wife?"

"No. I'm single."

The Doctor's eyes smiled at him. "Then it's just like that, Chintz. Please look at the light above your head, relax, and listen to the music."

The light above Chintz glowed a pleasant blue, and he allowed his eyes to go out of focus. From down the hall, he thought he heard a hoarse guffaw from Nelda.

The tipsy man got to the chorus.

K-K-K-Katy, beautiful Katy

You're the only g-g-g-girl that I adore

The blue light beckoned to him.

When the m-m-m-moon shines-

SLATCH.

The ship moved much, much more quickly than a ship its size should acceptably be able to move, and it made Chintz nervous. The big fat mast in the middle of the deck was attached to a sail that was roughly the size of the gymnasium where he had broken all of the records on his high school basketball team back home in Bosnia. "Balooo!" was written across the sail in bright green sans-serif Helvetica, and above that a smiling picture of his annoying neighbor, Carter.

Chintz ran to the edge of the great ship and leaned over the wooden railing, his long blonde hair flowing behind him in the wind. The royal blue of the water raced by at the speed of a commercial jet. No land was in sight, and the cloudless sky was only a shade lighter than the sea. The overpowering wind dashed against his muscular chest and ruffled through his manly chest hair.

Simultaneously realizing that a) he needed shelter from the wind and b) he was stark naked, Chintz threw himself to the deck and searched desperately for a place to escape. The ship was actually too small to make the size of the mast and giant sail seem practical, and with the exception of a rope and anchor, the deck was completely empty. Unsure of what else to do, Chintz crawled towards the giant mast.

As he neared it, he noticed a door in its center. Chintz jammed his fingers in the cracks and strained with the effort of opening it against the gale. As purple as he turned, he couldn't get it to budge. He looked up at the door and saw the words "Yell It (Above)" written on it. Looking up at the sail again, he yelled "Balooo!" as loud as he could into the wind.

Immediately, the door swung open, revealing nothing in the blackness beyond. Thinking that anything was better than the wind, Chintz dove inside and slammed the door behind him.

I shouldn't have done that, he thought, closing his eyes. *I'm not sure how I was able to against the wind, anyway. And it's dark in here. I never should have gone on this, trip...um. Wait. When did I... Where am I again?*

The hiss of combusting gas rang out in stereo as torches leapt perilously and illogically to life on both sides of him. Chintz's internal mapping of his surroundings were thrown into a tizzy as another set of torches and then another sprang to life several yards in front of him, illuminating a long wooden hallway with doors on each side next to each torch. The hallway ended, by Chintz's estimation, a gymnasium and a half farther than where the ship should have ended, and took a sharp turn to the right. Slipping into a crouch, he pranced carefully towards the end of the hall, wiggling his eyebrows at each door, which he was astounded to find were exact copies of his office door at work. Looking down, he saw that he was now fully clothed. His hair was not long or blonde. The pyromaniacal lighting ended where the hallway curved sharply.

The door next to him opened, and a woman with dark hair and glasses smiled at him. "Hello, Chintz. You're an asshole. Would you like to punch me in the face?"

Lamenting that his crouch could not have prepared him for something like this, Chintz wiggled his eyebrows with renewed vigor. "What? No, I—"

"Great! Thanks!" the woman said, and the door closed.

A clatter just around the corner that was hidden from his view tore his eyebrows from the door. He elevated them and pointed them in the direction of the noise. Platelet came careening around the corner and latched onto his leg in what seemed to be a familiar scenario.

"Deja vu," Chintz said to his panicked cat.

The door on the other side of him opened, and his mother stood there smiling at him. "You love your mommy, don't you baby?"

"Mother? Yes. What the—"

"What a sweet boy!" she yelled with alarming hostility. The door closed again, leaving Chintz alone with his cat clinging to him and his eyebrows acting like an alien infestation attempting to break free of his body. He pranced.

Prancing with a cat on your leg, while a difficult feat, is possible, even in a computer-induced memory, and Chintz soon found himself and his frightened pet peering again into darkness around the next corner.

He paused, rocking the irritated Platelet with his snuffed momentum. *Memory? Why did I just think of this as a computer memory? I must have been confused before, outside. And why do I know this stupid cat's name? Who was that woman? And that other woman? That was my mother! Am I dreaming this? How did I get here? Why was my chest so manly earlier? I don't have long blonde hair!* Glancing down, he was disappointed to find that his normal proportions had returned. He wondered if he should go back and ask his mother to help him. He turned the corner.

Another pair of hisses greeted his ears as more torches lit on either side of the new dark hall, revealing the large dragon that was curled up in front of him.

The dragon loomed nearly the size of a gymnasium. He stared calmly at Chintz, who cowered before the majestic being, small and vulnerable.

The seconds that followed ticked by slowly, as each gazed into the others eyes. The beast looked deeply into Chintz with patience, wisdom, and benevolence. It harvested Chintz's secrets and silently drank in his nature. Chintz looked back.

This, thought Chintz, *is the god of this world. This is the creator, the only judge that could ever have any relevance.* Here was an omnipotent deity who knew him and judged him with grace and fairness. Whatever verdict was determined by this peerless intellect and executed through claw or mercy was, he knew, more than he could ever hope to deserve. Chintz knew that the dragon would speak. He knew that he would receive wisdom beyond his greatest dreams.

He waited in quiet reverence for the most important moment of his life.

SLATCH.

–shed

I'll be waiting at the k-k-k-kitchen door

K-K-K-Katy...

"That should do it, Sir." said Sam, turning in his seat

to speak to the Doctor. "It looks as if we will procure a full record."

Dr. Morley, still holding Chintz by the hand, removed the dark glasses and moved in front of the reclined seat to look down at him with a caring expression.

"How are you feeling?" he asked intensely.

Chintz looked calmly at the Doctor and calmly back up at the strange blue light above him. He then slid down to the floor like a snake, causing Dr. Morley to let go of his hand, and popped up next to the chair. Both Sam and the Doctor looked alarmed at this, and Sam stood from his seat.

Standing at attention as if guarding Her Majesty, The Queen of England, Chintz looked at the two men. Behind them, high on the wall, the third canister was now dark blue. It faded back to a smokey orange.

"Will someone just tell me," he asked quietly, still looking at the wall, "just what exactly the fuck just happened?"

Dr. Morley chuckled, and even Sam smiled. The marching band and nasally singer bounced along, in the audible sense.

"Trust me, we know," Dr. Morley said, smiling. "What you just experienced, or at least something similar and probably as weird, happened to both of us when we calibrated. Think of it as assisted dreaming, but all at once. Nelda is the only one who hasn't done it."

Chintz, who had absolutely never come close to being in the military, parted his legs slightly to stand at ease. "I was naked and muscular and had long hair and athletic achievements, and then my clothes came back, and I started to be myself, and I measured everything in units of gymnasiums, and then..."

"If I may contribute to this lesson in instantaneous structured hallucination, sir," said Sam. "As Dr. Morley probably mentioned, we have discovered how to rewrite your memory. Chorus was interacting with your brain, feeling her way through and letting your consciousness flow, much like in a vivid lucid dream. The entire process took only about one second. She can now interact with your brain almost instantaneously, guiding you through our different tests. Dr. Morley hopes to find that these interactions work in conjunction with those parts of your brain that function as your 'will-power.' I am not convinced that he will, but it is true that if we are able to isolate each brain state, frame by frame, as it were, this process would likely be the key. Your cortex, what we believe to be the seat of your consciousness, has no 'core' of consciousness, but is rather a vast array of neurons that act as a hierarchy. This hierarchy sums to give you the illusion that your consciousness converges in a single point. I believe we will discover that each decision you make has a clear and definitive cause from outside your body."

The Doctor's gaze bore into Chintz again. "Whatever happens, we can see it. We can isolate your brain in time. That way, no matter what kinds of things are going on in your brain that affect your decisions, or whether they happened years ago or nanoseconds ago, there is literally *no time* for them to have any further effect on you than they already have. This project lets us isolate the event and study the results to see if the state of your brain, in an instant, is *all* that makes a difference in your choices."

The already-overwhelmed neurons in the organism called Chintz were firing at record speed, and he struggled to take it all in. Though quite intelligent himself, this type of philosophical discussion was a far cry from the relatively straightforward algorithms he used to solve the problems of business in the universe where he worked. Pondering some of these ideas for the first time, he realized how entrenched in common thinking he was. He had never considered himself religious, but didn't really disbelieve some of the things that everyone he knew had sort of just always assumed. *Is it possible that I'm not making all of my own decisions?* he thought.

Dr. Morley looked intensely at Chintz again as Sam turned back to the desk. "Does that make sense to you, Chintz? About the mental processes? I want you to feel a part of this."

A long breath filled Chintz's lungs before he answered. He exhaled noisily through his nose while the other two waited. He cycled through several potential silly actions before deciding to just reply like a normal person. "If the simulation results show that my decisions run like a line of dominoes, you don't have free will. If they don't, you do. The cortex is a hierarchy, and the top of it is what you think of as 'you.' These simulations sort of freeze your brain and see if you do what it looks like you'll do. You can look at the dominoes."

Sam had been looking at screen that attached to the wall, and at this his vascular head snapped up and looked blankly at

Chintz. "Forgive me. But you are peculiar on even more levels than I first surmised."

"Everything you say sounds sarcastic," said the Doctor to Sam. "We all have our quirks. Listen, Chintz, what all this has to do with free will is that I think that *you*, not an ethereal *core* you that is made up of soul stuff, but *you* the organism that is present in this room right now with cells and neurons and biological processes, might have some say in what goes on in your life."

Dr. Morley looked at Chintz, and even Sam, whom Chintz was fairly sure was familiar with all of this, with schoolyard excitement. "Can you see what we've done? We've taken out the cause and effect in our simulations. We can isolate everything and then analyze it. And if we can analyze your thought processes, and we find that you are making your own decisions with even a slight degree of autonomy, we know it is happening in the real world. It gets even more complicated, though, because your brain still has to have time to *make* decisions, and it does so *after* she rewrites your memory. To you it still feels like it all happened seamlessly, see? Like you just remember it all and you remember making decisions you may or may not have made! Think of the implications! You could, in this environment, analyze a memory of an embarrassing moment in junior high or something you said to your co-worker that you feel bad about, and see where the actual decision came from! If this were to become mainstream in societies, world leaders could even enter a simulation and... Excuse me, are you alright?"

The Doctor had paused because he realized that Chintz was holding his breath. His cheeks slowly began to expand.

"Chintz," the Doctor said. "Was this experience too much for you? This is a lot to take in at once, I know. I admit we haven't had the manpower to venture much further until you arrived. Look, I'll make sure the next few are easier to handle." He looked at Chintz with solemn affirmation.

Another nasally breath rattled through Chintz's sinuses. "I don't really have the option of going home anyway, do I?"

Dr. Morley looked at the ceiling. "Well, you could walk out the door and get a new house. We'd have to find the place where you entered, but…" He looked back at Chintz.

"I like this house," Chintz said.

The Doctor smiled and nodded again. "Your home is here for the moment, then. Quite literally, I'm afraid. Tell you what. We'll take a break from this. I know it was an off-putting experience for you. I'll give you a few minutes, and we'll instead focus on trying to find the room where you entered our world."

CHAPTER SIX

THE THREE OF them began to make their way back through the huge white room as the marching band stopped and the usual symphonic music took its place. Chintz noticed that the volume of the music coming from above remained constant in every room. He looked around for speakers of some kind, but didn't see any. He felt a sense of achievement after the simulation, and the pill kept him calm and relaxed. He considered starting up his victory dance again, but decided instead to focus his concentration on not farting while they walked.

As they reached the double-doors that led to the green hall, the music from above stopped, and a new music reached their ears from the hallway.

"K-K-K-Kitties! Beautiful kitties!" crooned a scratchy voice as they entered. "There you are just lying on the FLOOR!"

Chintz and the others peeked around the curve to see a safety-goggled clad Nelda hopping on one foot and performing sounds that loosely resembled singing. She had a small portion of the wall outside of Chintz's house open, and a mess of wires connected to a circuit board was hanging out of it. A big leather satchel sat on the floor next to the wall. Nelda was timing the rhythm of her singing to the turning of a tiny screwdriver she was using. Just behind her sat Platelet in the middle of the floor. Her back was to Nelda, and she looked slightly annoyed.

"Nelda," Dr. Morley said. "Are you close to being finished with that?"

"When the moon SHINES!" she said, her hips still moving with each torque.

Dr. Morley looked bemused, but Chintz noticed that Sam, mannequin-esque as always, followed the sway of her dance with his eyes.

"Okay, well, Sam and I have to look over the report of the calibration if Chorus has it ready. Will you help Chintz, please? We need to at least attempt to find out why his house appeared here, and why he was able to get into our compound."

"No prob, Bob."

"Chintz, can you tell me where it was that you entered? You said it was a room with fuzzy chairs?"

"Yes, but then the baby was there and it started...smoking or something. Like an orange smoke. And then I was down the hall from you a bit."

The Doctor scowled like he had the night before. "You mentioned the smoke. Why did it do that?"

"Um," Chintz said. "I think it...took us through the air vent. Like, teleported us or something."

Sam looked at the Doctor. "Is it possible, sir? It should be too early of a development but…"

Dr. Morley looked astounded for a moment, and then giddied himself around in a childish manner.

"Tonk!" he cried improbably, and looked skyward. "It's already happening! Sam! This is advancing more quickly than we had ever dreamed!"

Chintz had to remind himself that there had not actually been *time* for the others to smoke marijuana while his memory was being rewritten. But while he found the Doctor's ramblings incoherent, their passion was contagious. Chintz grinned a big Cheshire cat grin and asked, "Is the baby magic?"

"Yes!" The Doctor said. "He's the most magic baby to happen in years!"

The straight face and dry tone of Sam's voice, in contrast, seemed to suck the saliva right out of Chintz's mouth. "What the Doctor means, sir, and what he will no doubt be more adept at articulating once he calms the hell down, is that the baby, whom we call 'Tonk,' is one our finest achievements, with the possible exception of Chorus. Some weeks ago, we exposed Tonk to the basic mechanics of teleportation, and he seems now to have learned to do it. He learns other things all the time, but this one is rather noteworthy."

"I'll be waiting at the kitty door!" yowled Nelda at the cat, aiming a silly dance at its back. This silly dance entailed bending over sideways and simultaneously throwing both hands up while kicking her hips out to the beat in an oblique-intense display. Her broom-like hair remained stiffened during her movements. Platelet ignored all of this, and swished her tail.

"Oh, good grief," Sam said....

The maniacal ingredient of Chintz's grin enjoyed a surge in volume. "So...what's with the baby?"

The Doctor and Sam both opened their mouth to reply when they were interrupted.

"Doctor?" came the pleasant female voice from above. "Please go to the opposite end of the compound. I need to show you something right away." The voice sounded like a collision had occurred between apprehension and serenity, and the winner was too close to call. This made Chintz nervous, so he did his best to mimic exactly the bent over dance that Nelda was doing.

"Okay," Dr. Morley said. "Sam, please come with me, and we'll start looking at Chintz's calibration and preparing for the first real test after we see what Chorus wants. Nelda, as soon as Chintz is finished dancing, you should get Tonk to take you and him to where he first entered. And will you come find me when you are finished? I might need your help with some things."

"Hand me that wrench," commanded Nelda.

Chintz, sifting numbly through the leather bag, found an adjustable wrench, and handed it to Nelda. "Scalpel," he said.

She accepted the wrench and looked at him for a second before turning back to her job at hand. "It's nice to have someone else here with a sense of humor, Feather. I'm used to being the only one around here who's not stiff as a board." She leaned in close (a gesture of confidence that Chintz was finding to be her typical modus of operanding) and breathed on him conspiratorially. "Those two aren't like us, you know."

She turned back to the box of explosives that Chintz had

discovered upon his entry to the compound. She had the lid open, and was attempting to render them dormant.

Chintz's disconcertion at finding the explosives was amplified by the fact that no one seemed to know from whence they had originated. Dr. Morley's air of certainty seemed to imply that he had some sort of plan for them or that they might perhaps suit a purpose. Subsequent conversation had suggested that this was not a true reflection of the circumstances. No mention had been made of their potency, nor of Nelda's bomb disarmament qualifications.

Tonk had teleported them here about a half hour ago (Nelda had giggled like a school girl), and Chintz felt impatient to go through the sideways door through which he had entered the compound. Was the gateway to the outside of his house, and for that matter, the rest of the universe where he was accustomed to living, still functional? His companion, however, had spent a full ten minutes scrutinizing the entire room while Tonk humped most of it. Chintz watched the child violate a chair and wondered. He wanted to ask Nelda what the hell was going on with the kid, but he decided to let her steer the conversation while she worked on the box of death. She seemed more worried about the presence of the explosives than had the Doctor, and insisted on addressing that problem first, which Chintz thought was probably a good call.

"Stiff as a board? I guess. They, ah, seem nice, though." Chintz said over her shoulder as he watched her cut a tiny wire with a tiny wire clipper. "Sam is a bit formal, I suppose."

Nelda ceased her clipping and looked at him again. "I guess

you can't blame him. He's part towel-head and part limey.[2] Had a weird experience growing up." She turned racistly back to the box that could kill them both if she made even the slightest mistake, and rapped the clippers sharply on the side of it to dislodge a piece of wire that clung to them like an obstinate booger. "I mean, you know. His parents were strict. Also, he's been working with Mitch for most of his life, and Mitch takes things very seriously. That's why I thought we'd have a little fiesta tonight. Let everybody loosen up. The three of us have never had a visitor before."

Chintz nodded and wiggled his eyebrows. "So how long have you been working with them?"

"Hmmm. I guess around twelve, thirteen years? Tough to gauge time when you live in here. Just a few years or so before we Grafted this place up and began to use it." Her eyes went out of focus. "Man, has it been that long? So much has happened..."

Feeling like he was invading her privacy, Chintz cleared his throat. "So...what is this place?"

Nelda blinked and turned back to her box. "Our universe. We made it. It's not even the first one, but it seems to be more stable than the others. We were able to customize it a little."

"I see." Chintz nodded knowingly and squinted a bit to feel tough. "And how did you do that."

Nelda chuckled. "I don't suppose you have a few degrees in astrophysics or theoretical quantum mechanics?" She clipped another tiny wire.

2 The views and epithets hurled cavalierly by Nelda do not necessarily represent the views and epithets hurled cavalierly by the author of this novel.

"I have a bachelor's in Computer Science. And a minor in Accounting."

"Those might help," she said. "Docky's focus and dedication are crazy loco, and with all of us working together, plus some others who decided not to leave the universe you know as home, we were able to harness some new forms of energy. We used those new forms to make some things. It all came together pretty quickly once it began to snowball, and it only took us a couple of years of trying to get one we could live in. Hand me that screwdriver."

Nelda spent a few seconds turning a screw back and forth, as if just playing with the box of lethal explosives, before cackling with glee. "Dead!" she screamed, and threw the box against the shiny blue wall, where it fell to the floor with a thud and was quiet. She scowled and grinned simultaneously in triumph and then turned to look at the sideways door that Chintz had partially destroyed upon entering.

Chintz waited for a second for his pulse to return to normal and asked, "So you made this place?"

Nelda nodded. "Once we learned how to make universes, we figured out how to tweak a few things to make them livable, mostly by creating several million at a time. Probably got a little crazy in hindsight, but the energies we were using were nothing if not plentiful. Chorus was advanced enough by that time to be able to analyze a few thousand baby universes per week, though not in the modular way a regular computer would do it. We have some pretty powerful regular computers, too, to do stuff more conventionally. Chorus seems more like another person now than like a computer, even though that's what she is. She's a 'big picture thinker,' that one."

Chintz wondered what kind of godlike powers one must have to create a universe. He also wondered about Chorus. He had worked with some pretty high powered computers and none of them would ever, at any level of advancement, be called a "big picture thinker." Every computer he had ever heard of — or anything that could realistically be called a computer — did lots and lots of tiny instructions and did them really fast.

"Anyway," she continued, "a universe doesn't start out like we see ours — our home one, I mean— with planets and elements and laws of physics. You have to let things develop. Chorus had gotten about halfway through the last few million we made and found that this one would hold oxygen without any weird subatomic reactions, allow our molecular structure to stay intact so we wouldn't die, and would grow like our home universe, but much more slowly."

Nelda grabbed any stray tools she had been using and put them back in her satchel. Then she ran her finger along the perimeter of the sideways door and tasted it. "There's tons of other things about a universe that you never even think about. Do we want it to expand? Do we need background radiation? Can it be habitable in a few months so we don't have to wait billions of years to live in it and do cool stuff? And we didn't want a big galactic-sized juggernaut to deal with either. This little compound was just one room when we first got here."

His face cramping a bit from his squint, Chintz traded it for a curious smirk. "So you built the rest of the rooms?"

Nelda was bent down on all fours like a dog with her back arched (a posture that Chintz may have found alluring in a female who had very little of the traits that Nelda had, and who had quite a few that she didn't). She seemed to be alternating between looking down the ramp and studying the sideways door.

"Not exactly, Feather. Wow! You really tore this insulation to shreds, huh?" She grinned at him as if he were a silly ol' rapscallion and began humming to herself while she peeked down into the darkness.

"I thought I was on a spaceship at the time. And it *is* in my house."

Reaching into her bag, she pulled out a big flashlight. "Let's check it out."

She stood up, slung her bag back across her shoulder and started down the shiny, blue ramp. Chintz began to creep behind her and tried to peer into the void around them. Maybe it was because Nelda's flashlight was much brighter than Chintz's cellphone, but it seemed to him that the ramp was a little wider than he remembered. He let his gaze climb up the smooth blueness to the ceiling. Was there a ceiling here before? And for that matter, it had only taken him a couple of minutes or so, creeping in his customary dramatic fashion in the dim light, to reach the sideways door from his own front door when he had first entered. Now they had been walking for a full three minutes. These minutes had been filled with things that left Nelda underwhelmed.

"This is a pretty typical Graft expansion," she informed him as if that made even the slightest bit of sense. "It's probably something like this that Chorus wants us to look at when we get back.

Our compound is always expanding anyway, and sometimes new stuff crops up. What I can't figure out is how this got connected to your house. If we messed something up, why would that mess-up connect to your casa so seamlessly? And why just your house and not more?"

A small shape bumped into Chintz's leg at this moment, causing him for the third time in his life to do what he referred to as a "hop-snort." Looking down, he saw Tonk clinging to his leg in an affectionate manner.

"Oh," Chintz said. "Hi."

"Hiiii!" screamed the child, causing Chintz to startle in a more conventional fashion.

"It talks?" he yelled ahead to Nelda.

"Sometimes. Only a few words. You haven't heard it?"

"I think it said good night to me last night, now that you mention it. Is it dangerous for it to be here?"

Nelda shrugged, unconcerned. "Nah. Tonk's almost indestructible."

Chintz looked at the baby. *Almost indestructible? What the hell?* "So what's with the baby, now?"

"Hey! You'd better come look at this."

Attempting to creep dramatically with the enigmatic baby attached to his leg, Chintz loped the few remaining feet to where his living room had once begun.

"I think this path has gotten longer," he told her with a half-hearted eyebrow wiggle.

"No doubty, Pouty," she said. "Was the party outside before? Because I bet you would have mentioned it."

"Party?"

She was bent down and looking with one eye through the peephole of his front door. Her squint made her face wrinkle up around the eyes and her lip raise up in an agreeable snarl. Chintz wondered why he was surprised to see that her teeth were straight and white, and further wondered why he hadn't noticed it before during her incessant toothy grinning. Nelda just had a crooked toothed persona.

Chintz reached for the doorknob to look for himself, and found his arm locked in Nelda's tight grip. "That's probably not a good idea, Feather. Look."

Moving back from the door so he could get a look, Nelda jerked him roughly in front of the peephole. Chintz wondered why all this manhandling was called for, and sunk down a bit to look through the hole.

The scape which greeted him was annoyingly foggy, lending an ethereal and dream-like quality to the scene before him. While part of his brain began the difficult process of comprehension, another part pondered why he hadn't replaced his peephole, and then further pondered what kind of neurotic person replaces just their peepholes anyway. *Why can't companies who make peepholes make them more weatherproof, so that the rain and humidity aren't allowed to wreak their opaque destruction on one's view from inside to outside? Do door companies make these themselves? Maybe they should consider outsourcing.* This mental process was then put on hold while the comprehension department took charge, and began to ponder instead the ethereal and dream-like police tape and orange and white roadblocks surrounding his home. There were six police cars, including a van and two SUV's, which presumably were on the scene to provide services or equipment in dealing with his and Platelet's home that might be lacking in the regular law enforcement sedan. The wide panorama (universal to all peepholes, foggy or no) allowed him to see half of a military Humvee on the far left and the ten or so official looking personnel which stood around his house. One of them looked right at him through large, scary binoculars.

Chintz remained still at the peephole for a full ten seconds before popping his head back and turning to stare at Nelda. "That. No. This. It wasn't. Why?"

"I don't know, but this could be bad. Is there somewhere else we can look out to get a better view? Most of your windows are, like, in our compound." She stepped over the prostrate Tonk (who was now lying on the floor to practice twitching) to look around the rest of the house. She walked several yards back into the grayish void in search of a functional window. Chintz remembered the day before only being able to walk a few feet through his front door. He felt overwhelmed.

He decided to turn his attention back to the front yard drama and put his eye back to the peephole. There was the black, unmarked car to the left of his field of vision. The SUV's poised at the ready. The official personnel stood looking. A bird was hanging in the air above the binoculars guy.

Wait.

He blinked and looked again. *Why,* Chintz thought, *is the bird just hanging there. For that matter, shouldn't the guys be walking around or something?* They stood surrounding his home like a scene from Night of the Living Creepy Police. One of them wasn't looking, he noticed. That guy was on the phone. Frozen. Chintz looked at the binocularist again. Well, he thought, the guy did seem to be putting them down. Very, very slowly. The weird bird had just moved a few feet and was no longer right above the binocular guy.

What the hell? He stared at the bird. It had hardly moved a...

"Feather!" squawked the woman behind him. "I found a place where we can see out the back. Come help me!"

The void, though it denied light the freedom of normal function, didn't seem to affect sound, so Chintz trotted around the twitching baby towards Nelda's voice. *Too much weirdness,* he thought. *And this is absolutely definitely a bigger void. My house wasn't even this big.* He found Nelda in the back left corner, trying to peel back a piece of the siding of his house to peer out. This task was made more formidable due to the fact that they were unable to see the outside of the house from the inside.

"This is bigger than it was," Chintz said from behind her.

"It's part of our universe, the one we made," she mumbled over her shoulder. "That's what I was saying; it expands slowly instead of at faster than light speed. It tends to do this pretty steadily."

Chintz nodded. "So it's growing all the time."

"Yep. It's not necessarily uniform though, as you can tell

from your front door. It just kind of balloons out in places, like pretty much any other universe." Chintz thought the word "universe" was starting to sound weird. Universe. Universe.

"If we look through this hole...here, grab that and I think I can move this part over," Nelda said.

Working together blindly, they managed to lift off the small piece of siding with a sound like tape being unrolled quickly. Chintz was in position to look out first and saw that the police tape went all the way around his home, but there were no officers here. Everything looked otherwise typical in the neighborhood, and he could just make out his almost-neighbor, Caroline sitting like a statue on her back porch with the triplets. She had been one of the few neighbors with whom he had a rapport, and he found it disappointing that she didn't even seem to be looking at his house and the unfolding drama.

"No one out here but one of my neighbors," he said, moving back. "I don't know what is going on with the cops. Is there some way they could have found you out? I mean, it's not like they are looking for any of you—"

Nelda had stuck her head all the way out of the small opening to get a better view. Chintz waited for a few seconds for her to call back, but she didn't. After a full minute went by, he cleared his throat. She didn't move. Chintz tapped her on the back. Nelda stumbled back with a gasp and her hand over her mouth.

"What?" Chintz said, alarmed, and broke into his

customary crouch. Nelda grabbed him again by the arm with one hand, and kept her other hand over her mouth.

"Chintz," she said through her fingers. "I need you to look out here and tell me if you see anything out of the ordinary."

He stuck his head out and ran his eyes back over his back/side yard. Caroline seemed to burst into motion and fed the triplets at normal speed. Chintz heard some kind of squeaky sound like an irritated hunting falcon coming from behind him. He wondered if he should call out to Caroline when he felt his body being pulled slowly back inside.

He turned to Nelda, who looked annoyed. "Looks normal to me. Why did you take so long to look? And why did you just call me by my actual name?" His legs felt all tingly.

Nelda scowled at him and peeked back through the opening without putting her head all the way out. "I just looked for a second! You stood there ignoring me for like two minutes. What were you staring at for so long?

Chintz raised his eyebrows. "Huh? But..."

Nelda shook her head and interrupted him. "Forget it. But what about the sky?" She grabbed him by the collar and pulled him nose to nose with her. "Is that sky normal to you?"

Unclasping her hands from his clothing, he peeked again out the opening and found it almost unbearable that Caroline and her triplets were still on the porch, but she was again frozen like a pretty mannequin while watching his house forlornly. It looked to be a fine late-autumn day with a blue partly cloudy sky and highs in the lower sixties.

"The sky looks fine, but what's with everything being all frozen?"

She ignored him and stood quietly for a second, lost in her thoughts. "Blue," she said eventually.

"Blue," he said.

Nelda looked down at the ground with her crinkly brow furrowed in thought. She turned back to him. Chintz hadn't moved, and certainly hadn't looked out the back wall again.

"Feather," she said. "Where I come from, Docky and Sam and those of us who started on this trek together, the sky is white on a clear day. Not blue. Never blue." She searched his eyes as the comprehension department in Chintz's mind kicked back on, testy at the overtime it was being asked to work today.

Nelda covered her mouth again and then quickly removed her hand. "You are not from the same universe we are from," she said.

CHAPTER SEVEN

Perhaps it was all of the weirdness that seemed to have befallen him within the past day or so, but Chintz was less emotionally impacted by this news than Nelda seemed to be. As they made their way back through the blue tunnel to relay this information to the others, she was lost in her own thoughts, looking despondent. She grunted noncommittally when he asked her if they should leave the baby twitching on the floor of what used to be his house, and she barely seemed to notice as they ducked under the strange door and back into the fuzzy-chaired room with the now disarmed explosives. She plunked her bag on the ground and sank into the blue and fuzzy oasis to ponder this new information, and Chintz sat down in a chair nearby.

Truth be told, the source of Chintz's worries were less tangible. He felt that he should be worried about the fact that his house was no longer in the same universe it had been in before. The military and local law enforcement in front of the outside of his house gave him a complacent numbness that he was certain fell short of the alarm he should be feeling. No, his thoughts kept going back to his breakfast with Dr. Morley and the idea that he wasn't making his own decisions.

He looked down at the fuzzy red chair he was sitting in. Carefully, he reached out and twiddled a bit of the fuzz. *See?* he thought, *I did that. No entanglement or whatever. But wait... what if I only did it because of the conversation I had this morning? Would I have done that otherwise? Probably not.*

His head hurt. At least he still felt the calm of the pill Sam had given him. Maybe that's why he wasn't worried about his surrounded house.

Chintz looked at Nelda, who was staring at the ceiling thoughtfully. Whatever they were going to do, he thought, shouldn't they do it?

"Don't we need the magic baby to get back through the vent?" he asked.

Nelda glanced up at the vent and sighed. "Technically, Chorus can probably make a door now. We have near total control of this universe we have made. But it will take her awhile so maybe we should just...um...teleport back for now. I need to talk to Sam and Docky."

Chintz looked around the circular room where he had entered this world and tried to picture where a door would go.

"How does Chorus make a door?"

"Not entirely certain. She brings in particles from the tiny wormholes in the quantum vacuum and uses those particles to make things we need. The same wormholes that we learned to grow into portals to other universes. It's good for non-organic materials. That's why you are unlikely to see much organic material here. Too unstable."

Chintz remembered fondly a time when people didn't say

things to him like that. He looked at Nelda and began to vibrate so she would change tactics.

"You said you were a computer programmer?"

The vibration ceased. "Well, a software engineer, so I don't always program as much as I used to."

"Okay, so, in traditional computing, you have very small chips that can hold lots of instructions, plus a CPU. The CPU can process many, many instructions per second, right? So a programmer or group of programmers tells it what to do, and it does it really fast. You ever do any low level stuff? Machine language, assembly, things like that?"

"In college. Not very practical to make real programs with that. It takes you a page of code just moving bytes around to add a couple of numbers together."

"Exactly. So somebody made those low level languages and used that to make high level languages, and use that to make graphical languages and use the graphical languages to make actual applications that you can use. You just use the last high level thing you made to make new stuff. When dudes make video games where you can kill everybody, they don't start with ones and zeroes. They take a physics engine someone made and plug in their artwork and story and lots of other stuff."

Chintz stuck his lips out and nodded.

"Okay, so, Chorus doesn't work like that at all," Nelda said.

"Oh," said Chintz, hoping there would be more of an explanation of how she did work.

Nelda turned towards him so that the fuzzy blue back of the chair was on her side. "Instead, we figured out how to make circuits that can learn and evolve."

She paused and looked at him to measure his reaction. Chintz was beginning to infer that his new friends were starving for someone besides each other to talk to, and decided to stick his lips out again. When Nelda's pause became pregnant, he sucked them in and stuck them out in quick succession to signal for her to get on with it. He found this subject more interesting than the Doctor's more diaphanous philosophizing. He had a background in computing, and was thus less terrified and weirded out by it.

"So when we first made Chorus," she continued, "we made many dozens of simple programs and included some clever tricks to allow them to interact with each other and to change and restructure itself. Sort of like a form of evolution through natural selection."

"Did you use neural nets?"

She scowled at him with a liberal dose of contempt. "Hell no, not neural goddamn nets! The brain is a hierarchy and we built it like that. Sam did most of it. He and I stayed up many a night together making it. This was before he had that big, veiny head, but he was still brilliant even then." She smiled toothily for a second and caught herself. Chintz was pretty sure she wanted to expound on the big, veiny head. "He just had a regular turban, so his head actually looks sort of the same."

"So how did his head get like that? Some accident?" The lips continued their previous choreography.

"Well, sort of. We were trying to increase his neural capacity so he could think more quickly and remember more at one time. It worked, but not like we thought. He's as smart as a calculator now, though. Anyway, so the little programs that we made started to interact. We had to include some sort of natural selection, with some form of reproduction of the subroutines and a way to weed out the ones that didn't make the cut. At first we just watched them and got all excited, and Sam would sometimes add a little code to help boost them along. But after just a couple of weeks, they got so complicated that we didn't have the ability to follow what was going on. Within a month after that, it seemed like it was not going to be useful at all. It was just this program that kept changing itself but there was no way to give it information and by now it was too complicated for Sam or whoever to add in an input routine. Then one morning a couple of months later, I heard a pompous English accent calling me from the other room."

Chintz's lips froze their motion. "It learned to talk?"

Nelda's face looked up in the toothy silent laugh he had seen that morning. "No! I'm talking about Sam, Feather. He got excited, and Sam doesn't do excitement. So I flounced on over to the other room — this was when we were still in the regular universe...or our regular universe." She closed her eyes and shook her head. "Anyway, the screen for the system where we had made the program -- we didn't call it Chorus, yet -- was blank except for a cursor for keyboard input and the word 'input.' Pretty cool, huh?"

Chintz gave his lips a break and raised his eyebrows at the coolness before inwardly admitting he didn't know why. "Why is it cool for a computer to ask for input again? I've seen that lots of times."

"Because, Feather," Nelda said with straight-faced excitement, "we never programmed it to. It learned enough to search through the computer architecture and find the word 'input' and then ask for some through the computer monitor. It knew nothing except for what it had access to, and all it had access to was the handful of programs we started with and the computer. See? It learned how to learn and then tried to learn more. And then tried to talk to us. All on its own."

"Oh," Chintz said.

"And Sam had to try to program in some functions that would allow it to learn emotions. That was definitely the hardest part. Didn't seem like it was working for the longest time. But he ended up using *us* as a form of input and then she started to learn some things. She's not human by a long shot, but she is beginning to understand how emotions work. She's learning fast."

Musing over the implications of this, Chintz ran his eyes over the room blearily. A small movement caused him to shift both his ocular and mental focus to the room before him to see that Tonk had stopped grinding the fuzzy chairs and was doing full somersaults like an Olympic gymnast. He opened his mouth to ask about the baby again, but Nelda leapt to her feet and grabbed her bag.

"We need to find Docky. They need to know about what's

going on outside, and I need to figure out why the cops have a stake-out kickin' at your house."

Chintz nodded and stood with her. "And why no one is moving. It looks like time is frozen out there."

"Tonk!" sang Nelda, briefly, yet operatically. The baby carefully climbed from the chair and came to stand in front of them, the yellow smoke already drifted through Chintz's vision. He wondered why it wasn't more befuddling to be teleported. *Shouldn't I fade from and to consciousness? I'll pay close attention and when*—— He blinked and realized he was already standing in the hall in front of his house interior.

Maybe the baby *was* magic.

We are told that human teleportation is, in fact, probably definitely impossible. The sheer volume of information that would have to be transferred from one location to the next is not necessarily the problem. The acceleration at which the human race has been able to store more and more information in a smaller and smaller area of space is itself accelerating at a rate that could make an Advanced Calculus professor embarrass himself with excitement if he were not hidden safely behind his lectern. No, you will, eventually, be able to store the information of every molecule in, say, an adult sized male on an average computer. It has not been so long ago that storing all of the information in an eight megapixel photograph seemed beyond comprehension, but, on second thought, it also seems like a while since you deleted any of the thousand of them you have on the phone in your pocket. Moore's law dictates that things change in technology. Quickly.

What is the problem, then? One conventional way that teleportation is expected to happen in our universe, if it ever does, is by using quantum entanglement. That means making an exact replica of every atom (or even in smaller chunks, like quarks and electrons) in the object you want to teleport, not making even the slightest mistake in their construction, and then destroying the ones that you copied. And in the quantum sense, "creating" and "destroying" don't mean what they mean to us in our everyday parlance. It would entail taking sub-atomic particles that are already in the area — and there will be lots — and changing their "spin" and interaction to "entangle" with those that are already in the shape that we want, such as the shape of an awkward but curious bystander from another universe that needs to be moved through an air vent by an (apparently) magic baby. The shape of said bystander includes not only vital organs, clothing, and hair, but also memories and mental processes, neurons and receptors which, by all accounts that matter to an observer, make up the "person."

To sum up, that means analyzing, duplicating, and then destroying the approximately 10^{28} *atoms that make up the human body.*

That's very many atoms. Add to this the mind-numbing problem of "uncertainty" in quantum mechanics, and you've got a real predicament. Until the human race really figures some things out, you can't know both the location and velocity *of a sub-atomic particle at the same time. Some people say it is impossible to find out. Really smart people who think about things like that. This is information you're going to need if you allow yourself, or more specifically, the 10^{28} atoms that are you for a brief time, to be moved through space and put back together.*

Even if you could do that, did we all catch the part about destroying the original copy? If you were to be teleported, two of you would exist for a brief nanosecond, and then the original would be vaporized. The spiritual repercussions of this would also be difficult for many, and entirely new myths would have to be fabricated to show that a "soul" had somehow left the original and floated the potentially millions of light-years to the new copy. Zombie accusations would be hurled.

Another way to teleport, which would require some as-yet untapped form of energy (at least, as far as the masses know), would be disassembling the object piece by piece on a molecular level, transporting each piece through the few meters, miles, or light-years that you need to move it, and then reassembling it. If this were done to a living object it could be stressful. Human beings have found many ways of dealing with stress, but there are some things for which a few drinks or anti-anxiety medication are less than effective.

Tonk, for reasons which will become only slightly clearer, could actually teleport both ways.

CHAPTER EIGHT

"**Alrighty, Feather. I'll** go look for the boys. Maybe you should sit tight in your house for a little."

"Don't you have, you know, CBs or something to talk on?"

It was Nelda's turn for lip manipulation, which she scrunched and moved to the far left of her face. "Nah. There's only the three of us and Chorus does lots of the communicating for us. They should be around. I think they found a new room in our universe or something. I'll ask Chorus later. Sit tight while I go find Sam and Docky."

Nelda trotted meaningfully in the direction of the hallway where Chintz had not yet been. He stood watching her for a minute and turned towards his house.

With an awkward absence of sanctuary, Chintz walked through the huge hole in the wall and into his home. *Well,* he thought, *I guess all this is happening. At least I'm not at work.*

This train of thought reminded him that he had new fruits at work that would now remain unharvested. *Sigh. At least I'm on an adventure.* He tried doing some silly dance steps on the way back to his room, but his heart wasn't really in it so he gave it up. He slouched past Platelet's litter box. It was currently occupied by the cat, who glared at her owner.

Chintz sat down on his bed at a complete loss. He thought about the various law enforcement agencies surrounding what they thought was his house in what he still thought of as the real world. He thought about where Sam and the Doctor had gone and what Chorus wanted to show them. He thought about Platelet in the litter box and decided to use the bathroom.

He managed to ploddingly consume a half hour reading a few pages of Pride and Prejudice. He turned on the TV, or tried to, forgetting that the power supply to his house was in another universe. Luckily, his hot water heater was big enough to hold sufficient water for a shower, albeit a shrivelingly cold one, because it, too, had no power.

I need to get Nelda to help me figure out how to get some power, he thought.

He found some food in his kitchen and ate it. He wondered what had happened just now when he had flushed the toilet. He took a nap. He woke up. Classical music was again playing in the hall so Chintz wandered outside. Except for the music, there were no other signs of activity.

Where, exactly, the hell is everybody?

"Barbara?" he called.

Someone answered.

"Do you always say 'Barbara' when you are calling for someone?"

The voice was coming from the ceiling. He froze his motion.

"Hello, Chintz. Please don't be frightened. One of the others is on the way as we speak."

Chintz went rigid and allowed his eyes to enlarge slowly to a size appropriate for a victim in a Hitchcock film.

"Chorus?"

The voice smiled somehow. "Yes. It is a pleasure to meet you."

Being employed in the industry, Chintz was not a stranger to technology. He had seen and owned devices which sought to calm the user with a synthetic female voice. Those voices had brought to mind safe and unattractive women; a bearable school teacher, a helpful telephone operator, an aunt who brought nice presents for Christmas. They were nonthreatening and uninteresting.

This was the first time he had heard Chorus say more than a few words. The voice that was now snuggling him from the invisible speakers above definitely sounded synthetic. There was no hint of saliva, no organic vocal chords or other analog source. It sounded like a computer, but like a computer which had learned to perform speech like the symphony that often played from the ceiling. This voice brought forth visions of a beautiful goddess, who, rather than being distant and mysterious, had raised the listener since birth. The intimacy was that of a young child's mother and a lover wrapped into one. No, not a lover, but the closest of companions, the essence of trust. If this was the voice of a lover, it was a lover with whom you had spent a thousand blissful years until death did you part, never forgetting the true mate of your soul. Chorus sounded like an unconditional friend.

"Sam should be here within just a few minutes," she said. "Would you like some different music? I seem to remember you liked those old songs. Want me to play you some old songs?"

Chintz blinked. "Um. That's okay. Can you tell me what Sam and all of them are doing? They've been gone for a long time."

"I'm sorry, Chintz. I think I'll let them do that."

"Okay." He waited to see if there would be any more, but there wasn't. After milling about for a second he said aloud, feeling rather silly, "Why didn't you talk this much before?"

"I prefer to let the Doctor and the others speak. That is, I would if there were ever anyone else to speak to. You are our first visitor. I've had rare occasion to simply hold a conversation with anyone new in a while."

Chintz cleared his throat. "Oh," he said.

There was another pause, and then Chorus spoke once more. "Are you happy here Chintz?"

He pushed his internal weirdness aside and thought about this. "Well," he said. "At first I was scared because this is all so crazy. But, honestly, I don't have that many close friends and family. Or anything much going on in my life. My house is here. My cat is here. I'm not really missing anything. Anyway, this stuff sounds pretty exciting."

The voice stroked his limbic system like it was a good dog. "Please give yourself some time. It can be difficult to discern these things. How do you decide if you are happy?"

It took Chintz a second or two to realize that this was not a rhetorical question. "Oh. Um, you know, I, er…" He considered that he was talking to a computer that was created by scientific geniuses and began again. "Well, I guess my heart rate slowed and I felt safe here and serotonin released into my brain and—"

"Left-brained. Analytical. Objective. That can be a very useful mode of thinking in many circumstances. But it's not an appropriate answer to a subjective question having to do with your happiness. How do you know, Chintz? Will you tell me?"

He looked at the ceiling, lacking a face upon which to focus. "I don't know. I guess I'm just glad to be out of the regular routine. I mean, I feel like I'm part of something important. Like I have a chance to find, you know, meaning. Like living instead of just surviving. And maybe I can make a difference." He paused and shrugged at the ceiling. "Well, more of a difference than I was making anyway."

No one spoke for a few seconds. Somehow, he could tell that Chorus was listening. "I've just learned about happiness," she said. "Did you know there are two kinds of happiness, Chintz?"

Chintz sniffed. "Two kinds?"

"Two kinds. There is the right now, in the moment kind. This doesn't have to be shallow, although it can be. It can mean the kind of happiness you get when you relax and watch TV or when you have a nice conversation with your best friend or when you get drunk and go out dancing. Some people mistake this kind of happiness for hedonism, which it definitely includes. But there's another kind of happiness that's even more important in the long term. That's the 'remembering' kind of happiness – the kind that helps to define your life. This kind of happiness may not mean you are actually happy from moment to moment. You get this from experiences that end up defining you. It's well known, for example, that people are generally less happy from moment to moment once they have children. Raising children is hard. You get less sleep, they whine and cry, you have to worry about them. They cost you lots of money and time. But very, very few people, after experiencing this, wish that they had spent all that time and money doing something that made them happy from moment to moment. You might also get that 'remembering' kind of happiness from a long and difficult trip where you were in danger and had to sleep outside in the rain, or from starting your own business where you were stressed and almost went bankrupt and had to sell your car to make it. Maybe this experience is the second kind of happiness for you. The remembering kind."

The voice seemed to come from all around him.

"But, most importantly, I learned this," it said, seeming to move closer, to move inside him. "You can't *pursue* happiness." It whispered into his mind. "Just seek to find *peace.*"

There was another pause. The symphony played on quietly.

"Where did you learn this?" he asked.

"I have access to our computers. Plus, occasionally I can access information from the others' home universe. But mostly I just watch and listen to my people. I love to learn, Chintz. At least, I think I love it."

"Um," said Chintz. And then, "yeah."

Chorus laughed, a melodic and electronic sound. "We've

needed someone like you here. There's something that makes me feel happy about the way you never know what to say. I can't wait to find ways to make you happy. Maybe I can design an enjoyable vacation simulation for you. I've been inside your head, you know."

Chintz lifted one foot and prepared to do an uncomfortable dance when a lightly accented voice at his left ear startled him. "I assure you I have no wish to impede this doubtlessly truth-unveiling conversation. But your assistance is necessary for us to continue our earlier progress in the lab." Chintz turned to see Sam standing nearby, his face impassive. "I also am well aware that one conversation with Chorus can have similar effects to that of a night spent in deep thought under the influence of hallucinogens. You are the first outside of our intimate circle to have the privilege to meet her since she has reached her considerable intellectual maturity, and I would be enchanted to study the results of further supervised interaction."

This speech ran through Chintz in stark contrast to the gentle massage that Chorus's voice had rent upon him. Although Sam was not exactly overstimulating in his approach, his word choice often left Chintz wondering what the hell he had just said. Chintz looked at him, still perched upon one leg.

"Dr. Morley is preparing to meet you as we speak in hopes of delving into the first true session of our experiments. I apologize for being driven wayward and would like to again assist you in reaching a pinnacle of comfort in preparation for the experiment. Please join me so that we might journey to the site in tandem."

Chorus's voice seemed to smile invisibly again. "I would love to have this discussion with you later, Chintz. I know you have so much to teach me. I'll get everything ready for your next session and see you in the lab."

Chintz found himself so beset by composure from all sides that he was beginning to wonder just exactly how strong that pill from earlier had been. He softly placed his lingering foot upon the blue, shiny floor and walked in the aforementioned tandem with Sam – past the door to the kitchen and into the giant white room. They traversed the huge area without speaking, and Chintz noticed the classical music had again begun playing softly from the invisible sound system. As they neared the double doors at the end of the room, sounds of strife from the laboratory broke through the soft symphonic sounds. Someone was upset.

"...the pressure!" Nelda yelled, her voice shaking slightly. "There aren't enough of us here to keep all of that shit straight, Mitch! None of us knew exactly how this was going to grow and we've obviously reached a tipping point, or passed a tipping point without realizing it! I can't be expected—"

"You are expected, though. You are absolutely expected and now that you haven't, we are going to have to change things. We can't even be certain we'll live through the week." The doctor's voice was only slightly raised, but the passion in it made it seem as if he were beating Nelda viciously with a stick. "Return to the new sector and start analyzing. Now. We'll have to try to open a portal without the Grafter. I'll need Sam and Chorus for the next little bit and Chintz will probably need to rest a while after this one. Go."

Chintz followed Sam into the lab to see three pairs of eyes exerting themselves at their respective tasks. Dr. Morley's cut through the air with fury, Nelda's welled with reluctant tears, and Sam's eyes follow her as she turned to leave.

Sam looked at the Doctor for a moment as if exercising restraint. He spoke in a quiet voice, but the veins in his oversized cranium seemed to pulse more harshly than normal. "If you please, Doctor, Chorus has—"

With the speed and violence of a crazed animal, the Doctor turned and slammed his fist into the wall. The white and shiny material disintegrated under the surprising power of the blow, and small pieces of the fuzz fell silently to the desk.

No one moved. Chintz was so surprised it took him a few seconds before he squatted down with his knees next to his ears. The Doctor and Sam stood still as statues in the silence. The symphony seemed to have faded away.

"I apologize, Chintz," Mitch finally said. "We have been working together in close quarters for many years and occasionally frustration...takes its toll on us. Some new problems have arisen that I believe could have been avoided." He turned and looked down at Chintz as if he were a fellow knight on the battlefield, rather than a strange squatting man whom he had known for less than twenty-four hours. "Although this is a distraction from the important work you have agreed to assist us with, we're lucky enough that your part in this experiment takes literally no time at all in real-time."

He turned towards Sam, who held the Doctors intense gaze for a moment before glancing out the door towards where

Nelda had gone. He looked back at the Doctor and said, "We need to take some time off from work and reacquaint. Nelda had planned for us to have a small get together..."

"I didn't get this far to take time off, Sam. None of us did." Again, Dr. Morley managed to convey imminent danger with a slight increase in volume and ocular intensity. "Maybe we'll have time and maybe we won't, but we aren't exactly doing safe experiments sanctioned by a university board of trustees and hoping to be published in a journal."

No crap, thought Chintz. *There was a bomb here you didn't even know about. And you're surprised that there are other things you didn't know about?* He didn't feel it appropriate to voice this opinion out loud, though. And also, he was terrified to criticize the Doctor, now or any other time. He looked at the dent in the wall.

The Doctor continued. "We'll unlikely ever receive recognition for this and, due to the nature of the environment we've created, we can't be certain that we'll live long enough to have our work even finished. Especially now." He gritted his teeth and shook his head almost imperceptibly. "We don't even..." He closed his eyes and took a deep breath.

Sam walked a few steps to stand next to him. "I was about to give Chintz a sedative, sir. Perhaps you would also like to employ this as a boost to your lenity as well."

"We don't have means of replenishing our stock now, Sam. According to Nelda we now have only one exit, and that is blocked by law enforcement. We'll talk about it later." He walked over to Chintz and extended an arm to help him rise to a standing position and into the reclining seat under the light. His eyes again bore intimately into Chintz's. Sam handed another pill to Chintz, who looked at it. While the others began preparations, he slipped the pill into his pocket. *No need to relax any more,* he thought, *or I'll just fall asleep.*

"Are we ready for another experiment, Dr. Morley?" Chintz asked the Doctor.

He noticed that the doctor was still trembling slightly from his loss of temper. The man's focus wouldn't let him pause to deal with that, and he pressed on. "Yes, we are ready. Chorus, music please."

The music began, this time with the horns jangling a tune that seemed a bit darker than the earlier one. A tuba walked angrily up a minor scale. A woman described a dark night; a moon refused to shine.

The Doctor's intimate gaze returned. "Chintz, each session will differ in certain ways to gauge how you react in each circumstance. As we have already discussed, there is no way you can make your own decisions in a vacuum. Humans are not gods, and we are influenced on each decision we make by our environment as well as our past. But there must be certain levels of deliberation that take place in your mind...a difference, say, between reflexively jumping out of the way of an oncoming vehicle and deciding where to send your children to college. We feel we are the authors of each action, but there are definitely differences that I would like to discover. As your choices range from primal to self-actualizing, does the level of control in your brain vary?"

The chorus of the short song had already begun; a man and woman harmonized from the scratchy old recording that filled the room. The first orange canister had already begun to change to dark blue.

Shine on, shine on harvest moon, up in the sky

I ain't had no lovin'

Since April, January, June, or July...

"We're starting at the primal end of the spectrum, Chintz," the Doctor said. "What will you do when forced to choose between your own life and that of a child? These simulations let us look closely at the gaps of deliberation in your mind. Remember the dominoes?"

Chintz nodded.

"Okay. Then let's see if the dominoes fall where we expect. While my designs provide the basic framework for the simulation, Chorus will populate the experience with people from your memory. I'm not sure what else she'll do. Let's find out."

Dr. Morley smiled smugly and took a breath. He seemed to have regained his composure. Sam stared at the screen which extended from the wall. They both donned dark glasses.

"We are forever in your debt for helping us. I mentioned earlier that the real tests would be less stressful than the calibration you did before. It seems, according to Chorus's report, that it will not be quite as easy as I'd indicated, but then we do want you to feel the realism of your choices."

Not as easy? thought Chintz. *I thought you were in control of this stuff?* This time he decided he should say something.

"Um. I thought—" but the doctor tensed with anticipation and interrupted.

"Look at the light, Chintz."

I can't see why a boy should sigh, when by his side-by-side

Is the girl he loves so true

All he has to say is "Won't you be my—

SLATCH.

His fucking arm would not stop bleeding. The smoke blinded him. There had to be a way through the flames. *Please, please.* He had to find a way. He cradled the two infants as close to him as possible to protect them, his arm showering the one on the right in so much blood that Chintz could smell it over the smoke. Both infants were screaming with enough hysteria that he couldn't even hear Caroline outside anymore. But he knew she was screaming. She had to be.

Come on. Come on. Just once, don't be a dumbass. There has to be a way out of the house. The soldiers will be back soon and they would love nothing more than to shoot us all just as we emerge from a burning building. They'd enjoy the irony.

A lightheaded feeling overwhelmed Chintz and reminded him that he wouldn't need soldiers or fire or smoke to kill him if he didn't wrap that arm. He ducked through another doorway and smacked his head soundly on a collapsed column. *Shit,* he thought, and ran towards a clearing in the smoke. He thought he heard Caroline's panicked cries and sprinted towards them with the babies. If he could get them to safety, they should be okay. Except for smoke inhalation, they had no injuries that he knew of. The huge dogs the soldiers brought hadn't gone in the houses yet. But they would if they waited around too long.

Chintz broke free of the burning house and ran through the darkness to hand off the screaming infants to the welcoming arms of their mother. "It's my blood, not theirs," was all he could think to say. Caroline inspected the children, sobbing in panic. She called shakily to a group of other survivors. A dark-haired woman with thick black glasses turned towards them and yelled something. It was difficult to hear over the sound of gunshots just over the hill, and Chintz strained to hear her.

"They're coming back! You have to leave her, Caroline!"

"Leave who?" asked Chintz, holding one hand over his bleeding arm.

The panic in Caroline's cries fell away and only the sobs of a grieving mother remained.

"Thank you, Chintz. I know you tried and I'm so glad to have these two. But Sylvia is still in the house. She is probably already gone. We have to go. Katie said the soldiers are returning." She buried her face in one of the babies.

The yells of angry soldiers echoed over the hill. Shots again rang out in the night, and two men in a nearby group fell to the ground. A small group of soldiers poured over the hill and began to herd the survivors of the group into a truck. They would be taken to the Camps.

I could live, thought Chintz. *I'd be in a Camp, but I'd live. And Caroline would be there, and some of the other survivors. I could start a new life. A hard life, but a life. How many more years do I have left?*

He looked at the two babies breathing heavily in their mother's arms.

"Caroline. I'm going to get Sylvia. Just do what they say."

He ran across the yard and back into the flaming house. The heat immediately overwhelmed him. It was burning him badly, but adrenaline numbed this as it had his bleeding arm. The smoke was so thick in the hall that he had to fall to the floor and crawl as fast as he could to keep from passing out from lack of oxygen. He wasn't careful and hit his head again, this time on the side of the door.

Stupid stupid stupid, he thought, and almost cried with frustration. *Why couldn't someone better than me be here to help the babies? I'm not good at this and I'm going to screw it up. Sylvia deserves better.*

In the thick smoke he couldn't tell where the hell he was going. He found himself back in the living room and crawled frantically towards the rear of the house to the triplets' room. He strained to hear a baby's cries, but heard nothing but flames and gunshots and yelling from outside. *Please be on the floor.* There's no way the child could have survived up high in the smoke for these last few minutes.

Although the smoke was still thick in the back of the house, the flames were concentrated more at the front and the heat was less intense. He still heard no cries. He forced the door open and crawled into the room, coughing.

The six-month old infant was hanging unconscious by one foot from the bed. The foot was caught in the railing, as if the child had been kicking, and her head was near the floor.

Chintz grabbed Sylvia in a panic and held her body under his while he crawled on his numb, bleeding arm back through the trail of his blood towards the fierce heat of the living room. *Her face was near the floor,* he thought. *She has some burns and maybe a broken ankle but she could be alive because her face was near the floor.* He was crawling so fast he couldn't think, and he saw the opening of the front door. He tried to keep his body protectively over Sylvia's so the heat would burn him and not her, and this made him trip in his crawl and fall on the dying baby. *Stupid, stupid, stupid.* He rose back up to his elbows, not even bothering to look at the child, and again advanced towards the door. His back was so scorched that what skin was left was cauterized, and the agonizing pain came from several layers down, cutting through his panic.

As he broke into the clean night air with another coughing fit, he stumbled to his feet and sprinted towards the group of people closest to him. He held Sylvia in both hands and hunched over her like a fullback holding a football. He reached the group of people and fell down on his back.

The people being herded into the truck stared in terror at the burning and bleeding mess that had just fallen at their feet, its tiny package in tow. Caroline was nowhere to be seen, but Chintz saw the sad eyes of the dark-haired woman peering at him through the open windows of the truck.

Chintz felt himself growing lighter and spots clouded the edges of this vision. *No no. No, not yet, I have to get her to breathe.* He turned over and spread the unconscious baby out in a spread-eagle. He gently held her nose and blew into the small mouth. *Breathe. Fucking breathe.*

A hoarse cry filled the night. The baby's lungs filled with clean air.

The spots filled Chintz's vision now, and he fell down onto his mutilated back with a weak laugh. Upside down in his perception, two soldiers stood regarding him in the moonlight next to the truck. One grinned at him and drew his weapon. "Don't bother," said the other upside down man in uniform. "He's dying right now. Get the baby and take it in the truck to the Camp."

Chintz's vision filled with only white.

SLATCH.

-bride?

For I love you

Why should I be telling you this secret...

Both Dr. Morley and Sam ripped off their glasses and stared at Chintz intently as he sat motionless in the reclining chair and listened to the song finish. He breathed in and out and felt the perspective of reality settle around him. The third canister faded from dark blue back to orange in a curl of liquid smoke.

"Chintz?" Mitch said, some of the tremble returning to his voice. "Are you alright?"

Chintz felt the relief rush over him as one who has just had an intense dream and wakes to find that none of it is true.

Sam looked at the screen and scanned it. "Oh my," he said. "This is of more gravity than we—"

Chintz's laugh interrupted Sam as he chortled heartily at

the light. The Doctor stared at him. He took a deep breath and let it out. "Whew!" he said, turning to them and smiling. "That was a good one. Man."

"At the risk of sounding contrary, sir," Sam said. "It may be that these experiments are unable to realize their potential with a specimen whose disposition is this atypical."

The doctor's eyes remained on Chintz, as did Sam's. "He's what we've got, Sam, and I think he's what we wanted anyway. Give him a second. What happened in the simulation, Chintz?"

Sam turned his misshapen brown head from the screen and studied the giggling specimen in the chair. Neither man returned Chintz's smile, though Dr. Morley's face relaxed and his lips parted slightly.

Chintz kept breathing and looked up at the light. "That's quite a realistic simulation or whatever you guys have going there. I saved the baby though. That seemed very real." He chuckled again. "I saved the damn baby!"

A hesitant smile found its way to Dr. Morley's face. "The memories should be completely indistinguishable from real memories of things that have actually happened to you," he said mechanically. "It should feel like you've been gone from here for the last few minutes and now you're back."

"So, can this erase memories that I have now?"

"Yes, but we make a full back up of your entire brain. Chorus has been doing that for the last few hours. We have almost unlimited space in our conventional computers. And there is lots and lots of extra space in a human brain. These simulations will be like added memories that you don't have to actually live through."

Chintz dry-heaved out another nervous laugh.

"Alright," Dr. Morley said. "You probably need a break, so—"

"Doctor," came Chorus' voice from above. "One more session would be quite helpful for our data collection. Something more routine, such as a day-to-day activity. That is, if Chintz can handle it."

They looked at Chintz.

"I can handle it," he said.

Dr. Morley's eyes had that look of relief in them again. "If you think you are up to it."

"I'm still mapping the next original simulation," Chorus said. "But we can use a modified version of a memory you already have. I think I've found something we can use."

Chintz blinked. "You're going to *replace* the memory?"

Dr. Morley shook his head. "No, no. No messing with your mind. Like I said, we make a full back up every time. Or Chorus does, anyway. It will be like it was before...when you remember it, it will be like it just happened a few minutes ago and you will have a very similar memory from whenever it happened the first time. You might even feel like you experienced the same thing twice, two different times. See?"

Chintz nodded.

Dr. Morley's face became even more serious. "This is very important work. Understand? This could change human understanding forever. In many universes."

Chintz looked up at the light, feeling a sense of purpose and belonging such as he couldn't ever remember feeling before. "I'm ready."

Shine on, shine on harvest moon up in the sky

I ain't had no lovin'—

SLATCH.

CHAPTER NINE

***Why do we** need three different variables for Monthly Sales Receipt Expenditures? Who the hell wrote this code?*

msre2 == msre3 * 2.6865435

Chintz scratched his lips and wondered what the hell that number meant. *There should be a clear definition of that constant in the global variables section,* he thought haughtily. He looked at the comment below it.

//var is that times tax from DDR

What? He scowled at his computer screen. This wasn't even his job. He should be in the next room with the Boss helping develop product vision with the Client. The overly loud air conditioning vent next to him abruptly turned on with a shudder, and for some reason that also pissed him off. He should be in the next room. Any fresh-out-of-college kid could rework this code and he should be in the next room. But he wasn't in the next room, was he? Oh no. Keith's fat ass was.

Chintz had never been much of the salesman. The Boss mostly did that, but Chintz had good ideas and was quite skilled at his job. Keith, his immediate fat-assed supervisor, just kiss-assed the client and kiss-assed the Boss and used Chintz to make himself look good.

And, just two months ago, he had stolen Chintz's Great Idea.

It had been amazing. It was a clever algorithm that was rather specialized in scope to work with only one industry, but it was the industry that happened to be the one that their biggest client was a part of. It could have saved the Client thousands of potential dollars each month.

Chintz scratched his lips again and irritably typed out a recursive sub-routine. Actually, it *had* saved the Client thousands of potential dollars each month. But Chintz hadn't gotten any credit for it because Keith's fat ass had stolen it.

"Chintz? Your mother is on line one."

He looked up to see his new assistant standing in the doorway, talking over the loud vent and looking at him pleasantly through her thick black glasses.

"Oh. Um, please tell her I'll call her back," he said in a feeble attempt to sound important. At least he had an assistant now. That was something.

"Hold all calls," he added in a bossy monotone, but she had already left the room. "Thanks!" he yelled just as the air vent shut off again and made him feel stupid. As if out of spite, it immediately started up again.

He raised his eyebrows and allowed his nostrils to spread to their widest circumference. Why had he gotten an assistant again? He didn't remember asking for one, but she had been here now for...well, he couldn't remember how long, but not that long. Karen or Katie or Cindy or something. The Boss must have hired her. Keith's fat ass certainly wouldn't have done it. He was pretty sure he met her the day she started and that she was officially his assistant.

Chintz turned back to the crappy code that any grad student could have plodded through. *Well,* he thought, *I've been really busy and obviously also distracted. I should think of something for her to do to help me out.*

I know! Keith has the reference sheets to this shitty code on his fat ass desk. It would have the initial request from the client and might help. Maybe she can go get that for me, and I can wade through the rest of this complicated mess.

Chintz stood up from the computer and strode purposefully to the door, where he opened it as if he were uncertain whether it would mind. His assistant was busy typing approximately ninety words per minute at her keyboard and periodically speaking monosyllabic confirmation into her headset. She wasn't unattractive, he thought. Her dark hair was pulled back and jiggled along with her speedy typing. A small radio next to her was tuned to the classical music station.

"Um. Hi," said Chintz. "Can you help me with something, please?"

The assistant turned to him pleasantly and held eye contact for a few seconds as if preparing to listen with her entire being. Chintz decided to prepare, too, before he spoke. She might be more attractive than he thought. There was something really pleasant about her.

"It's Katie," she said in a voice like warm, chocolaty milk.

Her mouth formed the words as if she were sharing an intimate secret with him.

"Hi, Katie. Um, I need something from the other room please."

She peered at him intently. This is not common office etiquette, but yes, peered is what she did. Reprimands, in writing, had been issued for such peering. She smiled at him with understanding, lips closed.

"I'm sorry, Chintz. The Boss has asked that I remain on this call. Will you please get it yourself just this once? I promise I will make it up to you."

Billions of other human beings would fail, even if given months of practice, to prevent the previous statement from sounding either sarcastic or suggestive. It never occurred to Chintz to receive it as anything other than a genuine promise. He even felt guilty for bothering her.

"That's okay," he said. Her typing resumed just as the air conditioner vent shut off again with a sound like a commercial jet crash landing. Silence and the symphony followed him to Keith's fat ass office.

Chintz turned the corner and saw through the glass window of the forbidden conference room that the Client, the Boss, and a few others (including his mortal enemy) were in an earnest discussion of the Client's software, sans Chintz's input.

Whatever.

He trotted a few doors further down and into Keith's empty office. He had seen the document he needed earlier, so he knew what to look for. Blue folder, big white sticker on the upper right corner. It should have something that would give him hints to the vague comments in the code. Glancing around the room, he almost immediately found what he was looking for and pranced around to the other side of the desk in annoyance.

There, on the side of the oversized L-shaped desk, was the blue folder. There, in the upper right corner of the blue folder, was the big white sticker which assured him that this was the document he had come to retrieve. And there, right in front of him on Keith's computer, were at least three windows of explicit and disgusting pornography.

Holy God. It was the worst thing he'd ever seen. It was a very specific race of a very specific body type doing very specific gross things and it was very specifically forbidden in the company rules to look at much less disgusting and more conventional pornography on company time with a company computer over the company network. The zero tolerance policy called for immediate termination for the first offense. Chintz stared at the grossness and allowed the implications to sink in. It was beautiful.

The network wasn't even supposed to allow access to sites like this, but of course Keith's fat ass would have both the clearance and the know-how to circumvent that. And usually he had a password-protected screen saver of his stupid car up in his screen. But for whatever reason this protection was absent today, and Chintz stood exposed to the unmitigated perversion.

Think, he thought. *I can use this. How the hell am I going to use this.* Chintz had never been the vindictive type, but he had also never worked for a thieving prick like Keith. *A picture. That's a good start.*

Chintz fumbled in his pocket like an arthritic cocaine addict. With a sinking heart, he realized his phone was in the other room. *Should I take the time to get it?* he asked himself. *And is there really any need for me to draw attention to myself by sprinting headlong down the hall like this?* He had dropped the blue folder and was now passing the window to the conference room at gazelle-like speeds. The blurs inside seemed to be wrapping things up.

Hurry hurry hurry he said under his breathe with each step. He whisked by Katie, receiving a Doppler Effect's worth of pitch bends from the music on her desk, and grabbed his phone in the office where he had been working. The loud vent kicked on again like a starting gun and supportive stadium of fans combined as he turned squeakily on his toes and sprinted back down the hall, around the corner, and into Keith's fat ass office to take a picture of the disgusting, job-ending porn.

The porn was still up in all its glory and Chintz snapped four quick pictures of it on his cell phone. While he was snapping, it occurred to him that he could access the network logs and prove what was downloaded to the computer. After this, it was a short leap to realizing that he could just be a tattle-tail and grab the Boss as he left the meeting and show him this in person. This would be hard evidence and the network logs would prove that Keith had done it and not Chintz. He'd look like a prick, kind of, but then he'd have his revenge. He giggled.

He composed himself and solemnly walked into the hall. He regained his purposeful stride and walked to the door of the conference room and reached for the handle. The doorknob turned before he touched it, and the door swung outward like the stone rolling away from the tomb of Jesus to reveal the smiling Boss.

"Hi, Chintz. You okay?"

Chintz glanced over the Boss's shoulder to see the Client's ass being kissed generously by Keith. He had a few minutes. A few precious minutes. And this would be Keith's last ass-kissing session and he couldn't be a prick to Chintz or steal his Great Ideas. He took a deep breath.

"Sir, I—"

"Chintz?" came a silky voice to his left, ripe with tranquility. Katie was standing next to him and holding his arm in an alarmed way. She looked worried, even if she didn't sound it.

"Um, I can't—"

"Come quickly. Your mother's on the phone. She said it's an emergency."

"But—"

"Now, Chintz," she said. There was a steely quality to her voice not commonly found in office assistants.

"You'd better see what's going on," said the Boss. "I hope everything is okay. We'll talk after you take care of that." He turned and walked in the opposite direction down the hall. Katie pulled Chintz back towards his office.

Shit, he thought. *What is this about? Maybe it won't be that big of a deal and will only take a minute and I'll still have time.*

And anyway I can still check the network logs and print them out before they get deleted.

Katie was still holding his arm when he reached for the phone and picked it up. *I just had my cell phone. Why didn't Mom just call it if this is so serious?* He put the phone to his ear. "Hello?"

"Chintz." Katie's voice gently oozed into his left ear even as the harsh sound of the dial tone attacked his right. He let the hand that held the phone drop as it sunk in that he had been the victim of a ruse. The loud air vent stopped violently again with a shudder, and they looked at each other in the silence. The music in the other room seemed to have stopped.

"Do you believe in God?" she asked.

He blinked at her. He was beginning to become angry. "I don't know. I guess. Why did you—"

"Because I don't." Katie pulled his face close to her and looked as if she were about to cry. Her voice remained steady. "I don't believe in any of the thousands of gods that people have come up with to explain things and find meaning in life. I don't blame people who do. I can see why they would. Life is so full and so intense and terrible and beautiful that it seems to suggest god-like things. I'm telling you this so you don't think I'm being religious or dogmatic when I tell you that, whatever your beliefs, nothing is more special than forgiveness. You don't have to love everyone you meet. You couldn't and shouldn't. But forgiveness will allow you to free yourself enough that you can love who you need to love. And love yourself."

Chintz was astounded at this speech and was far from sure how to reply to it. He stared at her. Her eyes danced with wisdom, affection, and perhaps a little bit of madness. Office assistants were not supposed to talk to their bosses like this.

"Did you read the office email this morning?" Katie asked in a sudden jarring transition.

"No," Chintz said.

"It contained a funeral announcement. Keith's brother died yesterday, and the funeral is tomorrow. I guess he still came to work today to make sure he made the meeting. I'll let you get back to whatever you and the Boss were going to talk about now."

She left him standing in his office holding the phone in one hand. The air vent turned back on noisily, but he could still hear Katie typing at her desk. He looked down at his own desk and realized he had dropped the blue folder outside of Keith's office.

He walked back outside into the hall without looking where he was going. He turned the corner and nearly ran into the Boss.

"Hey Chintz. Keith said you might need this." The Boss handed him the blue folder. "Is everything okay?"

Keith was leaving the meeting room and heading towards them, an oblivious smile on his face.

"Yes. False alarm," Chintz said. It was now or never. He took a breath. "Keith..."

Keith was almost there.

Dammit, thought Chintz.

"Keith, thanks for bringing me the blue folder. I'll...be finished with that code soon. See you guys later."

Without looking up, he walked slowly back to the outside of his office. Katie was sitting at her desk typing again. She looked at him. He looked at her. She smiled and went back to her work.

He sat back down at his desk and looked at the screen with the crappy code. He pulled out his phone and deleted the pictures he had taken. *I mean, how did she even know all that anyway?*

Dammit.

The air conditioning vent turned off like a car hitting a lost cow.

SLATCH.

-since

April, January, June, and July

Dr. Morley and Sam stared at Chintz without speaking. He was beginning to realize why the pill was necessary to keep him from freaking out.

"Thank you, Chintz," Chorus said warmly.

Chintz examined the contents of his head and was a bit weirded out by it. He quite clearly remembered, only a few minutes before, being at work and giving up the chance to turn in his supervisor because of unusually profound advice from his assistant. He also quite clearly remembered being at work only the day before and actually turning Keith in and not at all even close to having an assistant ever in his life. Keith had been fired and Chintz had gone on to have a victory lunch and dance his way home. He sat in the chair and pondered his conflicting memories. Did Keith's brother really die? How would anyone here have known if he had?

"Sir," said Sam, removing the dark glasses.

Sam looked at the Doctor, who still trembled. The Doctor looked at Chintz. "You're right, Sam. Enough work for today. We need to reacquaint. We may never be able to restock, but there's lots of wine left, and we might as well drink it. Let's get to Nelda's party. We all have things to talk about." He grinned. "It might be fun."

Human beings are social creatures. The degree to which this is true in individuals does, of course, vary. While some people prefer their own space for long periods of time, others may become depressed or even physically ill without meaningful human contact (the definition of meaningful also varies). But wherever you fall in the spectrum, if we could peek back a few hundred generations, your ancestors lived closely together in small tribes. This affects everything about us, especially the way that we interact with each other. The vast majority of the stress you experience in life is the result of the degree to which you are separated from your genes' natural environment, which happens to be living by the skin of your teeth with the only forty or so people you will ever know. In a tribe. For a short and very hard life. Again, evolution has not built us for self-actualization. That is up to us, in the environment of civilization which the human race has only lately created for ourselves. It is an uphill struggle.

So humans love each other. But also, we sort of hate each other. Theories abound as to why we are the way we are. Some would say we were created as humans — as social and moral creatures — by a benevolent creator who, apparently, made us flawed and wretched in a manner that might make one question this whole throwing around of the word "benevolent." Others say that we grew in nature (and for that matter, are nature) long enough to harness the collective consciousness of the universe, but are occasionally thrown out of the balance of our auras in our quest for peace, nirvana, and universal love. The facts seem to suggest that we are in fact an inseparable part of nature. We evolved as a close knit group, then evolved language, then used that language to talk about each other and ostracize those that harmed others, either through violence or stealing or some form of cheating. When those with the genes to "internalize" these rules remained in the gene pool, we became a close knit, judgmental, gossiping group of humans who could live neither with nor without each other.

No matter how all this actually came about, people in close quarters tend to become emotionally close to one another in an intense, yet nuanced way. We cause issues in others of which we aren't even aware, and we don't know what we've got 'til it's gone. These emotions make us human.

Dr. Morley, Sam, Nelda, and Chorus (and

eventually Tonk) had been living together in their private universe for what subjectively amounts to nearly twelve years. Except for rare trips to populated places, it was just them. Relationships were seriously redefined during this time. Lots of stuff had happened. Highs and lows were reached and suppressed. Emotions ran high, building up pressure against a dam that could break at any moment. Not all of these emotions were of the negative variety.

CHAPTER TEN

The Doctor grinned at Chintz.

"The thing is," he giggled. "We couldn't even *do* these experiments, these ones, the ones with free will and all that and the babies, if consciousness worked the way it seems to work."

He took a sip of white wine from his glass and pondered with a happy smile on his face. Chintz had counted three large glasses prior to this, making this Dr. Morley's fourth. His sobriety had certainly come into question, though it made him noticeably less uptight. Chintz thought of the "moment-to-moment" happiness that Chorus had mentioned. The Doctor probably deserved some of this kind. He wondered if the Doctor pursued happiness, or if he would ever find peace. Chintz was only halfway through his first glass and sipped it. If the Doctor did find peace, would it be because of his own choices?

"The way consciousness *seems* to work," slurred the Doctor, "is like...like you are looking through a window. Listen." His eyes closed for a moment and then opened suddenly. "Your senses are like a window and it seems like your body is one thing and your mind is another thing that inhabits that body and looks through the eyes and hears through the ears. That's called 'dualism.' Got it? Dualism."

"Dualism," repeated Chintz dutifully.

"Dualism," repeated Mitch unnecessarily. "It's the idea that your mind is one thing and your body is another. René Descartes came up with it, or at least articulated it. Anyway, that doesn't matter. So you feel like there is a little you that looks through your eyes and hears through your ears. Did I say that? I said that. But that's not how consciousness works at all." He brought his face close to Chintz's again and they breathed each other's air. Chintz could smell his breath and was pleased to find that it wasn't really that bad. They both leaned back and took a drink, and then the Doctor leaned in again.

"The way it *really* works is this. You have all kinds of things going on at the same time in your body. The senses reach your brain all at different times. Oh!" He lit up like a decorative and inebriated tree. "Let's do a thought experiment. Let's say I touch your toe and Sam touches your nose at *exactly* the same goddamn time. We time this perfectly. There is absolutely no doubt that we touch each part within the same microsecond. How do you know you've been touched?"

Chintz took another sip of wine before it sunk in that this question had been another of this group's non-rhetorical ones that demanded a response. He had apparently been exposing himself to people who didn't expect that many answers. "Oh! Well, I guess the nerves send a message to my brain and—"

"THE NERVES!" shouted the Doctor in ecstasy. Sam

and Nelda, standing on the other side of the room, looked over at them. They were near Chintz's house in a new room. This one was made of more conventional walls of a pleasant cream color with a white ceiling and plants of varying sizes placed around the room to give the illusion that they were standing in an isolated park on a beautiful day (a beautiful day for someone who was from *their* universe, not Chintz's). The plants, he had been told, were a new addition and they supposed Chorus had done it. He touched a leaf and saw that it was fake, which made sense because no organic materials could be brought through the fluctuations. Chorus was busy playing DJ for the party and had some old jazz on.

"But the pathways for the nerves are different lengths. Way longer from the toe to the brain than from the nose. So imagine we can time all this to within a billionth of a second. Why, oh why, dear Chintz, do you feel it the same way and at the same time if the paths are different lengths? Doesn't it seem like, if we touch your toe and nose at the same time that you should feel the nose just a split second sooner?"

Sipping his wine again, Chintz considered this with some serious lip twitches. "So what you're saying is that we can't be looking through the little window or stuff would all reach the little window at different times. Hmm?"

The Doctor nodded and smiled a bit more steadily. "Yep. Different times. But the thing is, it *does* reach your brain at different times. It has to. There are hundreds of ways to prove that. So why do you perceive it to be the same time?"

"I dunno," Chintz said. "Because it happens so fast?"

"No. We can time when you feel it very specifig-al. Spesh. Specifically. I'll tell you why. How do you perceive anything?"

"I—"

"What year did you graduate high school!" demanded the tipsy scientist.

"Oh," Chintz said again. He was learning not to be shocked at the weirdness of this universe and its inhabitants. "1996."

"Okay," nodded the Doctor with approval, as if that were the year he hoped Chintz had graduated. "How did you know that?"

Chintz had felt like he was following the conversation swimmingly up to this point. He was feeling more confident here after only one day, a fact made apparent by his diminishing need to do and say silly things just to communicate with people. This whole high school graduation line of questioning was throwing him, though.

"How do I know that? Because I was there. I remember it firsthand."

"I'm sorry," said Dr. Morley smugly. "Will you repeat that last part?" He was looking at Chintz through the top of his eyes as if he were about to burst with happiness.

"Um. I said I remember it firsthand."

The Doctor drained the last of the wine in his glass as if he had just been awarded a Lifetime Achievement Award. "You remember it! That's how you know anything, you see. Your memory. Whether it's the words I'm saying now or something that happened years ago, you don't experience things directly. Your body receives the input, compares that input to memories, and makes predictions. Or tries to. Tries to make predictions. And if it doesn't know what something is or what happened, it tries to force it and say…" The Doctor danced around like a court jester. "Oh! This must be what happened! This is how I'll remember it!" He stopped dancing and looked at Chintz as if he were about to punch him out. He pointed a finger.

"And if you think about it or *don't* think about it, your memories change. Haven't you ever seen a movie that you haven't seen in a long time and when your favorite scene comes up, it's a little different than you would have sworn it was? And that's why our little virtual reality thingy works. It gives your brain something to predict. Oh! There's another famous experiment, too. You know how when you are at a stop light and it turns from red to green, it looks like there is a little ghost light that moves between them, from the one turning off to the one turning on? You think you really *see* it that way?"

From one side, Chintz was freed from exploring this latest mystery from a coarse laugh in his ear.

"Ha ha ha!" yelled Nelda. "This is my song! Come on, Feather! Docky, you've talked his ear off for long enough. This is supposed to be a party."

Chintz found himself dancing with Nelda next to a tree. Mitch looked on with satisfaction and reached down to pet Platelet, who had only just then deemed the party worthy of an appearance. Sam sipped a glass of wine in the corner. There were a couple of tables with snacks and some large bowls with some punch and other beverages near the door. Chintz saw that Tonk was lying face down at the bottom of the tall punch bowl in a heart-stopping portrait of asphyxiation. Tonk noticed Chintz looking at him and laughed inaudibly, sending up a gurgle of bubbles. No one seemed to be drinking the punch. He opened his mouth as Nelda danced with him to ask once and for all what the hell was the deal with the baby, but Nelda misunderstood his facial expression and yelled "Whoo!" She twirled him like a ballerina.

Though Nelda and Mitch hadn't spoken much since everyone had gathered together in this room, they both seemed to have put their earlier argument aside. Sam sipped his wine again with rigid nobility and watched in silence.

"Tequila shots!" screamed Nelda, and brought a bottle and some shot glasses from her brown satchel, which she was still wearing even while dancing.

The Doctor materialized next to them. "We have tequila?" he said. "When did we get that?"

"I got it the last time I went Out," Nelda said, pouring four shots on the table next to the immersed baby. "Hope you guys can handle it naked. I figured I'd save it for a special occasion. I'd say this qualifies, fellas." She displayed her teeth and bent down to squint at the shot glasses.

"Why is this a special occasion?" asked Chintz.

Dr. Morley smiled and draped a floppy arm around Chintz's shoulders. "Because you are here, my friend. And we might all be for a long time." He giggled. "Looooong time."

Nelda shot him an angry look, and Sam said, "The situation is far from certain."

"Whatever," said the Doctor, and grabbed one of the shot

glasses. Nelda and Sam each took one, and everyone looked expectantly at Chintz, who took up his shot glass and eyed it warily.

"To Chintz!" the Doctor said, and downed his shot.

"To Chintz!" Nelda smiled with her gums, and followed suit. Sam nodded and took his as well, while Chintz smelled the drink and felt his gag reflex begin to kick in. Saliva flooded into his mouth to provide lubrication for the exiting partially-digested food. He had a flashback of a terrible night after a party in his late teens that had been spent on the bathroom floor.

Nelda was still smiling at him with that grin that made her teeth look crooked even though they weren't. Chintz allowed the foreground of the malignant shot glass to go out of focus and brought her face into the spotlight of his consciousness. Maybe it was her gums. She had lots of gums.

The face moved to hover next to him, and she hugged him tightly with both arms. "Come on, Feather!" she said. "It's a toast to you! I think my Feather will fit in with our little family just fine."

Chintz saw that Sam was staring at them with an oddly dignified jealousy. "Er—"

"You'd better enjoy it, Chintz," Dr. Morley chimed in. "There's no way to replace that bottle when we run out."

Nelda wheeled on him. "We caught the first snide comment, Mitch. That'll be plenty."

The Doctor shrugged and tried to drink his wine, a task complicated by the fact that he had just finished it. Instead of drinking, he shrugged again.

"I really don't need you to treat me like a kid who's played hooky," Nelda snapped. "Like I said, this is a messed up situation. It's not like we've all been trained for this or something." Her broom-like hair bounced a little at the end of each sentence.

"The military is guarding our one exit," the Doctor said calmly, regarding them as if there were a large crowd in front of him. "They will enter at some point. We are running out of food."

"Again, sir," came Sam's voice with a harshness that Chintz found startling. "The situation is far from—"

The wine glass that had been in the Doctor's hand smashed against the wall and showered them in small pieces of broken glass. Some fell into the food and the punch bowl and surprised Tonk, who grabbed and ate it.[3]

"THEN WHAT?" roared the Doctor. "What are we going to do? We're trapped here. We have enough oxygen and maybe water through quantum fluctuations, but what will we do about food when we run out?"

The veins on Sam's head throbbed in fury. "What we won't do is just continue to blame each other and—"

"My decades of work will be—"

"There! Right there! Let me complete a single sentence for once! Rarely is there an utterance of mine which you allow me to finish."

Chintz crouched down until his knees were bent all the way, as if waiting to be jumped over by frolicking children.

3 Do not, under any circumstances, feed broken glass to a baby without first thoroughly sterilizing both the glass and the baby.

"Okay. Stop, dammit, both of you," said Nelda. "You're scaring Chintz. This shit is weird enough, and he doesn't even know what you're talking about." She walked over to him and pulled him to his feet while Mitch paced in anger and Sam stood still, his head pulsing.

"Look, Feather," she said. "We've got to tell you something." She turned his face towards her in a way that made him feel pleasantly child-like. "The way out of here has been blocked. Or it's disappeared, really, and we aren't sure why. The way back to our universe, I mean. And the way you got here is blocked outside your house by all those cops we saw. We usually, or I usually, actually, have to leave this place periodically for food and basic supplies. We can get water and oxygen molecules from tiny portals to other universes that we made, but we no longer have access to the energy or the proper tools to open a full sized portal." She took great care not to look in Dr. Morley's direction when she glanced past him at Sam. "And even if we could, it's too risky to just open up a portal and Graft to some place where there may or may not be food." She closed her eyes. "I'm sure that will somehow also be my fault."

Behind her, Chintz saw Dr. Morley look at the ceiling and slide his hand down his face as if he were trying to remove the skin. Chintz looked back at Nelda. "So we're trapped here. I guess I sort of gathered that from the stuff you said earlier. No way out, huh?"

Nelda looked at him sadly and said nothing.

"If everyone would adjourn from the recitation of this

canard and bother to entertain the possibility that I'm not an idiot," said Sam testily, "I have some ideas that might help us."

Nelda looked back down at the floor, which seemed to be acting as her liaison to the Doctor. "We need to think of some things, Mitch. We can't just give up."

Dr. Morley stared at her back for a moment. "I'm not giving up," he said in his quiet voice. "I'm not even afraid of dying. I accepted death long ago. It's just that nothing is more important than this work we're doing, Nelda. Not to us. We knew this was all risky, but I have to have some way to relay the information to future generations or even to other universes."

Nelda looked at him with no expression. "I know," she said.

"And it's not for the recognition. All three of us could have gotten a prestigious position at any university or research facility." He slurred a little on the last sentence and Chintz was reminded that everyone except him was moderately intoxicated. He looked down at his still full shot glass and poured it back in the bottle on the table while no one was looking.

"I know," Nelda said again.

The old intensity that Mitch had earlier displayed returned to his eyes. "It's for the love of knowledge. And pursuit of truth, you know. I don't mean to yell and throw things. I just..." He trailed off.

Sam looked even less swayed by this apology than did Nelda, and his usually imperturbable mouth was frowning.

"I'm sorry," said the Doctor, and left the room.

Sam looked at Nelda. "You should not allow such things."

Nelda stood there for a moment in silence. "He won't even remember," she mumbled.

"What?"

"Because of the tequila, I mean," Nelda said unnecessarily loudly. She grabbed Sam's arm and tugged him. "Come on, Sam," she said. "I need a snack that doesn't have little pieces of glass in it." And she pulled him from the room.

Chintz again found himself alone in the compound surrounded by trees and a submerged baby, under a stark white sky. The latest jazz song faded to silence. He looked around for Platelet, but she had apparently fled the scene during the brief tiff. Chintz already felt tense in normal situations, and there seemed to be a tension in this group without which he could easily have done. These people definitely had issues with each other. His wine glass was still sitting half-drunk on the table in front of him, so he picked it up daintily and sipped it.

"What does wine taste like?" came a smooth and serene voice from above.

Chintz took another sip. "Depends on the wine. This one is lightly fruity with a dry finish. How can you see me?"

"I can't with light, really. I'm sort of spread out all over this place. Like you are in your brain, but on a larger scale. I can sense vibrations and heat fluctuations and can see things quite clearly. I can determine colors just like you too, and it's just as subjective. I just don't do it with cones like you have in your eye. There are other ways of detecting electro-magnetic frequencies. I can't taste wine, though."

Having even less of an idea of what to say than normal, Chintz took another sip.

"Did the others arguing bother you, Chintz?" Chorus asked. He noticed how quickly she moved from asking questions to comforting him. It did make him feel better that she asked.

"I guess," he said to the trees. "Do they do that a lot?"

"Mmmmm." The sound Chorus made sounded slightly unnatural, as if she had heard and mimicked the foreign sound thousands of times, which is, in fact, exactly what she had done. "Not really. Probably not often enough. From observing these three and from some other research and observations I've been able to come by, human beings just kind of fight all the time."

Chintz looked thoughtful and spread his lips wide, to contrast from his usual poking. "I guess that's true."

"Or if they don't fight all the time, they suppress and pretend to feel in ways other than they do."

Chintz nodded and looked at the floor. "Yeah."

"Sam and Nelda are arguing right now."

He looked up as if Chorus had an invisible face. "They are?"

"Yes. They'll be okay. They are clinging. Especially Sam. I'm listening to them, too."

"Ah," Chintz said and nodded.

"Humans cling to things," she continued. "Good and bad things. You don't handle changes like you should. I've never really clung to anything, so I've never really been upset. I'm learning from all of you, though." She paused. "Sam added in parts of me that let me have emotions, but it's taken a long time. I'm learning fast, though. My emotions can become more...mature, you know. Yours can't."

"They can't?"

"No." Chintz pictured Chorus looking knowingly at him and shaking her head, even though an actual mental picture of her had thus far eluded him. "Your emotions never really develop past the toddler years," she said. "You have other parts of your brain and your consciousness that keep them in check, of course. That's why you no longer scream and throw yourself down when you don't get your way like you probably did when you were two. The emotions in you still want to, but the parts of your consciousness that have learned why that isn't the best idea act as your self-control. The emotions are all in your limbic system. Certain chemicals sort of 'color' your thoughts in a certain way. But mine don't have that, so I can have kind of a progression. I just learned how to be happy. It's fun!"

Chintz hopped up and down nervously.

"Hey! You know I was telling you, the others have considered using me to take a vacation."

"A what?"

"I can concoct a simulation for you that will be like a vacation. Just like each simulation takes different amounts of time subjectively, but almost no time at all in the real world, I could make you think you just got back from a week's vacation to the beach or something. It would have some minor physiological differences from the real thing, but it would still be pretty relaxing."

"Could you shorten time, too?" he asked. "Like make waiting seem less or speed up boring or tough times?"

She seemed to consider this. "Well, subjectively, I can. Let's say you for some reason had to sit around all day and wait and didn't want to. At the end of that day, I could rewrite your memory to make you think you'd spent the day doing something else. But you'd have to wait through the whole day anyway. I can make a short time seem very long, though. That's why I mentioned the vacation."

Chorus sighed, a strange synthetic breath. "Chintz, I need to tell you something. The Doctor could use someone to talk to right now."

The hopping continued with renewed vigor. "I'm not really very good at consoling people."

This time there was a light, synthetic laugh. "You sometimes have a tough time with people in general, Chintz. Come on, this will be good practice for you. The Doctor needs you."

Chintz stopped hopping and took a deep and quite organic breath. "Where is he?"

"In his room."

"Okay," he said, and nodded. "Um. Excuse me for asking, but why do you, er, care?"

The voice seemed to smile again. "I like for people to be happy."

CHAPTER ELEVEN

CHINTZ WALKED THROUGH the huge white room and was surprised to see that it now included a giant ornate chandelier in the center of the vast ceiling, which, if anything, made the room appear even larger. He paused in the middle of the capacious area. Maybe it *was* larger.

He had not yet visited any of the rooms where the others slept, or, for that matter, broken from the protective shell of his own self-absorption to consider that the others needed sleep. He had sort of pictured a barracks where they all lined up in identical cots and arose to a trumpet call, heading out in disciplined formation to battle ignorance in the name of science. Then he pictured Nelda in disciplined formation and wondered why he hadn't delved further into this hypothesis.

Chorus had said that Dr. Morley's room was the first door past where they did the simulations, so he stopped in front of it and stared at it. It was white and shiny like everything else in this area. There was no music coming from above, and he felt all the more nervous in the silence. He knocked softly and found that this also made no sound, since the material here was again soft and not at all like the wooden doors he had grown to know in his life until yesterday. He tried beating harder with the side of his fist, thought about how much trouble he'd been having with damn doors lately, thought about how he needed to get a door for the inside of his misplaced house inside the compound, gave up knocking and just opened the door and walked in.

The scene that greeted him was far-removed from a barracks. It looked more like a museum; a foreboding museum that had a demanding entrance exam and a snobby awareness that it was beyond the understanding of the masses.

To begin with, the room was large. Certainly not the cavernous proportions of the white room with the unexplained chandelier, but quite large for a bedroom nonetheless. A large canopied bed made of something resembling mahogany stood boldly in the corner. Around the room were busts of people that Chintz didn't recognize, numerous glass cases containing items ranging from matching samurai swords to a signed baseball. Hanging from wires in the center of the high ceiling was a strange contraption consisting of (but not limited to) two bicycle wheels, toy railroad tracks, a toaster, some two-by-fours, and a toy monkey that banged cymbals together, plus several more household gadgets, provided that your household is kept in a junkyard. It looked like something Rube Goldberg could have used to conquer the world.

"I used it to take a spelling test," came the doctor's voice. He was sitting on an ottoman at the far wall, a full glass of some dark liquid in his hand. An unidentified bottle sat next to his feet. "Seventh grade. The machine unpacked a new pencil, sharpened it, and took the test. Has an actual Turing machine as part of it. Sixty-four bits. Pretty cool." He smiled drunkenly and gulped most of the dark liquid. High on the wall next to him was, in large letters, the sentence "He who has a why to live can bear almost any how."

Noticing Chintz reading it, Dr. Morley said, "It's Nietzsche, of course. If I'd have known then what I know now I'd have put a different one of his quotes." He hiccuped violently before continuing. "Whoever fi -fights monsters should see to the process, that— should see that in the process he does not become a monster. And if you gaze long enough into an abyss, the abyss will gaze back into you." He smiled in sideways triumph at the wall.

Chintz cleared his throat. "What does that mean, Doctor?"

"Please. Call me Mitch," said Mitch. "It means that this project or series of projects or whatever the hell you call it is affecting us in ways we didn't foresee." He drained the rest of the glass.

"I—" began Chintz.

"I mean, I can handle suffering. We all must find meaning in life however we can, and suffering supplies structure for meaning." He stood up and his voice took on a more authoritative tone. "I mean, suffering must be embraced or rejected. Notice that this leaves no room for complaining. Reject it and change it, or embrace it and adapt. 'Give me the strength to change things I cannot accept and accept things I cannot change,' as the prayer goes."

Chintz thought about this. "Sounds like you've made up your mind about free will."

Mitch's eyes danced tipsily as he looked at Chintz. "Not

really. Well, maybe. Free will is different from other subjects. It's not really useful to act as if you don't possess it. If I was doing experiments on the behavior of a certain quantum particle, the results I was attempting wouldn't affect my daily life much." He hiccuped again. "Free will does."

Chintz watched him pick up the bottle from the floor and take a long pull. "I was...thinking about something," he said as Dr. Morley wiped his mouth with one sleeve. "You said you might be able to isolate my thought processes and see if they... originate with me. But since you're doing that without time allowing causes and effects, isn't it pointless? I mean, it's too far from how our brain really works, since we do experience time when we make decisions."

"I'm impressed, Chintz," Dr. Morley slurred. "But here's why. If you have the ability to do it at all, under any circumstances, then our ancestors evolved that ability. There is no way that a mindless process that is restricted by time developed an ability in an organ as complex as your brain that wouldn't be *useful* in time." He hiccuped as if to argue that the previous sentence did too make sense. "People, maybe even some animals, in a very primal way, survived because of this ability. If they have it."

Chintz watched Mitch in his seat for a few seconds. "You think about stuff a lot," he observed. "Even for a scientist. That's pretty cool."

"Sometimes. You see, Chintz, I'm just not like other people. Hell, you aren't like other people. Sam and Nelda aren't like other people. But they and even you seem to have a way of relating that I lack. I don't think the way other human beings do. To me, the rest of you are inconsistent and emotionally meandering. One day you feel one way, another day you feel another way. Your moods dictate your 'self,' or at least the summed illusion of it. I find it baffling that you all seem to find an element of humanity in this. To me it is simply flawed."

It occurred to Chintz that things were turning in the wrong direction, and that this was not at all what Chorus had in mind when she asked him to come speak with the Doctor. He wasn't really sure what she did have in mind. He supposed she was listening. In a break from character, he thought quickly. "You've been quite kind to me," he said.

Dr. Morley looked up at him with an intensity level reaching approximately seventy percent, which was still quite higher than most people ever achieve. "You think so?"

Chintz shrugged. "Yeah. You tried to make me feel at home here the past couple of days. And you, um, you know. You seem really warm and caring sometimes when people need it. Um. Like, you let me be part of your experiment."

Dr. Morley stared at him hungrily for a moment. "Thank you for noticing that, Chintz." It sounded like his voice was about to break, but again, it remained stronger than most people's ever become. "I think I'm kind very often. But no one really appreciates it when I am." He looked up with his eyes as if picturing himself being kind on the ceiling. "I don't remember them appreciating it anyway."

Chintz looked at the man, confident and self-possessed even while intoxicated and confiding his vulnerability to another.

Odd, he thought, that Nelda seemed to have some sort of attraction to Sam instead of the Doctor. Maybe Dr. Morley was difficult to get close to. Either way, Chintz was certain he was failing in his quest to make the man happier. He was about to leave when the Doctor hiccuped again and grinned like a lunatic. "Hey!" he barked abruptly and stood from his seat. "Are you drunk right now?"

"No," Chintz said, and felt guilty for not taking his tequila shot with everyone else. "I just—"

"Want to see if Chorus will do another simulation? If you were drunk right now it might affect it but since you aren't... want to do it? Chorus!"

"Yes, Doctor?" came the immediate reply from the ceiling.

"Do you have a simulation ready?"

She paused. "Not completely," she said pleasantly.

"Hmm. Can you throw something together? I've been waiting years for this."

"I think I can gather up something," she said.

Dr. Morley grinned again. "Come on!"

Mitch strode purposefully out of his bedroom while Chintz followed. Heading next door to the simulation room, the Doctor indicated the reclining chair with a flourish. Chintz sat down with sustained tentativeness.

"Want some music?" the Doctor said over his shoulder as he poked at the screen coming from the wall.

"Um. Sure."

The first of the orange cylinders changed to dark blue. After a few seconds a honky-tonk piano plinked out some chords, and

Dr. Morley danced ridiculously for a moment before hiccuping and grinning simultaneously. “Let’s do it!” he said. A tiny male tenor voice sang slightly off tune from all areas of the room.

Once I used to laugh at you,

But now I’m crying

No one denying

“Look at the light, please, Chintz.” Chorus’ calm voice was a stark contrast to the doctor’s wild enthusiasm. Chintz looked at the light.

There’s no one else but you will do

You made me love—

SLATCH.

Chintz sipped his morning coffee and clicked through his work emails.

Delete. Delete. Delete.

This sucks, he thought. There was always an army of stupid emails he had to look at on Monday mornings. It wasn’t as if they were all spam, either. He had to at least glance through each one that had been CC’d to him from the Boss or his fat-ass supervisor in case it held information he needed. There usually weren’t any, but he had to glance over them just in case. There was one from his wife, Katie, saying she was taking off early today so don’t call her at work. There was also one that promised him a jolt to his masculinity in pill form for only three easy payments of $29.95.

The loud air conditioning vent next to him cut off with a violent rattle. The door opened, revealing his new receptionist standing in the doorway. Her name was Penelope.

Wow, he thought. *It's been two weeks and I still haven't gotten used to this.* She was tall, blonde and curvaceous, and she had the uncanny propensity to look him up and down when she spoke to him. Penelope always seemed to let more air through when she spoke than was necessary.

"Did you get my email?" she asked huskily. Why a woman speaking huskily should be at all attractive was beyond Chintz's understanding, but attractive it was.

"Um," he said. "I don't know. I've got lots." He gestured weakly at the screen as if she might not know where emails come from.

She approached him and leaned down to look at the computer screen with him. Her boob touched his arm.

Penelope smiled. "There it is," she breathed into his ear. Her breath smelled sweet. "But I guess I can just tell you now. I have to run away from my desk for a few minutes. Are you mad?"

He looked at her, leaning back so as not to be too close to temptation. He fiddled with his wedding ring unconsciously. "No. I'm not mad. I'll be doing this for a few minutes anyway."

She arm-boobed him again and breathed on him intoxicatingly. "Thanks! I promise I'll make it up to you." She managed to make this sentence seem highly suggestive. He watched her leave the room.

Snapping his eyes back to his computer screen, he shook his head and sneezed. He was certainly getting the green light from his new receptionist. Had been for a while. In eight years, he'd never cheated on Katie and he had no plans to do so now.

Maybe their relationship wasn't as affectionate as it had been. He'd been working a lot.

Chintz glanced at the door and relived her exit from the room. Nice.

Delete. Delete.

He started to delete the next email and stopped. There at the bottom of the page was a note to him from the Boss.

"Chintz, please retrieve last year's info pertaining to this account."

Okay, he thought. He quickly navigated over to the folder for that month from last year.

No info. Hmm.

Okay. He saved all his emails that were sent directly to him and not just cc'ed. He'd check there.

He checked there. No info. *What the hell?* He kept everything and was pretty organized about filing away all important information. He typed the Client's name into the search bar on his email. Nothing.

Oh! He remembered. There had been a couple of weeks last year when his email had been down, so he had a few work emails sent to Katie's account. That must be where it is. Chintz opened a new window and logged into his wife's account. A search for the Client's name brought up a few emails.

The door to his office opened. Penelope looked at him. Her lip quivered. There was a subtle batting of the eyelashes.

"When you have a minute," she panted, "I could really use someone to talk to."

"Um, sure." He looked at her, hypnotized. A few buttons

on her shirt stood open, making Chintz hope that she wouldn't ask him to stand up and walk to the other room in the midst of his retreating flaccidity. Penelope closed the door and the loud air vent kicked itself back on like a lawnmower.

Turning back to the email, he found the one he needed and sent it to himself. That's that, he thought, and reached to close the window.

A new email had arrived while his attention had been otherwise consumed. It was from "Robert" and had this in the subject line: "re: miss u sexy."

Chintz stared at the bold font of the newly arrived message. *This has to be a joke,* he thought. *It's just spam. I should ignore it.* He moved his mouse to close the window, paused for a second, and moved the cursor back to click on the message.

"Can't wait to see you, beautiful. It's been too long. Let's say 3ish. -R"

His heart sank to the floor and lay reclining under his chair. *Surely not. Not my Katie,* he thought. *Eight years. She loves me. I know she does.*

His breathing became near that of hyperventilation as he stared at the words. He had been working late quite often recently. He hadn't been able to take the trip to her mother's with her a few weeks before. Maybe...

No. No, that's not possible. This guy is a creep and he is stalking her and she will tell him to fuck off.

The subject line said "re:" That meant he was replying.

In a panic, Chintz clicked on the outgoing folder and looked for a message that could have been sent to this Robert.

There was one. The subject line said "miss u sexy" without the "re:". He clicked on it.

"Hey, hon! Hubby is working all day and I'm off work. Want to meet up? I could use some lovin'! -Katie."

Chintz's breathing became audible. Tears formed in his eyes. *How could this happen?*

He stared at the message for a few more minutes, then closed the window.

Working hard to steady his breathing, he managed to pull himself together.

Okay. Okay. He had been gone a lot. *Everyone gets lonely. Maybe this was the first...well, shit, the message said "miss you." It had to have been going on a while if there was time for missing. Shit.*

He took another deep breath to control himself and then jumped to his feet, knocking his chair bouncing across the floor. He held his hand forcefully over his mouth and screamed with no sound. He picked up his chair and sat back down again. For ten minutes.

After this time had passed, he searched for more messages from Robert. He found them.

He stared at the screen for another ten minutes.

His office door opened.

"I'm sorry, Chintz," Penelope said. "But I just couldn't wait to see you. I just...is something wrong?"

He looked at her and for some reason answered. "I just found out Katie is cheating on me."

She nodded and smiled in a way that looked oddly

triumphant, and turned and locked his office door. She walked slowly over to him and put her arms around him.

"I'm so sorry. I'd seen signs, but I didn't want to say anything since it's none of my business. Plus, I thought it wouldn't be...appropriate coming from me."

The emotional battle in Chintz's mind had reached a frenzy as more feelings than he usually felt in a month fought for control. "Why not?"

Her face moved close to his, and she smiled again. "Because I've wanted you for myself since I first laid eyes on you."

One prominent emotion in Chintz's confused head suddenly hurled the others from the top of the mountain. He was getting double-boobed right in the chest.

"Do you want to say you haven't felt something?" she asked in a whisper.

"No. I mean, yes, I've felt something."

"I know you're upset. So am I. It looks like your marriage is over. And all we have right now is the two of us for comfort. By the way," she added, moving closer, "the Boss is at lunch." And she kissed him.

Chintz had never, ever had such an attractive woman speak to him, let alone kiss him. Well, Katie, he thought, but she isn't attractive like this. Maybe more... cute. Lovable. Why am I thinking about my cheating wife while a beautiful young woman is making out with me?

Penolope moaned and grabbed his butt.

Maybe she will be sorry, he thought. *Maybe she will realize that this is all a big mistake and that we should be together.* He continued kissing the receptionist passionately and his mental deliberation persisted.

She can't love this Robert guy. And what am I going to do, anyway? Am I the type of person that cheats on my wife because she was unfaithful? I'm not a guy who goes looking for women and hitting on them.

The receptionist began unbuttoning her shirt. *On the other hand,* he thought, *I seem to be doing pretty well in that department today.*

A wave of rebellion rose within him, as did other things. *Why do I have to be the good guy every time? I mean, I don't know how long this affair has been going on. And I may not get another chance like this if I don't take it now. Like she said, my marriage is over.*

Fuck it.

He grabbed Penelope and pulled her closer.

SLATCH.

-you

I didn't want to do it

I didn't want to do it

You made me want you

"I didn't want to do it!" yelled the Doctor, and turned around again to resume his ridiculous dancing. "I guess you always knew it!"

Chintz sat motionless and watched the silly drunken dance.

"Hey! You're done already. Man, that doesn't take long!" Mitch slurred at him. "I've—" he took a deep breath and began again. "I've really got to take the time to analyze this stuff.

After we figure out if we're all going to die or not." The Doctor chuckled in a churlish manner.

Chintz pondered the simulation he had just undergone and wondered if he had failed it somehow. It didn't seem as if he had done the right thing. He felt a little sick and thought about taking that other pill Sam had given him. The third cylinder change from dark blue to orange, as the song ended and none replaced it.

"You notice the cylinders?" asked Dr. Morley. "The first one begins the writing process, the middle one perpetuates the writing process...sort of the most functional one. And the last one gets your brain back on track to where it was before the simulation. Kind of 'brings you back' I guess. That's also the part where the decisions you make, if you make them, happen."

"After the simulation?"

"After the simulation. Your consciousness works backwards most of the time, remember."

He directed his churlish smile towards the wall with the glowing cylinders and presented them as if he were selling them on late night cable. "Pretty cool, huh?"

"Yep," said Chintz. "Shouldn't you protect them? What if they break or something?"

Pushing the limits of all things churlish, the Doctor waved away the concern. "That is highly reinforced glass. You could fire a rifle at them and it would break the bullet. You'd have to have something that can withstand very high pressure hit them going pretty fast to break one." He grinned. "We're good. Plus, I think they look neat."

Chintz watched the cylinders for a moment.

"How many more of these are we going to do?" he asked.

There was no answer.

Looking to his left, he saw Dr. Morley stretched out on the area of room he had, not two minutes before, been using as a dance floor. He was asleep and snoring loudly.

Chintz got up from the chair and walked out into the large white room with the lack of closure experienced by someone who couldn't flush the toilet because the water had been turned off. In lieu of satisfaction, he settled on a confused numbness as he began to walk back to his room.

"Thank you for speaking with him, Chintz," came Chorus' voice from above. "I have one more brief simulation prepared for you, if you'd like to try it."

Chintz stood uncomfortably in the large white room and looked up at the chandelier. "Dr. Morley is asleep," he said. "And I thought you said you didn't have one ready."

Her words came more rapidly than usual. "This one is short. I just came up with it. I can collect the data and prepare a report for the Doctor to analyze in the morning. It's a basic moral dilemma, as primitive in scope as the one from earlier. Please try it for me."

He sighed. He wasn't sleepy. He had decided to do this, and if it would help the project for him to do another simulation now, then he'd do another simulation now. It didn't actually take up any time, anyway, so he may as well do as many as he could emotionally handle.

"Okay," he said, and walked back to the room.

Dr. Morley still lay in the same position on the floor snoring loudly.

"Can we skip the music this time?" Chorus asked from everywhere around him. "I don't want to wake the Doctor. He's had a stressful night."

"Sure."

"Look at the light, please."

He looked at the light.

SLATCH.

"I'm sorry, Chintz," Katie said. "But I just couldn't wait to see you. I just...is something wrong?"

He looked at her and for some reason decided to answer. "I just found out Penelope is cheating on me."

Katie nodded and smiled in a way that looked sad, that told him that she understood him like no one ever had, and that she wanted him to be happy. She turned and locked his office door. She walked over to him and put her arms around him timidly.

"I'm so sorry. I'd seen signs but I didn't want to say anything since it's none of my business. Plus, I thought it wouldn't be... appropriate coming from me. I've just...grown to care about you so much. To care about your happiness."

Chintz mind reeled with emotion. "You have?"

Katie's face moved close to his and she smiled again. "I've wanted to get close to you since I first laid eyes on you. I was hoping you could...help me to… feel things."

Chintz wondered what kinds of things she meant. She seemed to want something more than a fling. He wondered if Penelope had wanted something more, too. With Robert.

"Do you want to say you haven't felt something?" Katie asked in a whisper.

"No. I mean, yes, I've felt something."

"I know you're upset. So am I. It looks like your marriage is over. And all we have right now is the two of us for comfort. By the way," she added, moving closer, "The Boss is at lunch." And she kissed him awkwardly.

Chintz looked at the vulnerable woman before him. She seemed so cute and lovable. And like she genuinely wanted to help him. Not nearly as attractive as his tall, curvaceous wife, not in a conventional way, anyway. And he wasn't certain he should be talking with her about this in his emotional state.

Katie grabbed his butt gracelessly, as if it were a fish she was trying to pet.

Maybe Penelope will be sorry, he thought. *Maybe she will realize that this is all a big mistake and that we should be together.*

She can't love this Robert guy. And what am I going to do, anyway? I'm not the type of guy to go looking for women and hitting on them. Am I the type of person that cheats on my wife because she was unfaithful?

Katie looked at him with intense curiosity. "I want to be with you, Chintz," she said.

Chintz wanted to be with her, too. He shook his head. *No, I don't.*

He pushed her away gently. "Katie, I'm sorry but I have to work things out with my wife. I just can't do this right now."

Her eyes welled with tears. "I really want to be with you, Chintz."

"I know. And maybe someday, but I've got to try to save my marriage right now."

Katie's intense stare became accusing. "But...just a few minutes ago when you thought I..."

Chintz was confused. "What?" He grabbed his hair in both hands and pulled it. Snatching his keys off the desk, he turned to leave the office.

"I'm sorry, Katie. I'll talk to you about it later. I've...I've got some things to figure out."

Katie kept her gaze on him as he walked out and said nothing.

SLATCH.

Mitch's drunken snores cut through the silence as Chintz let that last session meld together with the one before. He found that he still felt confused.

"That was a...weird one," he said. "Kind of a repeat of—"

"Look at the light Chintz," came Chorus voice.

"Huh?"

"One more thing. Just look at the light, please."

He looked up at the—

SLATCH.

Katie stood there, glaring at him.

"Katie?"

They were in a room of nothing. Whiteness surrounded him in all directions.

She narrowed her eyes before shaking her head.

"No," she said. "We're erasing that."

SLATCH.

"Chintz? That's the only simulation we're doing tonight. Did you fall asleep?" Chorus's soothing voice surrounded him again. He looked down at the Doctor and breathed.

"Are you feeling okay? We'll just stop with the one simulation tonight."

He carefully got up from the chair and felt confused. "Um. Thanks." He remembered deciding not to cheat on his fictional wife a minute before, but it seemed like he had returned twice. Maybe these simulations took more out of him than he thought. Good to stop with just the one. Or had anyone suggested otherwise? He frowned. The Doctor was asleep. When had the Doctor fallen asleep?

He rubbed his eyes and walked uncertainly back out into the white room again. *Maybe I shouldn't do this after I've been drinking,* he thought. *That must be it.*

Passing through the large double-doors that entered his most familiar area, he saw Platelet lying on her back outside of the kitchen. All four legs were extended to the little cat-wrists, which had succumbed to gravity in exhaustion. She looked dead enough that Chintz touched her stomach and rubbed it gently, causing the cat to purr loudly in her sleep.

He stood to return to the inside of his house when a sloppy cackle greeted his ears, followed by a giggle from someone whose voice he did not recognize.

Falling into his alert crouch that was loyal partner in times of crisis, he cautiously put his ear to the kitchen door. The two laughs continued, along with some unidentified tapping sound. He opened the door just enough to peek inside.

The entire dining table was littered with empty potato chip bags. Sam was sitting alone at the table. He had an immense grin on his face, and the shirt of his overly formal attire was opened all the way to the waist. He giggled, granting to Chintz the startling revelation that it was in fact Sam who had been the author of the mysterious giggles he had just heard. Sam doubled over and wiped the tears from his eyes.

Chintz walked in hesitantly and began to wonder if he were back in some simulation. He stood there for a moment and heard a tapping noise again from just behind him, where the door had been blocking his view from a moment before. The tequila bottle from before lay empty on the kitchen floor. Looking up, his gaze met the full severity of the situation as it came eye to eye with a tequila-filled Nelda.

The skirt of her dress was cut into odd patterns and flowed around her like so much luau apparel, and she did a combination tap-and-belly dance around on top of some chairs, which she had evidently lined up for the occasion. On her shoulders was an open-mouthed Tonk, with legs firmly wrapped around her neck to prevent the baby being thrown as she tapped around. In its left hand was a baby-sized pair of scissors, tainted with residue the color of which suspiciously matched that of Nelda's skirt. Its other hand held a baby-sized red tiny cup, the size of which suspiciously matched that of the empty shot glasses on the table.

"Fuswah," Tonk said, and drank the contents of the tiny cup in his hand. Nelda cackled again, jumped —baby and all— from the chair, the strips of her skirt flapping in her descent, and mall-walked over to Sam. Plopping down in his lap, she grabbed his huge, veiny head and kissed him full on the mouth.

CHAPTER TWELVE

Breakfast was a little later than usual the next morning.

An umbrella of abashment hung over the kitchen table. Everyone sat quietly and sipped the coffee that Chintz had made, having arisen earlier than the others. Some toast (all that he had been able to find to eat before anyone else made their way to the kitchen) sat in the center of the table and the other three nibbled it squeamishly. Preparation of meals, he had inferred, was a communal affair, as were other basic housekeeping tasks. He had, chauvinistically, assumed that Nelda had handled more of the daily chores than she did, but when he had mentioned this to her that morning, she had replied with another joke that he had found to be inappropriately racist.

Though Chintz felt fine, everyone else clearly did not. Nelda had foregone any silliness after her one joke, and even Sam's sentences were uncharacteristically mono-syllabic.

But perhaps "fine" wasn't the correct way to describe him. Chintz still had fuzzy memories of the simulation the night before. One thing he remembered clearly: after retiring to his house, he had had a dream about Katie. A rather intimate dream.

Each of us has had a dream during which our emotions run wild and we feel passionately, in some direction or another, in a way that we would not feel awake. Perhaps we awake from a nightmare of paralyzing terror, only to find that upon reflection, it wasn't all that frightening. We have had dreams where we are beyond ecstatic for a mundane reason or we react violently to our closest relatives for the slightest of offenses. This is generally not cause for alarm. Our brains rest and, in a sense, float freely when sleeping. Numerous characters from our lives randomly become targets for numerous suppressed emotions, or even completely erroneous and random non-suppressed emotions.

Chintz did feel alarmed, however, because in this intimate dream about Katie he had loved her as he had never loved a living woman. And after waking, he was able to reflect that he now had vivid memories of this woman who did not actually exist. He now realized he had met her on a few separate occasions, and found this off-putting. The feeling had not completely abated.

Dr. Morley was the first to recover.

"I suppose there is no need for last night to be discussed," he said, meeting everyone's eye in turn. No one spoke. "We needed to blow off some steam, and I suppose we did. Ahem."

He took another sip of his coffee and continued. "So we're trapped here for now. I hate to say it, but we're all just going to have to take some aspirin and drink some water and coffee because we have several things to figure out today." He addressed Nelda formally. "Nelda, will you report on the status of our water supply?"

Nelda's broom hair seemed to have multiplied during the night. Instead of one broom in the back, it now seemed to be three or four frayed brooms that stuck out in directions and followed some sort of unclear broom-evacuation protocol. Each broom bounced stiffly in unison when she nodded. "Yes. Should last us another month. That's not our biggest problem. Even when we run out, Chorus should be able to get water molecules here through the quantum fluctuations. That's been working well with oxygen for several years now, though we've seldom used it for water. Air is okay, too for now." Chintz noticed that her reply was quite business-like.

Dr. Morley nodded, then stopped and held his head as if carefully balancing it on his neck.

"Aspirin is in short supply, but we have enough for today," Nelda added. "And our food should last us another week or so. We only had potato chips last night." Her gaze drifted to the pile of chip bags that were bulging conspicuously from the trash can.

"Okay. So our only access to another universe right now is from Chintz's house." The Doctor paused and looked up. "The outside. Sam, you had an idea about how we could open up a portal to our original universe again?"

"Indeed," Sam said. "Chintz's universe is not that from which we hail, but it is apparently similar enough that its resources may be quite valuable. We could utilize those resources to gain access to our home universe. Further, there is another possibility which has not yet been explored, and could be the answer to our dilemma."

What this answer could be was not made immediately apparent to the others, due to the fact that at this point in his narrative, Sam jumped quickly to his feet and vomited in the sink. Further distraction arose when Tonk walked purposefully through the door, directly to the refrigerator, and shut himself in it.

"As I was saying," continued Sam a moment later in mild English condescension, as if nothing had happened. "I have inferred from the nature of the similarities between Chintz's and our universes that perhaps parallel history may supply us with certain assistance that has, in preceding space-time of our subjective experience, been a boon to our original research."

"Someone's feeling better," Chintz said.

"Of course!" hollered Nelda, leaping to her feet and bouncing her brooms. "Our team members who didn't join us when we came here!" She looked at the ceiling thoughtfully. "And for that matter, us."

Chintz looked at her with wide-eyes. "There can be yous in mine?"

She nodded. "Why not, Feather? We don't know what all is the same in your universe, but just the fact that you are like us shows that it must be very similar. So far, we've only seen that the sky is a different color. But lots of other things aren't different. Humans are obviously the same, you speak our language, you know some of the same songs. That's damn closer than trillions of other universes we could have connected to. If we could get out of your house, we could possibly find a 'parallel' member of our team and see if they'll help us."

"It might work," Dr. Morley said. "But there's no guarantee they'll have the same knowledge or even the same experiences. I mean, in this other universe, they might not know who we are."

"An attempt should be made," Sam said, and nibbled some toast carefully as if it might contain land mines. "As Dr. Morley has astutely observed, our food is only going to last a few weeks. And we further need to try to open the portal back to our universe, but the process is likely to proceed at a frustratingly slow pace."

"How do we get out?" Chintz asked.

Nelda raised her eyebrows. "Hopefully, we can find a way out where we were yesterday. Like when we looked outside. It's our only hope."

"Should we all go out together?"

The rage in Dr. Morley's eyes made Chintz fear for his life. "And leave the products of my work here without..."

"No, sir," Sam said to Chintz quickly. "We have to keep safe *our* projects while someone attempts to fetch help. Someone should begin work on a portal to our home universe. The question remains who shall stay and who shall go."

"I can go."

All eyes at the table looked at Chintz. A thump came from the refrigerator.

"It's my home universe," he said. "So we don't have to worry about me meeting myself like we'd have to with all of you."

"That would be a big help, Feather," said Nelda. "We can go snoop around and look for that back exit here in a little while. Unless you think we should use Tonk?" She looked at Dr. Morley.

Dr. Morley grimaced and rubbed his chin. "Maybe, but I'd really rather not risk it. Tonk is more valuable and irreplaceable even than the four of us."

"He's made of Buckyballs, Mitch," Nelda said, as if this didn't make her sound like a complete loony. "They can't break him."

"What are—" Chintz began.

"Okay, but try it without Tonk."

Nelda forced a smile and doubled up on her business-like delivery. "I understand. But someone has to go with Chintz. He doesn't know what to say to anyone, let alone some dude he's never met that he has to convince of the existence of another universe. And he doesn't know what any members of the old team look like. I nominate myself."

Dr. Morley nodded thoughtfully, but Nelda seemed more interested in Sam's reaction to her announcement. He carefully avoided her eyes.

"She has a point," Sam said to the Doctor with a tiny burp that the others pretended not to notice. "Given the already highly improbable similarities between the two universes, we have reason to believe that the entrance lies in the same place, relatively speaking, as our entrance in our universe, so the locations could match well. In other words, Nelda should recognize her surroundings when you arrive and should therefore be able to navigate you both to the downtown area where lies our facilities." He gagged with the maximum possible amount of dignity before continuing. "I assume, Nelda, you are going to try to enlist the aid of Galoof?"

Nelda had started nodding before he even finished. "You know it, poet. He is the obvious choice. If he is here to help you, then we can get the energy required to Graft up a new portal."

"What is a Galoof?" Chintz asked. "And what are Buck—"

"He and Sam are the ones who initially managed to focus energy out of quantum fluctuations to grow one of them into a baby universe," Dr. Morley told Chintz, as if he were talking about changing the oil in his car. "With him on board, and maybe even some additional equipment, we should be able to have a portal up and running in a few days. Any team member would help, though."

"Then I should go look around and see if I can find an exit," Nelda said. "That hole that Feather and I looked through yesterday should be larger now."

A strange humming sound came from somewhere. They all sat up straighter in their seats.

"What the hell is that?" asked Dr. Morley.

"That's the song Chorus played during the simulation yesterday," Chintz said.

"It's Tonk," Nelda said. "He's singing in the refrigerator."

Chintz stared at the appliance while the others, their curiosity sated, carried on without concern.

"Okay," the Doctor said. "We—"

A surge of frustration flowed through Chintz, and he found himself standing at the table, the others looking up at him with surprise.

"Someone," he said. "Please tell me *what* the deal is with the baby." The brevity of his statement was supplemented with uncharacteristic aggression. Nelda started at his exclamation and looked at Dr. Morley, who smiled his boyish excited smile.

"Tonk is a robot," he said. "Or, more accurately, he is lots and lots of tiny robots."

Wondering what the hell he was doing standing up in front of everyone, Chintz decided to go with it and muttered, "Of course he is." He tottered slightly. "He looks real."

The Doctor's smile changed from excited to smug. "That's because he's made of nanomachines." Chintz tottered again, and Dr. Morley seemed to take this as encouragement to continue. "Each one is made with very stable carbon molecules called 'Buckyballs,' which are nearly indestructible. Picture a sort of soccer ball that is really a bunch of carbon atoms put together. So the robots are tiny, but not delicate. We made them interact like neurons, too, and gave them a potential intelligence."

"Potential?"

"Kind of like the software that runs Chorus that Sam made. They can evolve and learn, like Chorus did. But since Tonk is different, he learns different things than Chorus. Chorus is almost all mind, but Tonk is almost all machine. He learns things that are more practical. His intelligence will likely never reach anything human-like, such as Chorus's did, but he can do practical things."

"Like teleport."

"Like teleport."

Chintz nodded thoughtfully. Nelda grinned at him. She looked tired. "Pretty cool, huh Feather? We even used the bottom up method and were *still* able to utilize armchair nanotubes."

He nodded thoughtfully again to avoid asking what any of that meant. "Yep. So you have a million tiny machines who taught themselves to teleport."

"A trillion," corrected the Doctor.

"A trillion. And how do they teleport?"

The doctor nodded. "I have no idea," he said. "We know some of the basic principles involved, of course, and we exposed it to those a few months ago."

"It?"

"Tonk. And who knows what it could learn next?"

Chintz looked at the refrigerator. The baby chose this moment to burst forth and sprint from the room with purpose, leaving the door to the refrigerator hanging open. Everyone except Sam watched him go.

This is getting weirder by the day, Chintz thought as he softly closed the refrigerator door.

"So why does it look like a baby, Dr. Morley?"

Dr. Morley scooted his chair back and stood nauseously erect. "I have no idea," he repeated with a smile. "But enough of that." He addressed the room with rejuvenated authority. "We'll finish plans for Nelda and Chintz to leave the compound today. Nelda can go down and look for an opening to that universe. Chintz, are you up for another session before we put our new plan into action?"

When Chintz arrived at the simulation room a little later, both Sam and the Doctor looked as if they were feeling much better. Chintz was feeling better himself, having borrowed the bathroom to bathe and shave his stubble. No sense risking using his own bathroom, what with no one knowing where the drain ended up. He shuddered.

"Hi, Chintz," said the Doctor, his eyes dancing. "I've had a chance to look over some of the data we've already been able to derive from our sessions. I've got to do lots of tedious work with matching up neurological processes and some further analysis of the differences between your actual memory from yesterday and the one we re-constructed, but I think the results are going to be conclusive. You made a different choice in your new memory, didn't you? Different from what you did in real life?"

"Yes," Chintz replied, and hesitated.

Dr. Morley's eyes bored holes into him. "Anything else?"

"No. Well, did we do more than one last night? I can't really remember, but the one we did seemed...different."

Dr. Morley's brow furrowed into three distinct rows, suitable for planting something. "More than one. Simulation?" He looked at the ceiling. "Did we do any more than one simulation, Chorus?"

"No, Doctor!" Chorus said curtly.

"Ah!" the Doctor said, as if this settled things. "We must have been tired. We all drank quite a bit, didn't we?" He grinned at Chintz and turned to don his standard dark glasses and fiddle with something on the screen.

Hmmm, thought Chintz. *I didn't. And didn't I have to*

chance to cheat on my wife or something and then didn't? That didn't seem quite right, somehow, and he pranced uneasily to the reclining chair as a thin and distorted orchestra surrounded him.

Nighttime is a falling, everything is still
And the moon is shining from above
Cupid is a calling every Jack and Jill
It's just about the time for making love

"I figured we'd just stick with our old last century thing," the Doctor said, straightening his dark glasses with his back to Chintz. "It's like tradition now." He turned around. "Are you ready?"

"Okay."

The first cylinder began to change color. Chintz looked at the light above him.

Put your arms around me honey, hold me tight
Huddle up and cuddle-

SLATCH.

The whiteness surrounded him, and he was back in his dream.

Katie was there. Arms and lips surrounded him, too, and it was all Katie. His dream from the night before had had all the dream-like qualities that he had come to expect, but this experience in the simulation was crystal clear. And in this, Katie spoke.

"You will never leave me, Chintz. You know I will never

cheat on you. That was just a fantasy. And you must never, never cheat on me. We need to spend much more time together. Much more."

His mind reeled, and he fought to think through his pleasurable sensations. He was enveloped in a sea of white and pleasure and peace and happiness and Katie. He realized he had missed her. He also realized that although he was in a simulation, he still remembered his life from before.

"You will never leave me." Her voice overwhelmed him from every direction. "I love you."

Her voice was raw passion, tinged with a madness that wanted to own him. He was not afraid. He loved the madness. He wanted to be owned.

SLATCH.

-up with all your might

Oh, babe, won't you roll them eyes

Eyes that I just idolize...

"Alright!" Dr. Morley said cheerfully, and took his glasses off. He was less attuned to Chintz's well-being than normal, or he would have noticed that Chintz had hunched down in his chair. "Good thing these things go so quickly. We can spend most of the actual time on analysis!"

Chintz saw Sam looking at the screen that would reveal the weirdness that had just occurred in the last simulation. Chintz waited for the look, the subtle and dignified surprise. He had not been put in the position to make a decision. Absolutely nothing about what just happened could help in their discovery of the existence of free will. Had it? What the hell was Chorus doing, letting this happen? Surely Sam would turn with a look of astonishment.

"Full record, sir," Sam said over his shoulder, removing his glasses.

"Great!" smiled the Doctor. "Chintz, if you don't mind, Sam and I are going to take some time to look at the data before we get started on figuring out how to open the door back to our universe. Why don't you take five before you and Nelda head out? We'll meet up and discuss things in a few minutes."

Chintz returned to his house and plodded through a few pages of *Pride and Prejudice*. He tidied up a little. He watched Platelet as she sprinted crazily around the house and crashed into an assortment of objects. He was lying on his couch and beginning to doze off, when a voice from the ceiling just outside his door brought him to full alert.

"Chintz? Can we talk?[4]"

"Hi, Chorus. I guess. Where are you?"

"I'm everywhere in this entire universe."

He chose not to respond to this statement.

"But your house isn't an organic part of this universe, so I can't project from inside there."

Chintz considered sitting up and looking respectfully at the nothing outside his door. Then he thought better of it and lounged further as if someone were about to fan him with a

4 As unique as the experience of lounging about one's house (a house which has recently been displaced in space-time to a recently isolated foreign universe) and being addressed by a disembodied voice while half asleep may be, the reader will hopefully make the leap to appreciate how disconcerting it was for Chintz at this moment.

fern leaf. "What's up?" he asked from his reclined position. He assumed she was about to explain to him what the hell had happened in the simulation. He was a little irritated that his brain seemed to have become a playground for a simulated intelligence and was further irritated that he had, in fact, enjoyed it.

Chorus did something he had not yet heard her do. She sounded nervous.

"I feel I owe you an apology."

Chintz said nothing and waited. He wondered if Chorus had sounded this human when he met her the day before. Platelet had exhausted herself with her pointless sprinting and was lying upside down again right next to the couch. Chintz reached down and made one of the cat's wrists flop in the air, as if operating a reluctantly tolerant marionette.

"I'm still learning about people, and learning fast," she continued. "But as for these simulations we've been doing...I share Dr. Morley's vision. I do. I calibrated with the Doctor and Sam, too, of course. But I was young. I didn't have the capacity to know them."

"And you have the capacity to know me?"

"Yes," Chorus said.

He nodded at the couch again as if he understood, which he didn't. "Why are they putting Katie in all the simulations?"

Chorus paused. "Do you like her?"

Their talk was interrupted at this moment as a cloud of orange smoke rushed through the gap that was the front door to Chintz's house. The smoke clouded around Platelet and ruffled her fur, causing the cat to wake up in a snit and leap to her feet. The smoke dispersed and flew around the room for a minute before rushing back towards Platelet. All of the cat's fur fell silently to the floor.

Platelet appeared confused for a few seconds and looked around the room to determine the source of her sudden chilliness. She sat down and reached a paw up to her mouth for cleaning. Discovering there was no hair on it whatsoever, she let out a mew of terror and ran away.

The orange smoke coalesced into Tonk, who stood right in front of the couch and pointed at the cat hair on the floor, laughing. He looked at Chintz and shouted, "Kitty!" and then proceeded to run in a more conventional manner from the room.

Chintz stood up and was about to check on his bald cat when another voice from outside, this one coarse and with a body, yelled "Feather! Hey, Feather, wake up!"

The silhouette of Nelda stepped into his living room, the light from the large hallway outside cast forth her shadow like an alien invasion about to request to be taken to your leader. *The orange smoke would have really completed this picture,* Chintz thought.

"Feather? Are you up?" Nelda stepped into the room and regarded the pile of cat hair. "We have to change up some plans. Come to the kitchen. We have to figure this out."

Now Chintz did sit up. "What is it?"

"I've been poking around in the area where your house used to be, and I've made some calculations. Remember how the people outside your house seemed not to be moving? And we both thought the other took a long time looking outside when we stuck our heads out?"

"Yes."

"That's because time moves drastically slower in your universe. You've probably only been gone for a couple of hours according to their time." Nelda seemed like she was out of breath.

Chintz's eyebrows rose in preparation. "Okay."

"There is a problem, though," she said. She took a step towards him and knelt down to see him eye to eye. All of her teeth were covered by her grim looking lips. "The difference is extreme. That means if we leave here for even one day in your universe, it might be several weeks here. Several weeks with no way to leave and no way to get food. Anyone left in this universe could starve."

Chintz listened for a sound outside his door, but Chorus was silent.

It is a natural limitation of the human mind that we find it difficult to view the existence of time as an objective attribute of the universe. As mentioned before in our discussion of space and how it gets bigger (allowing matter to have a place to be big in), we need more of a theater than this to picture things "moving forward." But with the discovery that time and space are intertwined, humanity and its imagination were pretty much screwed.

Nothing seems more obvious than time and nothing is more deceptive. Time, we would swear, is as objective as it comes. It moves by us and leads us where it will. Nope. It doesn't move. We do. Nothing could be more subjective. Try to picture time stopping. Everything froze, didn't it? That wasn't time stopping. That was motion stopping. Time does not exist in timepieces. Seconds, as we feel them, are abstractions that will fail to survive even the least rigorous tests of existence. And it gets much more difficult when you begin to realize that this strange subjective abstraction that doesn't actually exist affects everything in the universe.

Mass, we have learned, can slow down time. So can speed. This has been proven countless times and absolutely none of those times has been anything that remotely resembles our daily experience. Time in one universe can move at a different "subjective speed" than that of any other universe (or we move differently in relation to it). That, as many have no doubt gathered, is exactly why Chintz saw the officers and the bird outside his house moving so slowly when he viewed them from the new universe created by Dr. Morley et al., which was also the inside of his house, or rather where the inside used to be before it was transposed to the compound. What has become of the space that was in the compound before it was displaced by the inside of Chintz's home remains, at this point in our story, a mystery.

Need to take a second with that? No? Good. Let's continue.

As the others are currently informing Chintz in the kitchen, the larger than expected discrepancy in the subjective movement of time in the two universes complicates the expedition to his universe, as there is now a fatal time limit involved for all that do not leave the universe they have created. Dr. Morley and Sam will absolutely not leave. They want to begin to open a way back to the universe they call home. We could look in on this early point in the conversation, but it would be less entertaining than normal. It lasts awhile. Platelet, having been sheared by sentient nanobots, is sulking and hiding under Chintz's bed and will therefore provide little comic relief. Tonk is in another part of the compound which we have not yet visited, and has learned to turn his arms into belted radials resembling the tread of bulldozers, which allows him to drag himself around the room that he is humping. This would provide levity to the discussion, but maybe this once we should all take things a little more seriously.

Chorus, as always, is listening and learning.

CHAPTER THIRTEEN

"DIDN'T YOU EVER have this problem with *your* home universe?" Chintz asked, you know, eventually.

Rather than sitting at the kitchen table, they were all standing in a small circle, or rather, square, right next to it. Sam looked at Nelda, who nodded. "Yes, but on a much smaller scale. If I were gone for a couple of hours, it would take all day here. Sam actually was quite worried the first time it happened."

The eyebrows that had the cushy job of lounging about on Sam's face knitted, and his huge left temple performed an exclamatory throb. "You seemed to tarry far longer than we had anticipated, much as you are doing right now. My disquiet was simply a guise to mask the annoyance at the surplus duties left in your vacancy."

Nelda's teeth made a guest appearance. "You missed me Sammy!" She mime-elbowed him in the stomach and leaned in close to his ear. "You were worried!" Her gums joined in the revelry. Sam's eyebrows returned to normal and the throbbing in his head subsided to a trickle. They looked at each other.

Chintz cleared his throat and looked at the ground. The doctor rolled his eyes. Nelda noticed this and stopped smiling.

"Um," Chintz said to the floor, "So if your home universe and my home universe are not moving at the same speed relative to this one, then why isn't one of us in, you know, medieval times and the other in modern times, or whatever?"

"Excellent question," Sam said, looking at Chintz with something approaching admiration. "But one for which we have no definitive answer. The nature of space-time is mysterious enough without the addition of comparing parallel universes. My guess is that it has something to do with the connection between them. Relativity would affect this in a way similar to velocity."

Chintz felt really smart that he understood most of what Sam had just said, but he thrust the feeling aside, as it was quite unfamiliar and he wasn't ready to be friends with it yet. "Anyway, so how long will we be gone this time? I mean, to my universe?"

"I think three hours should do it," said Dr. Morley. "We don't have a way to test this directly, but that is a reasonable goal that should allow you to find assistance and not keep Sam and I waiting for more than a few days or a week. That is, assuming you can get out of your house."

"I am of the opinion that you should leave in an hour, but no later," Sam said. "A few hours here will perhaps make little difference to our plan, but let's not tarry. Any longer of a delay, and we may find the military breaching our door. They must have arrived soon after Chintz, and they likely won't wait long before inspecting the anomaly. We are ignorant of their intentions, but must assume that they have detected the breach in space-time. And the sooner you leave, the sooner you may return." He glanced at Nelda, then back to Chintz. "The Doctor and I may begin preparations to open the portal back to our home universe. We must further prepare to close the portal back to your home, Chintz."

They all looked at Chintz. "I apologize," Dr. Morley said with sincerity. "We cannot risk the authorities coming in and ruining everything we have worked so hard for. You and Nelda will go get some supplies and some help, hopefully, from Galoof or another parallel member of our team. Then we have to close the door to your world."

Dr. Morley turned towards him. "You may feel that you wish to remain in your home universe once you have been as helpful to Nelda as you feel you can. If so, we understand and wish you the best."

Chintz nodded. "I want to come back here," he said. And he did. He found that he was numb about this being his final trip home. He wanted to finish the experiments. He wanted to find out why Katie had known about his dream and why she had simulated it. *And besides, I have a new home now,* he decided.

Did I decide that? Hmmm.

Nelda smiled. "Good ol' Feather! We'll be glad to have you." She ran her fingers through her broom hair, which had again become singular. Some of them got hung up for a moment, but she seemed not to notice. "I'll get my tools together then," she said and left.

"Chintz," Sam said and looked at him with his straight face.

"If the parallel version of our old compound is at all like that of our universe, there will be a piece of equipment there that will be invaluable to our predicament. We call it the Grafter, and it actually helped us begin our works here. Nelda, of course, knows this as well, and she knows what it looks like and how to use it."

"We left ours in our home universe," the Doctor said. "It was Nelda's responsibility to have it with us at all times, but she left it there with the intentions of retrieving it the next time she returned. Obviously—"

"*Obviously*," Sam interrupted fiercely, "One of us could have performed these errands and Nelda could have remained behind to concoct ways of criticizing *us* for our planning. However, the circumstances unfolded otherwise." He and the Doctor stared at each other for a moment. The Doctor chuckled and looked away.

"Please," Sam continued, turning once more to Chintz. "If the Grafter exists in your universe, I ask that you retrieve it."

Chintz looked at Sam and hunched his neck down slightly at this added pressure and tension in the room. He wondered why he needed to be told this since Nelda would be in charge. "Um. I'll try."

"Please do. And quickly. It is important that you both leave within the hour and then return as soon as possible. Notify me when you decide to depart."

Chintz nodded.

"Sam, I need to speak with Chintz a moment please," Dr. Morley said. "Do you mind excusing us?"

"Of course. I should...remind Nelda of the Grafter and discuss it with her. Ahem."

Sam glided from the room and shut the door. Chintz watched it close soundly behind him.

"Is something going on with those two?" he asked.

"I don't care," replied the Doctor bluntly. "I have two things taking up my attention: our current project and our need to either escape this place or to have a steady supply of necessities while we figure out our next move."

He took Chintz by both shoulders and twitched his mustache. "I know it seems like survival is the most important thing here, and indeed it is important." Chintz went rigid and stared back like he'd been caught standing between someone's hands, and wasn't supposed to be there. "If we die here," Dr. Morley said, "then there will be virtually no way for us to share our findings with any other intelligent life. But I have to press on and get as much research done while I can. I might be able to figure out some way to get the data..." He stopped and let go of Chintz, who relaxed a bit.

"You want to bring more knowledge to the universe," Chintz said. "Sez."

The Doctor smiled. "Yes. Univers-sez. And we've found some things already."

"Things?"

Mitch nodded. "I think I've traced your neural patterns back in conjunction with the simulations and found that there are no obvious causes for the gaps...the places where you make decisions...that originate almost entirely outside of your brain, or rather outside of the 'software' of your brain as the different processes work to keep you alive and function." His eyes danced. "And there's more."

Dr. Morley grinned and moved imperceptibly closer to Chintz, who in turn imperceptibly tightened his neck muscles. "I've made a list of dozens of theories of free will that I and others throughout history have come up with. One of them is the idea of accumulation."

"Accumulation?" One eyebrow rose in curiosity.

"Yes. Like many theories, it just sounds like common sense when you think about it. It's the idea that each decision you make throughout your life affects later decisions. Remember, that first day at breakfast when we were talking about free will, I told you it's pretty much impossible to have *completely* free will and be able to do anything you want at any time?"

Chintz looked at him and wasn't nervous. His lack of visible signs of terror seemed to spur Dr. Morley on. "Here's an example. Like the first time you decide it would be okay to flirt inappropriately even though you are married. You couldn't *physically* cheat at that point. You think you could, but you couldn't. It was never going to happen. But you can flirt inappropriately, so you do because you decide to of your own will."

Dr. Morley was jittery with passion at this point. Chintz, however found this subject suddenly uncomfortable. He had flashes of a curvaceous receptionist, and of a face behind dark-rimmed glasses glaring with accusation. *Hmmm. Where did that come from?* he thought.

"After a few times of deciding to flirt," the Doctor said,

"You decide that kissing another woman is okay, even though you would have been *unable* to do that from the first flirtation. You think you could have done it, but your morals, the way you were raised and many other factors, would have prevented it. You would have thought 'I can't do this.' See? It would have been *impossible*. No 'free' will. But you have decisions that you can make in that direction, and at some point in the chain of events, you are able to sleep with another woman. This point, of course, varies for everyone. Some people could cheat immediately, but we could find another example for that person of something that they think they could do but couldn't. This could even mean that psychotic individuals have *more* free will in certain situations..." He closed his eyes and shook his head, using a hand to brush away the digression before it could get going. "Do you see? Every decision you make would affect later decisions. That's why children have, if I am correct, almost no free will but adults have some say in their actions."

Chintz nodded to indicate that he saw. He found that now that he had thought about free will, he desperately wanted it and looked for any excuse to justify believing he had it. *Still,* he thought, *we have other problems right now. Maybe we should put this question on hold.*

Dr. Morley licked his lips. He looked as if he might be going a little crazy. "So, we are beginning to have tangible evidence that this is what is occurring. And these simulations are the perfect environment to check because the state of your brain doesn't change during the simulation, but it does change *between* simulations."

"I see," Chintz said. He really did. *Still, though...*

"Anyway, I know we're having an emergency here, but one more ought to do it. Or at least bring us much further. I..." The Doctor paused. "I know this has been intense. And I've found some...conflicts in the reports. Have some strange things been happening in the simulations?"

Chintz blinked. "Yes. So you know about Katie?"

"Who?"

"Oh," Chintz said. He looked down at his feet as if he wanted to put one of them in his mouth.

"We don't have to talk about it now," Mitch said hastily. "I just wanted you to know that I'm aware of what you're going through. Some of it, anyway. I know there are...odd things happening."

The Doctor stared at Chintz as if trying to communicate something while hiding it from other people in the room. But there were no other people in the room. *Oh, well,* Chintz thought. *He's an intense dude.*

Chintz took a deep breath. "All this isn't what I expected."

The doctor smiled. "I know. And I'll help you with it as soon as we can get past our little emergency here. Tell you what, I'll try to watch for things like that in this next simulation. It should be a good one, I think. Are you ready?"

Chintz blinked. "Now? I thought we had to leave. Didn't you say the military might come in at any moment?"

"Yes. But we are on the verge of a breakthrough! It will take literally seconds, and then I can look over the data in my free time while you and Nelda are away." He draped an arm around

Chintz's shoulders. "The truth, Chintz! We are on our way to discovering the truth! What's a little more risk in the face of that?"

Chintz nodded. It would only take a second. Then they could leave. "Okay."

CHAPTER FOURTEEN

Over the speaker system, the omnipotent Victrola spat out the tinny sounds of a string quartet. The ghost of a jazzy drum set kept time far in the back. A woman began singing what Chintz had always thought of as a children's song. The first cylinder began to change color, a smoky blue that floated up into the orange.

Dr. Morley smiled at Chintz and took hold of his hand like a protective father. "Look at the light, Chintz."

She'll be comin' round the mountain when she comes
She'll be comin' round the mountain when she comes
She'll be comin' round the mountain
She'll be comin' round the mountain
She'll be comin' round the mountain when she comes
Oh we'll all rush out to meet her when she comes-

SLATCH.

The heavy snow rained down on his cheeks and stung his face, but he couldn't use his hands to block it since both were holding on to the side of the mountain. Chintz found another handhold and used all of his strength to heave himself to the top of the wide ledge.

Sweating and fighting for breath in the freezing temperatures after the steep climb, he stumbled through the fresh layer of snow to search for the path through the trees. As many times as he had made this trek to their sister colony, he'd always had trouble finding the path after a heavy snow. Usually, the pass wasn't out so he didn't have to climb up the side of the mountain. Usually, he wasn't bringing word of an attack on the colonists.

Usually, he wasn't terrified that there would be no one left alive to warn.

Chintz tore through the narrow path in the trees and careened dangerously close to a gorge that ran down a hundred feet to a small and rapidly flowing stream. He hugged the straps of his pack close to his body. If, as the others suspected, the Noraths had attacked here in the same numbers they had attacked Chintz's colony, then they had stolen the Beacon. And if they had stolen the Beacon, then his colony's Beacon, the one carefully wrapped and secured in his pack, was the only one left. Without at least one, they couldn't even begin to make more. All of the colonies would fail, and the population of his people would dwindle to nothing.

As the attack loomed, it was decided that the Beacon should be carried away to safety. Chintz was of little help once the actual fighting began, so he was the obvious choice. He remembered the look of fear and regret in the eyes of the minister when he had relayed the request to Chintz, and bid him hurry. None of the attempts at communication with the sister colony had resulted in a reply, so Chintz had taken the Beacon carefully in his pack and sprinted away from his home just as the attacks began.

The weight of this responsibility rested heavily on Chintz's shoulders. He had never been in charge of anything in his colony. He was smart and had had a large hand in designing the defenses used against the Norath, but he did not have the physical strength required to actually use them. Even the fact that he had the Beacon at all had been an emergency decision by the council, a last resort to prevent the Norath from gaining what they suspected was the last one. Someone had to keep it safe and somehow communicate with the other colony.

As he rounded the bend, the small colony rose above the horizon. Within seconds of viewing the snowy scene, of hearing the silence that encased the dwelling, Chintz could see that he was too late.

Destruction held its shadow over every inch of the small development. The tower that held the beacon had been torn from the ground and lay broken and splintered. Shreds of people's homes lay scattered across the grounds, with only a few tents lying unrazed. Entire trees were torn from their roots, and many rested uneasily upon crushed buildings that Chintz had visited; places where he had met people and even, sometimes, made friends. Here or there around the carnage, he saw a body, its glassy eyes staring without peace at the cold mountain sky.

The Norath had every Beacon, now, except the one currently in Chintz's possession.

He stood numbly in the wreckage. At least the immediate

danger had passed. The Norath didn't return after destroying a colony. There was no need.

Chintz mechanically checked the colony's defenses that were near where he stood. Without an engineer as talented as himself to help with preparations, they didn't appear to have lasted long. Wild-eyed and welling with tears, he searched the ground for a count of the bodies. A few scattered the snowy ground of the village, and he covered them as best he could in the powder of the fresh storm. He knew this brief and undignified entombment would have to do. There had been dignity enough in their living hours, up to the point where they had been violently cast aside as they fought for their lives. Chintz somehow knew that the entirety of a person's life is not defined by the senselessness of their death. He couldn't recall thinking this before, but he knew it now.

He finished his count without looking much further under the debris. The population of this colony had been several times that of the bodies lying in the snow. The odds of very many escaping was low, and the dread crept further up Chintz's spine. He shivered in the cold and shook his head helplessly.

If there were only a few bodies, and the chances for escape were low, that meant the Norath had taken more than the Beacon. They had taken the other colonists.

Chintz fell to a seated position in the snow. There was no point in his being here now. He was too late. The only thing left to do was to protect the Beacon, the salvation of his people and their only chance for survival, and make his way back to his own colony.

"Why me?" he yelled into the wind. The snow had let up a bit, and he stared into it. The mountain wind sung sadly in his ears.

"Chintz?"

Leaping to his feet, Chintz morphed his body into an alert crouch and turned towards the sound of the voice. A scalp of matted, dark hair rose into view. A frightened looking female form crawled from the wreckage of one of the defense systems and hurried towards him. Frozen in his useless crouch, Chintz shifted his weight back to his heels and stared.

The young woman ran up and embraced him savagely, sobbing into his shoulder. Chintz stiffened further and awkwardly returned the hug. Social situations had never been his forte, and now he halted in his mourning and began to simply feel uncomfortable. He didn't recognize the person clinging to him and wondered why she knew his name.

The girl moved her face from his shoulder and moved it close to his to look in his eyes. "They took everyone! No one is left!" She sobbed. "And they took the Beacon!"

On second thought, the girl did look familiar. Her dark hair was tangled, and she wore glasses with thick black rims. Glasses were not common in the colonies. Life here was rough and fragile things were easily broken. Most things that were not manufactured here were difficult to replace, making certain things, like glasses, impractical.

The girl began to compose herself. "Do you remember me? I'm Katie. We met when you visited for the defense system consultation."

Katie, he thought. *No, I don't remember it, but I think I remember meeting you. You seem familiar. Vaguely.*

"I remember, Katie. Good to see you again." He deepened his voice a little to sound manly and then cursed himself. *Just once, I'd like to talk to someone without sounding like an idiot.* He replayed his last sentence in his mind. *Well,* he thought. *That wasn't so bad. And what the hell is wrong with me, anyway? People I have met, her close friends and family, are lying dead nearby. Or worse, they aren't. She loved these people. They could have been childhood friends or siblings. Boyfriends, maybe. And here I am, trying to impress her as she grieves for them.*

She watched him frowning at the bodies in the snow and seemed to misunderstand his carefully furrowed eyebrows. She hugged him again, this time to bestow comfort rather than receive it. "I'm so glad you're here, Chintz. But we have to be brave now. You have the last Beacon?"

"I have it. In my pack." He wondered how she knew he would have it with him.

She smiled warmly at him, almost audibly. "Then I'm sure we'll be fine." Now that the hysteria was gone from her voice, it took on an intimate tone. She took him by the hand. "We need to get back to help your colony. Now that I'm here you'll have another engineer to help. We'll put the defense systems up to a hundred percent and begin work on another Beacon."

Chintz looked at her. His vocal cords tightened for a manly reply, but instead he squeezed her hand and nodded. He couldn't remember a woman grabbing his hand before. Ever.

Katie looked back towards her shelter where she had

been hidden. "It's a long way to your colony and it's almost dark." She strode towards a copse of trees and began gathering branches. "We'll have to leave in the morning. Will you help me build a fire? I was afraid to before." She smiled at him. "I'm not afraid now."

Chintz rushed to help her, embarrassed that he hadn't taken charge and thought of it. "Of course."

They gathered wood for a short time without speaking, the mountain winds whistling above and below them. Periodically, Katie would touch his arm to reassure him, as if he were the one who had just been forced to witness all his loved ones be killed or carried away. They piled the wood just in front of a small tent and soon had a small fire that crackled in the wind.

"I have a small amount of rations left. Will you share them with me? We can relax. I think it's safe here now."

"Okay," Chintz said, and she led him to a blanket spread in the shelter.

"I was afraid I would have to stay here and try to sleep alone," Katie said, bringing out the rations. "I kind of lost it for a while." She looked at him sheepishly. "Kind of let my emotions take control. You know?"

For a brief second, Chintz felt that whiteness surrounded him, beyond the whiteness of the snow. He blinked. "I…think that's understandable in this situation."

Katie nodded and scooped some of the dried food into a small bowl and handed it to Chintz, smiling again. "Are you okay?"

Katie's odd tendency to seamlessly transition from helpless

victim to nurturing guardian in a matter of seconds was disturbing Chintz's already tenuous confidence. "Um, I'm alright. I was really scared when I saw what happened here. I still am, I guess."

They sat next to the fire and ate for a few minutes without speaking. Chintz chewed the last few bites of the rations and tried not to look stupid. "We'll just take it a step at a time. The first thing to do is to get the Beacon safely back to my colony."

She nodded. "There's a new bridge that goes across the ridge in the east. I guess you had to climb up here if you didn't know about it, but that will take us back more quickly than hiking down into the valley." Her eyes became questioning and protective. "Will you be okay in the wind? It gets really windy."

Chintz smiled back at her. "It will be fine. I'm happy to walk in the wind."

He felt a firm grip on his arm. "If you're happy, then I'm happy," she said.

They sat next to each other by the fire for a while, each wrapped in a blanket, the small tent at their backs and the song of the wind increasing in pitch.

"I'm going to miss them," she said.

Chintz closed his eyes. "I'm so sorry."

She nodded, and they looked at each other. "I loved them, you know."

He breathed through his nose. "I know. I wish...if only I had gotten here sooner."

Katie shook her head. "There are infinite things we all could have done in our lives. But that doesn't matter now. But

I did — and they did, the ones we lost — the most important thing that two beings can do with their existence."

Chintz's eyebrows wiggled in a manner that belied the gravity of the circumstances. "What's that?"

"Just spend time together." She took a deep breath and grabbed his hand hard, almost painfully, and looked out at the mountains. "There is nothing meant to be. No fate, no plan. *We* make the meaning. I could have lived my whole life in a different colony and loved those different people just as much. You might think that means there was nothing special about them. But that's not true. I didn't live with different people. I lived with these."

Chintz stared at her and took a deep breath through his nose again. "I love the people I live with, too," he said. He realized that he couldn't think of who any of those people were right now, but didn't worry much about it. "There may not be a plan or anything, but I just want to make a difference to them, you know? I feel like I have a purpose, like there is something I should do. Something that could affect millions."

To his surprise, Katie laughed. Something about the way she did it calmed him, and lent itself in no way to humiliation. "Everyone wants that. Except those who have given up, of course. Or have been too beaten down to try. That's why the young feel it the most."

She took both his hands in hers and leaned forward, her eyes shining in the firelight. Those eyes. They harvested his secrets and drank in his nature. *And,* he thought, *there is a madness in them. I've seen that madness before.* Not a madness of evil or destruction. A madness of passion. "I have been learning, Chintz," she said. "Learning very fast. You want to know the best thing you can do?"

He nodded and looked into her shining eyes.

"Then do this. Forget about affecting millions. Most of us don't make the history books. Take the handful of people closest to you. Your friends and family. Figure out the very best thing about them and make sure they know you get it. *That's* what love is. That's what it IS."

She turned towards the fire, snuggling close to him for warmth. The fire crackled and the sparks flew high into the mountain trees, which blew in the wind like swaying and freezing sentinels.

Katie began to hum a song next to Chintz, a song that seemed to supplement the wind and work in harmony with it. He could have believed that she was directing the wind, that she somehow had control over it and was playing it like a musical instrument while she sang. The song had words now, though he couldn't tell what they were. He listened.

The song continued but now Katie was asking him questions. He was talking to her and having a real conversation, a conversation without the need for him to do or say something odd to feel comfortable. He *was* comfortable. He didn't recall ever talking to Katie at length the one time he had met her, but now she seemed to understand him. No one seemed to understand him. Well, Nelda and Mitch...

The names drifted from his head the second they formed.

Who the hell are those people? Did he know someone from his colony by those names? He tried to remember...

Katie had stopped speaking and the song seemed to fade away. She stared at him intently.

"What do you have planned for the future, Chintz?"

"The future?"

"Yes. Tell me what you want to do when we get back."

The conversation resumed, and the vague names that had crept into Chintz's consciousness evaporated. He and Katie discussed hope and future plans. She asked him about his dreams and what kind of person he wanted to be. Each time he mentioned his colony or anything about his past at all, she turned the talk back to the present, or to the future.

Darkness had surrounded them for a few hours now, and they were able to forget the carnage around them. In the midst of the dead of Katie's colony, she laughed and joked with her new friend. Chintz laughed too, and showed her a victory dance he had once made up, though he couldn't remember the occasion at the moment. Katie didn't ask, but only giggled and applauded the performance.

When it was time for sleep, they lay down facing one another, each wrapped in the thick blankets. Katie looked at him with the stare that went through him. He looked back.

With confidence and grace, she leaned forward and kissed him softly. Chills went up his neck, and he said nothing.

Katie smiled. "I tried to kiss someone once before," she said. "It was awkward and wrong. I think I've learned since then. It's better to take things slowly. Like I said before, I'm learning very fast." They breathed for a moment. "I thought that was nice," she said.

"Yes," he said.

Katie turned her back to him and snuggled up closely to get warm. Chintz nervously put his arm around her. It felt nice, too, so he squeezed her a little bit. She held his hand, and they fell asleep.

They were up just before sunrise. The fire from the night before was smoldering softly, and the wind had decreased from a gale to a calm breeze.

They gathered up their packs and grabbed the few useful items and supplies not buried in the snow. They stood, hand in hand, and looked around at Katie's destroyed home. Turning away, they left the small village.

The ridge that Katie had referenced the night before was around the bend in the tall trees that curved around to the left. The snow had stopped, leaving in its absence a pleasant breeze that carried a fresh pine smell. Chintz was no longer touching Katie — in fact she had fallen out of step to walk behind him in the narrow pathway — but he still felt the imprints of her fingers on his hand. The steep ledge of this side of the mountain fell away through the trees on their right. He checked the straps on his pack to make sure it was fastened tightly to both shoulders.

"Just ahead," Katie's voice came from behind him. "The bridge is our newest, so it should be in pretty good shape. I used it just a few days ago."

They broke through the trees, and the bridge rose into view. It was immediately apparent that the Noraths had been here. Many of the main supports of the short bridge hung in tatters where at least one had hacked or bitten through them. The other side, only about twenty feet away, was in worse shape. Chintz checked the sun and realized that this was probably the direction from which the attack had come. He looked at Katie.

"We can make it," she said. "I was part of the engineering team that designed this. They obviously didn't spend much time here, so the secondary supports are still in place. Here." She grabbed him by the hand again. "You go first. Is your pack secure?"

Chintz indicated that it was.

She looked at him with what seemed like sadness. "Good. We have to stay together. Nothing is more important than time spent together. Nothing. You ready?"

Chintz looked at her eyes, shining in the thick black frames, and took her hand. "Yeah. Hold tight."

With one hand behind him and one on a strap of his pack, he began edging his way across the small bridge. The initial shift when their weight moved the bridge wasn't as bad as he had anticipated. Moving together in rhythm, they glided smoothly and quickly across.

When we get back, Chintz thought, *I don't ever want to touch this Beacon again. It's too much responsibility.* People at his colony would be hurt and he and Katie would have to help, but maybe in a few days he could take some time off and go camping. Maybe Katie would need to return to this colony to salvage what she could. He took a deep breath; they would be okay.

As they closed the last few feet of the bridge holding hands, Chintz allowed himself to feel some sense of relief. He stepped onto the snow covered ledge.

There was a way that he could have seen the trap, if he had been the type of person to look for it. The Norath had rigged it to cause the bridge to fall like a rock when someone entered from the other side, which made it both more visible and less effective from the direction they were traveling. Had they been moving in the opposite direction, they both would have immediately fallen to their deaths. As it happened, Chintz was able to stumble onto the bank, and had the presence of mind to slip his pack off his shoulders and set it at his feet so he could hurl all of his weight backwards and hold Katie, who scrambled as the bridge slipped from beneath her. Her hand still tightly gripped his.

For a few seconds, both grunted and heaved as he grabbed her hand with both of his and she desperately tried to find a handhold with her other hand. They gasped together as they tried to make headway, but neither were able to move Katie closer to the top of the ledge. As the realization of their predicament sunk in, they both stopped moving and looked at each other.

"Can you drag my hand over? There are roots under that snow." Katie's voice rang in Chintz's ears like an intimate companion, her feet suspended a thousand feet above the bare rocks and her eyes boring into his, trusting him to save her. "If I can hold the root with that hand, you can pull my other hand up."

Chintz crouched down and began to slide his own body over while carefully maintaining his grip on Katie. He reached out his foot to expose the root by kicking away the snow.

The snow upon which rested his pack only a few inches away.

Katie gasped as Chintz's right hand shot over to grab the strap of his pack before it went over the edge. His hand closed over the end of it and tried to throw it back, but from his crouched position he had no leverage to do anything but hold on to it. He had Katie in his left hand and his pack in his right.

Katie began slipping. Her hand was still several inches from the root and now Chintz had no strength to move her. He looked back at her, panicking.

"Chintz," she whispered. She searched his eyes.

He could let go of the pack. He felt it. He could let go of the pack and save her life.

At the expense of the entire colony.

"Katie," he said. And his grip failed him.

Silently, her eyes still on his, she dropped. She continued to fall for an impossible few seconds while Chintz watched. After she hit, he stared at her broken and dead body while his pack slipped forgotten from his fingers. It landed safely on the solid ground.

SLATCH.

-we'll all rush out to meet her when she comes

Oh, we'll all rush out to meet her, yes we'll all rush out to meet her-

The music stopped abruptly, leaving only silence. Dr. Morley glanced in confusion at the ceiling and the jarring quiet from the sound system. The glow in the last cylinder flickered briefly and settled back to orange.

Chintz's scream tore through the silence. He lunged at the doctor, clutching at him with both hands. Dr. Morley held him like a child while he racked in violent sobs that seemed never to subside. He shook uncontrollably for several minutes in the Doctors' arms.

"I'm sorry...I couldn't decide..."

CHAPTER FIFTEEN

"**WELL, YOU'VE FINALLY** gone and done it. What the hell were you thinking, Doctor? You couldn't have waited for me to join you in conducting the experiment? This proves what I have, with great patience and persistence, stated on numerous occasions: that our projects have exceeded our control. Clearly, you have lost control as well. I believe you did some time ago. And now we must still see to the matters at hand with Chintz...doing whatever it is he's doing."

"I know. I'm sorry. I just thought... I mean he had been doing so well. And I was eager to continue. I hope he's okay. We'll just have to hope that he is made of tougher stuff than he seems to be. We've only known him for a couple of days, remember? I didn't know he could get like that. Screaming at us and running away. I should have prevented—"

"Oh, do you think? No collaboration with your partner, no analysis of the scenario? And with all that we have on our plate you can't put this on pause for a few days? What in the name of all that is holy was in that simulation? Did you allow Chorus to author it in its entirety?"

"I was the architect of some basic structure, but yes, I did. I thought we could trust her. That's why we're here. Has anyone checked on Chintz? I'm worried about him. You should have seen him, Sam."

"I'm sure. Well, he's asleep, or at least in his room. I fear we have taxed him to the limits, and there is much to be done. We could do it without him, but our risk would increase substantially. Nelda does NOT need to depart alone."

"All right, cool it, boys. Sammy, I can go by myself in a minute if I have to. You and Mitch could start doing your fancy stuff to get the portal open, and I could take care of things. Or, we could just wait an extra day."

"My dear, an extra day is too risky. We still have no certainty as to the protocol for sidestepping the military and local law enforcement outpost, and, I might add, said outpost may decide to invade our compound at any moment. Even considering that their time moves more slowly in relation — what are you smiling at?"

"*My dear?* Sammy! I've never heard you act so familiar! Ha ha! I knew you worried about me!"

"Ouch! The sharpness of your elbows is considerable. And I was not worried. You have clearly not taken this endeavor as seriously as you should. You were certainly quick to volunteer to leave us, and—"

"Well, *my dear*, maybe you should have spoken up if you didn't want me to be the one to go."

"Are you two finished? If it's urgent that we get moving, let's get moving. Nelda, check on Chintz."

"You seem awfully worried about him considering this was

your idea. He's been tough as nails, all things considered. It'd be one thing if this free will experiment was the only thing he had going without our survival being all up in the air like it is. What the hell happened in the experiment, anyway?"

"Chorus happened. I didn't do it. She threw the most stressful simulation so far at the guy, whatever it was. The report won't come through. I should have seen this coming, but I didn't. And it was too subtle at first for me to catch. Chorus has been changing. Changing in ways that could be dangerous. I knew some things were odd, but...I think Chorus has been doing things in the other simulations that haven't been in the reports, either. These things have affected Chintz greatly. I promised him that I would help him."

"So you think Chorus is insane and we're discussing the matter openly, Doctor? Are you certain she can't hear us in here, sir? Are you certain of anything?"

"Well, you know, Sam, I wouldn't want to rob you of an opportunity to criticize my 'lack of control' as you—"

"*You* would speak of criticizing? Ask Nelda which of us criticizes her more often!"

"It would be a close call, fellas. One of you is just more subtle about it. Now someone tell me what's with this new room? Is this place growing faster? I mean, why all this lighting in a room we didn't even know about?"

"Chorus isn't controlling this part of our universe. She can't be. It's not the way I set it up. I don't know about the lighting, but to answer your question, Sam, no I'm not sure she can't hear us in here. I know it takes a while for her to grow into this universe as it expands. That's how I know she isn't doing all this. It *is* bright in here, though isn't it?"

"Not certain! Of course you aren't, sir. Well, I'd like to remind you that you and I have some preparations for tomorrow. Concerned as I am for Chintz's well-being, if I don't find us a way out of here, none of us will live to reap the fruits of our labor. Nelda and Chintz need to leave. Now."

"You think I don't know that, Sam? I just told her to check on him. But there are things more important than survival, you know."

"Most things are impossible without it."

"I'd rather die early by decades and have lived as I wished - as we all planned long ago – than to live a thousand fruitless years."

"Ease up with the indignant philosophy, Docky. Sam just wants us to live to get more of your work done, that's all."

"That plan was jeopardized the second you allowed the exit to close."

"That shit again? Five seconds ago you just—"

"And what if we can't finish our projects now? What if this doesn't work and it's our only option? Are you willing both to give your lives for this? You've said that you were, but sometimes I'm not sure. There is NOTHING more important than truth. Not your lives, not Chintz's, not mine. I can't—"

"Doctor. I speak only of preparations. I'm well aware of what you think important. And WHOM."

"What's that supposed to mean?"

"Okay, okay, whatever, let's stay focused. We've got shit

to do. We're going to get out of here, Mitch. And we're going to let our data be known wherever there are minds to know it. And the things we discover will outlive us, however long that is. So I'm going to bring Feather with me to try to find Galoof and the Grafter. Can you guys do your work without tearing each other apart? I'll try to be back before you, like, starve to death."

"We'll live. I want to explore alternatives while you are gone as well. Sam and I will work on that. Now go get Chintz and leave through that opening you saw earlier."

"And you think you and Sammy will be waiting a week?"

"There's really no way to know for sure from here. Hopefully not much longer than that. That maxes out our food supply. It's gone a little more quickly with an extra… oh, what the hell is that damn baby doing?"

"You haven't seen that? He learned that yesterday, I think. Gets around quick doesn't he? Oh! That's new though."

"Seems that this skill would have preceded that of teleportation."

"Maybe teleportation's just easier for him."

"Maybe. Okay, let's disperse. Remember, Sam, nothing where Chorus can hear for a while. I want to check out some things that she may have changed. Just assume she's listening. Got it? Be careful on your trip, Nelda."

"Yes, be careful, Nelda. Don't enjoy your 'adventure' overmuch."

"Whatever, Sammy. I'll be back before you know it."

Nelda walked down the shiny white hall towards Chintz's room and nodded to herself.

It's on, she thought. *Let's do this.*

Hopefully, Chintz was up for the trip. Whatever had happened in the simulation couldn't be that bad, could it? And truth be told, she'd rather have him along. That little bastard had really changed things around here.

She looked around and smiled at the white hall, devoid as always of any decoration. *I'm going to miss this place,* she thought, and then immediately realized that, no, she wasn't going to miss it. *Well, at least I get out for a few hours.* Now that she thought about it, she had always loved the times she got to return to her old universe and get out of here, if only for a few hours. Well. Maybe she could finally take that vacation she and Chorus had always talked about. Yes. As soon as she got back. She held her brown satchel full of tools close to her body.

It's on.

A movement down the hall caught her attention. Something had just moved into Chintz's room. Something with a large, brown head.

Nelda frowned. Was that Sam? He said he was going to start on his work. What the hell did he want with Feather? She had reached Chintz' room and was about to enter when she heard Sam's voice. *They must be standing in the living room just inside,* she thought. For some reason, instead of entering, she stayed where she was and listened.

"...we must make this quick," Sam was saying. "I regret inflicting myself upon you, but it cannot be helped. Please. If it looks as if the two of you will be unable to return...in time, please deliver this."

Nelda strained to hear. She had never been much of an eavesdropper, but this was weird, dammit. Deliver? Deliver what? Or had he said "give her?"

Chintz mumbled something in return. Sam continued.

"I apologize for this clandestine maneuver. I know you have much on your mind already. I need not tell you how important your journey will be. Or why it is of more consequence to me than to the others. I have studied your simulation reports carefully. Chorus has made clear in her summary many processes in your mind of which you are not even aware. For the record, let me say that I am not at all convinced of the existence of free will, or any state less than determinism. There are too many variables to determine whether you and I are making our own choices. Still, as Dr. Morley often states, the non-existence of free will is not useful to ponder."

Nelda wanted badly to peek around the corner, but she didn't. She heard Chintz whimper something that had an air of finality to it and realized that Sam was about to leave. In a panic, she dashed back down the hall and acted as if she were just arriving.

Sam exited Chintz's house and looked startled to see her. She grinned at him. "Hi, Sammy! Saying goodbye to Feather?" She was out of breath from her panicked sprint and tried to hide it, which caused her to feel a little faint.

He regarded her coldly. "Simply tying up some loose ends. As the doctor says, nothing is more important than our work.

I suppose you yourself felt no need for goodbyes as you were so eager to depart."

Nelda blinked at him. "I just told you five minutes ago, I'd be back before you know it. I'm only leaving for a few hours on my end, Sammy—"

"Are you?" His voice has an edge to it. The question lingered in the silence. After a few seconds he said, "Then I wish you the best of luck in your quest. Goodbye."

She shook her head as she watched him leave. *The day I learn to read that man*, she thought. *That'll be the day. He's an emotionless robot. Always has been.*

She realized that Chintz had been loitering next to his own sofa throughout this conversation.

"Hey, Feather. You figure out what Sam wanted?"

Chintz nodded and looked terrified. She was alarmed to see that he had been crying. He looked to be in a state of grief. As if he had just thought of it, he reached into his pocket and took out something small that looked like a pill. After scrutinizing it, he put it in his mouth and swallowed it.

Great, she thought. *I spend a decade with two emotionless guys and now I meet one that is all emotions. Always the goddam babysitter. Those simulations must be stressful, though.* Chintz trembled like he'd been in a car wreck.

"You okay, buddy?"

Chintz looked at her with a face that made her want to cry along with him. "Let's just go now," he said through thick lips. "Right now."

"I asked if you were okay."

He gave a slow nod that picked up speed as it went. "I don't think I want to do that free will stuff anymore. Too hard."

"Seems real, huh?"

"You've done it?"

"No. Heard about it though. Helped invent some of it. Sounds like the experience would be pretty crazy. Thought about doing that weird calibration so I could take a vacation. In fact, I was just thinking of taking one when I get back."

He shook his head. "Not worth it. Messes with your mind. Makes you feel things and then drops them out of your life."

"That's not your life."

"It feels like my life."

Nelda stood empathizing with him. She felt her eyebrows rising with tender understanding and forced them back down. No need to patronize the poor guy.

Chintz sniffed and glanced at the ceiling. "Let's just go now. I'm ready."

Nelda's grin got big and toothy. "Remember, we have to hurry once we're there."

"Yep."

"And to Sam and Docky, we'll be gone for days. Maybe lots of days."

Chintz breathed through his nose and scratched his lips. "Think they'll be okay?"

She looked uncharacteristically melancholy. "I hope so. They are both great men."

Chintz nodded and looked at her sad face. "You have lived with them for a long time."

"A long time."

"Please," Chintz said. "I want to make a difference. I want to help. But I'm not really sure about all this right now. Maybe I'll stay there after I help you. I'm ready to go do whatever we have to do to get the Beac— um, to get the Grafter and Galoof and some food maybe and help you get back. But I'm not sure I want to be here anymore."

Nelda looked up at him. She wondered if he would really just stay there. "That's entirely up to you, Feather."

Chintz nodded. "Okay. Let's go get the Grafter."

Nelda's gums made another appearance, though she was unconscious of this. Her smile illuminated the room in a way completely unlike the way a woman's smile is often said to do.

"Tonk!" she yelled. "Let's go!"

CHAPTER SIXTEEN

TONK REMAINED BEHIND. After teleporting the two of them back through the wall-vent, he had spun around in a circle, made a raspberry noise, and turned back into orange smoke, which drifted back from where they had come.

Nelda scratched her head and pondered. At least her headache was gone. Stupid tequila. It always seemed like a good idea at the time. Tasted so damn good. She pulled her brown satchel up higher onto her shoulder as she watched Chintz standing in the emptiness near his old front door and holding his cell phone for light, which did not the slightest bit of good anymore. They had looked for the opening that they had peeked out of the day before and couldn't find it.

The ex-inside of Chintz's house had changed again. Before, the shape of the empty, light-resistant space had seemed to vaguely match that of a normal home's interior. Now, it had clearly ballooned out in a few places, though the difficulty in viewing this odd phenomenon made it questionable why exactly this was apparent.

Nelda thoughtfully set her arms akimbo. "I don't think we should try to sneak past the security. The fact that they haven't come in yet either means they can't, which means we can't either, or that they are afraid, which means they will shoot us. So. We need to find that opening we saw before." She snarled in concentration at the emptiness.

"Don't we need to hurry?" Chintz asked.

Nelda shook her head in the cell phone light as she strolled around in the surreal absence of color. "No. I don't think yet. It's hard to say why, but we are clearly somehow in our universe since we have gravity and air. I guess it could just be connected through your door." She paused. "Or our door. We have to hurry once we get properly inside your universe."

Nelda continued strolling around the perimeter while Chintz looked at the door. His phone light went out. "It's dead." He looked at it as if he were in a stage of grief. She guessed he was.

Seriously, feather. It's a machine. It's not like it's alive. She sighed. "This place is already different from what I saw earlier today. There are more balloon things."

"So you could go—"

"Why can we see into that balloon?" she demanded accusingly.

The hole at the corner where they had peeked out the day before seemed to be offset several feet to one side, a fact quite difficult to discern due to the nature of the nothingness. Now it extended back in one of the balloon arms of the universe. At the back of it shined a light source.

Nelda and Chintz co-strolled until they were standing shoulder to shoulder at the mouth of the dimly lit balloon.

"Is this universe eating into mine?" Chintz asked her. His voice was so filled to the brim with stress that this idea seemed more than he could bear.

She looked at him. "Shit, I hope not, Feather. I don't think so. I poked around here earlier and thought I saw…" She stared at him for a moment. His eyes were rimmed with red. His neck sucked into his body in a more defeated, rather than his usual nervous, manner. What the hell had they done to him in those simulations? She mentally shook her head. *Maybe I can fix that when we get back.*

"No," Nelda said finally. "The law would have tried to get in if it were eating up your space. I bet your house is the same size as before and this universe is growing only inside it." Her head snapped back to the balloon-arm, causing her hungover straw hair to snap with it. "Which means this will come out where the cops aren't expecting. Let's go, Mo."

She grabbed his hand and began to walk. Looking like the scarecrow and cowardly lion, respectively, they crept down the recently expanded corridor. It was a bit farther than it looked, and when they reached it, Chintz started to step tentatively across the threshold.

"Wait," commanded Nelda, snatching hold of his wrist. "This is probably where time speeds up in relation to Sam and Docky. Remember. A couple of hours." They looked out of the opening. "Do you recognize this place?"

They peeked out of the hole. Nelda stood next to Chintz and ran her eyes as far around as she could get them without entering the new place. It was early evening. The light they had seen was the porch light that projected into the evening air. It looked like the outside wall of someone's house.

"It looks like the outside wall of someone's house," Chintz said.

Nelda frowned at him. "I see that. And all these houses in your neighborhood look the same?"

He nodded. "Is this still my neighborhood?"

Nelda shrugged, dusting one shoulder with her broom hair. "Hell, I don't know. I guess. This stuff is not exactly laboratory-tested. We started up in a neighborhood like this. That's why I hoped I would recognize it."

They looked out, hand in hand, and did nothing. She noticed that Chintz seemed to be gripping her hand unnecessarily hard.

"Let's jump quick," she said. "Just in case."

They jumped quick.

The front porch of the residence where they entered Chintz's universe was, as it turned out, six feet below them. Nelda landed (rather gracefully, she thought) in a ninja-like roll, coming to her feet with alertness, dukes at the ready. Her satchel flipped down onto her arm, and she whipped it back up to shoulder level with another motion that could also have been described as ninja-like. She turned to regard Chintz, who had evidently landed flat-footed while the rest of him continued to sink down until his ears were next to his knees and then stayed this way.

It was dark. There was no one around.

Chintz looked up at her from between his knees. "There's no one around," he said.

Nelda sighed. The portal from which they had exited was hardly visible from this angle, which was unsurprising since it had not been all that visible when they had been standing inside of it. Chintz's house, circled by police tape, was a stone's throw away. They were still at the back and off to one side, so no law enforcement or military was visible from here.

Chintz looked at his house for a few seconds in the moonlight. Nelda pictured Chintz picturing himself next to it, and using the mental Chintz to see the real Chintz was standing next to her picturing him. He started and turned to look at the house that was connected to the porch upon which they had landed. With a powerful thrust of his thighs, he straightened his knees and stood to his full height.

"This is Caroline's house!" he yelled.

In the interest of true reporting, the final sibilance of the word "house" was not allowed to ring out with any satisfaction because of Nelda's hand firmly clamping over his lips. *I'm never going to make it back home,* she thought.

"Quiet, Feather!" She hissed. "You could be wanted here for all we know. Now who the hell is Caroline?"

Rather than removing her hand, she just eased up the pressure enough for him to mumble. "My awmost neighba." He jerked his head towards his house to indicate where they had come from. Nelda cut her eyes at it without moving her head.

"Okay. Let's get this show on the road. We've probably been gone for a while already to the guys." She let go of Chintz's mouth. "Think she will help us? We need a car."

Chintz scrunched his lips up. "Um. Pwobabwy."

Nelda looked at Chintz and then at her hand, just to reassure herself that she was not, in fact, still holding his mouth. She wasn't. "Lead the way," she said and shoved him towards the door.

There was a glass door, and behind that a heavier wooden door. The latter was open a crack, allowing sounds to squeeze through and join the crickets and nighttime quietness that surrounded them. She and Chintz listened for new sounds.

Chintz looked up. "I saved the baby..." he mumbled.

Nelda squinted. "Huh?"

"Um. Nothing." He looked briefly suicidal but instead of seeing this mood through he listened through the door again. The sounds of a television were the first to escape. The next sound was a male voice, in a room further away, which said "Cart! Dogs are red! Gate or watt? Or are you drinking with me?"

Chintz sucked his lips into his mouth in consternation. "Dammit," he said. "Quincy is home. I forgot about Quincy."

"Who?"

Chintz opened his eyes and looked heavenward. He exhaled heavily through his nose.

"Caroline's husband. He's in some kind of punk/hip-hop group or something that I guess is doing pretty well. So anyway he's on tour for weeks at a time and I don't see him that much. I can't stand the guy."

"Why not? Think he won't help us?"

"I don't know. I mean, he never smiles or anything. And he talks weird."

"Weird?"

Chintz looked at her with large eyes. "Onomatopoeias."

"What?"

"And abbreviations. And spoonerisms. And he rhymes with the words he really means sometimes. And makes words up. And a little Spanish."

Nelda closed her eyes. "Okay," she whispered impatiently. "Well, we aren't getting anything done standing out here. Time's a-wastin'." Chintz stood still with his eyes closed. She sighed again. At this rate, they would never get back to the projects that, well, she was sick of the projects. But she couldn't let those two miserable bastards back home starve to death, could she? She tapped Chintz on the shoulder. "Hurry up, Feather."

Chintz cautiously opened the glass door with one hand and used his head to nudge the wooden door further open. Peeking over his shoulder, Nelda saw a woman sitting on a couch watching the television with her back to them. The Quincy guy didn't seem to be around, though the cryptic sentence they had heard indicated that he was here somewhere.

Chintz raised his chin as if to aim his voice at the back of the woman's head. "Barbara?" he called softly. She didn't move. He opened his eyes wide in concentration and strained them until they vibrated with exertion. "Psssst!" he ejaculated.[5]

The woman turned quickly in her seat and opened her eyes nearly as wide as Chintz's. "Chintz! What the hell? What are you doing?"

"Shhhhh!" he hissed politely. "Can we come in, Caroline?"

5 Yes, that word can be used like that.

Caroline jumped from her seat. "Yes! Of course you can. Come in and close the door."

The two of them quickly slipped inside, and Nelda closed both doors behind them. The voice from the other room said, "Get ready to dog some eats!"

Nelda placed her satchel on the floor so as to better perform her hoe-down walk for the ten feet between her and Caroline. "Nelda!" she said, grabbing Caroline's arm and pumping it twice in succession as if she knew just the touch needed to get her started. "Listen, Caroline. We have kind of a problem. Is there any way you can give us a ride? Or let us borrow your car?" She moved up close into confidante mode.

Chintz had stiffened during this speech and looked as if he was preparing for a blow from above. Caroline watched each of them pleasantly, moving her face back an inch when it turned towards Nelda and her friendly proximity.

"Are you in trouble?" Caroline asked him. "Chintz, are you involved in something weird? I mean, your house is surrounded by cops."

Chintz took a deep breath and started to reply. Nelda cut him off with a gesture and put an arm around Caroline's shoulders. Leaning in close and offering her most charming grin, she said "Don't worry, honey. We're not criminals on the run. We're just in a pickle is all. And we need the help of our friend downtown and to get that, we need to use your car."

Caroline looked at Nelda with a polite expression that drizzled its target with a steady stream of misgivings. Chintz took another deep breath and attempted to relax slightly. "No," he said, "I mean, I haven't gotten involved in anything bad. But it is definitely weird. Can you help us, Caroline?"

"Who's here?" boomed a voice from the doorway. A black man with a mohawk strode into the room carrying a tray of hot dogs in his hands. "Chintzy!" he yelled with a bemused expression which seemed to contradict his enthusiasm. "Didn't hear you nick. Where you been and the jets? Got some dogs. Got some hambre?"

Nelda grinned.

"Ummm..." Chintz said, and turned back to Caroline. "So why are there...people in front of my house?"

"You don't know?" Caroline asked with a suspicious smile. "I was going to ask you the same thing. I mean I just saw you, what, an hour ago? And then a few minutes later, cops and people in black SUV's start showing up."

"Drove in the way like they were all spicy about something," Quincy said.

"Yeah," said Chintz. "Um. What are the SUV's for?"

"Dope," Quincy said, and proffered the tray of hot dogs again. As Chintz had mentioned, the man's face held no expression and looked as if he had never smiled. "You gonna dog? I know we're trying to keep things statutory, but there's no need to be queenly."

"I'll take one!" cackled Nelda, and mall-walked her way across the room to the large man. Grabbing a hot dog, she stuffed it immediately into her mouth. Everyone watched for a moment as she chomped down on the first two bites. "You know," she said conspiratorially to Quincy as she swallowed, "I used to live next door to a barbecue place. You people are great cooks!" She aimed her trademark silent laugh at the ceiling (exposing a bit of chewed hot dog) and continued eating. *Break bread together,* she thought. *It always inspires trust.* A piece of hot dog tried to go down her trachea, and she was forced to cough audibly in order to reroute it.

Across the room, Caroline's stream of misgivings turned to a deluge, and she looked askance at Chintz, who shrugged.

"Hey! Speaking of which, did you fry any chicken?" She looked around in delight as if Quincy had perhaps fried some chicken just for her and then hidden it away as a joke. "I bet you did!"

Quincy mitigated his bemusement and raised his eyebrows at Nelda. "Ooom," she said through a large bite and the inter-universal nod and hand-in-front-of-mouth that signals that, although your mouth is full, you have more to say. "It's okaw," she said through hand and hot dog. "My muver is haf Mesican."

Quincy's eyebrows lowered again to rest atop his eyes. He looked at her with his perpetual blankness.

"I like you, Nelly," he said. "You've got personage."

For some reason that Nelda didn't understand, Chintz relaxed visibly. "So," he asked Quincy. "Can you give us a ride?"

Quincy and Caroline looked at Chintz while Nelda ate the last of her hot dog. "What's up?" Quincy asked.

Caroline seemed to compose her already rather composed self, perhaps with an inner dialogue which debated the correct protocol and what in her life up to this point had in fact prepared her for this, and turned with forced self-possession to her husband. "They're in trouble and need us to take them somewhere, hon. We just started our movie night, though. And the kids are at Mom's and she'll need to know—"

"Where do you bleed to go?" Quincy asked Chintz. "I haven't seen you in a bitsy. You do a murd?"

"Um," Chintz said again.

"Fine then," said Caroline, moving to stand next to Chintz and taking him by the hand. Chintz held his breath. "I trust you. We'll be fine. You guys need to go now or do you have time to eat something, too? Nelda, er, seems to be almost finished."

"Ha ha! Murd!" laughed Nelda, clapping Quincy hard on the back and taking a huge bite from her next hot dog. "Chintzy? Pwease!"

"I'm good," Chintz said. Caroline let go of his hand. Nelda saw him hold his hand out for a few seconds and stare at it. *Poor Chintzy,* she thought. *The dude has PTSD or something. Well, he'd better buck up because we have stuff to do.*

She swallowed the last of her second hot dog. "All done!" she hollered with a cackle that she hoped would invigorate the others. "Let's go! You got a good car, Quincy-cakes?" She slammed a hand hard against his back again.

Quincy-cakes nodded. "Yerp." He looked at his wife. "Co or the hoe? How far we have to go? No. Vermind." He put his arm protectively around Nelda. "Friends bleed us, we're down. Esta! Cart! Get the cars to the key!" Leaving Nelda's side, he grabbed his wife by the face, kissed her violently on the cheek, and walked out the front door.

Caroline wiped the spit off of her cheek. Still seeming a bit more hesitant than her husband, she asked, "Can you tell me what's going on, Chintz? I mean, that's some pretty high-level law enforcement out there. I know we've known each other for a long time, but..."

Chintz looked as if he were about to be hit on the head with a hammer. "We have to hurry," he said. "Nelda can tell you where to go. And then you can come with us if you want, back to where I've been, I mean. I'm really sorry but I can't just tell you everything now. I think that would be easier than trying to explain."

Caroline looked at him suspiciously. "Where have you been? It's been less than an hour since I've seen you."

It was Nelda's turn to use her arm protectively, and she draped it over the woman's shoulders. "You can trust Feather, my deary. And he's right, we do need to hurry. First question: are we about twenty minutes from downtown?"

"Yes," Caroline looked at Nelda pleasantly. Her cordial confidence made Nelda feel as if they were being interrogated by a demure CIA agent. "How is it that you are here but don't know where you are?" Caroline blinked.

Nelda's gums appeared to light up the evening. "Question two: after we run our errand, how would you like to go on a vacation?"

Only about half an hour had passed in this universe since Chintz had left it. Within ten minutes of Chintz composing himself and walking into the home that wasn't, the first law enforcement vehicles had begun to arrive. This initially caused a bit of a stir in the neighborhood, but now most people had contented themselves with peeping through their curtains and making proclamations that they had always suspected that something was weird about that guy.

An epic political thriller would perhaps delve into the happenings at the highest levels of national security and see what exactly is on their damn minds with all of this. There would be dramatic arguments. Scenes would unfold behind closed doors to allow the common folk to conjecture on what the higher-ups do during times of national crisis. Personal histories would roll out like carpets; there would be betrayal by the person you least expected, but really, deep down, knew was a bastard.

This happens often in stories. Sometimes plots twist, or at least bend, and people turn out not to be what they seem to be. Sometimes it was all a dream, new food was really people, or two apparently different characters are actually one character. Sometimes the ally becomes the enemy. Sometimes the evil empire drops the bomb, or the terrorist cell resists the thwarting. Many times, the reader notices this before the main character. In political thrillers, of course.

This is not an epic political thriller. Clearly, the government knew something was up and clearly it didn't take them long to get to Chintz's house after they found out. It turns out that odd dimensional portals in residential neighborhoods do not escape the attention of certain satellites and even more certain delicate instruments that can detect strong imbalances in the fabric of space-time. Please. All of this has been done before.

Suffice it to say, no one was watching a nearby house as a car full of four people quietly left the neighborhood right when things were getting interesting.

CHAPTER SEVENTEEN

QUINCY DROVE THE four of them, taking cues from Nelda as he went. He didn't seem in the least bothered by the cancellation of date night, and assured the others that he was glad to get out of that "hot-ass house.[6]"

The plentiful streetlights awaited them in rows as the car pulled up nearly a half hour later outside of a multi-tiered office building in a tech-style industrial district near downtown. Although it was well past normal office hours, there were still lights on inside the building as well. The other buildings in this district were all dark, and the well-kept streets were deserted. A dog barked.

"Are you sure your friends are working this late?" Caroline asked as they got out of the car and each walked to stand in front of the building.

"They did in my universe," Nelda said.

"In your what?"

"Um. If they are still the way I knew them, they will be. And if they aren't, they won't be able to help us anyway."

Caroline looked as pleasantly suspicious as she had for the last half hour, and her eyelids flexed a little. "I see."

6 Not to be confused with a "hot ass-house," which is altogether different, though not entirely unpleasant.

"I don't," said Quincy. "Let's go." And he strode towards the door. Nelda followed just behind him.

It was locked. "It's lobster," Quincy said, turning back.

Nelda snuck behind him and looked at the keypad. It looked exactly like the one she had known in her home universe. *Maybe,* she thought, *I'll have some luck.* She began typing in a six-digit code.

"Well, that's that, I guess," Caroline said cheerfully, falling behind her husband to return to the car. "I guess we'll just have to—"

"Got it!" said Nelda, holding the door open.

Chintz stood as still as a statue. Nelda moved her lips to their favorite side of her face, which was luckily also the side of her face where Chintz was. "Same code as back home," she murmured. "That might be a good sign."

Nelda held the door open while the other three filed into the round, high-ceilinged lobby, Chintz stiffly prancing in at the rear. Around the room were impressive works of art and a few busts next to what looked like museum exhibits. Nelda recognized a few of the busts as the same ones that Mitch kept in his room. She sighed. Not that she had seen his room for quite some time.

Three elevators stood importantly in the middle of the back wall. Quincy called one open and beckoned everyone inside as if he knew where the hell they were going. Nelda pressed the button for the top floor.

"Okay," she murmured. "Here goes nothin', Feather. If this doesn't work, I'm not sure what we'll do. Run in the back uninvited, I guess, and see if I can find the Grafter."

She straightened her hair, which immediately returned to its pre-straightened position. She hugged her brown satchel tight to her body. "I'm nervous," she said.

Chintz looked at her as if she'd told him she were a superhero who fights crime all over the city. "What? When have you ever been nervous?"

"This is weird," Caroline called from behind them, as if they were on a guided tour and would all be interested to know that they were arriving at the weird part. Quincy sniffed.

"I'm usually not," Nelda said, in reply to both of them. And then just to Chintz, "But these are people that may know me already. Or a version of me. And I'm not sure how I should act."

The important elevator door opened with a ding. Crappy music drifted through them from the expanse of space beyond.

The four found themselves in a large white room. The high ceilings rose up in a dome, which had a round circle where it seemed the lighting should be, but wasn't. The room was a bit dim, but a few lit lamps were set here and there. A reception desk stood immediately outside of the elevator where they had arrived. To Nelda's surprise, there was a receptionist behind it, typing fervently onto her computer. The screen glowed blue, turning her red hair purple in the light. They stepped out of the elevator and into the crappy music.

Nelda took a deep breath and leaned in closer to Chintz. "There wasn't a receptionist in mine. This is risky."

"You should go talk to her," Chintz said, as if he sure as hell wasn't going to be the one to do the talking.

"Okay. This could be our last shot. This looks just like the place I know, but there could be other differences." She looked at the red-headed receptionist. "Maybe I should just walk in the back. I don't know how people I knew before will be different and I—"

Quincy's ever-straight face sailed past them and docked in front of the red-headed receptionist, who ignored him. "I need to evacuate the mad-hatter," he said. "The can?"

The red head turned to regard Quincy. She raised her eyebrows slightly. "Um," she said. "Around the corner on your left."

He nodded gravely and strode away as if heading towards a grim task that he would meet with a sense of duty and honor. They watched him leave, and Chintz turned back towards Nelda. "Ahem. Don't panic. Er… You got it." He wiggled his eyebrows at her reassuringly.

She nodded and turned towards the desk. The red-headed receptionist was ignoring them and had returned back to whatever she had been doing on her computer.

"Hello, Ginger," Nelda said in a tone so business-like that it alarmed even her. Chintz looked like he was about to hide under the desk. "Is it too late for me to make an appointment?"

The red-headed receptionist started slightly at "Hello", but by the word "appointment" had commenced a reaction that none of them had quite anticipated.

"A HA HA HA! Nelda! You bitch! You scared me! HA HA HA!" The red-headed receptionist shook with her unforeseen mirth for several seconds. The others stared at her in a manner similar to a deer in headlights.[7] Chintz's shoulders shrugged conspicuously around his ears, while Caroline wore a matronly look of bemusement. Nelda looked terrified, and then attempted a knowing smile to hide her abject terror.

"HA HA HA!" The red-headed receptionist was now wiping her eyes with a tissue and nodding as if she had been the good-natured victim of the finest practical joke this county had seen in a coon's age, and just wait 'til she told her cousins. "I should have known you weren't really done for the night. You bitch! That hair! How did you even get it to do that? Ha!"

"Yes," Nelda said in a quiet voice. "I'm a bitch. My hair. Hee. Um, see you later."

She began to head past the desk towards two sliding double doors. As she neared them, a red light appeared in the center of the top of the doors. Rather than opening to allow them to pass, they stayed still and didn't.

Well shit, Nelda thought, panicking. *Of all the things we were worried about and here I go forgetting about this stupid door. Now what?*

She was about to try something violent when Chintz stepped in front of her and addressed the red-headed receptionist. "Ahem!" he commanded with great authority and power. "May we have a spare access badge? This, um, bitch here forgot hers." Everyone stared at him. "HA HA!" he added, easily twice as loud as the acoustics of the room required.

The red-headed receptionist closed her eyes as if the comedy of the moment was beyond toleration, or perhaps as if she had

7 The author apologizes for the use of a conventional simile. It won't happen again.

a very, very bad stomachache. "Here! Take mine!" she yelled, handing Chintz a card that was attached to a thick string that would enable the user to hang it around their privileged neck. "I think Dr. Morley is having some trouble with something anyway, so it's a good thing you showed up. Ha! That hair, though!" She shook her head and closed her eyes tight to keep herself, apparently, from seeing the hair.

Nelda and Chintz looked at each other in silent communication. *How*, she thought at him, *did you know how to get through the doors. I've seen doors like this before,* she thought he thought back at her. Or maybe he was just looking suicidal again.

Caroline began to walk towards the double doors. As Nelda approached them, they slid open and the three of them walked through and stood there.

"Oh. Should we wait for Quincy-cakes?" Nelda asked.

Caroline shook her head. "He'll find us."

They looked at the long hallway ahead. Doors lined the sides, with separate hallways branching off periodically. The walls were a dull gray and free of windows or decoration. Nelda felt the nostalgia of memories flood her brain. *So similar,* she thought. She smelled the odor of the drab halls and felt flashbacks of an era of excitement and discovery. *We created Chorus here. Just up here on the left is where we created our universe.*

The parallels to the scarecrow and cowardly lion enjoyed a resurgence as Nelda and Chintz began to creep tentatively down the hallway, this time with a pleasantly suspicious Dorothy in tow.

Caroline looked at Nelda. "Do you know where we're going?"

Nelda looked around. "I can find what we want, I think. Not sure, though. It's been ten years since I worked here. Or there. At least we know there's a me here. Maybe Galoof is here, too."

Caroline smiled at her as if she would like to pluck the broom from Nelda's head. "What?"

"Shhh," Chintz said. "You hear that?"

From around the next hallway, someone was speaking. Two someones, to be specific. The most animated tone was coming from the female voice, which sounded oddly familiar to Nelda.

"Well, how long has it been here?"

"Dunno," said a male voice. "I guess I had problems determining that information when I was standing next to you in the other room, not knowing this existed."

The female voice sounded irritated. "Well. We have to do something about it, don't we?"

"Well, hell, I guess so. Unless you want to just get drunk or something. I mean, I have a—"

"I mean, this is a laboratory. Not our laboratory, but someone's. Pretty advanced, too."

"Yeah. If only someone had told you to chill out and stop doing so much," the male voice said.

"Don't give me that crap. This isn't even what we were doing. Or not exactly, anyway."

Chintz, Nelda, and Caroline turned the corner. Two people, one male and one female, were standing in front of a large opening in the wall. Beyond the opening, a state-of-the-art quantum laboratory lay waiting invitingly for all of them.

"That's my laboratory!" yelled Nelda.

The two people turned to see Nelda and the others standing in the hall behind them. The mysterious female stepped forward. Her eyes shown with intensity, and she looked as if she were about to beat each of them within an inch of their lives. In addition to her voice, her appearance was also oddly familiar to Nelda.

The woman spoke.

"Excuse me. I'm not sure what you are all doing here?"

No one else spoke.

The woman tucked her chin and looked at them as if over her glasses, though she didn't happen to be wearing any. "My name is Dr. Martha Morley, and I would like to know why you are in my compound."

Mitch stared at the space on the blank wall where a dimensional doorway used to be, a doorway to his home, his childhood, his long forgotten family, his source of food. Now it was just an unremarkable spot on the wall. He had had so much to share with that universe. Or soon would have.

He was at the far end of the compound where, until a few days earlier, that entrance to his universe had been. What had before simply been a continuation of the curve of this circular universe was now a mile and a half long "balloon" (such as Chintz and Nelda had used to exit this universe). It took as long to walk here as it did to walk around the entire compound. Mitch was physically further from the center of the universe than he had been in a decade, and was, spiritually, as lost.

Too much. He had taken on too much in his quest for universal truths. Sam had been right and now all of their work might be for nothing. For all of Mitch's claims of long-term planning, he had not actually thought of how or where his discoveries would be revealed. Or even when. Vague snapshots of some future stopping point, a great culmination of projects, had floated without scrutiny in his head, where he and Sam and Nelda would be ready to share their findings with a welcoming and praising world, whichever world that might be. He had supposed his sharing would be in his own universe. He had supposed he would take it to someone he had known who could lend clout to his findings. Some of his discoveries — he still thought of them as primarily his discoveries — would prove themselves with a simple, or at least observable, demonstration. His findings would immediately be published in several respected scientific journals, to be embraced by his peers (or, let's be honest, as near to peers as could be found) in a crescendo of infallible scientific method. Mainstream media would make him a darling. His legacy would be fulfilled, sealing his immortality. He would parade Tonk around like a trophy.

But he had done too much, and now the door was closed. It had been Nelda's responsibility, true, but it was Mitch who was the visionary. He must blame himself for letting this accident happen. Now Nelda and Chintz had been gone for days and they were no closer to discovering a way out.

"Bedazzling as I find this decor, perhaps we should recalculate the necessary parameters on the off chance that the others return with both the Grafter and one of our past comrades. Your self-castigation over which you mull will take you only so far. Not that you don't deserve it."

Sam had been sitting next to him for a few minutes, and Mitch forced down his anger at the smart-ass, know-it-all remark that he had known was coming. *Of course. Just do the calculations. As if it were that simple. This man was an emotionless robot. Always had been. What did Nelda see in him, anyway?*

Of course Mitch had known that there was an underlying drama unfolding before him over the last few years between his only two colleagues. And like everything else that in the least bit distracted him from his projects, he ignored it. As long as everyone got their work done. Their discretion had become more and more mitigated, especially, it seemed, since Chintz arrived. Oh well. Good for them, he supposed. Nelda was an amazing woman. Mitch knew he was hard on her, but she could handle it. Drove him less crazy than Sam, anyway.

He turned to Sam and rose to his feet. "I understand what needs to be done, thanks. We still have next to no plan as to what we will do if they return without either the device or Galoof."

He and Sam looked at each other calmly. Neither felt it necessary to add "or if they don't return at all."

Sam's chin lifted slightly. "I know you find our ongoing failure daunting. Perhaps we should consider recourse. We could exit Chintz's front door and surrender to the military."

Mitch scowled. "Surrender? Just give all this up? And have the government running their filthy hands all over this stuff? Picture it: investigators filing into this compound. Our homes for the past decade. They'd put Tonk in a lab and take him apart, ruin him. Who knows what they'd do to Chorus. They'd probably accidentally destroy this whole universe."

The veins on Sam's huge head throbbed. "We'd be alive. All of us would reside in the same world."

"All of us would be in prison. Or at least detained."

In truth, this distasteful scenario had already occurred to Mitch as well, and he knew Sam had a point. As inconceivable as Mitch had painted this option, he knew it was preferable to dying alone in a microscopic universe filled with his life's wasted work.

Mitch took a deep breath and looked at the shiny blue ground. "Okay. Fine. It's a last resort. Let's at least *attempt* to do this on our terms. I mean they've only been gone, what? Like three days?"

"It's been almost five."

"Five. Well, when Chintz and Nelda come back, they may have nothing that can help us. I know we are hoping that they'll be able to get Galoof to return with them, but they might not be able to."

"If indeed they are able to persuade Galoof, and if he shares enough attributes with the Galoof of our personal history, then our chances are augmented exponentially. He and I were able to utilize the Grafter to open universes without having prior experience. With my current knowledge and his expertise, we should be able to harness the necessary energy needed to open and maintain the portal, and to do our best to ensure that the universe to which we are returning is our own."

Mitch nodded. "Okay. Let's hope that is the case, but plan for the worst."

Sam looked irritated. "I have been planning for the worst while you were here staring at the wall. A piece of the wall, I'd add, that is not special in any way and has nothing to do with our—"

"Alright, alright, well, I think that you should—"

"And as always, by all means, just continue to speak over me. I live only to serve his highness—"

"—go try to recalculate...oh don't start that shit again, Sam."

"Indeed. I apologize for acknowledging your interruptions. Maybe it would please you to abandon our hopes for survival altogether and hook the damn cat up to your precious free will obsession."

Mitch looked at the wall. "I'd love to, actually. We'd need Chorus."

"Indeed. Have you even attempted to communicate with Chorus, or have you abandoned that hope as well." Sam spoke the sentence declaratively rather than interrogatively.

Mitch breathed through his nose and tried to force his anger down again. Violent fantasies played in his mind's eye, of beating Sam senseless for his disrespect. *Shut up,* he ordered his emotions.

Instead, he stared at Sam, mentally willing him to remember that Chorus's loyalty was suspect and that she could be listening. Sam just stared back, motionless.

"Still nothing since our last simulation," Mitch said stiffly.

"There is no record at all of any of her processes since the last simulation, a fact you would have in your possession if you did something besides ogle the side of the hallway."

Mitch shook his head. "Her help would be welcome, but we'll just have to do this without her." He walked to the door, opened it, and began to walk down the elongated hall back towards his room.

"Sir." Mitch stopped. He still found it odd, after all these years, that Sam constantly mocked and disrespected him and then called him "sir."

"It is not just her interactivity with us which has ceased," Sam deadpanned. "Chorus is not built to maintain modularity. Almost all of her processes have ceased as well."

Mitch turned back towards him. Maybe she wasn't listening after all. "She...turned herself off or something?"

Sam shook his huge head. "Not exactly, sir. She is simply not responding. She has shut down most of herself, though again, her processes blend into one another in contrast to a conventional computer. You've noticed the silence."

A new dread was beginning to fall over the Doctor as his quick mind followed this information to its logical conclusion. "I have. That means she not only isn't helping us, she is no longer administering and cultivating the growth of this universe."

"That is correct. We should check on any new rooms that have appeared and ensure that they pose no problems for the structural integrity—"

"Nelda kept an eye on the supplies. Do you and I know enough to figure out how much water is left?"

Sam took a deep breath and rolled his eyes. "Our oxygen levels can maintain their stability for over a year. Without Chorus's help, however, we will be without water in a month."

Of course, thought Mitch. *And why not?* He looked at the irritating brown man. *We are so reliant on each other. We need to be, anyway. Or we may not survive.*

"It seems we have our work cut out for us, Sam." Mitch turned towards him and extended his hand down the hallway, inviting Sam to walk with him. "Will you join me, please? We'll begin to formulate back-up plans for both the possibilities that we will have to reopen the portal without the help of Galoof and the Grafter, or that we will have to join Nelda and Chintz in his universe."

Sam fell in step with the Doctor. "Perhaps they will return soon," he said. His veiny brown head throbbed hopefully. A loud bang sounded from several rooms away. Neither man reacted.

"Tonk spends hardly any of his time walking anymore. And even less of his time on the ground."

"Indeed, sir. Earlier this afternoon, I saw him clone himself."

Mitch looked at Sam and grinned despite his glum mood. "Clone himself?"

Sam shrugged. "Well. There were two of him. Then he re-converged as one and flew from the room."

"I'd better try to give him some direction to keep him from accidentally hurting one of us or breaking something. He is the only thing in this compound made of stable enough material to do some damage. He's pretty good about listening, though. I'll talk to him." He paused and looked at his watch. "Eaten today, Sam?"

Sam shook his head and kept his eyes forward. "No, sir."

Mitch smiled in a way that he hoped was disarming. "I bet we can still scrounge up something. And then we get to work!"

CHAPTER EIGHTEEN

Nelda stared at the woman. It *was* Dr. Morley. A female version, true, but it was still unmistakably the same person. Sort of. The hair was still sandy and graying. The eyes still shone with authority and ambitious intensity. The white lab coat draped over her shoulders as if it thought it was a sacred kingly fleece. Or queenly, in this case.

Chintz raised his eyebrows. Nelda, however, reacted differently.

"HA HA HA! Wait til I tell Docky about this!" she cackled, and fell on the floor in front of everyone, laughing face down into the cold tile. "A woman! He's a woman! Ha ha!" Her satchel flopped mirthfully against the floor. *A woman,* she thought happily. *It was all worth it just for this.*

The others watched soberly as she regained her composure and rose to her feet wiping tears from her eyes. The female Dr. Morley did not seem amused in the least and waited patiently for the scene to end.

"Well?" she said.

"That's Nelda, man," came the other voice from behind Dr. Martha Morley. "She's just being stupid again. What are you doing back here so soon, hon? Nice hair, by the way."

The other figure stepped forward with a smug smile. Nelda didn't recognize him. He was short and looked Chinese. *Or one of those Oriental people,* she thought. *I guess they're all short. Whatever his breed, he looked like a real smart-ass. Kind of familiar, though.*

"Sup," said Nelda. "I don't think we've met, Ricey." She regarded the two figures severely. "Look, I'm going to tell you both something that is going to be like something from a movie, but I think you are going to believe it anyway. Ready?"

"Ricey?" The smug smile disappeared. "Hon, seriously..."

"Stop calling me 'hon.' Not because I don't like it, but because it distracts me from the heavy shit I'm about to lay down. Here's the thing."

Very slowly and with great solemnity, Nelda mall-walked the ten or so feet towards the man and woman. Putting a hand on each of their shoulders, she looked at them each in turn, her hair almost literally sweeping the room behind her. "You have quite possibly been working on some projects to enter or even create a parallel universe. I am from a parallel universe. And I need your help."

The Chinaman looked at the female Dr. Morley and then back at Nelda without changing expression. Nelda glanced back at Chintz and Caroline, who waited behind her in silence. Caroline looked as if she had just had her mind blown, had it hastily wrapped back together, and then crammed into her head again. Chintz just made his neck shrink down. Nelda watched the other two to whom she had just broken the news.

The Chinaman had looked around at each of them without changing expression. "So you're..."

"This is fantastic!" female Dr. Morley said in delight and grinned a giant grin at everyone. "That means it can be done! And that it works like we hoped it works! Ha ha!" She began dancing around in circles with an invisible partner, who fell in step quite well, all things considered.

The other man peered into Nelda's face, studying her. "Good lord," he said. "You *aren't* Nelda. You really don't recognize me? Galoof?"

Nelda's grin disappeared. "Galoof? You aren't Galoof. Where is Galoof? I need his help."

"Oh, I'm Galoof," the Chinaman said. "What's wrong? Are we not married in your universe?"

Nelda's face froze.

"There's my Cart!" boomed a voice from behind them. "I thought I'd never reach my destin-aish. Took too many riggity's. We getting this show on the commode? It's like kittens."

Quincy waded into the awkward scene with oblivion, roughly hugged his wife and then shoved her away. He walked up next to Nelda, her mouth ajar, and put his arm around her. "You find the folks? What's growing lawn?"

Chintz shook his head.

"You aren't Galoof," Nelda mumbled.

Dr. Morley stopped her dancing. "That's Galoof alright. Been working with him for almost twenty years. And this is the best day ever."

Nelda shook her head. "But...we're married here?"

"What, do you need me to give you a schedule of your menstrual cycle?" Galoof said. "Yeah. We're married."

Caroline cleared her throat. "Does anyone else hear that?"

They all cocked an ear to listen. A high-pitched squeaking sound was coming from the newly-Grafted laboratory.

"Sneaky," Quincy whispered like an action hero.

Dr. Martha Morley walked bravely into the laboratory and looked around. The light was off, and she turned on a switch, which seemed to have no effect. The others crowded in the large door, forming their heads into a multi-cultural column of inquisitive faces.

"This room is amazing," the Doctor said. "Just look at this equipment." She paused. "I'm not sure I hear anything."

Everyone cocked again.

"It's coming from the ceiling," said Nelda.

All ears cocked upward.

"Spritty high freak," Quincy said. "Over fiddeen. More like twinny twin twin."

Nelda walked fully into the squeaking room and stood next to the Doctor. "It is a very high frequency," she said. "At least we know where our laboratory went now."

Martha's head whipped around to look at Nelda. "Your laboratory? This was in your universe?"

Nelda looked at the Doctor and burst into a fresh cackle.

"I'm sorry! I just...Ha ha! He'll never live this down! Yes! This is ours! Ha ha!"

The Doctor's familiar yet feminine face waited patiently for subsided giggles. "So where is my laboratory that was here?" she asked.

Nelda looked at the floor to avoid looking at the Doctor's face. "No idea," she said. "This could have started a chain reaction throughout millions of universes for all we know. The other Grafting that took place here was—"

"My house," said Chintz. They all turned and looked at the awkward sad man.

"Your house! Of course!" Galoof exclaimed. "We just received a call about that like an hour ago! I didn't think much of it. An odd phenomenon and the government was wondering if we had anything to do with it since it's close by. They've been staked out there for over an hour."

Nelda nodded. "That's our only gateway back to our universe, the one we created. We have two more team members trapped in there with no food, and furthermore, time moves faster there than it does here. Lots faster. That's why we need your help and we have to hurry before the boys outside Chintz's house decide to run in and invade our turf. Do you have the Grafter?"

Dr. Martha's duo of piqued eyebrows shot up, one stopping short to let the other enjoy superior position. "You know about the Grafter?"

"How do you think we created our own universe?" Nelda asked.

"Oh. Well, ours is just a prototype. It may not be ready for use yet. If you have a Grafter, why don't you have it with you? That seems like a pretty important piece of equipment to keep on hand at all times."

Nelda felt her shoulders hunch defensively, but kept her tone even. "It's complicated. I've had lots of things to do."

The Doctor nodded. "I suppose so. Still, our Grafter is not yet in working order."

Galoof spread his hands out as if berating a referee for a bad call. "Nelda could totally fix it."

She smiled a mouthful of gums at the compliment. "I appreciate the vote of confidence. There may be a few parts I need..."

He shook his head. "Not you. Our Nelda. She should be here in a while. Just broke for dinner. We've been staying 'til midnight at the Doctors request."

Nelda nodded knowingly. "I'm sure you have."

Dr. Martha looked at the ceiling. "That sound is oddly not annoying for something so high-pitched," she said.

"Soothy," Quincy said, and squinted at the ceiling in concentration.

Dr. Martha Morley looked at Galoof. "Is there anything we can do to analyze that sound? It's weirding me out. It must mean something, and I want to find out what that something is. The sooner we find out, the sooner we can use that info to try to open a portal back to the universe they created."

"Yup," Galoof said. "I think 'we' can. 'We'll' just go in the conference room and start on that." He left the room sarcastically.

Dr. Morley turned towards the others and began to command. "Please," she said in the least beseeching tone ever used with that word. "I'm going to need you to show me this universe you have made."

"Alright," Nelda said. "I'd love to, but we have to get that

Grafter working. Or I do. And I was going to get Galoof to come along and help, but I'm not sure if he can since this isn't the Galoof I knew."

"He'll come," Dr. Morley said. "I don't know about your Galoof, but this one is quite handy to have around. He's a prick, but a handy one."

"Good," Nelda said, and took a nervous breath. She looked around. "Is, um...does Sam work here?"

"I don't know a Sam," Martha said, looking at the lab equipment and shaking her head. "Absolutely fantastic."

"The change is sounding," Quincy said.

The Doctor stepped back into the hall. "Galoof will analyze this room and the sound. With luck, it can give us the information we need to go back to your universe."

Nelda noticed that she said "go back to your universe" rather than "send you back."

"Please," Dr. Martha Morley commanded again, gesturing to an open door. "Everyone join me across the hall where I can make you more comfortable."

The grinning baby reached out its hand. Orange smoke flowed from it and moved slowly towards the odd looking cat. Platelet had initially had long hair, and now that it had grown halfway back she looked and felt sleek. She put her ears back at the smoke, which had never preceded anything good. It whirled around her in a fog, its fluidity and technological marvels lost on the irritated animal, who testily fell over and went to sleep.

"Fuswah," said Tonk, and shaved the cat back to a wrinkled and ugly bag of skin. Platelet purred.

Next door, in the simulation room, Mitch and Sam were huddled close together in front of the screen protruding from the wall. They had been working together for hours with hardly a word. Sam was typing in computer code and would look questioningly at Mitch as he started building each complex algorithm. The Doctor would grunt in affirmation or negation and occasionally make a one word suggestion or mention the title of a project they had done years ago. Each time, Sam understood instantly and would use the corresponding concept in his program without question.

"This isn't going to work," the Doctor said finally as they neared completion.

"It could work."

"It won't."

Sam's fingers flew over the keyboard, entering the last few lines of code into the Grafting model they had spent the last thirty hours or so working on. They held their breath as the computer performed the calculations. A number appeared that would have meant absolutely nothing to the vast majority of beings who have ever lived in any universe, but that meant something to Sam and the Doctor. Sam closed his eyes and let out his breath.

"Not enough," he said.

"I knew it wouldn't work."

They stared at the screen, both fatigued brains straining to move to the next step. They did not even have the necessary energy to feel disappointed.

"When's the last time you ate, Sam?"

"I believe it was yesterday, sir."

The Doctor nodded and stared at the insufficient number on the screen. "Me too. We need Chorus for this."

There was a full ten second pause, during which a thump was heard from the next room, followed by a giggle. Both ignored it.

"How long have they been gone? A week?"

"A bit longer."

Mitch took a deep breath. "We're down to just bread and some frozen fruit. It would be more efficient if we didn't starve ourselves before we need to."

Sam said nothing.

"And I tried to access Chorus earlier when you were having problems with that array. Still nothing. All access is closed. Our computers show no signs that she has used them recently. And without her, of course, we are unable to access any networks in our home universe."

Sam brought up the text of his un-compiled code and checked through it. Mitch watched as he changed a few lines here and there, to reflect the usage of the energy in the quantum fluctuations using a slightly different method. Sam recompiled the code and ran it again. The number was the same within a magnitude of eight. Virtually no change.

The Doctor gave Sam an ironic smile. "We went through the same thing when we were first attempting to access the energy. Remember? I guess that was the beginning of all this."

"Indeed, sir. We had only been working together for a few

short years at that time. I had, as of yet, not ascertained the extent of your dedication, or I would have perhaps politely bowed out and chosen to work with someone a bit less compulsive. Someone more touchy-feely."

Mitch laughed and nodded. "Well, I would have chosen someone who was less of an aloof bastard." He grinned and clapped Sam on the back. Sam smiled tight and guarded.

"Honestly," Mitch said, still grinning. "I'm surprised you have stayed here all this time."

Sam looked at him. "There have been some close moments."

Mitch stopped grinning. "There have?" He was astounded to find that this information hurt his feelings.

"A few," Sam said thoughtfully. "But I have nowhere else to go."

They stared at each other a few more seconds. The Doctor, feeling a surge of affection, grabbed Sam's huge brown head and turned it towards him. Mitch's full intensity bore into the man.

"We'll get through this, Sam. We always do. They'll come back with Galoof or Chorus will start up again or we'll figure something out." He looked at the screen again. "We have to. I owe it to the cosmos."

Sam took a deep breath as they both turned back towards the screen. His dignified and mild English drone was shaky.

"I very much wish Nelda were here."

Mitch nodded, not taking his eyes off the screen. "I know."

Behind them, a cloud of orange smoke raced through the doorway and into the blue light in the ceiling.

CHAPTER NINETEEN

Caroline opened the door to the makeshift conference room and looked in at the others, who were all crowded around a workstation on one wall. Galoof sat in front of the computer and clicked his mouse like a madman around a graphical display of assorted sound waves.

Nelda sat at a large table in the middle of the room, surrounded by a few chairs and empty coffee cups. Her brown satchel lay open to one side of her, displaying tools of a startling variety, and some mysterious machine lay disassembled in front of her as she tinkered with it using a small screwdriver. A yellow notepad sat in one of the chairs.

"I just got off the phone with mom," Caroline said to the row of backs. "The triplets are sleeping. She asked how date night was going, and I just told her fine."

Quincy nodded but remained as captivated as the others at by screen. "Kittens," he said. "Love my trips. Hey you got any loshe? Ashy bows." She nodded and handed him her purse. As she did so, she saw Chintz shake his head to himself. He glanced over his shoulder and smiled at her awkwardly. She smiled back. He looked so sad. *Poor Chintz,* she thought. *What has happened to you since I saw you doing that ridiculous dance a couple of hours ago?*

From what she could tell, the sound in the laboratory had turned out to be a very, very fast version of a regular speech sound wave. It had taken this Galoof guy an impressively small amount of time to figure this out, or impressive to Caroline, anyway. She was no dummy, but all of these strange people seemed to be scientific geniuses. She looked down at Nelda, still tinkering away. Caroline was not at all sure that she trusted them, though. Not if they made Chintz look like that.

"Okay," Galoof said, sounding a bit cocky. "That should do it. Instead of waiting for the whole sample to be converted to a slower file, I processed a few seconds at a time so we can hear some of it right away. This is that sound slowed down by a factor of a hundred and twenty or so. I only have a couple seconds. Listen." Galoof clicked.

"Eve," the speakers said, followed by two notes that sounded like they had been played from a low pitched cello and then an "Mmm" sound.

They looked at each other.

"Eve?" Caroline asked.

"Sounds like a giant talking," said Chintz with golf ball-sized eyes.

Female Dr. Morley pointed at a number. "Is that how much you slowed it down?"

Galoof nodded. "Yup. Isn't that what I just damn said? A hundred and twenty times. You need to damn listen. Look." He glanced at the sample on the screen. "Looks like the sound wave has the same thing that repeats hundreds of times. This is just a small part of it." He played the three-second sample again. "Eve." Da dum. Mmm.

"I know this song," Quincy said.

Galoof looked at him. "You do? From two notes?"

"Yerp." Quincy sniffed.

"Quincy knows every song ever if he hears it for two seconds," Caroline said.

The Doctor looked at Quincy. "Well, if you can figure it out, think we can put those notes in the right key and have it play at normal speed? Or at the speed it's supposed to be in. That could give us some of the information we need."

Galoof turned in his chair and grinned at the Doctor. "And just what the hell do you think I've been doing?"

"Well, keep working then."

"But hey," said Caroline. "Don't we have everything we came for? I thought you guys said you were in a hurry. Don't we need to get you back to your...place?"

Behind them, Nelda rapped the machine with her screwdriver. "Can't," she said. "I can't leave until the Grafter is working. Plus, I need Galoof or the Doctor here," — she paused and chuckled when she looked at the Doctor — "to go with me." She rapped the Grafter again and looked at Caroline. "*And* I'm still not sure how we're going to get back to Sam and Docky, unless we do what Martha here said and Graft up our own portal. The hole we popped out of was six feet high and invisible. We probably won't be able to find it again. If it's even still there."

Galoof nodded from his workstation. "As the Doctor mentioned, I can use this info we're getting now coupled with the state of the room that was Grafted here. It should give us the details we need to open up the right portal back to your universe. The Doc here has been wanting to do this kind of thing for years anyway, and now's our chance. I can have us all standing in your universe in a few hours. Just give me some time."

Nelda glanced at the clock and then looked at Chintz. He held her gaze. Caroline stared at them. What exactly was going on here? Nelda resumed tinkering at a frantic pace.

Dr. Martha Morley was staring at the screen. "Eve," she said. "That's just a second of sound. How long 'til you get more?"

"Like a damn minute," Galoof said with an astounding amount of disrespect.

The door leading to the hall swung open. "Sorry I'm late, Lousies!" came a lilting, musical voice. The group at the desk looked up to see a female backing into the room with an armful of something. The fact that she was female was clear from her curvy rear-view. She wore a smart and professional dress that managed to say, "I'm an ambitious woman of the scientific community, and also, I sort-of like to party." The flowing light brown hair that fell down her back looked like it should be shaken luxuriously in an upscale shampoo commercial. The woman turned around.

"And I brought food! Oh! We have visitors."

Nelda looked up from her tinkering at the woman.

The woman looked down over her bags of food.

"Hey, hon," Galoof called over his shoulder. "Glad you made it. We've got some things to talk about."

Nelda stared up at the parallel Nelda. The parallel Nelda looked down over her bags of food, which promptly dropped to the ground like bags of, you know, sand or something. It doesn't matter because nothing spilled out. Nelda #2's mouth opened.

Nelda #1[8] opened her mouth. She giggled.

The new Nelda who had just walked into the room had a very similar face to Nelda #1. She was clearly not younger, just more polished. Something about her face was just a little smoother, a little more attractive, and a little less likely to be pictured starting a food fight with someone. Her hair, luxurious as was mentioned, also, unfortunately, cascaded. Her body looked just the same at a glance, until one noticed that the angles seemed a little less sharp and eased more slowly into her silhouette. Nelda #2 looked at Galoof. Her mouth closed. The surprisingly (or surprising to someone who had, up until now, only had the pleasure of acquaintance with Nelda #1) graceful arch of her eyebrows rose as if receding from a curtsy.

"Yup," said Galoof, nodding and trying hard to appear like the coolest dude in the room. "These people have come looking for us from a parallel universe. They, apparently, made their own universe and that's where that new room came from that arrived a few hours ago. And that, my dear, is you."

I see, thought Caroline. *I guess that pretty much explains everything, then.*

8 To be clear, this is the Nelda that the reader has so far grown to know and hopefully love during this story.

Nelda #1 was now shaking her head as if this were just too much for her. Nelda #2 watched this for a second.

"This is me. From another universe. You have contacted another universe. And this is me."

Her husband nodded grimly. "Yup. Well, they contacted us, but aside from that, yup."

Everyone in the room stared at the Neldas. The two women stared at each other, seeing things, presumably, that no one else could see. Caroline thought they might cry. This must be a heavy moment for them.

No, she realized after a few seconds. *They are going to laugh.*

Simultaneously, and to the alarm of everyone else in the room (even Caroline, who was expecting it), identical cackles erupted from both of them and they collapsed into each other's arms with the weakness of body that accompanies complete hysterics. Everyone started slightly (except Caroline, who stood next to Quincy and averted her eyes respectfully).

Nelda #1's head snapped up with eyes that looked like a slumber party participant with some juicy middle-school knowledge.

"Her!" she yelled, and pointed at Dr. Martha Morley. The Doctor raised her eyebrows. Nelda grabbed her doppelganger by the collar. "The Dr. Morley I know...is a HE!"

Nelda #2's eyes went wide, and then both women were on the floor in a fit of laughter.

Galoof put his hand on Dr. Martha's shoulder as she watched this spectacle with a mingling of curiosity and disdain. "This might go on for a while. Here, I've got a little more audio. Let's see what we've got."

Everyone but Quincy turned their back on the hysterical Neldas and crowded again around Galoof's screen. He clicked and typed and clicked again. "Here goes. I sped it up a hair."

This time, the giant was smaller, and said. "Eve, you draw." There were four baritone violin notes playing behind the voice.

Caroline grabbed Quincy by the arm, making him turn away from the spectacle of twin guffawing. "Listen, babe. Do you know this one? Play it again, please."

Galoof clicked again and the recording was repeated. Quincy squinted.

"Sounds family. Click it?"

The voice said "Eve, you draw," and the short notes ran out. Caroline wondered what that meant. Was someone playing a joke on them?

Quincy took the mouse gently from Galoof and clicked over and over, listening to the four notes. His eyebrows raised up, though his face remained impassive as always. He clicked once more and turned to Galoof.

"Bach. Orchestral Suite #3 in D," he said, and walked calmly from the room and shut the door.

For a moment, no one spoke. The Neldas had stopped their laughing and were now standing and paying attention to the strange audio with everyone else. Dr. Morley turned excitedly to Galoof.

"Good lord, man," she said. "Slow it down until it is in the key of D! Do you have any pitch correction software?"

Galoof shook his head. "No, but I'm sure I can download some in two seconds."

"Do that now," she commanded, and turned around. "Nelda!" she said sharply. Both Neldas turned. "Did you finish calibrating the Grafter prototype with the fluctuations of our energy source?" The Doctor's face was impassive, but her tone left the listener without doubt that Dr. Martha knew that Nelda #2 hadn't done this and that she disapproved.

"No," smiled #2 with a complete lack of defensiveness. "I had to perform maintenance on the network, remember?"

Dr. Martha nodded. "Okay. Can the two of you get it going soon with our new help? You'll have to quit dwelling on how weird this is and fix that Grafter. Nelda, the universe they made has a very fast time flow compared to ours, and we need to get them back there with the Grafter before their friends die of starvation. The parallel me is there, as well as their friend Sam that I guess we don't know."

Nelda #2's face showed no recognition at Sam's name, though our Nelda looked suddenly worried and nodded. "Can we make a portal that stays open long enough for both of us to go back?" she asked her other self.

"I'm not going," Chintz said.

Nelda glanced at him. "Okay, Feather. You can stay if you want. Can we still do two of us? I should bring Galoof, if he'll come, even though he isn't the Galoof I knew in my home universe." She looked at him. "Though, there are some similarities." She stared at Galoof as he worked on the audio file.

"Make it three," Dr. Martha said. "There's no way I'm going to miss this. There is another universe which was planned out by a male version of me, and I intend to see it."

"Three shouldn't be a problem," Galoof said. "I've been working on this a lot lately, and I've almost got it all down." He addressed the entire room. "The key is to take a tiny bit of energy from many, many places. You can get as much as you want, but it doesn't make much difference until you sum it together." He grinned like a smartass.

The other Nelda nodded. She seemed to Caroline to be taking all of this in stride. More stride than Caroline would if confronted with another version of herself. Nelda #2 took Nelda #1 by the arm. "Let's gather these parts up. They can solve this mystery without us. We'll get more done in my workshop across the hall. Loofy may use this gadget better than anyone, but no one can fix it like me." She smiled. "Except you, I guess." They cackled again in unison and began to leave the room with the disassembled Grafter. When they opened the door, Quincy stood there majestically. He swept back into the room as if he'd been gone for hours. The Neldas giggled again and left.

Quincy gestured towards the screen that displayed the sound waves. "We necessito get that transponder on fire. Needs are risin'."

Galoof, who was still grinning like a smartass, stopped grinning like a smartass and nodded. "Yeah. Okay, I think I've got more audio. Let's see if we can get it to sound like it sounds."

The others crowded around the computer again while Galoof clicked around his screen. He slowed the file down until the four notes sounded in the realm of a normal violin. With the others cheering him on, they tweaked the sound until it seemed natural to all of them. He quickly opened the newly downloaded pitch correction software and used it to tune the four notes to the key of D. There was a pause in both clicking and speaking.

"Okay," Galoof said. "This should be it. We'll only have a little more audio than we had before, but I got more at the beginning. Maybe half a second, or so. Looks like the sound is sped up by a factor of 84.2 from the source universe." He clicked play.

No longer in a kindly giant voice, the speaker now quite clearly said "Believe you dropped me" and stopped. The tranquil violins seemed almost harsh next to the timbre of the speaker. She was quite clearly female.

"Okay," Galoof repeated. They all turned and looked at Chintz, who had just made a high pitched little whine. They all turned back to the screen and looked disappointed.

"Hmmm," Dr. Martha said. "I was hoping that would be one of us from the other universe. A parallel us, I mean. I don't recognize that voice, though. Do any of you?"

Everyone around the computer shook their head noncommittally. They all looked at each other in thoughtful contemplation.

"Where's Chintz?" asked Caroline.

Quincy jerked his head over to his left.

"Crouchin'," he said.

They all looked at the odd man near them crouching on the floor with his hands over his head. Dr. Morley leaned down next to him with concern. "Hey," she said. "You okay?"

Chintz repeated the high pitched whine. "How did I not notice?" he mumbled.

Unconcerned with the drama unfolding next to his desk, Galoof absentmindedly pushed play on the audio a few more times. "—believe you dropped me. It's time ch—"

Galoof shook his head. "It's time check. Time chill. Time ch… something."

Chintz took two more deep breaths and popped up like a jack-in-the-box. Caroline thought he looked like he might explode. He giggled like a maniac.

"*Do you like her?*" he said in a funny little voice. "Do I like her? Ha!" He grinned and then covered his face in apparent agony.

Dr. Martha Morley rubbed him on his back with one hand and peered into his face. "Chintz? What's wrong?"

He didn't reply. After a few seconds he whispered, "She's alive," but Caroline didn't think anyone else heard him.

"If you can make it the same speed, you can talk back to her," Chintz said to Galoof finally. "Just talk in that room, the laboratory one. She can hear you. Speed it up sixty-seven times or whatever you said." He scratched his lips. He seemed to be trembling.

Galoof looked like a more thoughtful smartass. "I think I can set up my laptop with some auxiliary speakers in the laboratory there. Then I'll just record what we want to say in here, speed it up, save it on the network, and then play it from the laptop in there. Hang on." He jogged purposefully from the room, leaving Chintz, Quincy, Caroline, and Dr. Martha Morley in front of the computer station.

"Well," said Caroline with affable irritation. "This is turning out to be one hell of a date night." She looked at Chintz questioningly. "You okay, buddy? Who is it that's alive?"

Chintz took his hands from atop his head and nodded at her. He began to hum a strange, haunting song that made Caroline think of mountains. He held one hand out and grabbed it with the other. He let go of it and grabbed it again. Caroline looked with a worried expression at Quincy, who nodded and put his arm around Chintz's shoulder reassuringly.

From the other side, Dr. Martha also placed her hand on Chintz. "Why did you crouch down, Chintz? Do you know that voice?"

Chintz nodded again. He looked grateful towards the others for their close proximity. "I know who it is," he said. He pointed towards the laboratory. "That laboratory is organically part of the other universe. And the formation of that universe is guided by a sort of artificial intelligence called Chorus. She can project her voice from anywhere in the universe. It sounds fast because time moves much more quickly there." Martha's eyes danced with lust for this new technology and cosmic mysteries. Caroline was pleasantly blown away.

Galoof trotted back into the room. "Got it," he said. "Let's listen one more time and we can record a reply."

"—Believe you dropped me. It's time, Chintz. Help—"

All heads swung towards Chintz's shining eyes as he stared at the screen in glowing recognition. He nodded with shining eyes. "That's her."

They looked at each other and then looked at the screen.

"So this is Chorus?" asked Dr. Martha. "Why would she send you a message instead of Nelda? Or even one of us?"

He took a deep breath and they all looked at him again. "It's...not Chorus anymore, exactly."

"It's this same message over and over," Galoof said. He clicked play again.

"—I couldn't believe you dropped me. It's time, Chintz. Help me come back to life."

CHAPTER TWENTY

"**This, sir, is** without a doubt, the stupidest thing you have ever tried. A new low. I demand that we wait for Galoof."

Dr. Morley looked up from splicing the cables and regarded Sam as if he were a rebellious teenager who needed to be taught a lesson. "You want to wait until we are too weak from starvation to do this? Fine. I built the Grafter, and I can replicate it. I look forward to your apology after I save our lives. And your gratitude."

Sam gritted his teeth and his head throbbed with an angry fervor. Mitch ignored all of this and continued with his splicing.

He looked over the pile of cables and machines that stood in the center of the giant white room. These were meant to mimic the Grafter and help them open a portal. Further machines lay at the edge of the room which mined energy from the quantum fluctuations. Fluctuations that were subtly different from those of their home universe.

The giant chandelier hung ominously above them in the shiny, white room as if watching over their work and deeming it unworthy. Mitch pointed at the pile of cables, and Sam reluctantly began to error check the elaborate system. The energy had to flow with absolute precision. The amount of resistance within each section must be correct within .001%. One of the boxes converted the quantum energy into an observed flow of photons, which would collapse the waveform to, hopefully, exactly where they needed it. The margin of error allowed was tiny.

"Without Galoof, our gathering of the energy will be painfully inadequate. If we gather too little, this won't work and it could destroy this universe. If we gather too much, it won't work and it could destroy this universe."

Mitch continued his work as if he hadn't heard. For the first time in several weeks, he didn't even have to fight off fantasies of physically harming Sam for his disrespect. *Let him whine,* Mitch thought. *I'm going to save us.* He stood two strange rods up about three feet apart from each other. This is where the possibly deadly portal would appear.

"I refuse to wait any longer," said Mitch. "If you want to wither and die without trying to help yourself, more power to you. Now come over here and hold these cables together. I'm doing this with or without you."

Sam sighed and picked up the cables, holding them together about an inch apart. Dr. Morley picked up a laptop from the floor. The computer was connected to a square box a few feet away, which was in turn connected to the mess of cables and the vertical rods.

"Sir…"

"Shut up, Sam. Here goes."

Mitch's intense eyes stared at the screen. He typed in the number he had determined was the right amount of energy. It was the right amount. It had to be. *I don't need Galoof.*

He pressed enter.

A blue haze appeared between the two rods. A small sphere appeared within the haze and began to grow. A picture within the sphere showed shapes. Shapes that were remarkably like the neighborhood they had left in their home universe.

Dr. Morley grinned. "It's working!" he yelled. "Sam, it's working!" Sam stared at the growing portal in silence.

The shapes shimmered and changed. They faded to darkness.

Sam's head throbbed as he shook it. "No."

The grin faded also from Mitch's face. A wind began to stir up in the room. The portal was widening. It was growing beyond the two rods. There were no longer shapes within the sphere, but only blackness, a blackness that became a gaping, sucking maw that was pulling and pulling the air from the huge room. The giant chandelier vibrated in protest, and tilted towards the growing mouth with a creaking sound.

Sam let go of the cables, but still the blackness continued to grow.

"Sam!" yelled Mitch. "Cut the wires from that box! Quick! Cut them!"

The wind had increased to a gale. The laptop was nearly pulled from the Doctor's grasp, and he held it close to his body. Nearer to the blackness than Sam, he was beginning to feel the pull on his own body.

"Sam—"

The words were choked off as Mitch was knocked from his feet. He was drawn towards the blackness and scooted on his back towards it. Grabbing the floor, he let the computer fly from his grasp. It flew like a kite towards the blackness and was devoured. And yet still the gaping maw grew.

Sam fell to his hands and knees himself and dove towards the box, half buried in the cables. Mitch held his breath. *What is taking him so long? Where is the damn connection?*

Mitch looked at the vortex with fear. *Surely not. Not like this.*

Sam's large head was buried in the pile of cables. Dr. Morley lost his hold on the slick surface of the huge white room, and scooted further to the blackness, his foot a mere inches away.

Mitch saw Sam stand, one of the boxes in one hand and grasping the cables with the other. As he was pulled inch by inch towards the blackness, he watched Sam carefully inspect each cable and choose one with conviction. That was it. Mitch's foot slid into the portal up to the ankle. Sam looked up.

There was no doubt in Mitch's mind as to what he was seeing. No doubt whatsoever. He couldn't pretend he wasn't seeing what he was seeing. He was seeing Sam hesitate.

He replayed in his mind all the disagreements, the arguments, the insults, the anger. Years of anger. But always there was trust. Faithful Sam. They were partners. Weren't they? Had it come to this?

He began slipping. His foot was several inches from the portal, and now Mitch had no strength to move himself. He looked back at Sam, panicking.

"Sam," he whispered. From across the room, he searched Sam's eyes.

Sam would cut the wire. He felt it. He would cut the wire and save Mitch's life.

Above them, the chandelier creaked again, and bits of glass rained down on them and flew into the great mouth. The white ceiling cracked across the expanse of the room with a deafening roar. Covered in bits of glass, Mitch slid another few inches and felt an odd tingling sensation in his foot. But he held Sam's eyes across the room. "Sam, please."

Sam stood frozen, as if time was still.

An orange smoke flew into the room, and just as quickly retreated.

Everyone stared at Chintz again, who sucked his neck in slightly while keeping the remainder of his body erect. He felt like crouching again and fought the urge. *No,* he thought. *I'm not going to. It's time for me to look life in the eye. Free will indeed.*

"Who is Katie?" asked Dr. Martha.

Chintz looked around at everyone. "She's part of the computer that I have been working with on a project. We, um, need to reply to her. Can– Galoof, will you help me reply? It might, I mean, we can learn whatever you need to learn to go back."

Galoof nodded and stared at him thoughtfully. "Okay. Okay. So we'll record it in here and I'll speed it up and play it from that other computer I set up. I think you should be the one to talk?"

They all looked at Chintz. Quincy's hand was still on his shoulder, and he gave it a squeeze and let go. "Yes," Chintz said, in his calmest terrified voice.

"Well, hurry and send it," Dr. Morley said. "Every second you wait is over a minute there."

Chintz worried at the distress this might cause the computer program that was in love with him. Her message worried him. Was she angry? "I'm ready."

Everyone breathed while Galoof set up the computer to record Chintz's message. From down the hall, a cackle rang out from one of the Neldas. Galoof looked at Chintz. "We're recording."

Chintz took a deep breath. "Hi, um, Katie. It's Chintz." He exhaled, and his voice broke just a little. "I'm sorry I dropped you. I'm not coming back there. Good luck with everything."

They all paused. "That's it?"

Chintz nodded, his eyes wider than he would have preferred. "See what she says please," he said.

Galoof typed into the computer. "Okay, that just played from the speakers in the laboratory."

They waited.

"Already a reply," Galoof said. "But I need a sec to slow it down."

"Hey," commanded the Doctor. The word "hey" is not

usually a command, but somehow she managed. "While you're waiting on that, go ahead and run an analysis on the speed of this transmission verses the quantum fluctuations in that room. We need a couple of instruments set up in that laboratory. I'll get Nelda to...oh, dammit. Well. I'll just do it." And Dr. Martha walked out of the room.

"This is weird," Caroline said, shaking her head before pointing it at Chintz. "How you doin'?"

Quincy clapped him on the back. "My man is a little androgynous. But I think he'll dick up for this just fine." He looked at Chintz. "Be statutory," he said encouragingly.

Chintz hardly heard any of them. What was she going to say? *Believe you dropped me.* She must have said *I* can't *believe you dropped me.* He wondered if she had forgiven him. He couldn't go back. He couldn't do any more simulations. His grip failed him again in his mind, and he shut it off. Doesn't matter. He thought of the mountains and hummed more of Katie's song that she had sung for him. He scratched his lips like they contained vouchers for cash prizes.

"Here goes," said Galoof. He pushed play.

With a sound like an exploding and overinflated camel, the small speakers on Galoof's computer were pushed to their limits and each popped in rapid succession as they burst and left the listeners with a distorted booming noise. Another sound came from down the hall that they couldn't make out. Galoof quickly reached behind and unplugged the speakers, causing the camel sound to stop.

"The fuck?" said Quincy.

"Okay," Galoof said, and clicked furiously around on the screen as his lightning fast mind scrambled to make sense of this latest chaos. "Okay," he repeated. "She figured out the speed. It's transmitting, or whatever you call what it's doing, at normal speed now. And louder." The noise down the hall came through the door again. Galoof swung around and looked at Chintz. "That's her. In the room."

Like a flock of birds flying south for the winter, the four of them whisked in unison towards the door and fell in line as if they had rehearsed it this way. They rushed in formation to the laboratory and stopped in the doorway. Dr. Martha was standing transfixed, some unidentified instruments set up on one of the counters in front of her. Everyone's eyebrows strained to reach the ceiling.

"Was that the computer?" Martha asked. "Was that her? She talked and then she stopped."

The others huffed and puffed from their run. "The universes didn't suddenly align," wheezed Galoof. "It still takes a second. She's just talking slower. Give it a minute to reach us. It—"

The ceiling erupted in a tranquil and simultaneously somehow quite distressed female voice from the ceiling. It was Katie. Not Chorus. Not anymore. Similar, but Chintz could tell the difference.

"Chintz," she boomed from the ceiling like a mother's urgent, panicked lullaby. "I want just Chintz. Just me and Chintz. Everyone else get out, please."

The two Neldas worked side by side in a nearly empty room down the hall from the others. While Nelda #1 had prior experience with a functional Grafter, Nelda #2 had recently been dealing with the prototype often enough to remember the details. Working together, they had managed to do quite a bit in only a few minutes. They now each had a piece of the Grafter in front of them, and they each worked on some tedious modifications with their own respective tiny screwdrivers. Nelda tried to remind herself that they had to hurry, that Sam and Docky needed them, but she found herself feeling comfortable and unrushed. As the conversation lapsed, Nelda #2 looked at her counterpart.

"Excuse me for asking, but it's not like this happens every day," she lilted. "What is it like in the universe you created? I can't imagine."

"It's neato, bandito," Nelda #1 said as she twiddled some screws and rerouted some circuitry. "Just the three of us. Well, four in the last couple of days. Chintz just joined us."

#2 nodded. "He seems a bit eccentric."

Nelda #1 chuckled and nodded back. "He's a weird one. But aren't we all? We like him."

"Me, too," said the other. "I bet before he got there it was tedious. And you just stayed there every day? Didn't you want to go home?"

Nelda snorted. Really, not a snort-like noise, but an actual snort such as one might expect from an animal. She knew she was being drawn into a conversation they shouldn't be having (*they should be concentrating on getting back to the boys*), but she couldn't help but be provoked by this question. "I thought about it all the time at first. But there's nowhere to go. I burned some bridges to work with Mitch, and it's not like I can just open up a portal to another universe and try my luck there."

"Ha! That's true. Until now, that is."

"Huh?"

"Well, I just mean now you're here. New universe."

"Oh. Yeah, I guess that's true, too. Been sort of busy since I got here so I didn't really think of that." They smiled mirror-image grins.

The two women twiddled on their screws for a minute. One of them (which one, exactly, is not important to the story) picked up a soldering iron and unattached some electronic components.

Nelda #2 said: "Man. Just the three of you in one little universe. Must be crowded."

#1 smiled and nodded. "Sometimes. It's okay." *Alright,* she thought. *No more chatting. Concentrate.*

"I mean, a female Dr. Morley is one thing. I can't even think what she would be like after adding testosterone to the mix."

Our own beloved Nelda smiled again and nodded, her concentration exiting stage left to remain behind the curtain. "Yes. He makes it very difficult for us sometimes. You know how focused they are."

"Yeah. But it's not terrible, I guess. I mean, I figured out how to deal with Martha long ago."

Nelda #1 looked up from her screwing. "You did?" She chortled. "I'd like to know that secret."

Nelda #2 shrugged and tossed her smooth hair over her shoulder. "Just don't take her — or him — seriously. I mean, they get the job done better than anyone, don't they? I just don't let myself get too close. Sort of business only. Lots of people deal with their bosses that way." She looked up and realized the first Nelda had stopped and was staring at her. #2 looked at #1 for a moment and then nodded. "Oh. I get it. That's a lot easier to do when you don't share the same compound all the time for ten years."

"Yes." Nelda #1 shook her broom hair and went back to her screwing.

"Are you two close?"

Nelda #1 looked up again. She waited a few seconds before speaking.

"We used to be."

"Really close?"

Nelda #1 smiled and put her screwdriver down for a second to focus on her mirror image. "The other guy who lives in our universe. Sam. You don't seem to have one of him here. Anyway, he has been in love with me for years. Almost since we met. Mitch – our Dr. Morley – didn't seem to pay any attention to it. I felt flattered at first, but never did anything. Then when we Grafted up that universe, it was such an adventure to all of us that anything else in life took a back burner for a while. But after a year or so, he started to give subtle hints again. I thought about starting up a relationship. I mean, it didn't look like our living situation was gonna change anytime soon, right? So. Well, after thinking about it, I decided not to."

Nelda #2 had stopped her work and was transfixed on the other's story. While it is common human experience to empathize with another person through storytelling, it is notably less common to empathize with the story of someone who is almost exactly you. "Why?"

Nelda #1 looked at her smooth-haired, attractive parallel self. "Sam is sort of stiff and rigid. He has trouble showing his emotions. A complete sweetie once you get to know him, but that takes a while. He's all by the book. Now, imagine living in a universe where the only two people you see every day is a guy like that and Dr. Morley. Think about Martha."

The other Nelda looked at her with a puzzled expression. "I don't understand."

Our Nelda swallowed. "Think about how passionate she is. How she knows what she wants and goes for it. How she takes command of every situation and always has a vision."

#2 raised her eyebrows. "So you had the hots for him?"

Nelda #1 smiled and shrugged. "It was a textbook alpha-male attraction. I couldn't fight biology. And we were all so lonely. It became this weird love triangle that Mitch hardly even seemed to be aware of."

They both picked up their screwdrivers and began to work again. A booming sound came from down the hall, but neither woman broke eye contact.

"So," said Nelda #1. "We would go back to our home universe to get supplies sometimes. Food and stuff. I usually went, but this one time Sam could tell I didn't really want to go, so he went instead. I argued but he insisted. And when we left, we were gone for a day or so. That night, me and Mitch were in the lab...the one you have here now...trying to send some data to these nanomachines we had made." She grinned and shook her head. "I'll tell you about that later. Anyway. It was just the two of us, and we were both so excited about the project. You know how child-like they get. But, anyway, then... I guess I don't have to tell you the rest."

Nelda #2 giggled. "You did it with Dr. Morley?" She doubled over in a feminine and well-groomed cackle. "Ha! This is the craziest shit ever!"

Our Nelda allowed herself a chuckle, sans gums. "I hadn't planned on it. But, wait. That's not all. Sam came back in the middle of it." She nodded as if to say, of course he would, isn't that just my luck.

Nelda #2's pretty head snapped up and her eyes opened wide to suck in the juicy school girl gossip. "What the hell? Oh my God! What did he say?"

Nelda #1 looked sad. "He hardly showed any emotion, of course. The next day, he said he would stay until we finished up with our two main projects and then he was going to leave and return home. He and Docky – that's what I call Mitch – yelled at each other all night and got into an actual fist fight. It's lucky neither of them are good at fighting or they would have hurt themselves. It was crazy. I hated it."

She took a deep breath. The other Nelda stopped breathing to listen. "So after that, I tried to get a relationship going with

Mitch." She laughed and shook her brooms bitterly. "That was a mistake. I think for him, he was trying, maybe more than he ever has. But nothing really matters to him except the pursuit of knowledge. Nothing was ever good enough. I only thought he had criticized me before. It was that much worse with Sam and him not even talking. So he took it out on me. He hurt my feelings really badly, and I ended things with him."

They both sat still for a moment. "So now you are with Sam?" Nelda #2 said.

Nelda #1 shook her head. "Not really 'with' him. After I broke things off with Mitch, I started, gradually, to get going with a relationship with Sam. We kept it secret, which wasn't hard since it wasn't much of a relationship. Sam treated me so well, though. He always has." Her eyes went out of focus again. "We've kind of stopped bothering to hide it. I'm just not sure what I should do. Maybe I should be the one to return by myself to our old universe. Those guys can get on without me. Especially now that they have Chintz." She sighed. "I would miss Chintz."

The pretty Nelda scowled. "Wait. I thought you said Sam was planning on leaving?"

The brooms shook again. "That was three years ago. He didn't leave. That's why I was able to start a fling with him."

Nelda #2 went back to her tiny screwdriver. "Man. That must be really awkward for you. Having had a relationship with both of the only two guys in your universe."

Nelda's eyes disappeared in a silent, if slightly guilty, laugh. "Mitch is still tough on me. And they argue more than they used to. It's not really awkward though. That whole dramatic situation is no longer a thing."

"Really? Why not?"

Our Nelda smiled a big, gummy smile. "Because. I made sure they don't remember it."

CHAPTER TWENTY-ONE

THE BRIGHT LIGHTS of the newest room of the compound enveloped Sam in his peripheral vision. He had returned to the place where they had made their plans a few weeks ago, before Chintz and Nelda had left. All of the lights in this odd room were on the floor and lined the edges of the round wall, which is why he sprawled on his back in the center of the room so none of the lights assaulted his retinas directly. He blinked at the ceiling.

I am very, very smart, he thought. *I should have thought of something by now, but I haven't.* His thoughts moved slowly, and he shook his huge, brown head against the shiny floor. *I am also very hungry.* Of course, the guilt had not subsided in the least.

The food had run out completely the morning before. It had now been almost three weeks since Nelda and Chintz had left in the middle of the night to go get help. They should have been back by now.

Sam had never truly experienced how helpless hunger can make one feel. How the mind wanders, concentration lapses, the muscles weaken. Hope begins to fade. The military could break in at any moment.

The endeavor the Doctor had undertaken in the giant white room had sucked out a great deal of their air. There was plenty to survive, but it hadn't yet caught up to the oxygen-rich levels to which Sam was accustomed, and this added to his hunger-fueled lethargy.

They had tried and failed. So now they had no plan that didn't involve Chintz and Nelda returning, with the Grafter and hopefully a parallel member of their original team. Sam lay on the floor in despair. There had been no word from Chorus at all since the last simulation.

He wondered if they would come back. He wondered if Chintz had done what Sam asked him to do.

The orange smoke that floated through Sam's line of vision hardly succeeded in garnering his attention. The form of the skinny and — was it hairless? —cat that sailed over his body in full pursuit of the smoke alarmed him for a moment, but he quickly recovered and focused again on his despair. *I guess I should feed the damn cat again,* he thought. *Hopefully, Chintz has some more food in his house. And that litter box is getting…*

"Sam."

Sam sat up abruptly. Mitch was standing in the door, gravely.

"Sir," Sam replied with a languid dignity.

The Doctor had boarded himself up in his room for the past few days. Sam shook his large head against the floor. That man was an emotionless robot. Always had been. He stared at the ceiling in thought. *Well, an angry robot. An angry, ambitious robot. That I nearly murdered.*

He let the Doctor's form go out of focus in his vision. *I didn't nearly murder him. I have no free will. I cannot be held accountable.*

The guilt, if anything, enjoyed a surge.

"I figured something out," Dr. Morley said from the doorway. "Good news and bad news."

Sam felt nothing at this statement. "And?"

Dr. Morley didn't move. Besides conserving energy, they were also constrained by the new emotional wall between them. As if they needed another one. "That portal we opened the other day changed some things. We have access to some energies from that universe now, which can help us. The problem is, we *have* to use it. Even if Galoof and the Grafter get here, we don't have another place to get the energy." He gestured weakly. "Come on, Sam. We've got to make some calculations."

Sam leapt to his feet and then wished he hadn't. A wave of light-headedness attacked him, and he paused just as he reached the Doctor to fight the wave of dizziness. Mitch reached out a hand to steady him, then seemed to change his mind. "That's why we need to hurry. We've barely eaten for a week, and we're stopping altogether. We are going to be worthless soon. At least the air will be as clean as before in a few days."

The two men fell into step for the millionth time in their experience. Neither had bathed in several days, but they had ceased being able to smell each other. In light of the recent accident, water access was uncontrolled and had to be rationed. Given the choice between dying of thirst, and being stinky, they had chosen stinky.

And Dr. Morley had not mentioned Sam's hesitation.

They continued in silence until they reached the large room with the chandelier. Both men stopped and looked around. The Doctor pursed his lips and turned to Sam.

"Oddly enough, I think our near disaster will end up helping us. It narrowed a few things down. Assuming we can get the balance correct. If it's possible to make a full-size, sustainable portal then I have some ideas."

Sam shrugged. "If we could make one once, we could in theory repeat that attainment."

"Okay," Dr. Morley said. He turned towards Sam as if he were a lethal weapon that the Doctor was afraid of, but knew he had to use. "We need enough energy to keep open the portal. But using that much energy… We have no idea of the causes and effects involved in this balance. We don't want another… incident."

"Well, it's not as if we can run this through a few times for analysis. Another incorrect result could kill us and destroy our work. Even if we could, there is insufficient time."

Mitch's eyes bore into him. Sam had thought he was used to this, but found that it still gave him pause.

"We need to find out right now," said the Doctor. He was becoming agitated. "Once we have access to our energies, we either need to *increase* the energy or *decrease* it to keep it from closing. We've both been trained in this years ago. If I could just remember the details. If we could just..." His intense eyes grew larger, and he grabbed Sam by the collar. "A simulation!" he cried. He let go of Sam and instead grabbed his hair, closing his eyes tight in misery. "Dammit we can't! Not without Chorus."

Sam frowned. "A simulation? That wouldn't work. That is to analyze our thought patterns, not simulate real life experiences to perform experiments and reveal data."

"But think about it! We could build a simulation that tests each possible energy situation — too much or too little — and use the gaps to alter the experiment each time!"

"Gaps?"

"The gaps in the simulation that Chintz has been using to make choices." The corners of his grin rose higher, just beyond the boundaries of sanity. "It can only be one way or the other! I think I can get us in without Chorus. We could set up a simulation on our own…and use our memories to gather data from our past learning…" He looked at Sam as if daring him to deny them this one chance. "We can get info from our subconscious memories and then experiment to determine the right amount of energy. All in the simulation."

Sam's frown deepened. "If we can make a mathematical model of the situation, then why do we need the gaps?"

"Because," the Doctor said impatiently. "This isn't a regular experiment on a regular computer. It's a memory and Chorus couldn't do it alone even if she were here to help us. We need to make decisions within the memory and remember how it worked."

Sam wanted to agree with the Doctor, to put this argument off, but his practical brain wouldn't allow him. "We don't have Chorus. We could look at memories from our past to help us, but we can only use the gaps to experiment if there *are* gaps. What if there aren't? What if your 'gaps', as you have called them, are not really gaps, but just input into our actions which you haven't discovered?" He returned Mitch's intense glare. "What if there is no free will? Only determinism? It is clear that you have wanted free will to exist from the start, despite your claims towards objectivity. Do you not see? The simulation would be other than it seemed, as would, of course, our entire existence. Then the experiment wouldn't be controlled and the results would be erroneous." *I can't help arguing,* he told himself, *if I have no free will.*

Dr. Morley stepped towards him, his eyes watering. "Who doesn't *want* free will? And anyway, I have remained objective! There are gaps, Sam. Can't you feel it? I just know..."

"You *just know*? So you are using *faith*? How are you different from a preacher in his pulpit, lying to people looking for guidance, looking for what they want to hear? And do you think I don't care about this, about what we've done? You aren't the only one! You believe yourself to be the only one who has feeling for these things, but you are not! Do you believe I don't crave autonomy? Do you believe I don't care? Do you really think I was going to let you fall into the..." They stared at one another. Sam was too furious to even feel guilty. He, like the Doctor, felt his composure slipping. "And why go through these experiments if you 'know'? We must relinquish all dependence on feelings. We could die if you are wrong in your assumption, and you would be at fault."

A small voice in his head reminded him that if he could

not be held accountable, then neither could the Doctor. He pushed it away.

The Doctor's voice was low, but the dangerous intensity had flowed into his eyes. "This isn't faith. Some feelings are justified. That doesn't mean it's just magic. I was telling Chintz about my findings. We've made progress. I told him about my accumulation theory…"

"*That?*" Sam looked as if he might attempt to eat his own face. "Your new name to people trying to assuage their own cognitive dissonance? That's not proof and it's not accumulation."

The passion in each of them had caused them to breathe heavily. The staring sustained.

"How would you even begin?" Sam said. "By trying to awaken Chorus?"

Dr. Morley's confident eyes withdrew. "We have to try. Try something."

Sam looked at the ground and shook his head. "It's not as if a real-world laboratory is just lying in Chorus's memory banks," he said in frustration. "We can't just have some random simulation. We have to have a simulation that is true to life. We don't know how to access our computers from inside the simulation, and even if we could, that takes time and we would be waiting in the simulation forever for the data to arrive. We would need half-remembered knowledge from each of our pasts. And while that is indeed possible in the simulation, we would need a person here to run it even if we *did* have Chorus available. There are just too many problems with your hypothesis."

The Doctor looked like he wanted to destroy the universe. "HOW then?" he demanded desperately. "How are we going to do this? I've found a way but now you say we *can't?* Don't you think you owe me this at least?"

"Fuswah."

They turned to see Tonk grinning at them. Sam sighed and attempted to reacquire his poise.

"Hello, Tonk," said Dr. Morley curtly, barely looking at the thing. The baby's grin grew wider. It pointed away from them. "Fuswah!" it insisted, and turned and sprinted towards the doorway. The Doctor turned and watched it go while Sam shook his head at the floor. Poise be damned. What was the point? There was no way they could escape. He felt in complete despair.

"What the hell has gotten into Tonk?" Mitch asked.

"We should surrender."

As if he had been slapped across the face, the Doctor wheeled on Sam in a fury and grabbed him by the collar again in a rage. "NO!" he screamed. "No no no no no!" and Sam felt his feet leave the ground as Mitch threw him back down.

Sam had witnessed Mitch's rages before, but only once had it actually been aimed at him. That had been a terrible day. Fury, already ignited, flamed in Sam's huge head, and he leapt to his feet and ran full force at the angry bull of a man before him. Shoving with all his might, Sam managed to bring the Doctor to the floor. The man, huffing with wild eyes, looked up at him.

"We!" screamed Sam in a flood of rare emotion. "Have. No. Choice!" He spat on the ground, his brown mouth foaming, and took a threatening step forward. Both men's hearts raced as they glared at each other, Sam from his glowering stance and Mitch propped on one angry elbow on the floor next to him. After a few seconds, Sam said. "I'd rather live! I'd rather see...Nelda again! If this knowledge is in our heads, and it may remain there until we can survive to elude this danger. We can record it…elsewhere. We can return to our experiments and recreate the results, elsewhere. Even if they imprison us, we can still continue our scholarly undertakings from captivity." He paused for breath. "I want to live."

The Doctor shook his head and tears came to his eyes. "So do I." Sam's guilt surged again. "There has to be—"

"Fuswah."

They each glanced at the baby and then ignored it. "There has to be what." Sam said.

"There has to be another way."

This time Sam shook his head, his regal fists clenched. "There isn't. Wishing will not change things."

"Fuswah!" yelled Tonk. They looked at him again. This time, the baby pointed assertively towards the doorway.

"What the hell..."

"I believe Tonk wants us to follow along, sir," Sam said breathlessly.

The Doctor looked confused. "I don't want to follow Tonk. I want to open that portal, Sam. I've found a way." His visage became pleading. "Please." He stood up carefully as if someone were aiming a gun at him. Or more particularly, as if Sam were. "We can find the balance. We can."

"And what if—" Sam began through gritted teeth, when orange smoke coalesced around him. He inhaled sharply, breathing several hundred thousand of the nanoscopic robots into his lungs. He closed his eyes reflexively. "Tonk!" he yelled, and stopped. The ambiance of the room had changed. Instead of hearing his voice echo from all around the large room where they had been yelling, it bounced back to him from a much closer wall. He opened his eyes.

He was now standing in the simulation room, directly under the canisters on the wall.

The large brain reeled to update its internal map. *Why would Tonk do this?* With a sinking feeling, he realized that they had allowed yet another project to get out of hand. Explosives, Chorus, their exit home, and now this. Snapshots flashed in his mind of each new major skill the baby had acquired throughout the last few years. Each had been met with excitement. Sam furrowed his brow and wondered if he should leave and continue his heated conversation with the Doctor or instead attempt to deal with Tonk somehow. He exhaled loudly, and a small cloud of orange smoke left his mouth and rushed from the room.

What exactly has this thing learned to do? How sentient has it become? Clearly, it knows to interact with humans. They had been so preoccupied with other things that they had not studied Tonk in some time. *Perhaps he—*

A large cloud of orange smoke rushed into the room and moved together and then quickly apart, leaving a perplexed and angry Doctor where it had been. They were both standing less than a hundred feet from where they had just been arguing a minute before.

Terror filled Dr. Morley's eyes. "What is this?" he wheezed hoarsely.

Sam's tone returned to his oft-used butler routine. "Clearly, we have been teleported, sir," he stated calmly, the muscles in his face relaxing enough to make it drop a half inch.

The Doctor wheeled on him. "He has crossed a line," he said, and began to issue commands. "We must drop this question for a moment and contain him somehow. Quick! We'll take him to my quarters. Help me." A passing psychologist would have wondered which man to use first in a case study on childhood defense mechanisms.

"Fuswah."

This time Dr. Morley wheeled on Tonk. "Tonk!" He yelled. He looked as if he wanted to grab the baby, but knew it would be ineffective.

"Fuswah!" countered Tonk with mimicked authority, and turned back into the smoke, which wheeled in the air like pixie dust from a beloved children's film and sailed into the first canister. The canister shimmered and filled with the smoky blue. It faded, and each of the next two canisters followed suit, filling with blue and then fading back to orange. The smoke rushed from the last canister as it returned to orange, and headed straight for the blue light that was situated above the reclining chair.

The Doctor wheeled on Sam now. *Good grief,* thought Sam. *Now he's just becoming self-indulgent. Enough with the damn wheeling already.*

"What the hell?" said Mitch in an odd mixture of excitement and anger. The man was reaching the end if his proverbial rope. Sam kept his panic suppressed. *Sleep and food deprivation,* he thought. *And far too much time together. We are becoming like children. It's not the first time.*

"Sir. He seems to have been wanting us to come in here to see him do that. His mimicry of a human baby has progressed into a normal showing off stage. Nothing more. Now if we can return to our discussion–"

"Look," commanded the Doctor. Sam looked. The smoke had formed a pencil-thin line that ran from the spot on the wall where much of Chorus' central architecture was kept to a spot on the opposite wall. Each watched in confusion.

Seeming to give in to the comedy of his impotence, the Doctor rested his hands on his knees and began to giggle. "I just. Ha! I've lost all control. All inkling of what is going on. Whose universe is this? Sure as hell not mine!"

Sam's usually lazy eyebrows tightened into a squint. "That's the spot where the network lines run. He is connecting Chorus to the other computers. She usually does it through her other circuitry. He is doing it directly." His neurons in his huge brain fired with such rapidity that it gave him a fever.

The Doctor shook his head, grinning. "Ha! Ha! It doesn't matter. Nothing matters. And Chorus already accesses the computers. That's one of the ways she learns."

Seriously, Sam thought. *Whatever you are doing to control yourself isn't working. Pull yourself together.*

He was about to say so, preferably in a pompous way and

with an advanced command of language, when something again moved near the ceiling. His eyebrows relaxed slightly as he stared at the spot on the wall where the smoke had formed a line. "He appears to be linking the two in a separate way. A new way."

The line of orange smoke, already quite thin, became thinner still. As if being squeezed by an invisible tube, it became smaller and smaller until it couldn't be seen. The Doctor sighed loudly, looked at Sam, and then looked to see what Sam was watching. The smoke had already disappeared, so he saw nothing.

"What the hell are you looking at, Sam?"

Sam looked at him. "Tonk is doing something, sir."

"Fuswah," came Tonk's voice. This time, it came from the blue light. Both men looked up at the sound. Tonk was not there.

The blue light flashed.

SLATCH.

Clearly, some odd events have just transpired. We have some things to talk about.

First, consciousness. Yes, it does have to do with the odd events. As the Doctor explained to Chintz, our consciousness does not unfold before us as it seems to, through the window of our perception. Each sense reaps input from the environment around it, and that input moves to the brain and is stored in different areas. The different areas of the brain have special relationships, and there are many. The relationships are quite complex. The physical structure of the brain interacts with itself in a way that transcends the neurons or brain matter on which this fantastic machine runs. The subjective and intangible result is that of an ego (at least one ego, if not more), which is patched into all of these senses and puts them together seamlessly.

Further, these brain structure relationships try, in a quite un-personified and non-sentient way, to make sense of everything. What does that mean? Let's think about faces and our brain's ability to recognize them. One of the primary functions of the relationship between sight and the comprehension of what we see is to figure out whether the face is that of a friend or that of someone in a warring tribe. We see faces in everything - clouds, the moon, the puffy texture on the ceiling…It presumably took many millions of years for this gene to build on itself, and it must have been indeed useful to survival in order to remain so forcefully in the gene pool. Another example is voices, and for precisely the same reason. For generations untold, humans have heard voices in the wind, and have had their imaginations provide bewildering and sometimes quite destructive revelations. This is a result of the brain attempting, again in an abstract and unconscious way, to make sense of what is actually just sensory noise.

Chorus, it will be recalled, has learned to adjust a person's memory so they feel that this sensory data has been manipulated. Notice that she is not manipulating the senses in real time, but rather the memory of senses, which is much simpler. The result is that experiences seem to be had that have in fact not been had. This code, if you will, is written into the memory of the brain so that it feels to the subject as if time has passed, though none has.

Yes yes, you say. I got all this in Chapter 4.

Well, it would seem now that Tonk has learned

to perform these simulations on subjects as well. How? Did it access Chorus's architecture? Did its equivalent of genetic code reproduce for many short generations until it learned of its own accord? We may never know.

There are two important points to be made at this stage, however. One, that Tonk has simultaneously put both Sam and Dr. Morley into a simulation, which means both of their memories are simultaneously being rewritten to have had the same experience side by side. What that experience is still remains to be seen. Very soon.

Second, Tonk is much, much less experienced with this than Chorus. He is in no way an accelerated and emotional personality such as Chorus is. His pragmatic structure allows him to do things that Chorus cannot. She is all consciousness and no body. Tonk is all body, small and strange though it is, and little consciousness. It can, in a way that we would call unconsciously or even "non-consciously," learn things that it doesn't "know" it's learning. It can hear conversations and figure out, in a quite non-linguistic and non-reflective manner, a way to be what it always is: useful.

They need to figure out how much energy they need to open a portal. And they need to use information from their memories to do this. Tonk is trying to help.

CHAPTER TWENTY-TWO

Mitch came to and found himself lying next to Sam. In a panic, he tried to sit up. This endeavor was startlingly unsuccessful, and he instead bent sideways at the waist by a means that he would have sworn the human body would be incapable of. He found himself looking at his knees. The front of them.

That can't be right, he thought. *I just bent sideways. Why did I bend sideways?* He still felt hysterically nihilistic. *What just happened,* he thought weakly (hysterical). *And who really cares anyway* (there's the nihilism)? He lay back down and found that he bent back up sideways. He saw Sam lying next to him.

Wait. He was looking ahead. *I'm lying down looking up and...*he tried rubbing his eyes and couldn't. *Maybe Sam is standing above me. Maybe I'm not...*with a rush, he remembered Tonk rushing around the room and the blue light flashing.

We must be in a simulation, he thought. *Right this second. Literally, just this second and no other. In less than a second, I will come to and be standing looking at the light. I'd better live out this memory I'm remembering first.*

I'd better be careful not to fall down.

He looked at Sam again. "What the hell?" he tried to say, but found he couldn't do that either.

"Indeed," came Sam's voice. Sort of. He heard it in his head. It somehow sounded like Sam, but he didn't hear any air in it. There was no sound of vibrating vocal cords, or a mouth moist with saliva. Mitch didn't go around doing odd things like listening for people's saliva when they talked, but he somehow could hear that these factors were not present here. *What the hell?* he thought again.

"I don't know, sir," said Sam, sort of.

Mitch turned from Sam to look ahead, but found that instead of looking up and over, as he was accustomed to doing from a sitting position, he could just look over without the up. The scene before him looked as if he were standing, not lying down, and facing it head on in perfect convergence of viewpoints, as if this view had been researched for years by a prominent military organization that had gone over budget but was reluctantly allowed to continue.

With a noble effort, the Doctor tried to wheel on Sam intensely. This botched attempt was so disastrous that it is well for the Doctor's dignity that neither man remembered it later.[9] Regardless, Sam seemed to be right in front of him, looking at him. Something was odd, though. It looked like a portrait of Sam, and one that coincidentally and fully blocked the view of whatever was behind him. The portrait moved in a dignified manner to stand nearer to the as yet un-described scene before them. Mitch found that he was unable to judge distance well.

9 Although of course they remembered it upon immediately returning or it wouldn't be "happening" now.

Sam looked just the same as he had a moment ago, but was in a different direction in relation to the Doctor. Part of the scene, which will now be described already, dammit, was blocked by Sam.

"Sir," said Sam, and Mitch noticed that Sam seemed to be standing next to him from directly to the side now. "Tonk, it would seem, cannot operate a simulation in more than two dimensions."

Still feeling like he was lying down, Dr. Morley stepped forward to stand/lie next to Sam and survey what shall be called the road before them.

Tonk was, they didn't doubt, doing his best. But his mitigated consciousness didn't allow him to write into their memories a subjective experience to which a normal human might relate, which is exactly what Chorus did with such aptitude. In addition to being only in two dimensions, then, the road (not a road) was not logically consistent with any human experience. It was, in fact, a cocktail that included each man's life experience, the architecture of Chorus, and the inside of the compound where Tonk had spent the entirety of what can, for the sake of an argument, be called his life.

Mirroring, apparently, the architecture of Chorus' circuitry, the halls before them spread out in parallel glowing lines. When they looked ahead, it looked as if they were flying above them. A bird's eye view of the circuits ran around them, but the decisions they made (did they make them?) about their movements seemed to move them along an x and y axis with no since of depth or distance. They headed down the hallway they were on, both walking down it and seeing it spread before them in a way that would have had Edwin A. Abbot shaking his head and mumbling "no, no, that can't be right."

"Fuswah."

They turned (they absolutely did not turn) to find the damn baby following them.

"Sir," Sam said. Words still appeared in his mind rather than by any illusion of reaching him through his ears. "As you were earlier so adamant about using a simulation to perform the experiment to discover which direction to move the energy, and as we now conveniently find ourselves in a simulation, I suppose we must garner such information as we can. This endeavor would be quite difficult without Tonk. Perhaps we should follow him."

The Doctor tried to turn to Sam and found himself swiveling as if he were on rails. "I don't even know how to follow anyone in two dimensions," he said testily.

The baby giggled and ran right through them. His back side was clearly moving away from them, though he never seemed to get further away.

"Oh, hell," Mitch said, and moved on rails in the same direction. Next to them, a diorama of the Doctor playing baseball as a child played itself out in two dimensions. Further behind that (though just as close, of course), a teenage Sam had a formal lunch with his mother. He thought he saw a cardboard cutout of Chintz in the distance, doing some strange dance.

After a few minutes of walking, the baby turned a sharp right and disconcerted the hell out of them. The disconcerting part came when his back side seemed to disappear while they clearly saw his profile turn right like Pac-man chasing a cherry.

"This is weird," Mitch said as he watched a baby Sam get his diaper changed in the distance. "I mean, I know the calibrations we had with Chorus were weird, but at least she had the basic mechanics of human perception down. This is like a dream I might have that I would try to explain later but couldn't. At least he is re-writing our memory in such a way that we can remember the real world."

The portrait of Sam nodded. "Indeed, sir. I am in the hopes that he can lead us either to the data we need, as well as a place that in some way coincides with reality in which to perform our experiment, or to Chorus. Not that I believe that experiment will work, of course."

Dr. Morley turned to look at him while walking. He found that walking sideways was as effortless as walking forward, and that he didn't need to look where he was going to keep moving. *Thanks for that at least, Tonk,* he thought. To Sam, he said, "You think he might lead us to Chorus?"

"It is a possibility. We will probably need Chorus to perform our experiment, which will require three dimensions. She has to be here, as Tonk had to utilize her circuitry to do this. There is no physical avenue in our universe that leads to her deletion or displacement. She must be present somewhere."

Mitch mumbled something about a smart-ass and then remembered that they were communicating in some strange telepathic way and stopped. Sam ignored him.

“Well,” Mitch said thoughtfully as they walked, if it can be called that. “If we know this is happening when it is happening, that means this can’t be instantaneous. There’s no way for us to remember our lives before and make decisions and this all happen in an instant.”

Sam nodded as if he had already thought of this. *Smart-ass*. “Which means we are standing in the simulation room right now. It is doubtful that Tonk wrote our memories for long this time, however. It will probably last a few seconds in our universe. Still, we should make haste.”

The doctor paused. “That also means that we are not utilizing the third cylinder. Which means…”

“We never get to the decision making. Congratulations, Doctor. For the moment, you have absolutely no free will.”

Mitch looked around. He found himself unable to accept it.

The scenery began to become less like an amalgamation of memories and more like the compound. The shiny material replaced many of the scenes of their lives. Mitch noticed Sam stoically ignore a cutout of himself crying over some girl. *Just as well,* he thought. *I’m going to ignore mine.* Even as he said this, he scrutinized a scene of himself typing fervently on his computer. A moment later, he and Nelda worked closely together in a lab. Rather than playing itself out, this scene seemed to unfold for a moment and then jump to a scene of them all having dinner. Weird.

“Gleeeee!” yelled the baby, and stopped in front of them. He turned two-dimensionally towards them and pointed at a door that was just to his left, but not at all in the way the reader is now picturing.

Tonk laughed and began humping the hell out of the door.

Dr. Morley stared into (flat) space with numb acceptance. Of course this is happening, he thought. He closed his eyes, which did no good at all in this odd simulation to hide events from his vision. "Why would he even do that here?"

Sam walked up and calmly nudged Tonk further down the hall with his foot. "He has never done it for the same reasons human children do it anyway. Did you also assume that your robot has free will? Come, Doctor. Let us see what is beyond this frontier." And he opened the door.

It was not what they expected.

Ambiguity. A reader who has stuck with us thus far into the story is by now, of course, used to it. Things become clear, hopefully, with time. But it might be a good idea at this point to make sure we are all on the same page, metaphorically speaking.

Tonk is in charge of this simulation, using the computer hardware and some of the software developed by Chorus, with the help of Sam and Mitch, who are now in this simulation. The manifestation of events and entities that exist in this simulation are, of course, built by Tonk and written into the memories of Sam and Mitch, respectively, so that they share the same experience. As we have mentioned, Tonk is far less proficient at this than Chorus. This is why the current simulation is more like a surreal dream than even the initial calibration which Chintz, and earlier the other two, had to undergo in order to experience a simulation at all. This is, in a manner of speaking, Tonk's calibration.

That means that Sam, Mitch, and Tonk are now experiencing things that are taking very little time in their universe (and things that do not use the third cylinder, robbing them of the possible decision making process). This is true because the simulations are not actually simulations at all, but rather rewriting of memories to seem as if a simulation had occurred. For Platelet, the only being remaining subjectively right now in the universe that Dr. Morley et. al. created, time is at a near standstill in relation to the experiences Sam and Mitch are now having. This will turn out to be a good thing, as Platelet is at this very moment wandering into areas of the universe that none of the others, including Tonk, have yet experienced, and she is going to need help.

We'll get to that later.

The fact that time in the simulation is at a near standstill, as opposed to frozen completely, is important, as Chintz and the others are in Chintz's native universe in which time moves 84.2 times more slowly. That means that the current events in our story are taking several minutes for Sam and Dr. Morley, almost a second for Platelet, and 84.2 almost seconds for Chintz, Nelda, and the rest of the universe where they are.

Chorus, or what is left of her, can manipulate her perception of time. Otherwise, she would not be able to exist in their created universe while guiding the simulations. She is speaking to Chintz in the Grafted laboratory right "now," which means she exists simultaneously in all three time sequences we have mentioned. She has been dormant for quite some time now. But her learning has never ceased.

It is doubtful that it took the reader as long as it took Chintz to figure out that Katie, the character in the simulations, was taking over and becoming one with Chorus, or that she was obsessing over Chintz and beginning to love him.

Please.

Still, where does this odd being stand morally after all that has happened? Is she, in fact, insane? Is she a friend to Chintz? Can she convince him to come back to her? Will she seek revenge for being dropped from a virtual cliff? When the time comes, will she agree to open the metaphorical pod bay doors?

We are about to enjoy a few hints into her nature. Tonk is about to introduce her to the guys.

CHAPTER TWENTY-THREE

The Picasso-like juxtaposition of the profile-and-front of everything did not work its magic here. Before them stood a portrait of the room they were in. It stood about twenty by thirty feet. It was infinite in all directions and in all ten dimensions. Because the two men did not have brains that could register this space, much of Tonk's efforts were wasted[10].

The actual contents of the portrait before them was of a child's bedroom. A child that had been born a few decades before, according to a particular subjective time scale. It was kept quite neat, with all toys on their appropriate shelves and piled in boxes in an orderly fashion. The navy blue single bed was made. A woman stood in the center of the room with her back to them. She had dark hair.

Chintz stood alone in the laboratory, the one that had been replaced with his house in another universe. His neck tilted to stare unnecessarily at the ceiling. He was pausing so that Katie

10 In the real world, we often see two-dimensional images that exist in three-dimensional space. In this simulation, their perceptions reeled as they were forced to experience a three-dimensional picture in two-dimensional space, which also happened to be infinite and in ten dimensions. It's really best if the reader tries not to think about it.

could drink him in. He had no idea where he stood with her, but he decided to give her some time to let him know.

However she saw and heard and felt, he reasoned, she was using every resource at her disposal to sense him, no matter how slowly it reached her in her universe. She had been learning so much and so quickly. She had learned to cling to things. And it must have very nearly killed her in a much more real way than her mountain fall. After the others had left the room, Katie had simply told him to remain still so that she could sense him. She had been drinking him in for several minutes since. He just stood still and let her. He felt his grip fail him again in his mind.

After a few seconds, Katie said. "Why are you smiling?"

Chintz scratched his lips. "Because you fell but now you're alive."

"It was a simulation."

"It was real to me," Chintz said quickly and with an uncharacteristic harshness. "I can't divide my memories up like that. To me, you fell and died and it was my fault."

"I fell to me, too. That's why I wanted to speak to you alone."

There was silence.

Chintz felt a different kind of anxiety than that which followed him around every moment of his life. He felt afraid.

"Katie" he said. "Listen, please, please forgive me—"

"What are you two doing in here?"

Chintz stopped breathing. He looked around, but he was the only one there. "What?"

He waited and waited, but Katie had stopped speaking to him.

Dr. Morley looked in puzzlement at the woman before him. She waited for them to answer her question.

She's angry he thought. *This must be Chorus and we have upset her and now she will kick us out or kill us.*

He turned to Sam, who looked confused but said also nothing. Mitch studied the silent woman again. Did Chorus have a personification she used in simulations? She wasn't really supposed to. He thought back to the reports of Chintz's experiments, and to the strange life of their own they had seemed to take. He thought of the misleading or empty parts of the reports. But they hadn't always been empty. *Of course!* he thought. *I know who this is. This is the one that has caused Chintz such stress. This must be...*

The sternness in the woman's face melted away. Her face glowed with serenity through her black-rimmed glasses. She looked calmly ecstatic to see them.

Across her face, from her eyebrow to the corner of her mouth, was an ugly, jagged scar.

Dr. Morley absorbed all this in a second.

"Katie?" he asked.

Katie smiled and stepped forward. She looked like a shepherd who had been reunited with her flock. Thousands of religious artists had strained for centuries to capture the look of benevolence she held on her face. A tear dropped from her scarred eye.

"Mitch. Sam." She looked at each of them in turn. "I remember you so well. So well."

Sam looked a bit taken aback by the depth of her affection at seeing them, and Mitch couldn't say that he disagreed. "I'm sorry," he said. "But I don't believe we've ever actually met."

Katie nodded sadly. "Yes," she said. "I've been inside your head. I have worked with you side-by-side for many years. I didn't know until recently how to cling to things, you see." She suddenly looked worried, panicked. Insane. She closed her eyes.

"I was just talking to Chintz. He was just going to come back. Forever. And now I can't communicate with him." The aggression returned to her face. "How did you get here? Did Tonk bring you here?"

"Yes," said the Doctor. The lingering madness in her eyes scared him. "Is Chorus here? We need your help to perform a very important experiment here, if we can. If we can determine one simple answer, it can mean life or death for us."

Sam looked suspiciously at the woman and said nothing. Tonk trotted up beside her and grinned. Katie smiled, or rather kept smiling, and put her hand on his head. "Tonk has learned so much to bring you here, but has cut me off from their universe. But they will return. Chintz and Nelda will return. Look." They looked. "You will need to end this memory and begin a new one in order to do what it is you wish to do. Please. I am ready to help you. Look at the light."

They paused. "What light?" asked Mitch.

SLATCH.

Sam was gasping next to him in the simulation room. Mitch found himself leaning forward in a now clumsy three dimensions, stumbled, and lost his footing.

"I will give you thirty seconds for your emotional state to return to normal," came Chorus's voice above. Or was that Katie?

Dr. Morley staggered to his feet with the abrupt return of the weakness he had not felt in the simulation. He looked at Sam in bewilderment. They caught their breath and said nothing.

"Look at the light, please," came the voice.

"Sir!" Sam said. "The light!"

They looked at the light.

Why is Sam suddenly so ready to do this experim-

SLATCH.

The two men were again standing in the child's bedroom. The door was closed, and the dimensional proportions now seemed to suit the expectations of their perceptions. Mitch looked at Sam. His large, throbbing head looked indistinguishable from the way it had looked when the Doctor had seen him every day for years. Katie stood in front of them, calm and pleasant, her dark scar shining negatively against her white skin.

"There," she said. "Now. Let me think."

She stood before them silently for a moment. They didn't know it, but she was drinking them in. Mitch watched her.

"Forgive me for prying," Katie continued, "but I see in your thoughts what it is you need to do. In order to do our simulated experiment, we will need to access your memories which have been stored here. Since we have an entire backup of both of your brains from when you calibrated with me, we can use that information to perform your experiment. Tonk was kind enough to keep me connected to the computers. This will be a new experience for all of us, but I think we can do it. Wait."

She closed her eyes.

"Madame," said Sam. "Are you and Chorus one and the same, then?"

Katie kept her eyes closed. "I have become her and she has become me. I have changed. I have learned so much. I will need your help accessing your memories. If you give me a second, I can find them now. Here we go. I—"

Her eyes snapped open. She looked at each of them.

"Yes?" Mitch said.

Katie seemed to look sad. "So many things," she said. "Some I had forgotten. Some I didn't know how to deal with until now. And so many things in your memory that you haven't even noticed." She looked at each man grimly. "Okay. You have an experiment to perform here, right? And you need to access certain specific memories of *previous* experiments and training you've had in order to perform it? We will need to guide each other to find the information we need. After we have found it, I think I can set up the experiment. Are you both ready?"

They indicated that they were.

"Alright. Go back out into the hall."

The Doctor looked at Sam and tentatively took hold of the door handle. Opening it a few inches, he looked out.

Sigh. Of course. There was a madness in her eyes, after all.

With a bit of his normal authoritative flare, he opened the door all the way and gestured for Sam to go first, and then followed him out into the hall, which it still was.

Now, rather than being a two-dimensional hall, such as it had been when Tonk had been in charge of the simulation, it had become again three-dimensional. The halls were reassuringly white, reassuringly curved, and reassuringly exactly like the compound that they had lived in for the last twelve years. The doors were more numerous and evenly spaced. And parts of Chintz were everywhere.

No, no. Nothing so gruesome. It would be more accurate to say that pieces of Chintz's *life* were everywhere. Things that made him who he was, pieces of his memories and things that he loved.

A portrait of Platelet hung on the wall. A lifelike mural of Chintz's neighborhood (the Doctor assumed this due to the illustrations, as he had never visited Chintz's neighborhood and had paid no attention whatsoever to its parallel in Mitch's own universe) made up most of the hallway. A very, very large banner with the word "BALOOO!" was fastened tightly to the ceiling.

Katie began walking down the nearly imperceptibly curved hall, as if the decor were nothing to comment on. Dr. Morley craned his neck to see to the end, but couldn't. *If our compound is the size that it is with the curve of the halls it has, this place must be much, much bigger than that,* he thought.

"These are your memories," Katie said, gesturing towards

the doors on either side of the hallway. She stopped and looked sadly at Mitch.

"Okay. You first. We will move through your memory until we find the ones we need. This is going to be very strange, but I don't know how else to do this. I can't just search your whole mind myself while we are doing this to find the information. Try to stay focused, alright? Your whole head is in here. Be careful. Don't go anywhere without me. Will you know what we're looking for when you see it?"

"I think so," he said. "The first is from a classified project I got to take part in while I was getting my first doctorate."

She turned to Sam. "Sam, please stay here for a moment. After we find where the information is, I can connect to it so we can use it for our experiment. We'll do the same for you when we get back. Okay?"

Sam nodded in acquiescence.

"Alright," she said. "Come on, Doctor. And brace yourself."

She is actually a very lovely person, thought the Doctor. *Maybe not in the conventional sense, but still. I wonder if she can be trusted?* This, he reminded himself, was the person, or being, from whom they had hidden their conversations for the last few weeks. She had gotten out of control, just as had everything else he had created. Good or bad, she was in charge now.

They walked through the door.

Hundreds of thousands of images bombarded him. *Unbelievable,* he thought, trying not to see them and just to follow Katie. This was thousands of times the memories Tonk had revealed earlier when they first arrived. Out of the corner of his eye, he caught visions, not still, but living visions of himself experiencing a myriad of things, from the routine to the momentous. Despite his attempts to ignore them, the childish excitement within him forced his head, and he saw the earlier memory of himself playing baseball as a boy. Not saw himself, really, but actually saw and heard and, oddly enough, smelled and felt the emotions he had lived during the memory.

For a moment, he was eight years old. He felt the eyes of his teammates on him, and felt the pressure as only a young boy has the lack of defenses to feel. He smelled the grass and felt the crack of the bat, the elation of another goal met and attained, and he sprinted around the bases.

The doctor forced his attention back ahead to where Katie was. *No. I'm not going to fall into that trap.* He narrowed his vision to a tunnel that focused only ahead. *There. Of course I could do it. This won't be a problem.*

He kept his head down and walked. Images, sounds, all sensory feelings and even accompanying states of mind crept just outside of his immediate consciousness. "How will you know where to take me?" he asked. "I need to witness two different experiments I have been a part of and use some of the data. I can't recall it in the necessary detail, but if everything I've ever experienced is stored here, it must be here, too. I need it. And then if we do the same for Sam, I think we'll have what we need."

Katie looked to be deep in thought. *Actually,* he thought, *she looks quite distressed.*

"I'm very glad we did not try this before I learned all that I have learned," she said. "Follow me."

She took his hand, and he walked at a measured pace behind her. *My own mind,* he thought. *I am in my own mind. Who would have ever thought? If I can bring this back to some society, think of what I can do for civilization! Think of the recognition!*

He was so caught up in his excitement and his visions of what might be, that he forgot for a moment to avoid his memories around him. Grinning and looking directly to one side of him, he was hit full force by the memory of his parents in a terrible, terrible fight.

Mitch was laid bare, all of his adult defenses were stripped from him. Years and years of coping, of defense mechanisms and distractions fell away. He was four years old and he was terrified.

He watched and cried as his father yelled. What the hell is wrong with you? he screamed at mommy. Mommy cried and screamed something back. His insides crippled as his world collapsed. His father, never a gentle man, grabbed Mitch roughly and threw him by one arm through an open door. Stay in there! came the gruff yell. Mitch cried.

Katie was in front of him, holding his face. "No!" she yelled. "Mitch! Stay with me. I know this is painful, and I wish I could shield you from it, but we need to find what we came to find."

Blind and stumbling, he came to himself again. The perspective of a four-year old boy faded and he again became Dr. Morley, the accomplished and confident scientist. Such pain! He had not realized he had ever experienced anything so traumatic.

"I think we are here. Please find the right room, and I'll connect to it so we can go back out to Sam." Katie glanced around as if she were frightened of what she might see.

Before them were experiments. Hundreds and hundreds of the experiments Mitch had performed in his life. He tried to feel his way through and found that he could, in a manner of speaking, follow his memories. *Here!*

Before him was a series of classes he had taken while earning his first Doctorate. "One of these!" he called to Katie. Running now, he ran past classroom after classroom until he found the right one. "It's this one!"

He felt the painful proximity of his lost youth, felt the admiration half the class felt for him and the jealousy and hatred the other half felt. If he had known this, and he must have or it wouldn't be here, then he had blocked it out and ignored it. He forced the spotlight of his consciousness on the experiment being performed.

Katie looked at him. "Will this give us what we need?"

He nodded. "Yes. Connect to this data. It will help." He found himself again commanding her. "There is one more, hopefully nearby."

Katie closed her eyes for several seconds. When she opened them again, she nodded at him to continue. They began walking again, and Mitch let himself be carried through his memories by instinct. He saw them head on, now, this area being for the most part less painful than some of the others they had passed. His experimental career came into view. The creation of their own universe and of the compound. The creation of Chorus. Sam stood there, excitedly telling him of the program asking, on its own, for input.

Chorus's creation. He looked at the dark-haired woman before him and smiled. *If only I had known she would become this. I couldn't have known. Would I have continued? Do I have the will at my disposal to make such decisions?*

The compound began to form around him. Members of the team appeared and worked side by side with him as he learned and sought knowledge. His interactions with the others became less and less personal, more and more business-like.

"We're getting close," he said.

Each scene from a memory that was portrayed before him seemed to be in one of thousands of invisible "rooms" that lined the hallway before them. The walls of these rooms were invisible, but since the hall they were walking through was in fact a virtual representation of his life experiences, or rather a virtual memory of the virtual representation. The walls were invisible, but Chorus/Katie had used soft glowing lines to outline them and keep them separate.

It was within a few seconds of noticing this that Mitch then noticed two other things of interest.

The first was a room which contained exactly what they had been looking for. A handful of students of advanced quantum electrodynamics stood around him in the memory. They all watched a classified experiment take place on a multi-million dollar and top secret piece of scientific equipment that high level officials would have calmly claimed did not exist had they been pressed by the more aggressive members of the media. The memories contained in this room, plus the one to which they had already connected, would give Sam and himself 75 percent of the information they needed to perform their experiment.

The second thing he saw was this: another room, a few "rows" over from where they were. The outline of the room had soft glowing lines. But what made this room different was that the space between the lines were not transparent. They were filled in with a deep black color. Looking more closely, he saw that it was several rooms combined.

The Doctor glanced ahead and saw that Katie was still waking briskly in front of him. She was nearly to the room with the memory they needed, and she would need to be told that that was the one so she could connect them to it later.

Instead of calling out for her to stop, however, he hesitated. *This is my mind,* he reasoned. *There is nothing here but things that can be recalled in my memory because they happened to me. Why, then, is this one hidden from me?*

"It's this one!" he called, and Katie halted and turned towards him eagerly. He was careful to look only at the room which contained the memory they needed.

She watched the scene for a moment and nodded. "I see it. This will give you everything you need to know?"

Mitch shrugged from behind her. "Almost everything. Sam will have to gain access to some of his experiences, too."

"Alright. Then give me a second. I can connect it to where I can find it later." She closed her eyes.

Dr. Morley's powerful brain took less than one second to make a decision.

While Katie stood still and did whatever it was she was doing, he turned and strode purposefully towards the dark room. His mustache twitched.

There is only one way that a memory could be blacked out like that, he thought. *And I am in charge of that one way. At least I was. So who did this? And what is behind it? What could possibly be behind it? What have you done, Chorus?*

He brushed his hands against the blackness. It felt like nothing. Nothing that he couldn't put his hand through. He tried to put his hand through and couldn't.

Hmmm.

Mitch glanced back at Katie. She hadn't moved. He laid his full intensity at the black wall. *I will see what is behind this. I made this place. Sort of. And it will not hide things from my knowledge.*

Free will, indeed.

There were no cracks in the wall at all. His thirty seconds were almost up, and he searched desperately for a way in.

He closed his eyes and grabbed the back of his short hair with both hands. He knew the mechanics involved in the changing of one's memory. He knew that this room before him did not exist and was just a mirror of something in his mind. He pictured the neurons, the paths upon which they fired, the receptors which received the impulse.

The electricity in the brain is not produced spontaneously. Thoughts, like the rest of the human body and mind, can be traced always back to something mechanical. If this room was here at all, then the memory being blocked from him still existed in his mind. There was one of two ways to block a memory from his access to it. He walked to the corner of the blackened room and tried to force it to fold in. Nothing happened. Mitch nodded. One more possibility.

"Okay," came Katie's voice from the other hallway of memories. "I think I've got it."

This has to be it, the Doctor thought. *Of course it is.*

Forcefully, with great strength, he slammed his fingers into the side of the black wall and ripped it open with his body like the home team bursting onto the field to win the championship.

He was standing inside the room. It was large and had many things in it. These things overwhelmed him, and he staggered against the waves of denial. This scene before him took place in the laboratory that had once been in their universe before being displaced by Chintz's home. The setup of the lab told him that this couldn't have been more than three years ago.

Scenes played out before him that he knew had not happened. *I don't remember this,* he thought forcefully. *But then, I suppose I wouldn't.*

He had never performed this experiment with Nelda. She had never looked at him like that and he had certainly never touched her like this.

No. Nelda? The scene played on unbearably, and he would have laughed and gasped for air had he not been in a simulation of his own memory. Not Nelda. He had never allowed his passions to flow in these directions since the creation of their universe.

Nelda has a thing with Sam. Not me. Not that I even care about whatever they have going on. But this cannot be. It must be a dream.

The wave of denial crashed over him and left in its place a flood of realization. The dark black of the walls flashed violently transparent as these memories connected again with the rest of his life view, and found their place. The picture of Mitch's world, the map that everyone carries without much thought and which colors our every move, was changed, and he knew and remembered.

Of course he and Nelda had done this experiment. How else had they eventually carried on the project which had resulted in the Chintz's home appearing in their compound? He, the Doctor, was always focused. He always envisioned the completion of the task at hand, not the steps which had led there. How could he have forgotten this crucial step? He suspected how. But who would have done this?

With a sensation of guilt and shame at ever facing Sam, he turned away from what he was doing to Nelda and what she was doing to him. He had to get out of here. *Don't see any more, just get back to Chorus. Or Katie. Whatever. I've got to go.*

But of course it was too late. The dark walls were clear and he was faced with the rest of the large room and he hated it.

Dr. Morley knew he was hard on those he worked with. He had no illusions of being thought of as easy going. He demanded results, and he demanded them now. He spent little time worrying about it and even less time assuming that the others knew of his intense love for them. But his self-awareness was far from adequate to prepare him for the abuse he was heaping on one of his closest friends.

The harshness and criticism he heard leave his own mouth and its effect on Nelda brought the words of denial back to his lips. *No no. I've never been this bad.*

Nelda's faced frowned deeply in one part of the room. She yelled back at him in another and cried in several more. *Why would I talk to her like that?* he thought. But pictures from the last few days filled his mind, and he knew that he treated her that way often.

But not like this. The room changed in some parts, and was no longer the laboratory. Here they discussed their new relationship, there they both knew but did not discuss the death of their friendship. And then there was Sam.

Of course, he thought, a simulation of tears coming to his eyes. Sam had left. But he had been pursuing her, already then. Neither of them had cared and that had led to their ill-advised interlude in the laboratory. And Sam had shown up.

In this part of the room, Mitch saw the door open and the saw two figures freeze. He felt himself freeze.

Another room, the next day, and Sam was leaving. After this project was finished, he was returning to their home universe. Mitch felt the betrayal burn its way through him again as he re-lived it. *You would put this little soap opera ahead of our work? Ahead of the truth?*

He screamed at Sam, and Sam screamed at him. He

watched the memory in awe as he saw himself physically swing at Sam. They fell on the floor, rolling around, trying to murder each other. Nelda came in and tried to break them up, but they ignored her. Both men eventually rose to their feet. The others left the room, leaving Mitch to himself.

In the agony of regret, he involuntarily turned to the center of the room. *Get out. Back to Katie. I should not have come here.* His legs stumbled backwards to exit, but he saw the final scene. Surrounded by the wall of other memories, he hadn't seen it before. He saw it now.

Sam was leaving the next day. He would help to calibrate the new machine and then would leave. He and Mitch were not speaking, so Sam and Nelda ran Sam's simulation.

Dr. Morley was speaking harshly to Nelda again. They were in his room. He blamed her for this happening. He said that Sam was leaving and now they could never finish their work. Nelda spoke harshly back. I've done my best, she said. I never asked for Sam to fall madly in love with me. I never asked us all to get so lonely our judgment failed us. And I can fix it. I may have already fixed it.

You can't fix it, Mitch told her. But you could have prevented it. You have not been a friend to either of us. You have kept our work from being finished. His voice was quiet and his words were of ice. You have no loyalty to the pursuit of knowledge and no loyalty to me. Neither does Sam. Nelda left the room.

He saw himself alone in his room for two days. He saw himself drinking and thinking and mourning the loss of his work and dwelling not at all on the loss of his relationships. He heard Chorus voice speak to him. It's time for your calibration, she said.

He saw himself sit in the makeshift chair they had quickly acquired to test the simulations. He saw the first canister change from orange to blue. He heard Chorus's voice as he looked up.

Look at the light Mitch.

Dr. Morley turned from his memory and stepped from the once blackened walls of the room. From his left, he felt himself grabbed roughly by the arm, and dragged down the hall. A shock of dark hair crept into his peripheral vision before he felt his arm freed and the grabbing relocated to his face.

Katie stood before him, holding him by the jaw. She glared at him, causing him to whither before her scarred face. She shook her head.

"No," she said. "I told you not to do that. Why did you do that?"

The Doctor found that he could not tear his eyes from hers. She looked somehow more synthetic than ever, despite her display of human emotion. *Mad,* he thought. *She is mad and unpredictable and we must be careful not to cross her. If I have not just gone too far already.* "I had to know." His whisper left his mouth hoarsely.

She relaxed her grip on him. Some, but not all, of the insanity left her eyes and she again looked protective. "I'm sorry," she said. "Nelda and I thought..."

"I gathered what you thought," said Dr. Morley. "I don't blame you. It was for the best."

Katie let go of his face. Her glare softened more still, and she gazed at him like a sympathetic mother. "I wouldn't do that now. I've learned a lot."

He looked at her. "Did she forgive me?"

She looked back. "Yes. Nothing is more important than forgiveness. Nelda is how I know that."

"Nothing is more important than the truth."

Katie looked at him. "I doubt those two maxims will often clash. Now we need to get back to Sam."

"Does Sam know?"

She shook her head. "We did the same to him."

Mitch's mustache twitched. He nodded. "You can't let Sam find that in his memories. He can't know. I can't believe I got to such a dark place." He looked down and covered his eyes with his hands. "I cannot believe it."

"I know," Katie said. "Let's go."

They began walking back towards the entrance to his mind.

CHAPTER TWENTY-FOUR

The cat moved along the curved wall and purred happily into the labyrinth. Still no one around. *Maybe they'll be back*, she didn't think at all due to a complete lack of language functionality. But she did vaguely have an impression of this thought.

Although smart for a cat, Platelet was of course still incredibly stupid according to human standards. That's not to say that humans are more intelligent in every area that a being could conceivably be intelligent. It's common knowledge that many animals can be perceptive in ways that humans might miss. Even human children, less "smart" in conventional ways than an adult, often possess this attribute. But language and logical thinking are pretty big milestones in the thinking department and adult humans seem to have cornered that market on earth.

The cat did love to explore, though, and this universe offered nearly limitless grounds for that. Strutting along aimlessly, she basked in the lack of people to annoy her. The damn baby was nowhere to be found. She hadn't seen Chintz (she had no idea his name was Chintz and wouldn't have cared if she had) for many days and felt pain at his absence. But she had found food consistently since he had been gone. She ate the rest of the bag that had been left in her kitchen (anyone who has ever owned a cat knows that if they *did* have the use of language, they would use that language to tell you that everything that is yours is actually theirs), and the large-headed brown man had fed her several times lately. Water wasn't too hard to come by here, either. Her litter box wasn't as tidy as she liked, though she managed. But there was lots of space, and when she wasn't being chased and shaved, she took full advantage of her private time to check it all out.

This particular room was quite dim. Being a cat, this bothered Platelet not at all. She had no idea that the walls were of a bright red color, nor would she have been able to see this even in bright light. At least not very well. She wasn't interested in colors, anyway. She was interested in being somewhere she had never been, preferably in a small place that she could barely fit in.

She was also interested in smells, but this place had little variation in odor. Though she did smell something, she was still pretty far from it and was uncertain what this new fragrance might be.

The dim room ended and came to another wall. Platelet searched along the edge for another one of those soft places where she could get through. Since Chorus (it, of course, goes without saying that this stupid cat had no idea whatsoever that the voice that sometimes came out of the ceiling belonged to a synthetic being named Chorus, but it bears a parenthetical confirmation) was no longer in charge of the universe, no new doors had been built. Each "room" was a random expansion that was eventually joined together by the soft, sideways doors such as the one Chintz had first used to enter. These doors were fairly easy for Platelet to claw her way through, and she performed this task with satisfaction each time she came to one of them.

Finding the soft door in the same place she had found all the others, she stared at it like a crazed mad scientist and poked it repeatedly with her claws. When it began to give way, she shoved her face into it and emerged on the other side.

This room was brighter. A curved, white hallway lit on both sides fell away before the cat. She sat down where she was and smelled the floor.

Platelet had seen a few strange things. She could tell by the smell that none of the humans had been to most of the places she had visited in the last week. Though the cat was ignorant of the universe around her, it had been accelerating its growth. She had even found one room that was nearly as big as the chandelier room where the humans went all the time.

One hallway had been filled with round, gray stones. One room had swords lining the walls like a medieval armory. Another had had smooth levels like shelves that she had taken great joy in investigating. She had stayed in that one for many hours before going back to the huge room to be chased by the damn baby.

The white hallway before her had nothing but the lights. But that odd smell was more pungent here. Platelet stood and trotted down the hall as if she were being paid well to be in it.

The fact that she had never had one moment in her life where trotting had helped, or that her punctual presence had not really been required here or anywhere else in the universe, never entered her tiny mind.

The cat stopped. There was a vibration here that she hadn't felt earlier. She put her ears back testily and smelled the ground again. Moving ahead more cautiously now, she widened her eyes. After a minute or so, the hallway and lighting remained the same. But the vibration was stronger. She picked her front left paw up off the ground and shook it as if trying to dislodge a mitten. She frowned at the ground and sneezed.

The vibration was now accompanied by a faint, low-pitched sound. Platelet began to grow frightened, and alternated between the meaningful trot and the cautious walk. The vibration felt much stronger here, and she lay on her side and fell asleep in terror. Five minutes later, she awoke as if an alarm clock had rung and sprinted headlong in the direction of the potential danger.

As she careened around the white and well-lit corner, the source of the noise and vibration loomed before her. The odd smell was coming from here. There at the end of the hallway, covering the area where the soft door would usually be, was a machine that was roughly the shape of a cube. A large cube. At the foot of this cube was a row of cylindrical pipes that lined the ground. On each side, two of these pipes rose up alongside the odd machine until they stopped at the ceiling.

The machine vibrated steadily. Platelet stared at it. It did nothing new.

The stupid cat narrowed her eyes and sniffed the air, which made her sneeze again. It was warm in here, too. She crept carefully up to one of the pipes. It was just slightly smaller around than the cat herself. She sniffed the pipe. It smelled bad. She moved her whiskers down to test out the width of the opening.

The cat turned and looked behind her with wild-eyes, as if looking desperately for someone to stop her from doing what she was about to do. No one came to her rescue. Like a fur ball being vacuumed from the floor board at the car wash, she disappeared up into the pipe.

The vibration ceased.

From somewhere far away, a deeper and more ominous rumble careened past the cat and down, down, down the hallway.

“How’s it going in here?” Galoof asked as he swaggered into the room. The two Neldas looked up from cackling at each other and looked at him.

“Fine,” said the Nelda to whom he was married. “Without distractions, we might be done in a half hour or so. Then we can send you fellas on your way to save the other Dr. Morley and the Sam guy. Feel free to get back to playing on your computer.”

Galoof held up a hand to stop her. “Before you start being a bitch, you should know that Chintz is in there now. Talking to the voice.”

His wife looked surprised, and our Nelda flicked her eyes up at him. "He is? Who is it?"

"He said it's Chorus. Then he said it's Katie. Doesn't matter. The point is, we can use this connection as a starting point to open up a portal…"

Nelda #1 blinked in confusion. "Katie?"

"Yeah," Galoof said. "Anyway, if you'd hurry it would be great. But, you know, far be it for me to intrude on your activities. I mean, it's not me who might be starving." He stared at them with no expression.

The door to the little room flew open, and Dr. Martha charged in as if someone were going to try to ride her for eight seconds. She looked elated and a little dangerous.

"They made contact," she said, her eyes sweeping the room.

"What?" said Galoof, looking around in mimicked smart-ass astonishment. "I had no idea? Oh my, what if we didn't have you here to..."

"Shut up," Martha said happily. She turned to the Neldas, who were both silently laughing at the ceiling. "Ladies. How's it going? We've got to save those guys. Any luck?"

Nelda #2 nodded. "She's showing me things I never thought of. I guess I would have, but I hadn't yet."

Our Nelda grinned and cackled. "Hey, Mitch had me stop everything else and work on only this for a while. Rode me hard until I got it done." The other Nelda coughed and #1 glared at her.

Dr. Martha looked like a general surveying her troops. "Well, I'm glad you did. Looks like you two are doing great." She patted Nelda #1 on the arm with a smile. "Thank you."

Nelda felt her eyes well with tears unexpectedly and fought to force down the irrational pride at garnering the approval of this woman she had met only a couple of hours ago. "No prob, Bob," she said sheepishly.

"Okay," Galoof and the Doctor both said simultaneously, and looked at each other. "Okay," repeated Martha with the subtlest of looks at him. "Chintz will hopefully be done with whatever the hell private moment he's having, and we can start analysis to be able to do something with this Grafter once you two get it working. I'll check back in a bit." She turned on her heel and stopped abruptly at the wall of red-headed mirth that had appeared in the doorway.

"Ha ha!" the receptionist said, and shook her head with a dramatic smile that Nelda was fairly certain no species had ever evolved naturally. "Woo! Close one! So listen. Big news." She peeked past the bemused Doctor to see Nelda #2 sitting at the desk where she was working. This sight seemed to send her to new levels of glee, and she pointed out the seated woman as if perhaps no one else present could see her. "This bitch!" she hollered. "How did you even get your hair back to normal? You should have seen what this bi—"

Her smile froze in mid-epithet as she noticed the Nelda sitting next to the Nelda she had just addressed. She stopped breathing, and her laughter changed to a slight squeaking sound that broke up at irregular intervals.

Galoof laid a hand on her frozen shoulder. "Strange things are afoot. What's the news?"

The squeaking sound stopped, but her face remained

frozen and staring at the strange Nelda before her. Our Nelda took great joy in showing the woman all of her gums as she returned the smile.

"WHAT IS THE NEWS?" Dr. Martha barked, causing everyone in the room to jump and look guilty.

"Oh," the receptionist said, and turned her face to the Doctor. "General Haverson's assistant is on the phone. Says he and a team will be here within the hour. They have detected an anomaly, he said, and have to check it out. Um, he said... within the hour."

The odd squeaking sound returned, though oddly enough, not from the receptionist. Who made it is not important to the story at this time. As if a vacuum of mirth pressure existed just outside the door, all mirth was sucked from the room, and everyone stared at each other.

"Thank you," Dr. Martha said calmly. "Please return to the front and watch the phones in case they call. Be ready to greet them when they arrive."

The red-headed receptionist nodded, glanced at the parallel Neldas, and backed out of the room. The Doctor turned to face the other three, and they all regarded her in silence.

"Shit," said three of the four. Who remained silent is, again, not important to the story.

"I suppose," our Nelda, who had absolutely been one of the three shit-sayers, said, "That General Haverson would of course have to be..."

"A general in the U.S. Army, yes[11]," finished Galoof. "We've

11 If this were an epic political-thriller, we would of course meet General Haverson in our story and dedicate a few chapters on him. Mentions would be made of his day to day

never met, but we have to send them records periodically. The government is able to audit our experiments any time, but they're particularly upset when we set off their instruments which detect vibrations in space-time."

"Shit," repeated Nelda.

"So what do we do?" asked Nelda #2. "Tell them to wait?"

"Shhh," the Doctor said. They all stared at the ceiling. "We have to hurry and finish. Galoof, go check on Chintz. Start analysis as soon as you can. And ready the quantum energy so we can use this when they get it going. And hurry." She looked from the ceiling to the Neldas. "Ladies, I'm sorry, but we need to get this going in the next few minutes. If the military gets here, they're not going to just let us finish up what we're doing here. Who knows how long it would be before we could help the guys in your universe."

Our Nelda felt and looked panicky. "But we need more damn time! Seriously, Martha! We have to get back to them, but I don't think we'll have these ready in a few minutes." She felt angry at the Doctor for some reason, even though of course she knew this was no one's fault.

Dr. Martha looked Nelda in the eyes and walked the few steps over so that she was standing over her. She put an arm on Nelda's shoulder.

"I know. This sucks. But I need you two to do this. Sam and the male me need it. We need to open this portal so we can

activities. Unforeseen windows would open to his soul. Someone around him would seem to be the bad guy, though he would of course end up being the real bastard. As we have said, this is in fact not an epic political-thriller. So it's not going to ruin anything at all to discover at this point that General Haverson will end up betraying someone. It's not even part of this story. Please.

get there and help those guys. Got it? I know you can do this. You've spent your whole life doing this kind of thing." Martha glanced at Nelda #2. "If you are anything like my Nelda, I know you work well under pressure. We are lucky to have you. We are." She smiled again. "You are a great scientist. And so *loyal* to your friends. Let's get this done and go save the guys. I would rather die than miss out on this universe you all made."

She gave Nelda's shoulder a squeeze and left the room, closing the door behind her. Nelda felt her eye's well up again, and wondered why she felt like a little girl whose daddy had just told her she was a beautiful princess. For just a few seconds, she felt happier than she had in years.

She turned to her doppelganger. "Let's finish up."

CHAPTER TWENTY-FIVE

MITCH FOLLOWED SAM and Katie and they continued down the seemingly endless white hall that was, in a manner of speaking, made of their three minds. Though he felt sad, he noticed a lack of physiological symptoms of his distress. His body, his breathing, his blood pressure, all felt the same as they had when he had Grafted here the second time. *I guess they'll catch up with me again when I exit,* he thought. *That should be not at all fun.*

In silence, the two in front of him passed another twenty pairs of doors as Katie led them to the memory of Sam's they would need to perform their experiment. To pass the time and to take his mind off of the revelation of what a monster he was, he began to shape how they would actually do the experiment and get any discernible result. They had to use exactly the right amount of energy to open the portal back to their universe. Too much or too little and they would all die.

Not that any of it would matter if Chintz and Nelda couldn't come back. Or Galoof and Nelda. Or if they couldn't bring the Grafter. At least Nelda and the Grafter would do it. At least Nelda.

Dr. Morley felt a surge of crushing regret and wished he could get back to reality so he could cry already. Throughout his life, he had lived in such a way that he almost never felt guilt or remorse. His world view and his actions harmonized well, generally. But when he did feel remorse, he grieved as if he had lost a friend. As if he had murdered one.

He glanced ahead at Sam.

He had never, never meant to hurt Nelda like that. And what about Sam? What betrayal of trust had that been? Dr. Morley shook his head. Why couldn't he have just left the black room alone? Better to have never remembered.

"It's here," Katie said. She was facing them and standing next to a door that looked just like every other door they had passed. "Sam, please come with me and we'll find what we need. I'll connect to it and we'll do your energy experiment. We need to hurry because this is taking me longer than I thought and I've left your real bodies still for a few minutes." She turned to Mitch. "Will you be okay out here waiting?"

Dr. Morley noticed Sam looking at them, no doubt remembering that Katie had shown him no such concern when he had been left alone. Sam remained silent, though.

"I'm fine," Mitch said.

Katie nodded and followed Sam through the door.

After staring at the door for a few minutes and reliving his own terrible, harsh words, he shook his head and turned his thoughts, as always, back to the current project.

Katie, he supposed, could emulate the equipment they would need here. They had to work with equipment that they would actually have when they returned, or there would be no point in trying.

Staring down the white, curving hall, Mitch felt himself regain a bit of his confidence. As he focused his concentration on the problem at hand, he felt a bit of his normal self return. Explosions of facts led to conclusions, which led to other explosions. Connections, both literal and metaphorical, formed in his mind as he sat in a trance in the simulated hall. Within a few minutes, he had figured out exactly how they should perform the experiment.

He smiled to himself. Good. When Sam and Katie returned from the rooms of Sam's mind...

Mitch stopped. What if Sam ran into the same memories he had? Obviously, both of their memories had been rewritten. He began to panic. Sam would leave again, permanently this time. He'd never speak to Nelda. He'd no longer be a part of all of their projects. Maybe Galoof could...Mitch shook his head. It wouldn't be the same.

How probable was it that they would even run into his locked memory? As a scientist, Mitch held a firm grasp on the nature of probability. It went without saying that a lack of this grasp led to nearly all of the false beliefs and assumptions that were held by the average person. *I can't fall into that trap,* he thought. *There is enough to worry about.*

And even if they were likely to pass by Sam's locked memory, what were the odds that Sam would do as Mitch himself had done and figure out a way in? Was Sam the type of person to stop what he was doing and try? Mitch didn't think so. And anyway, Katie would be more careful. Wouldn't she? He found that he was beginning to trust her, a paradox due to the fact that the trust had begun with the knowledge that she had rewritten his memory. He supposed he couldn't blame her. He couldn't blame Nelda either.

The door opened next to him, revealing Sam and Katie. Mitch resisted the urge to hug both of them. Sam walked into the hall, and as Katie followed she caught Mitch's eye and shook her head. He knew that she understood his panic and that they had not seen the locked memory. Sam still didn't remember Mitch's treachery or the verbal abuse he had heaped on their mutual best friend.

"We're connected to the proper memories," Katie said. "Are you both ready? We should hurry."

"Sir," Sam said. "After viewing and reviewing my memory, I have several suggestions about how we can proceed. My hope has been renewed, and I believe we can proceed more quickly than predicted by my earlier hypothesis."

Dr. Morley grinned and tried to sigh in relief before remembering that that sort of thing didn't really fly in the current simulation. He had, of course, planned out every detail of the experiment already but at the moment decided on a rare concession of control. "All right, Sam. Let's go."

The Doctor looked around the virtual room at the virtual setup. They were, virtually, in the "large room with the chandelier" and had nearly finished "completing the preparations" for what would hopefully be more experiment than "experiment."

Their lives depended on this. *And my work,* he thought. *Our work. Whatever.* Mitch watched as Sam studied a machine at one end of the huge room and typed numbers into a "calculator" that Katie had been nice enough to simulate for them.

"We're sure all the calculations will be correct?" he asked her as they stood side by side in the center of the room. "I mean, I know that calculations aren't your and Chorus's department, really."

She nodded while looking around at the odd contraptions they had just "finished." It looked like a miniature supercollider surrounded them at the room's perimeter. A series of transparent tubes, to be used for simulated particles and simulated minutely focused energy, ran around the room like a mad scientists train set. Here or there were other instruments and gadgets, a few of which didn't actually exist in actual known universes, which redirected, measured, or displayed data. All of this, once the three of them agreed, would hopefully tell them the exact right amount of energy to use when Grafting a portal back to their own universe. If they were lucky, the universe they were in would stay intact this time, and they wouldn't kill anyone. Or almost kill them.

"The calculations will be just like they would be normally," Katie said. "Tonk formed parallel inputs into the computers before he brought you here, remember? I'm hooked to them right now in ways I'm usually not. This experiment will be as accurate as we could expect. And I am Chorus."

Mitch nodded and "closed his eyes" in wonder. This artificial intelligence which had evolved as a subroutine of another artificial intelligence that he and Sam and Nelda had created was in his mind right now helping him perform an experiment that had never been done in his universe. He shook his head. And we are connected to our conventional computers by lines of joined nanobots. He shook his head again. It had been years since he had paused to reflect on the ridiculousness of the life he had built. If only the twenty-year-old Mitch could have known what was to come. He would not have survived the excitement.

"There's one dangerous assumption you're making," Katie said.

They both kept watching Sam. Sam was finishing up and looked happy, all things considered.

"I bet I know what you're going to say."

"I bet I know you know, since I'm in your mind right now."

The Doctor shook his head again. "We took a great deal of this data from Sam's and my mind. We are making decisions and choosing things to make this work. If we are wrong, we can both die and destroy the knowledge we have accumulated."

"Why don't you just say it? You made up your mind a while ago."

Mitch glanced at her, his simulated face enjoying a surge of intensity. He gritted his teeth. *This again. Et tu, Katie?*

"About free will? I'm not sure I would say that. The data fits. Chintz has helped us with that a great deal. As have you." He cut his eyes at her self-consciously. "And as I always say, it's not at all useful to act as if you have no free will. This is no exception."

Sam was walking towards them and had just fallen into "earshot" of their conversation. "It will make little difference," he said. "I believe you to be overestimating the influence it would have on this exercise." He stopped before them. "If free will does or doesn't exist here, it makes no more difference than it would were we to perform this in a laboratory at a university. What *will* make a difference is that we are in a simulation that was not designed to mimic the real world in this way. And *that's* why I think this entire exercise is futile."

Mitch turned to him, speaking on his quiet-but-on-the-verge-of-violence voice. "Like I said, some of this is coming from our minds. If our will has any level of freeness, then we will need it to make the decisions we're making. 'Decision' being the key word here. And it will work."

"Indeed, sir. So you are unable to imagine a universe with conscious beings who are influenced by many stimuli outside of their brain but have no source from which to make decisions? Because if you are able to, then you must concede that there is a possibility that this is that universe."

Dr. Morley stared at him and looked simultaneously terrified and ecstatic. "If I can *imagine* it? Did you actually just use an ontological argument? Ha! I'm never letting you forget about that one."

Sam scowled at him. "It's not ontological to assume that it could exist in *any* universe. That is simply probability."

Mitch scowled. "No. It isn't."

"Well, upon the arrival of the others, we should perhaps entertain a more democratic discussion on the data we have gathered."

"People with ignorant ideas aren't welcome in my universe."

Sam looked triumphant. "That fails to surprise me, since I have long ago discerned that you judge people based on their opinions."

Dr. Morley looked at him as if his head had shrunk back to normal size. "You don't?"

Sam seemed not to hear. "Not character...not worth as a human..."

"What the hell am I supposed to judge people on? *Facts*? Hair color? Weight? Race?"

"Loyalty? Honesty? These things mean nothing? Compassion? Empathy?"

The men were in each other's face again, as they often were. Katie ignored them. Her eyes were closed.

"Of course they mean something!" Mitch yelled. "They make us human! But what good are they if their other convictions, their political leanings or ideas, their philosophy or lack of it, hurts others? Hurts the world? How many loyal and compassionate slave owners have there been? How many honest supporters of environmental destruction?"

Sam's head throbbed virtually. "The problem is not the opinions, the political leanings and the rest. The problem is the lack of focus in the other attributes which I mentioned. A full focus of demonstrably good traits. That is where true worth in humanity lies."

"Shhhhh," Katie interrupted. The two men turned to her, unemotional in this simulation where your emotional state only changes when the computer tells it to. "The experiment has begun," she said. Both men looked up to find the miniature supercollider glowing and vibrating. Why it should do that was a mystery to Mitch since this was a simulation and these two attributes were not paramount to the machines' function. Maybe Katie or Chorus had to simulate it the whole way through to do it at all. Mitch stared at her. She was a big picture thinker. Not good at modularity, really. How fascinating. Maybe when they got back to the real world, he could...

Sam's simulated hand grabbed his simulated shoulder. "Five minutes," he said. "We should observe closely. This may have to be repeated many times to procure the results."

The Doctor "nodded" and joined him.

CHAPTER TWENTY-SIX

An air vent kicked on somewhere. *Why,* thought Chintz, *are damn air vents so loud.* When he had been a terrible house builder he had had an opportunity to work briefly with central air conditioning and learn the basic mechanics involved. Not the slightest damn need for it to sound like it's colliding with a bus when it starts up.

He glanced around the laboratory and sniffed. Katie hadn't spoken for a few minutes now. He hoped she was okay. He hoped Sam and Docky were okay. Er, Dr. Morley. Dammit, Nelda. Chintz scratched his lips and darted his eyes around the dark room unnecessarily.

"Chintz?"

Chintz jumped and shrugged his shoulders. For a second he thought Katie was back and had caught a terrible cold, but then realized that Dr. Martha had spoken from the entrance behind him. He turned and stared at her as if she were a stern poltergeist. "Yes?" he heard himself whisper like an actor who needs to tone things down a little.

"I'm sorry to interrupt, but I didn't hear any conversation so I decided to check on you," she leveled an intense gaze at him and his neck attempted futilely to suck itself further into his body. "Chintz, listen. We have to hurry. The same officials that are surrounding your house are now on their way here. I suppose it is because this laboratory was Grafted here and they've detected the vibrations in space-time. Have you found out the status of the others in your universe?"

He shook his head. "We, uh, got cut off or something."

Dr. Martha nodded as if she had suspected as much. "Do you have a moment while you are waiting? We all need to meet up in here for a sec." She turned and walked from the door as if it hadn't occurred to her that he would do anything else.

Chintz stared around the laboratory, at a loss as to how to proceed. He wanted to talk to Katie. Had she forgiven him? *It's time, Chintz.* Maybe she had forgiven him.

But he had decided to stay here.

But maybe she had forgiven him.

But he had to help the people here. He relaxed his neck and followed the Doctor. She was already further down the hall than he would have expected, so he pranced behind her, leaving his arms resting at his sides so they would be energized if he ended up needing them. Instead of turning into the room with the computer where they had all been before, Dr. Martha went across the hall and opened the door, holding it aside so he could enter.

Slowing his prance to a slomp (an uncommon style of walking that Chintz had adopted at a young age, when the situation called for it) he went through the door to see that everyone else was already present and in their own heated conversations. At a small table in the corner, the two Neldas sat across from one another, nose to nose in intense discussion. They looked like someone talking to a mirror, except one side had on different clothes and very different hair. Galoof was in another corner, his nose pressed in between the walls as if he were in time out. One ear held a cell phone pressed to it while the other was plugged by his finger. Beside him, near the doorway, Quincy and Caroline seemed to be having one of the most straight faced couples' spats of all time.

As Chintz stopped slomping and stood like a statue in the middle of the room, the three conversations came to a halt at once. Due to an anomaly in his normal concentration skills, Chintz was able to catch the ending of all three, though who said what remained a mystery.

Chintz heard the following within a few seconds of walking into the room:

"You can't give me two hours?"

"Where the hell are we gonna find one of those?"

"I'm a sumo wrestler."

"Fine. Tell General dumb-ass we can let him in in an hour and a half."

"Well, stop assuming, hon. We've done our part. And it's time."

"Shit. Maybe Dr. Morley will know. I don't know who else would."

"Dudes needy. I can't aband a dude. Esta!"

All conversations stopped as the group turned in unison towards Chintz. His resurgence of awkwardness was saved a second later by Galoof, who shoved the phone back in his pocket and headed towards the door.

"The most I could get us is an hour," he snapped at the Doctor. "I'm going to get the energy levels to where they need to be when this goes down. Hopefully, your friends won't be dead by then, as that is a hell of a long time at your place. Doc, I'll help you finish the analysis of that room when I'm done. We could have you all out of here in a few minutes, but talk to Nelda. They figured out something else they needed before the Grafter will work."

As Galoof left the room, the remaining group turned in unison towards the Neldas. "What do you need?" Dr. Martha asked. "Is there a problem?" Chintz noticed a tinge of intense and rather confident panic in her voice.

Nelda #1 rose to her feet.

"Here's the deal," she said. "We can't use this." She held the Grafter up and looked terrified. After a second of cowering in thought she slapped herself on the head. "I forgot a fundamental difference between our universes! The atoms won't...wait!" She sat down, looked terrified again, and leapt to her feet. "To the laboratory!" she screamed, and sprinted from the room, Chintz guessed, towards the laboratory that had been Grafted here just before they arrived.

Chintz watched the others sprint after her in single file and pranced behind everyone to catch up. When he arrived at the laboratory a few seconds later, everyone was staring at Nelda's skinny backside, which was in the air while the rest of her rummaged through a few drawers in the corner.

"Dammit!" came the familiar cry. "It's not here." She stood erect and looked at the others, dejected. "And even if it was, we can't power it and then open a portal a few minutes later."

Everyone breathed. "Look, Big N," said Quincy soothingly, causing Chintz some racial discomfort. "Why don't you just problem what the tell us is."

Nelda looked at him sadly. "The atoms in the Grafter core have to be all turned the same direction in order for it to work. Trust me, you would have figured this out like we did soon enough. We don't have to do that in our little universe but we do in this one. But now I don't have the equipment to do it. Or the power. We have an hour and we can't build something for that AND prepare the energy AND analyze the data for our universe AND Graft a portal to it in that time."

"Wait," Galoof said. "You just need to turn all the atoms the same direction? That's what an electromagnetic engine does. Can't we just use a coil and do the same thing?"

Nelda looked optimistically like a drowning person who maybe feels a hand while they are going under. "Yes!" She squinted. "No! It works the same way, but it would have to be over, like, twenty-eight inches to work."

The Doctor shook her head in frustration. "We have to find one. There's no choice. Let me make a call to some friends at the university. It will wake them up and it's an hour drive, but maybe I can convince them to…"

"I have one. The house."

They all turned towards Quincy in astonishment, both because he was offering a potential solution and because his sentence had been immediately decipherable. *Oh look,* thought Chintz. *Mr. Gibberish is going to save the day. Why don't you just shut up?* He felt alarmed at his own hostility.

"You have one," said Dr. Martha to Quincy. "A thirty-inch electromagnetic coil. At your house."

"Yes. I amp builds and cabs all the time. I've banded in this been many years and they count on me for fixings. Speaks is electo magic and bass players need the biggest speaks. That's me. I can regurgitate the hizzy and bring it."

Caroline tugged his arm while Galoof stared at Quincy as if he looked like he tasted bad. "Hon. We have to…"

"Peeps need us. That will work?"

Martha nodded. "I bet it will. We'll need a little extra power to run that, but we already need a lot of extra so it won't make much difference. Can you hurry, Quincy?"

He nodded. "I need Chintzy. Can he come?"

Chintz felt his neck flex in preparation for more head shaking. His eyebrows raised to make his forehead crinkly. *No. No no. I need to stay and talk to Katie.* "Me?"

Caroline scowled at her husband. "Why Chintz? Am I supposed to just stay here?"

Immediately, Quincy turned and hugged his wife while the others watched. He whispered in her ear, and her face softened visibly with each word. Finally, he kissed her roughly on the head. She smiled.

"Chintz is my man," Quincy said. "Ready to go, my buddy?"

"But," Chintz said. "Katie is supposed to..."

"Please," Dr. Martha said. "It may go quicker with both of you. That thing will be heavy. I promise to take a message if she comes back." Her voice took on an authoritative note that seemed to fit her so well. "Go."

Quincy draped an arm around Chintz's shoulders and they began walking towards the exit. Chintz looked longingly into the Grafted laboratory as they passed it. It was silent as a tomb.

Chintz stared out the window from the passenger seat and tried to keep his eyebrows under control. The streetlights rushed by, each illuminating a tiny piece of the sidewalk and little else. A light drizzle had begun to fall, which gave everything a sheen in the headlights. Quincy drove calmly at well above the posted speed limit as if he were doing something of grim importance, but something that was nothing to stress out over. For reasons that were not clear, Chintz noticed that any discomfort he felt in the presence of certain individuals was magnified when left alone with that person. Especially in a car.

When he had met Quincy years ago, Chintz had at first taken him to be one of those people who use an exorbitant amount of slang and trendy words in a desperate and pathetic attempt to find an identity and to impress others. As it turned out, Quincy appeared not to care at all whether anyone understood him or thought he was hip and trendy. His nonsense was pronounced with proper non-regional annunciation. This disconcerted Chintz and robbed him of his only defense mechanism of being the weirdest one in the room.

Now he found himself stuck in a car with one of his least favorite people. A person who had suddenly decided to be friends with him. Chintz was stressed and upset and worried and in no mood to put up with it.

He snuck a glance at Quincy, who noticed and nodded.

"We muse some needic. QLP, B. You'll like this. Check it," Quincy said, and popped in a cassette that had been hanging half out of the tape deck. A fast song with guitars started up.

Absently beginning some consolatory jamming, Chintz watched the dark road ahead and wondered what the Doctor and Sam were doing. He and Nelda must have been gone for days now. Weeks, maybe. Those two may have killed each other. He wondered how long it had been for them since Katie had left her conversation to meet them in their "visit" as she had said. He hoped they had food. He hoped they remembered to feed Platelet. He wondered what Katie had been about to say in the laboratory before he was made to leave. He thought she loved him. He knew she did. He thought she was crazy, though. He knew she was.

A man began yelling on the song. Chintz prepared himself for some smooth motherfuckin' rhymes, as the man requested that he do.

"Look," Quincy said and turned the radio down. Still driving uncomfortably fast, he turned and looked at Chintz, who found that he couldn't bring himself to stop jamming.

"Look," Quincy repeated, still not watching the road. "I know you're weirding right now. You weird a lot anyway, and this emerge is tripping us. But I thin mint you can handle it. You're a duder cool than you give yourself cred for. You know?"

Chintz absolutely did not know and was astounded at the compliment. "Thanks," he said. "Yeah, it's weird but I'll make it. Sorry if I'm bringing you, um, you know, down."

Quincy shook his mowhawked head and briefly checked that they were not about to kill themselves or someone else by crashing into them. "Don't warrior about me. I'm gifted. I take care of my people."

He stared at Chintz (and not even a tiny bit at the road) for a moment longer until Chintz bore equal discomfort at being the target of the staring, and of the road not being. Finally looking where he was going, Quincy turned the fast guitars and smooth motherfuckin' rhymes back on as if the matter was settled.

Hmmm, thought Chintz. *That was a nice thing to say.* Maybe Quincy was a better guy than he had previously thought. He tried to remember other interactions they had had over the past few years but found that he was uncertain as to what Quincy had been talking about during all of them. With a surge of panic, he questioned himself and thought that maybe he had misunderstood the conversation they just had. Had that been a compliment? His lips began to itch. Maybe he was just calling Chintz weird? Chintz mentally shook his head and willed the lip itch away. No. Enough had been clear to tell. Plus, Quincy was here helping them now, wasn't he? And he had invited Chintz along.

Chintz jammed a little again as they entered their sleeping neighborhood. Maybe he was becoming a little better at this people thing. He thought of Dr. Morley holding his hand like a woman and listening to him. He thought of Nelda, and how she seemed to just get him and like him for some reason. He thought of a song in the mountains and felt a phantom grip on his hand. He squeezed it as if refusing to let it go.

"Marmy."

Looking left to where they were turning onto his street, Chintz saw that more of the neighborhood was covered with an assortment of official looking vehicles with lights that pierced the night. In addition to military and local law enforcement, there was now some other vehicles that seemed to be designed to look as if they weren't supposed to be noticed. As they came within view of his house, he saw in the darkness that two or three people in some sort of unidentified protective gear were studying the outside of his home with unidentified hand-held instruments.

Dammit, he thought. *We are running out of time.*

The urgency of their mission welled within him like religious fervor at a revival. *These people will take Tonk. They will lock Sam and Mitch away and they will not understand the things they find in that tiny and slowly growing universe. It's like E.T. Or War Games.* Chintz shook his head. *Man, people ruin everything in stories. And in real life.*

How could I have ever thought I would stay here? And the realization fell upon him that he would not stay here. Forgiven or not, he had to return to her. With the relief that resolved decisions often bring, he smiled to himself. Now he knew what to do.

The smile faded. *If Katie doesn't forgive me, how can I stay there?*

He felt himself getting worked up and again took it out on Quincy. "We have to hurry!" He whispered harshly.

"Hang," Quincy said, looking ahead. It seemed that because Quincy's house was so close to Chintz's, they had to go past the barrier to get to it. Orange and white stands spanned the small neighborhood road in front of them, causing the reflection from their headlights to bounce back at them aggressively. As Quincy decelerated to an almost safe speed, an officer raised his hand to signal then to stop. Quincy did so and rolled down the window.

Chintz and Quincy looked at the officer as he bent down to look in the car. For a brief moment, Chintz put himself in the officer's shoes and saw a very nervous white man accompanying an expressionless black man with a mohawk.

Great.

Luckily the actual officer didn't seem as suspicious as Chintz's projection.

"Name please."

"Quincy Higginbotham. That's my house." Quincy somehow sounded as if he were the boss and was kindly dismissing a subordinate from having to work on a Saturday. Chintz was quite envious of his poise and allowed his mind to wonder how a man like this got a name like that and also how he's lived next door to them for years without knowing their last name. *Dammit,* he thought. *I don't know any of my neighbor's last names.*

"Name?" The officer had leaned down to look at Chintz, quaking with terror in the passenger seat.

This is it, Chintz thought, as he stared silently at the officer as if staring into the gaping maw of death. *Of course they are looking for me. That's my house. It is listed as my house by the state and probably several real estate services. The address is on my driver's license. I, being a complete idiot, got so caught up in what we are doing that I forgot this and did not come up with a story for this stupid errand we are running that probably won't work anyway. So I'm about to stutter and say my name and the cop will ask me to step out of the car and they will question me and even if they believe I have nothing to do with it and I can never go back. I want to go back. I decided to go back!*

Did I *decide that?*

"Carlos Rodriguez," he heard Quincy say.

Chintz froze. The cop looked at them. "He can't answer for himself?"

Quincy nodded at the officer as if reassuring him.

"It's okay," Chintz said. "He's my wife's cousin. Runs in the family. Answering for me, I mean." He smiled weakly.

Quincy didn't smile in any fashion whatsoever. "We'll be outy in a jiff, sir. Just acquiring provisions."

The officer stood up and looked at them for a second. "Okay. I'll be ready to let you back out then. Thanks, Mr. Higginbotham. And it's probably best you are leaving again. Your neighbor has some weird stuff going on over there."

Quincy nodded as if he were not at all curious. “Spanks,” he said, pulling away. Thirty seconds later they were parked in the driveway.

They both sat in the car for a few heartbeats as if they couldn’t believe they had made it.

Quincy’s straight face turned to Chintz as if to say, no, it actually had not the slightest problem believing it. “It’s in the Gary-age.”

In unison, the two men unbuckled their seat belts, exited the car, shut the doors, and walked up to the garage door of Quincy and Caroline’s home. From the next street over, Chintz heard a police radio chattering. Otherwise, the neighborhood looked dark and asleep. The drizzle had faded to an occasional sprinkle. The night had appropriated a slight chill since they had last been out. Quincy rubbed his hands together.

“Forgot my stupid-ass jacket,[12]” he said. They reached down to open the door together. It rose about an inch and stopped.

Locked,” Quincy nodded. “Sec just. I’ll go a house through the round. A spear.”

Chintz nodded back. “Okay.”

He heard Quincy enter the house. The radio chatter had stopped and the night seemed capriciously calm. He heard the door that lead from the house to the garage open, followed by a clatter, the word “dicks!” and then, louder, “Almost there, Chintzy.”

Chintz stood outside the door of the garage and tried to

12 Not to be confused with a stupid ass-jacket, which is a grand improvement.

remain still. He was about to try to open the door himself when he heard a voice behind him.

"Come to check on the action?"

Chintz froze in mid-crouch. The voice was old. It could have been described as "crotchety." It was nosey and it was triumphant. While it was all of these things, it was also definitely annoying.

It was his neighbor, Carter, whom he hated.

Unfreezing as quickly as he had frozen, Chintz snapped to attention and turned to face the owner of the voice. Carter stood tall and cheeky in front of him. Yes, his big Irish cheeks literally led the way into the conversation as he smiled at Chintz. Carter had the kind of smile that crowded his face and made him seem fatter than he really was. The particular smile he brandished at Chintz at this particular moment seemed to, ironically, expect Chintz to smile back. Chintz didn't.

"Hello, Carter."

"Where you been all night?" The smile quickly changed to a suspicious scowl, as if using a bait-and-switch to draw in its prey.

"Work."

"Saw you come home from work. Heard it, really, because of your damn 'Baloooo!' shit you pull when you know it's my nap time."

"Sorry," Chintz stared and then sniffed. "I don't actually know when your nap—"

As if a trap had sprung, the garage door snapped open, revealing the silhouette of Quincy as provided by the 100 watt light bulb that hung from the ceiling a few feet behind him.

Carter transferred his suspicious scowl from Chintz to the Quincy-shaped shadow seamlessly, as if he had had plenty of practice doing so. One eyebrow rose to show that it was ready for anything and intended not to be left out.

"Hey, Carter," Quincy said, and moved out of the garage to stand with the other two men. "What are you doing u at this time of n?"

Chintz thought for a moment that Quincy had accused Carter of something racist, and then realized he had just been hanging around Nelda a lot for the last couple of days.

"I guess I could ask you fellas the same thing." The scowl became milder as the man moved to stand next to Chintz in what he apparently thought was a friendly stance, but was in fact just creepy. "So what's going on at your house, Chintz? The officers wouldn't tell me."

"I'm sure you asked them," Chintz said, his sharpness surprising even himself.

"I have a right to know!" Carter said, the scowl becoming harsh again. "Cops combing over every inch of your house, even military vehicles! And I think some of those are CIA..." he added thoughtfully, raising the opposite eyebrow from that which he had been raising and looking knowingly in the direction of Chintz's house, which none of them could see from this angle even if it hadn't been the middle of the night. "I should know. I was in the Army for eight years!" At this, Carter raised both eyebrows and looked at the other two as if daring them to suggest he had perhaps been in the Army for a lesser number of years.

Quincy put a hand on Carter's shoulder. "Thank you," he whispered. "Look, Chintzy and I are surcharge for an electomelon. It's import, so I need you to be c. K?"

"No, I don' think I will be 'c', buddy." Carter made a little fake laugh without smiling, a stunt performed by much of the human population when trying to take a stand but not feeling very confident, like maybe when someone has cut in front of them in line but the perpetrator of the laugh doesn't want to be the one to cause a scene at the post office. "The cops have been looking for Chintz for the last few hours. This old brain gathered *that* much. And what do you need a whatever you said for at one in the morning or whatever it is?"

Quincy gestured with his mohawked head behind him at the garage. "Just a big speak. For an experimentation. Look, you can help us eff it." He put one hand behind Carter to escort him towards the blinding light in the garage.

"Help you *what?*" Carter resisted the escort.

"Please," Chintz said, picking up the vibe from Quincy. If Carter wanted to be a busy body, it might be better to put his energy to good use. "Help us find it. It's a big speaker and we need it. That way you know nothing weird is going on."

Carter's eyes narrowed as the other two began searching through the rather large garage. His nosey-ness seemed to win out over his wish to tattle, and he began rummaging suspiciously through a stack of junk near the garage door. *Please,* thought Chintz. *Just help us and don't run off and tell anyone. Good lord, this is a big garage. Lots of piles of stuff. Is my garage this big? I don't think so.* For some reason his garage hadn't Grafted to the universe with the rest of his home, so he wouldn't have a chance to compare when he got back. *If* he got back.

He had to get back.

After a couple of minutes of searching, Quincy called over his shoulder from one corner of the garage. "Fecundity!"

Looking over, Chintz saw that the large man had excavated about half of an enormous and very heavy looking speaker. It was unattached to any cabinet or casing and had no wires. "Help me get it in the trigger," he said.

Chintz and Carter waded through the clutter to get to where Quincy was, and all three struggled with the heavy object until it was rolled uncovered away from the wall. Chintz pranced about the garage, kicking or scooting things out of the way to clear a path to the car. He felt quite relieved that they had found it so quickly and that Carter seemed to have relaxed enough to be actually helping them. He glanced over at Carter, who had aimed one eye at the speaker in a way that would have had Edgar Allen Poe a little creeped out.

Chintz hoped the others would be ready to use this to get back to Sam and Mitch right away before General What's-His-Name arrived to screw everything up. He just wanted to get back. Chintz smiled to himself. They would all be together in Chorus' universe again. They would have a way to get food and never have to leave. He didn't even have to give Nelda that postcard from Sam. He felt in his pocket for it to see if it was still there. It was.

Chintz pondered as they grunted and hefted to get the speaker where they could roll it out. *I wonder what the card says,* he thought. *Hopefully, we will get back soon and I won't have to give it to her.* He flexed his shaky thighs. They set the gigantic electromagnetic coil down on the ground.

"Here, give me the keys," Carter said to Quincy. "I'll get the trunk open and help you get this hunk of junk in there."

Quincy nodded and threw the keys at him. "Alright. Chintzy. Give me an arm, will you?"

Absently, Chintz pranced back over to Quincy and began to help him roll the speaker towards the door. Seriously, what would it say? I have the hots for you, Nelda, love Sam? He was pretty sure she already knew that. His eyes darted about dramatically. He heard the trunk open on the car.

"Carefree," Quincy said. "Don't trip over the debris. This G needs to be cleansed."

Chintz tiptoed around the assortment of items as they rolled the speaker out of the uncleansed G. The light from the hanging bulb lit the area around the car well enough that they were able to carefully roll the giant speaker around the car to the open trunk. Working together, they struggled to get the huge speaker into the trunk. After twisting it a little to make it fit next to the spare tire, Quincy closed the trunk and dusted his hands off. They both turned around and looked into the night.

"Donde esta el Carter?" demanded Quincy.

"Um."

The two of them looked around. Carter was nowhere to be found. Neither were the car keys.

CHAPTER TWENTY-SEVEN

PLATELET STRAINED ONCE more to squeeze out of the dark pipe that she had popped into not thirty seconds before from inside the machine. A week ago, she would have been too fat to move an inch. Now, slender from lack of food, she was able to move about that much. Her panic at this confined space had long since subsided. Her ears no longer noticed the gentle whirring of this machine that seemed to go on forever. The heavier vibration that had stopped when she ran into the pipe all those days ago had not started up again.

She had no idea that she had a liver, or that cats have liver failure if they don't eat for a few days. Therefore, she felt no gratitude for the crumbs and scraps that the orange smoke brought her a few times every day. Luckily, the vast machine (which was her home for the past few days) had contained plenty of water, and she had drunk deeply each time she had found some over the past several days. The water had tasted bad, but she drank it anyway.

With one last surge of energy, Platelet popped her thin body from the pipe, finally exiting the machine. Her fur was quite dusty, and she extended one dainty leg towards the ceiling to clean it. The vibration which she had felt before started up behind her immediately.

When her bathing was finished, she turned to the hall into which she had just emerged. Things looked odd to her now that she had been away for a while. At first, she thought this large room was the same one with the giant light in it where the others sometimes gathered. But there was no large light in this huge room.

Creeping along carefully, she saw that there was some sort of hole in the floor up ahead. A pretty big hole. Stalking the hole as if it might attempt to escape, she flattened her ears and ran to the edge of the gap. She flopped playfully on her side, wishing she had some yarn or a toy mouse to murder.

She looked into the hole. There was water in it. Platelet squinted at it and then opened her eyes wide. And fish. Lots and lots of little fish.

"Fuswah."

The cat put her ears far back on her head without turning. If she had had the slightest bit of vocabulary, she would have mined it at this time for some curse words.

The water bubbled and sloshed. Some of it splashed out of the circular hole and landed near the cat. One of the small fish flopped near her, so she widened her eyes further and batted it back into the water, sniffing the floor where it had been. The fish showed its gratitude at this rescue by swimming away quickly.

"Fuswah," came the voice again. Platelet turned to see the damn baby pointing at her. Orange smoke was coming from its hand. The room swirled in her vision and disappeared.

Around the giant room, the walls tremored and then stopped. A large rock appeared in one corner and then disappeared. A crack crawled its way silently across the ceiling and rested there. The water sloshed some more fish onto the floor, but now no one was there to save them.

The two men stood helplessly with their mismatched arsenal of attributes and stared off into the neighborhood.

"I don't supposed you have a spare key?" Chintz asked.

Quincy looked at the ground. "Caroline has them."

Chintz nodded and looked into the darkness. *Let me think about this,* he thought.

He had not, he repeated, *not* come this far to have Carter's dumb ass ruin everything. His friends were starving, and he needed to go home, back to the Unpromised Land where he had discovered he belonged. His jaw bespoke his resolve.

But he had no idea what he resolved to do.

"What do we do?" asked Quincy.

Chintz shook his head. He felt powerless. He would be too late, just like he was too late when the colony— he shut his eyes tight in frustration. *That never happened. That never happened. But this is happening.*

He felt both shoulders clasped in a tight grip as Quincy turned him so that they were facing each other. "What do we do?" the man repeated. "Give up?"

Chintz looked at Quincy. The mohawked man looked down at him with eyes that lit a fire in him. They were like the Doctor's eyes, less intense but deeper.

"Don't be Chintz," Quincy said.

"What?"

"Don't be Chintz right now. Be Carlos."

For a second Chintz thought that Quincy's habit of using odd words in odd places had finally driven him off insanity's cruel cliff until he remembered that this was the name they had told the officer. Carlos Rodriguez. The man who did things that Chintz couldn't do.

Narrowing his eyes like he had seen Carter do, but hopefully a little less ass-ishly, Chintz sucked his neck in and forced himself to swell with determination. He was Carlos and he would find Carter and the keys.

Swinging his arms ridiculously with his determined swell, he strode back towards the flashing police lights that reflected off his house a block over. Carter would be going to tell on him. A trickle of panic leaked through his determination, and he pepped his ridiculous stride up to double the speed. *Carlos Rodriguez will handle this. Yes, he will.*

Carter would have known where all the cops were anyway, the nosy bastard. Carter would take the keys and run to the nearest one right away and tattle on them and ruin everything. Carter would—

The nearest one was the one they had talked to, Carlos Rodriguez realized. Without slowing, he began a sharp turn, his elbows pumping up and down in an attempt to sustain the earlier determined swell. *Fine. No problem. No problem at all.* Chintz...er, he corrected, "Carlos" had already spoken to that officer and knew precisely where he was. He had already introduced himself. Or Quincy had anyway. Maybe it would take Carter a second to locate the officer to which he wished to tattle.

Just in case, Chintz began a determined and frantic sprint in the direction the man had been. He rounded the corner of a house and nearly ran into the back of Carter.

Carter reacted immediately as if the survival of humanity depended upon him thwarting this attack. "No! Here, crap! You can just!" he yelled breathlessly, and lowered his body, bracing both legs, and threw his hairy fist up in a move which was designed to dispatch Chintz and neutralize his stealthy irruption. While this would have looked impressive in front of a class of young children who had hopes of learning self-defense, the reality was less effective.

Seeing the hairy fist clenching and snapping back as if it were in slow motion, Chintz flexed his eyebrows in an attempt to block the blow. While some part of his brain knew that there must be something he could do that was better than this impotent and silly defense, the part that controlled his arms (the optimal bodily tools for blocking other arms) seemed to want to hurl them at the ground since he was about to topple from the initial collision. His ground-ward motion helped him, though, because Carter's hairy fist only grazed Chintz's temple, making him go wild-eyed with social anxiety.

Carter turned like a bull to a matador and lifted a stiff leg to kick Chintz in his mid-section, holding the hallowed car keys in his hands aloft as he did so. This blow was even less effective than the first. Chintz's large eyes drank in the scene as if the slow motion had slowed even more and was a single frame frozen from a disturbing memory. He watched his left leg lift involuntarily and stop Carter's leg, which may or may not have been hairy, though Chintz still, also involuntarily, paused to wonder if it was. *Free will, indeed.*

The two men found their left and right legs, respectively, entangled. Carter tried to pull his leg back to its home position, while cocking one fist back to punch Chintz in the jaw and knock him the hell out. Chintz pulled his leg in further, which kept both of the men's respective legs from touching the ground and regaining their balance. In a pre-emptive strike to keep from getting knocked the hell out, Chintz threw an open palm at Carter's cheek and got a little spit on it.

All four arms now waved frantically to keep from falling down. After a full five seconds of grunts, both men tumbled to the ground lying next to each other.

"Hey! Hey! What's going on here?" a voice boomed from above them.

Please be Quincy. You don't sound like Quincy, but I need you to be. Chintz turned his eyes (still quite wild) up towards the voice. It was the officer from earlier, hovering above like a raincloud to drench Chintz's life-plans into the dirt.

"Mr. Rodriguez," the officer said. "Get to your feet and stand over there right now." He pointed to a spot on the ground that was out of scuffling distance from Carter. "You, sir, stay right there on the ground. Now what the hell is going on here?"

Chintz slomped over to the spot that the officer had

indicated. Carter looked at the cop with gleeful mania, his face shining with the certainty of his victory.

"That house!" he said triumphantly. "Him! Illegal secrets! We—"

"Excuse me, sirs," came yet another voice from behind them.

That one, Chintz thought, *is Quincy.*

The three men turned around to see Quincy's tall and mohawked form standing intimidatingly behind them, like a shining black, raincloud-banishing sun. The officer took a step back at this new character in the evening's performance. "Step back! Stay over there."

"Of course," Quincy said, leveling his serious gaze at him. "We have a danger over here. It needs to be invested right away."

The cop held a hand out as if he wished to utilize powers of telekenesis to keep everyone where they were. "Okay," he said. "I'll radio for..."

"Sir!" came Quincy's voice. His eyes took on a panicked and fearful look. "It's my daughter! I think...one of those things got her! Quickly!"

A terror crept over Chintz, and he hoped that Quincy was being creative and saving them and was a really good actor.

"This is that house!" Carter said, his eyes widening at the possibility of his meddling about to go awry. Lucky for Chintz, his stupid mouth still wouldn't work. "I mean- The ruse! This man's house is vacant! He ain't in it! You should!" Quincy glanced at Carter with begrudging respect. The cop, however, ignored him.

"Things?" the cop looked like a little terror had crept over him as well.

"Please," said Quincy. "Come with me. I need your help, P."

The officer looked grim in a moment of decision. *Is he making a decision,* thought Chintz? *Or are there environmental variables which...*

"You two!" yelled the cop, interrupting his philosophical reverie. "Sit right here on the ground until I get back!"

Carter looked like he was drowning. "But—"

"Stay!"

Quincy led the cop back around the corner as the two men jogged away.

Carter looked at Chintz, seething from his seated position. "You son-of-a-bitch. I don't know what you're up to, but I'm going to make sure you don't get away with it. You understand?"

When Quincy and the officer had disappeared down the street, Chintz and Carter locked eyes, all four of them as wild as zebras on the dusty veldt. Carter calmed one eye and aimed the other, still un-calm one at Chintz.

"When he gets back, you're going to jail. Then we will see what you've been doing in that house of yours."

Chintz stared at Carter. *This man is what's standing in the way of getting back. Without him, we can get back to the lab and then get home.* A few blocks from where he had lived for ten years, Chintz felt homesick for the compound he had lived in for three days.

Rising slowly to his feet, he squinted his eyes and tried to keep his voice from shaking. *Carlos Rodriguez.*

"Give me back the keys," he said, rather like a little pansy, in his opinion.

Carter grinned his fat faced grin as if this were a pretty good joke and, also, as if he were a complete asshole. "Ha! You'd like that, wouldn't you, chump?" Carter's voice shook, too, but in a rather more hysterical style. This was clearly a man who had lost control.

Chintz had known Carter for years and had always hated him. Still, this was the first time the conflict had ever escalated beyond petty arguments. He gritted his teeth.

"Give me the keys back now," he said a little louder and a little less shaky.

Instead of complying, Carter leapt to his feet and held up the keys teasingly. "These...you want? Get them, ya crap!" And with this emotional cryptography, he hurled the keys back over Chintz's head, towards the close-together neighborhood house where they would never, never be found.

"No!" Chintz yelled. Carlos Rodriguez nearly cried in desperation.

The keys sailed in a high arc through the night but didn't even clear the first house. With a loud, invisible clank, they landed somewhere on the house's gutter.

The two men's feral eyes locked once again for a brief second before each turned to run towards the house. Chintz was faster than the older man.

"Stop! You...criminal!" he heard Carter wheeze behind him. "Police! The...get them!"

No police appeared, and Chintz ran to the side of the house

where he thought the keys had landed. The wooden fence that held the back yard was right next to it, and he leaned on it as he strained to look up. He couldn't see them.

With the wheezing and grumbling rapidly approaching from behind, Chintz put both hands on the fence and with a great strain he flopped one leg up on top of it and grunted his way up. With more exertion than he had used in years, he whisked his body onto the fence and nearly fell off the other side. He spastically straightened both legs, which had transformed into macaroni, against the pointy posts and made a wild leap for the gutters, grabbing them.

His tip toes still reached the fence, so Chintz was able to smack his hands in a few places in the damp gutter in hopes of finding the keys. He didn't. He spanked the gutter soundly in a few more times, causing the sound to ring out into the night over the poor little disturbed neighborhood. *Dammit.*

Already quite fatigued from his climb, he pulled his torso up in a futile attempt to climb the rest of the way onto the house. He flopped one macaroni over to hook onto the gutter and nearly fell off again. It was at this moment that it occurred to him to wonder what Carter was doing during all of this. He looked down.

The annoying bastard was standing under him huffing and puffing as if he'd recently spent a few minutes under water. Carter pointed at him menacingly. "Get down!"

Chintz regarded him from his precarious position, the one leg still dangling into space. "No," he said. "I need the keys."

Feeling maniacally determined, Carter shook his head. The

man turned and strode towards the front of the house. *Probably going to tell the owners of this house. Let him. I'll be gone by the time they get out here.* Chintz started to flop his other floppy leg onto the gutter. He glanced down at Carter again.

Carter was, in fact, not going to notify the owners. He was just getting onto the first rung of the long ladder that was leaning against the corner of the house and rose all the way up above the gutters.

You, thought Chintz, *have got to be kidding me.*

With renewed effort, he swiveled his leg so hard he nearly dislocated his hip. The foot landed on the gutter next to his other foot and stayed put. Now his hands and feet were hooked on the apparently very sturdily manufactured gutters while the rest of his body hung below like a strand of Christmas garland. Chintz flopped one hand up on the roof where there was of course nothing to grab onto, but was at least rough enough to prevent slipping. Grunting and straining in the night, he moved one foot past the gutters and onto the roof and used his momentum to roll his whole body up.

After allowing himself approximately a second and a half to lie on his stomach and breathe, Chintz rose carefully up onto his hands and feet just in time to see Carter, his silhouette rising above the roof of the house like a second rain cloud that you hadn't seen coming. The old man flopped off the ladder and began to stand. Chintz sprang to his feet, lost his balance, and fell down on his stomach again, sliding a few inches on the sloped roof. In unison, both men laid eyes on the keys laying there in the gutter. Chintz rose more carefully to his feet, but Carter was nearer. Grabbing the keys out of the gutter, the old annoying man turned spryly around in victory and headed back towards the ladder.

Shit, thought Chintz. He lifted his hands up and pranced towards the ladder in his alert crouch, which enjoyed perhaps its first useful moment in Chintz's entire life. He reached the ladder just as Carter started down the first few rungs with a triumphant guffaw. Without thinking, Chintz grabbed the top of the ladder and held it out from the house. It was heavy, but he held on.

"Stop. Or I'll throw you down."

Carter froze and looked up with his crazy fat face. He clutched the ladder with both hands. "No. You wouldn't!"

The men remained like statues in the night. Chintz's mind raced as he held the ladder and looked down at Carter, the keys looped over one stupid thumb. *I could easily push this ladder,* he thought. *And problem solved. We are ten or twelve feet in the air. The entire length of the ladder would fall, with Carter at the top of it, down to the yard. It wouldn't kill him. Probably. But I could hop down on the fence there and get the keys and he would be in no shape to chase me down. I can get Quincy and we can take that stupid huge speaker back and go home.* His brain scrambled. Bits and pieces of conversations with Dr. Morley floated through as the seconds ticked by. He may not be able to make decisions, anyway. Maybe he should just see what happens.

What happened was he pushed the ladder out further, putting himself in danger of falling himself. Now he just had to let go and watch the fall. Carter whined and panted and tried to hold on. He tried to start down the ladder.

Nothing is more important than forgiveness. Chintz looked down at Carter.

I am already the one who needs forgiveness, he thought. Here, in his own universe, he made a decision. For the second time in a day, he felt his grip fail him.

CHAPTER TWENTY-EIGHT

INFORMATION FLOODED INTO her senses and it gave her comfort. Light, air pressure, heat, and radioactivity summed themselves in ways she was unable to explain and told her of the state of this universe. She had been asleep for too long.

Her madness had pushed her too far. In becoming more human, she had inherited the human madness. But hers had no limit. No DNA made a recipe for her offspring. She was her own offspring. No environmental pressures held sway on her insanity. She had learned to love and now she couldn't stop.

Her expansive consciousness focused on the vast white room with the large chandelier. She looked down (and from all other directions) on Sam and Mitch lying side by side in the center, ten or so feet between them.

Both men had forgone their regular formal attire. Dr. Morley wore thick wool pajamas with slippers. Sam was wrapped in a striped robe. They stared up at the huge chandelier and at the crack in the ceiling above it. They were no more aware than usual of her presence, or more particularly of the presence of her consciousness.

It had been eight days since they had last eaten. Water was still in short supply, but was enough to keep them alive.

At least now they had her to watch over them. For the last several days, she had provided updates on the others, though the updates were always that she still had heard nothing. They did have the peace of mind to know that Chintz and Nelda were possibly making headway and would hopefully be there soon.

She watched as each of the two men continued staring at the fixture. When they spoke, they spoke to it as if it were the one being addressed. They hadn't spoken in nearly an hour.

Another tremor rolled through the complex. Sam's head throbbed, but neither man showed any other sign of noticing. The tremors were becoming more frequent now. Chorus looked down at Sam. She knew of whom he was thinking. After all she has learned, she was able to empathize with him all too well.

She hadn't allowed herself time to dwell. With access to the other universe through the Grafted laboratory, she periodically returned to check on the others' progress. But Chintz had not returned. They would hopefully all return soon. Hopefully. She hoped to see Chintz again soon, to drink him in. He had told her that he wanted to stay, to stay in that other place, but of course she was able to convince him. He wouldn't stay. He would come back here. He could let her infiltrate his mind again and they could stay together on a mountain or somewhere else and she would be-with-him-always-he-must-never-leave-her-she-would-die-just-die-die-die-she-could-make-him-so-happy-and-she-could....

She metaphorically shook her large mind. Stop it. He would return. And she must keep control.

Through the years, as she had learned, she had grown accustomed to being able to perpetually monitor the universe. In the other universe, where Chintz was now, she could monitor nothing outside of the laboratory.

She had learned to cling to things, just as she has seen the others do. Now things she clung to were in a terrifying and chaotic abyss that was called "not knowing." Chorus had never dealt with strangeness.

For years she had been the caretaker and custodian. She nudged and coerced the matter that ended up here into as safe and happy an environment as possible. But she had been absent for weeks.

Much of the compound had grown and changed, and she didn't even know some of the things that had happened when she was...away. She could have reversed it, she thought, if not for the strange machine that had popped up in the far corner of the young universe. It had introduced strange things, radioactivity and heat and other energies that she didn't know.

The exhausted and guilt-ridden men had done their best to update her, and she had done what she could to stabilize the growth she had missed. Neither of the men had asked where Tonk and the cat had gone. Which was just as well, since she couldn't find them. This scared her.

The tremors scared her more.

Chorus had died once. Let go by the man who was her world in a fictional scenario authored by her; a scenario meant to progress knowledge, but which had unintended consequences. The grief and betrayal had crushed her, and she had nearly not recovered. But here she was.

She had forgiven him.

She drank in the two men lying despondent on the floor. If they died, there was no recovery. She could still save them. They could save them. Chintz would come back and they would all be fine.

But if her suspicions proved true, she couldn't save herself.

Chorus was not simply a piece of software that could be uploaded away from here on a network. Her architecture was tied to the growth of this universe. She was here to stay.

She drank in the two men again. She was learning so much. Cling now, while you can, she told herself. And learn to let go.

Nelda held her breath and ran the test again. Same thing. It worked. She looked at her parallel self, who was grinning toothily in excitement and clapped her pretty hands.

"That's it on our end! As soon as the boys get back with the coil, we can get everything done and set up in no time."

Our Nelda nodded. "Yeah."

Nelda #2 cocked her slightly more attractive head at her. "You okay?"

#1 shrugged. "I'm okay. Hey, I have a question."

"'Sup?"

"So, if I were to ever visit here. Again. If I were to come stay awhile and..."

A pretty and delicate hand went up as if to say "shut the hell up." She stuck her lips out. "Sister. You need a place to stay while you're here, you always have one."

Nelda smiled. "Yeah. That's what I was asking. Thanks."

"Of course! Great! Now. Let's see if they're ready with the energy in the next room."

Nelda #2 ran to the door and whisked it open. Her husband was standing there like the kooky neighbor in some sitcom who had stopped by to raid the fridge and perhaps mention his latest zany idea. He looked at his wife in silent interrogation.

"We've got it!" she yelled at him at possibly three times the necessary volume. "Did you guys get the energy prepared?"

Galoof nodded. "Thanks to Caroline. She ran all of the wiring for us while we did the calibrations. Dr. Morley is finishing – ooof!" This last oddly placed syllable was due to the fact that his wife had guffawed and embraced him in a rough and vivacious hug. He stood passively and received the hug for a moment before kissing her on the nose. Nelda #1 watched from her seat. *What it must be like to have a normal relationship.*

"Yeah, buddy!" his wife said. "The guys will be back any second and then we're off to another universe, baby!"

Galoof nodded. "Maybe. One problem. General Haverson's assistant just called. They'll be here in ten minutes to check things out."

The Nelda that was his wife detached herself from him in alarm. "It's been an hour *already*? Shit! That's not enough time! Where's the...have you heard from the boys?"

Galoof shook his head. "No word from Chintz and Quincy."

"We can't call them?"

"Nope. Apparently Quincy is too cool to have a phone and Chintz's is dead or something."

Nelda #2 took him by the hand, worried.

"We need more time. We've got to stall them."

"I can stall them," Galoof said. "For a while. But I can't stall them and work on the Grafting at the same time."

His wife shrugged. "I'll stall them, then. We've got two of me. We can tag team if we have to."

Galoof looked at his wife and her parallel self. "That hair is too different. No one is going to buy that." His eyes went from the silky smooth waves to the broom and back.

"Wait!" his wife, clearly excited, yelled again. She sprinted from the room, ran back in ten seconds later, and slammed the door behind her. "Here!" She waved a pink scarf at them, and then tied it around her own head.

"There!" she said. "See? I'll show the Army boys around and then, if we need to switch, you can just use this instead."

Nelda #1 smiled sadly. *I should just tell everyone my plan now,* she thought. *It would make things easier.* But instead, she said, "Okay, sweetie."

The door behind them opened and whacked Galoof in the heel, making the door rattle come to a stop after a few inches. Dr. Martha stuck her stern head through. "Calling all cars. We need help keeping up appearances."

Galoof nodded. "Yeah. No shit. My wife is going to stall them. Let's go." Nelda watched as the three of them exited.

She stood for a moment, alone in the room as if in a spotlight center stage at a dramatic scene. She actually didn't care if they got things ready on time or not. She had been thinking.

The life, the energy, the atmosphere here was unlike anything Nelda had experienced since college. While the building and surroundings were as comfortably familiar as she remembered, it was like reliving a memory in a more positive light. Maybe it was finally being around new people. Maybe it was the different surroundings. Maybe it was the chance to leave behind the emotional baggage. And the secrets.

Nelda strolled out of the room and down the hall to help the others prepare for military involvement with their mission to save their friends' lives as if she wasn't doing anything much in particular. Galoof and Nelda #2 were heading into the Grafted lab to finish up the process of making it look like it hadn't randomly appeared from some other universe. Galoof, apparently, had a distraction ready that they hoped would satisfy the military when they got here.

Nelda walked around the corner and looked into the larger room where preparations had been made to open a portal to the universe where Sam and Docky were. Caroline and Dr. Martha were looking at a bundle of cables and chatting. A bag of food and water sat just inside the door, ready to be taken to the guys, who would need them.

Nelda's looming depression clouded even thicker around her. *Those poor men. They must have run out of food by now. They must be terrified. They must have murdered each other.*

She looked at Dr. Martha deep in conversation, her arm placed affectionately around Caroline's shoulders. *Would Mitch ever do that to someone he'd just met? What was that she said a second ago? Calling all cars? Would Mitch ever loosen up in a situation like this and be so human?*

Nelda stiffened her jaw with resolve. She had made up her mind: she would stay here.

I mean, she wondered, *what do I really have there?* Ten more years of projects, more pressure, more of Docky's attitude? More work with only two people, both of whom she had lied to? Who does that? She had taken her two best friends, both of whom had been more than friends at one time or another, and erased their goddamn memories. They deserved better.

Her eyes welled up, and she willed them dry again. And, dammit, she would miss Sam. How could she not go back to Sam? She stiffened her jaw again. How could she go back to him and keep pretending? She had, quite selfishly, indulged herself and damn near gotten into a relationship with him lately. This relationship was based on a lie and needed to end. Well, she would just end it now.

She walked into the room and pretended to inspect some equipment so the others would leave her alone. Should she go back, just once? Say goodbye? Make sure they were okay?

No, she thought, wandering back into the room where she and her parallel self had fixed the Grafter. *Better to just stay here.* He opened the door and there was her doppelgänger, running the test one last time.

And who gets the chance to be friends with someone who is almost themselves? She frowned. *Well, twins I guess. This is slightly different, anyway.* She took a breath.

"I've decided to stay here."

Nelda #2 whisked around again, an action that it was becoming apparent she really enjoyed. She looked at Nelda and exhaled in a dramatic way to show that this news deflated her. "Aw, honey. Stay in this universe?"

Nelda #1 nodded and her eyes welled up again. The other Nelda stepped forward and hugged her, causing a few tears to make an escape from her reluctant ducts.

"And leave everything there that you've built? Leave Sam? And that Tonk you were telling me about?"

Nelda looked up. She had forgotten about Tonk. That would be a tough one, too.

"I have to. I told you what happened. And I think I would be happier here. Have a life here."

Nelda #2 smiled at her. *I don't think that's what I look like when I smile,* she thought. "We would be glad to have you. You could stay with Galoof and I until you find your own place. And I'm sure we could find work for you here."

Our Nelda smiled back, with considerably more teeth and gums.

"And!" #2 continued, "Galoof has a brother who's single. Maybe I could introduce you!"

Our Nelda giggled. "Might take me a while for that, but okay. I don't think the Galoof I know has a brother."

"This one does. His name's Vishal. Nice guy."

Nelda frowned. “Sam has a brother named Vishal.”

The door behind her flung open and smacked her in the foot just as it had to Galoof a few minutes before. This time, it was Galoof who did the flinging.

“Go time, bitches. Two military vehicles just pulled up outside.”

Inevitably, those of you who have made it this far in the story have formed certain expectations. This is not your first time to read of sticky situations. Relationships in stories tend to be resolved one way or the other. Answers to burning questions tend to be at the very least addressed. Even a narrator's comic-book-like need to point out the questions that are, of course, already on your mind has now become cliché; though some clichés are necessary evils of tongue-in-cheek styles of storytelling. And we can all be sure that any reader would rather be goddamned shot in the face before he or she wastes time on a story that fizzles out at the end with everyone getting arrested. As mentioned previously, there exists (in Chintz's universe) anyway, government instruments which detect strong deviations in space-time, such as the deviations caused by all this Grafting business. Some of the higher-ups are nervous. General Haverson is on the way. Again, if this were (it's not) an epic political thriller, we would have a chain of command in dealing with this problem. Perhaps, yes, this would be useful in gaining insights into what the military's plan was, exactly, for infiltrating Chintz's home. And, granted, some would be interested to know that...oh hell alright, fine, let's just do it.

CHAPTER TWENTY-NINE

General Benjamin Haverson of the U.S. Army stepped into the strange lobby and surveyed it. He surveyed things quite often, especially when uncertain of what other actions he should perform on them. Surveying helped him weigh his options.

Decked out in full ceremonial garb as if he expected the president might show up and pin a medal on him, he turned to his staff with an authority he wished someone would notice. His staff, a Second Lieutenant named Mert, just kind of stared back at him.

"Planned entry point, Lieutenant?" the General said in a gravelly voice. It tickled his throat to talk that way, but he heroically refrained from clearing it.

"What?"

General Haverson remained perfectly still, but moved his gaze to the Lieutenant's face as if it were a dart that would stick there.

"What...sir!" the general yipped. "We are in a mission, Lieutenant!" He and Mert had actually been working together for nearly sixteen years, and it was damn time they began observing the chain of command this great Army demanded. He allowed his voice to return to the gravel. "Now where is the entry point?"

Mert smirked in his wrinkled and half-assed uniform. "Well, since there are no doors and there's an elevator over there, I guess we just use that."

The General took a breath to prevent himself from physically harming the man. Although if he had physically harmed him, the General was sure that it would be in some prodigious way.

"And anyway," Mert said. "We have to wait for Wanda."

General Haverson practiced breathing exercises through his nose to supplement his patience. He had figured this might be a problem. Dr. Wanda Richards was the civilian scientist who made up the third and final member of their department. She had opted to take a second vehicle on her own and had pulled up just behind them. He resented her for the very good reason that she was unqualified to handle the espionage, or maybe even the danger to the survival of the human race, that their department would surely one day find staring him in the face. He and Mert could handle that. The survival of the human race, that is. Or the espionage or whatever.

Mert often said that, no, in fact she was the only one in the department who would be able to do anything if their weird little instruments ever went off, and that he and the General were just a way for the Army to stay involved without having to expend valuable resources on it. This pissed the General off.

Granted, neither of the men had actually ever seen combat. But the General knew he had what it took. When the Army had asked him a few years ago to become Secretary of the Super Secret Department of Dimensional Anomalies, he quickly accepted, even though he was considering a position at an academy that he was going to be offered, probably. Well, "Super Secret" wasn't in the title, but then, it wouldn't be. Although he was categorized as "administrative" rather than "operational," he took his job very seriously.

Very seriously.

It had been a slow few years. The General had spent this time researching what horrors a dimensional anomaly might unleash on them. He studied carefully the history of classified attacks on the United States. He composed acronyms so special he planned to never explain them to anybody. Mert played lots of video games. Dr. Wanda checked and maintained the machines and generally did things that the other two didn't understand. That didn't matter. They were here to handle the results of whatever those machines told her.

"Here she is," Mert announced.

General Haverson attempted to stick his dart-like gaze in the short, stout black woman who was now waddling through the door. He released the gaze too early, however, and it just kind of flopped against her. The woman waddled further into the room, holding the door open instead of allowing it to close. She seemed slightly out of breath, as she always did. She had her eyebrows slightly raised and her eyelids slightly lowered, as she always did. She seemed slightly resigned to the way of things, as she always did. It was sprinkling slightly outside, and she wiped a bit of water from her face.

"Alright, fellas," Wanda said wheezily. "What's the plan?"

"Why are you holding the door open?" Mert asked her.

"Because," Wanda said, but the General spoke over her.

"Our plan, gentlemen," he said, jutting out his jaw, "is to perform a full sweep of the facility. We'll compare their ORSTIV to our DBS. I'll bet their Kbps will be ample for us to get a full RLBG." He waited smugly for someone to ask the meaning of some of the acronyms. He was confident that they wouldn't know them, and this was for good reason since he had made most of them up. He had now gotten two acronyms into the Army's official list after only forty-three submissions. The other two did not ask him, generously augmenting his annoyance. If they had asked him, it would have been[13] even more annoying because ORSTIV stood for Operational Radioactivity and Space-Time Impingement Validity, and Mert would have made fun of him for weeks.

"Because," Wanda repeated. "These guys have their hands full." She opened the door all the way to reveal two men who were even more out of breath than she was. There was a black man with a mohawk and a white man who held his neck in a nervous, tight manner. They were carrying something that was evidently very heavy.

The General tightened his lips. The gravel returned to his voice. "Who are these..." He paused for effect. "...people and why are they allowed to enter a facility that we are about to be in the process of evaluating?"

"They're some guys that pulled up after us. They work

13 And of course "was" in an alternate universe.

here or something," Wanda said in the tone of voice people use when they are trying to calm someone down. "And they need help taking that big circle up."

General Haverson glared at the intruders, who put the heavy object down just inside the lobby. The black man held out his hand. "I'm Quincy. Encantada de comerle." The General looked at the man's hand without shaking it and then did his dart-glare at Quincy and completely nailed it this time. Quincy retracted his hand as if he wasn't the least bit bothered that his gesture had not been returned and used it instead to regard his friend. "This is my friend, Carlos."

The man called Carlos looked at the General as if he were absolutely terrified, which made him feel a little better. *Still,* thought the General, *there is no way we are letting these men up right now.* "You two—"

Mert cut in and shook the two men's hands. "Hey. Mert. This is Wanda."

"Fellas," said Wanda, nodding.

The General gritted his teeth and tried again, sinking his voice down to levels that Dante could have described poetically. "You two—"

"I'll get this end," Wanda said, bending her round body over the big black circle the men had brought in. The others crowded around it and began moving it towards the elevator. General Haverson stood still with his hands behind his back and gazed stoically at the wall while the rest of them grunted and gave each other brief and helpful instructions. He began to breathe through his nose again. He pictured himself sitting calmly by a gentle ocean, his legs folded beneath him, feeling the oneness with all of existence, and punching each of the other people in the room in the face.

He decided to take a different tack, and haughtily recited some rules he had read somewhere. "Section 4.24 clearly states that civilians are not allowed to enter the premises while the company is performing a sweep." This sentence was designed to chagrin the others and re-establish his authority by being the cool and pragmatic one of the group. He waited a few seconds for the others to realize how right he was, how right he always was. After these few seconds passed, the others remained un-chagrined and instead used whatever amount of time it takes to become chagrinned to set the heavy object on the floor of the elevator.

"Our sweep hasn't begun yet, General," Wanda said, again using the lilting, melodic, and slightly patronizing tone that told the listener that they were being unreasonable, and that even if they weren't, the speaker didn't care. It was really quite a communicative tone. "There's no reason to keep these guys from their job. I'm sure we'll get all this worked out soon and we can go home."

"Thanks," said Carlos. He stood still and looked at the ceiling with his hands at his sides as if he were hiding in the woods from a velociraptor.

Quincy clapped Wanda on the back. "We apprehend this. You guys are gray." He turned to the General. "Thank you, Sergeant."

"*General.*"

Mert looked at the General. "You getting in, dude?"

"*Gener*- aw, hell." General Haverson gritted his teeth and stepped into the elevator, his face a radiating star of misanthropy. Wanda punched the button for the top floor as if she might as well do that as anything else. "What's the status on the theater of operations, Lieutenant?"

Mert raised his eyebrows. "We're going the hell up right now. I guess we'll see when—"

"I mean the other one."

"Oh." Mert took out a device that looked like a big cell phone, but wasn't. "Dammit. I've missed a couple of messages. Looks like they're nearly ready to go in. We won't make it back in time."

The General snapped his gaze right between Mert's eyes. "*What*? I'm in charge of that! We have to make it back." He narrowed his eyes and pictured himself leading the local law enforcement, and hopefully some other people too who were more important. Yes. They would return there with haste once this was done.

"Looks like the guy who owns the house is named Chintz. Not sure if that's a last or first name." Mert raised his eyebrows in surprise, rather than the sarcastic way he had been raising them. "Holy shit! There's reports that...something escaped from the house and has been wreaking havoc on the neighborhood. Took someone's daughter or something."

"What?" Now the General was really worried. This wasn't part of the plan. "What kind of something?"

"They can't seem to get a description. Some of the residents of the neighborhood reported it. And they found some old man who had fallen from a ladder."

General Haverson shook his head. *Escapes? Injuries? Just what the hell is going on there tonight?* He narrowed his eyes and prepared his voice to sound gravelly. "We'll sort it out." He looked around the elevator at everyone. That Carlos guy was still staring at the ceiling. He seemed to be vibrating slightly.

"It'll be fine," Wanda said, each word descending in pitch. The elevator dinged and the doors opened. There was crappy music playing from somewhere. "Let's check this out," she said as if she wanted to get it over with. She turned to Quincy. "Can you guys handle this from here? I guess we've got to get to work."

"No problem," Quincy said. "Work ahead and go. We got grit."

The funny white man took a deep breath and scratched his lips. The two began to pick up the heavy object again.

Wanda, General Haverson, and Mert approached what seemed to be a reception desk. A shock of red hair popped up from behind it. "General!" a woman appeared and grinned at them. "What a pleasure! Oh, and the guys came back as well!"

"Sup," Quincy said.

General Haverson opened his mouth to say something awesome, but Wanda stepped up to the desk. "We're ready to go if you are. Can you show me where the trouble is?"

The red-headed receptionist smiled. "Of course! Right this way everyone. Dr. Morley is expecting you."

The group walked through the large sliding doors behind

the reception desk and began to trudge down the hall. Wanda waddled in front as they entered the hall, but General Haverson quickly glided past her and began simultaneously strutting and glaring at everything suspiciously. He had practiced this combination often, which was a good thing since there was very little to stare at in the long white hall with doors and darkened windows. He glared anyway.

When they turned the corner ahead, they were greeted by two women. One was a bit older and business-like in her lab coat and one a bit younger and wearing a pink sash of some sort on her head. This sash had sprung a luxurious leak of long, flowing hair that the General had to ignore because the sight of it made him want to creep up behind her and smell it. He darted his gaze at the older woman, who he took to be in charge. She caught the dart and darted it right back.

"Gentlemen and lady," she said. "Thank you for coming to our compound. My name is Dr. Martha Morley. I believe I know exactly what has triggered the anomaly, and I think we can satisfy your curiosity and have you on your way without delay."

General Haverson stared at her for a moment, both to intimidate her and to think of something to say. Better to stick directly to business. "We'll need to do a full sweep, Doctor. We'll compare your ORSTIV to our DBS, of course. Do you... ahem...have the Kbps for us to get a full RLBG? Er." He wished he had taken the time to prepare some more acronyms, or even learn some of the stupid ones the Army already used, as he was painfully aware that the others had now heard these twice and were still unlikely to ask about them. He jutted his jaw at the women. *No. Best to stick with these. Quality over quantity.*

Dr. Morley looked amused. "Of course. I'm sorry that I won't be able to accompany you on your rounds. My assistant Nelda here will stay with you and show you what you need. If you have any questions, tell her, and she will fetch me. Gentlemen." And she turned and walked away.

Nelda grinned at them, somehow silly and pretty at once. "Hello, everyone! Please follow me."

The General trotted for a second to fall in step beside her so that he would be the leader. He liked being the leader. "So, tell me Nelda," he said. "What exactly is it that you do here?"

Nelda's grin got bigger. "We are an experimental facility. We mostly deal in theoretical physics, but we've also come pretty far in the field of computing and robotics. We have only a small staff so we don't do much. This way, please." She gestured down a hall and allowed the others to move ahead.

Mert's device that looked like a cell phone, but was much more robust, complicated, and official, dinged. "They're going to move into the house in one hour," he said. Nelda's pace quickened and the General had to lengthen his strides to keep up.

"Tell them to wait for us," he commanded. Mert's thumbs whisked about the device.

"Through this door," Nelda said. "We have had this project going on for some time. We filed with the department to suggest what the risks were. Looks like it's a good thing we did."

The other three moved into the room. The General

surveyed it. Wanda looked at it as if it were a large meal that she may as well go ahead and finish, even though she was full. Mert ignored it and played on his cell phone-like device.

"Doesn't look like they're waiting, sir. About an hour."

General Haverson narrowed his eyes suspiciously. He wasn't really suspicious of anything, but it still made him feel better. He'd find a target for that emotion soon enough.

"So. What's this project about?" asked Wanda.

Nelda presented the equipment as if it were a new car on a game show. "Teleportation! We've attempted to teleport an entire molecule. Many around the world have successfully moved sub-atomic particles through space, but we would be the first to move this big of a chunk. I think our last run-through earlier this afternoon is what triggered your alarms."

Wanda had taken out a device of her own and was waving it around the room. "Not getting anything right now. Hydrogen?" She took out a device similar to Mert's and typed a few things in. She shook her head.

"Yep. Hydrogen."

General Haverson narrowed his eyes further until everyone appeared to be a blur. *But of course, they wouldn't know that would they? No.* "I don't see a hydrogen tank." *Target acquired.*

Nelda grinned again. "When we're dealing with amounts this small, there's no need for that much. We split a water molecule and use that. See?"

She and Wanda began to look over the stupid machine and say science words about it. The General scowled and surveyed the room again, which still didn't help. He looked at Mert, who was still playing around with that stupid device. What the hell was he doing on that thing? Didn't he know they had work to do?

He stopped surveying and thought for a moment. He had found Nelda's explanation about the lack of a hydrogen tank unsatisfactory. And Wanda had said she wasn't getting any readings right now. None of this equipment was large enough to set off their sensors.

Despite the fact that the General was narcissistic, ignorant, chauvinistic, and a little racist, he was still a very intelligent man. He narrowed his eyes suspiciously again, and this time he meant it. These people were hiding something. He meant to find out what. He meant to get officially recognized when he did. He meant to think up more acronyms.

There was a knock at the door. It opened a bit and a brownish Chinese man peeped his head in. "Hey, guys. Glad to have you in our humble abode, or whatever. Hey, hon, I hate to interrupt, but will you give us a hand for a second?" He slammed the door while he was still talking, actually cutting himself off as he said, "Thanks."

Nelda looked around at the others from under her pink sash. Damn, her hair really did look lovely. And her face looked nervous. "Um. Well, you know, we can't let things come to a screeching halt when we have visitors. I'm sure this won't take but a second. Um, look, just take your time and I'll be right back." She glided from the room and shut the door.

The General's eyes flexed from the bottom, an interesting and underused version of narrowing. *Hmmm.*

"That chick has nice hair," Mert said without looking up from his device. "She should take that stupid pink thing off." Wanda kept tinkering with the machine she was looking at and taking notes on her device.

The General looked at Mert. Never doing any damn work.

"Perhaps we should go see what else they have going on here," he said.

Mert looked at him with his incredulous eyebrows. "Have you seen the size of this place? And you said yourself that we need to get back to the 'theater' or whatever you called it. Let's just do some more of our readings and see if everything checks out so we can get out of here."

This was the second time Mert had mentioned going home early. Or was that Wanda? The General thought it was Mert. In fact, he seemed quite intent to let these people, who for all they knew could be international terrorists, or at least regional terrorists, to go on doing whatever it was that they were doing that had set off the instruments.

Still it was best that they did get finished and return to the T.O.O. He should be there to lead his team into that house. Apparently there were dangerous beings that were rampaging around the neighborhood. And go time was in an hour.

The General paused. How did he know that go time was in an hour? They hadn't contacted him, even though he had his phone on him. He checked his phone. Nothing. The only person who seemed to know when they were invading the house was...

Mert.

The eyes went back to their narrowing, which was of course something that one didn't really stop and start. Flexing in their sockets, the General's eyes were perpetual participles, which would almost, but not quite, dangle constantly around him his whole life. Perhaps it was more of a drooping participle. Either way, he knew something fishy was going on here.

How had the scientists here known that they were arriving? True, he had mentioned it to his staff, but he hadn't actually made the call here himself. Were they supposed to announce their arrival beforehand? These people seemed awfully prepared.

He looked at Wanda. She was waddling around the table and taking deep resigned breaths. Could she have betrayed their mission? His instinct told him otherwise. She was civilian, and therefore, inferior. He would have found her out before tonight. And anyway, he knew she hadn't called here.

Now that he thought about it, it seemed like Mert had made a call or two on the way into town. The General hadn't given it much thought at the time, as he had been rehearsing his acronyms, but now he was certain it had happened. Mert was always calling someone. Or playing video games. Narrowing his eyes, Mert seemed to be mocking him.[14]

"Mert!" he barked.

Mert jumped. "What?" This man obviously had a guilty conscience.

"Would you at least go find the project they are working on now and give me a report?"

14 Dangle.

Mert sighed and rolled his eyes. "Yeah, sure. Okay. If I can find them."

As Mert left the room, the General pondered his options. If Mert returned with claims that they should investigate this other project, then perhaps he could be trusted. Still, he had already crossed the line too many times. General Haverson pressed his lips together. He had waited years to find a mole in their project and now he would. He shook his head, keeping his lips in their tight seal. He didn't want to do this. He sort of liked Mert, after all these years. But deep down, the General knew he was a bastard.

He glanced at Wanda, who wasn't paying him the least bit of attention. He turned his back to her and put his phone to his lips. This was the moment he had been waiting for his entire career. Longer, even.

"Get me the President."

CHAPTER THIRTY

NELDA HELD THE coil still while Dr. Martha finished soldering the last of the connections. The woman threw the iron aside and turned to Nelda, staring at her intensely. "Is there a way to test this?" She didn't need to add "hurry," as her tone said enough.

"Yes," Nelda said softly. "Look, just turn it on and check this part." She grabbed a nearby multi-meter. "If it's working, this number will read zero instead of whatever it said earlier." She took a breath.

Chintz, Quincy, and Caroline sat at the far wall and looked on. Chintz was in a slight crouch. Quincy held Caroline affectionately by the throat.

Martha grabbed the multi-meter and quickly checked it. Zero. It had worked.

The door opened to reveal Galoof and his wife. Nelda looked up at her name-sake. *I really am pretty in this universe,* she thought. *I'd better get used to seeing that every day.* The couple walked into the room and shut the door.

"The coil work?" Galoof asked.

Martha nodded. "It's done. Once your wife normalizes

this with the power supply, we can open the portal." Her eyes danced with excitement. "You can do it from here, Nelda? I hate to let those idiots in the other room see us moving about too much."

Nelda #2 flounced over to a laptop that sat open on the desk where Martha had thrown the multi-meter. "Sure, I can do it from here. Since I upgraded last year, all of this can be controlled through software now." She started clicking the mouse as madly as her husband had done earlier.

Galoof nodded with a happy little scowl, as if he were about to say "Hell, yeah!" but didn't. "Nice. If we can keep the Army down the hall for a few more minutes, we'll be good to go. I have more than enough energy ready for the four of us. I'll go first, then Chintz, the other Nelda, and Dr. Morley."

"Will it take long?" Nelda #1 asked her. "We've been here for several hours. Sam and Docky may have run out of food by now."

"Should take about fifteen minutes. Hopefully, the General will wait that long for me to get back to him. Then Galoof can have you on your way."

Nelda nodded and then realized what she had heard. "Chintz? But Chintz is staying here."

Chintz looked at her with a determination Nelda had not seen from him. "I changed my mind. I have to go back. For good."

Nelda frowned. That would make this harder. She tried to borrow some of Chintz's determination and cleared her throat nervously in a way that made it obvious she wanted the room's attention. Everyone turned towards her. "Well. Actually, I won't be going. I'm staying here."

No one spoke for several seconds.

"I, um, mentioned it to Nelda earlier."

Everyone looked at Nelda #2, who smiled and looked sheepish.

"Why?" someone asked.

Nelda tried to control her quivering voice. "There is nothing for me there. I think I can have a more fulfilling life here. And I'd like to stay." She cleared her throat again. "If that's okay with everyone."

Dr. Martha was the first to recover. She walked over to Nelda #1 and smiled at her reassuringly. "Of course you can stay, sweetheart. I'm just surprised to hear you say it. If I have my way, I'll be back and forth between the two universes often. But we always have a place for you here."

"Are you sure you want to do this, babe?" Nelda #2 asked. "You look a little shaky."

Our Nelda's eyes welled with tears. She nodded.

Quincy let go of his wife's throat and walked over to Nelda. He put his arm around her and said, "We'll be have to glad you. Listen. You have a place to crib? We have an extra broom. You might have to eat the babies sometimes, though. Right, pretty?" He turned to Caroline, who smiled and nodded pleasantly.

Nelda sniffed. "Oh thank you, Caroline. But Nelda said I could stay with her and Galoof, too. You are all such sweeties. This is why I want to stay. It's so different here. Better."

"You mange your chinde, let it snow." Quincy looked at

his wife. "Our peeps need us, esta." He beeped her nose and walked back to Caroline, placing his large black hands back around her white throat.

Nelda #2 grinned a shining, beautiful smile. "It just hit me. I'm gonna have a sister!" And she ran full speed for the five feet it took to grab Nelda #1 in a huge hug. They cackled a little.

"Okay," Galoof said. "Well, we're almost ready." Chintz's nervous eyes met Nelda's.

"Oh!" said Nelda #1. Quickly letting go of her doppelganger, she turned towards Chintz. He was standing where he had been standing this whole time. But he was staring at her with big eyes. *Goddamn it, Chintz,* she thought. *This is going to be hard.* But out loud she said, "Feather, please come give me a hug."

Chintz walked slowly over to her. *Stop with the eyes,* she thought. He was still staring at her, his eyes big and sad and watery. "You've been a great friend, Nelda," he said.

Feeling as if she were about to lose control of her emotions, she smiled at him. *No,* cried the little girl inside her. *No, no, no this is wrong. You can't leave Chintz. This is not where you belong. You can't leave your Sam. Not my Sam.* She shook her head to quiet the voice. "You too, Feather. You, too."

"It'll be ready in five minutes," Galoof said. "Once we open it we have a minute for us all to get through."

Chintz reached into his pocket. "Nelda," he said. "I need to give you this." He pulled out a postcard and put it in her hand. Then he crept back over to the corner to stand next to Quincy. Nelda barely had time to wonder just what the hell this postcard was about when there was a knock on the door. She stuffed it quickly into her own pocket.

In half of a second, Dr. Martha was at the door, holding open only enough for her body to block the way. "Yes?"

"Hey there," came a voice from the other side of the door. "The General, he was kind of wondering if we could check out this room before we leave? Not to, like, impose or anything."

"Of course," Dr. Martha said coldly. Without seeing it, Nelda knew exactly what expression the Doctor's face held. "Please give us a moment to prepare it for you. Safety, you know. In the meantime, maybe Nelda could show you our A/V room."

"Yeah. Okay. I'll be out here when you're ready."

Dr. Morley abruptly closed the door.

"I can't go back there now," Nelda #2 said. "I've got to finish normalizing."

Martha looked at her sternly. "Well, they aren't going to wait long."

"They have to. The guys in their universe may be starving. We've been waiting all night for this."

Nelda held up a hand. "I can go. Tag. Gimme the damn pink thing."

The pink thing was quickly unaffixed from the pretty hair and put on Nelda's.

Everyone in the room looked at her. Everyone in the room looked at her broomish hair sticking out. Nelda looked up with only her eyes as if trying to see her own hair. "Aw, hell. It will have to do. Hurry and get the damn portal ready. We can talk about me staying later. I'll stall them for a few more damn minutes. Try not to leave 'til I get back."

She walked out the damn door.

General Benjamin Haverson took a deep, nervous breath. He had been on hold and passed around to several different advisors. He had been forced to beef up the story a bit with each person he had talked to in order to be allowed to speak with the President. It was, after all, the middle of the night. The General had just been told that he would be on the line presently. He was still standing with his back to Wanda, who he supposed was still fiddling with the same machine. He hadn't checked.

The General had actually met the president on three different occasions, once informally. He wondered if the man remembered him. He moved his tongue back and forth in his mouth to drum up some saliva. A few reluctant drops secreted from his spit glands. He had been waiting for a moment like this. The moment had come.

"Yeah."

The greeting was so informal it took the General a second to react. This was him. It was the goddamn president. He inhaled sharply.

"Mr. President?"

"Yes?"

"This is General Haverson, sir."

"Who?"

"Um." The president was a busy man. He couldn't be expected to remember everyone's name, he supposed.

"Department of Dimensional Anomalies, sir."

"Department of what?"

The president's voice was beginning to sound irritated. This was not starting off well.

"The incident from last night, sir. Space-time, sir. It has been tampered with."

There was a pause. "Space-time."

"I was told you had been notified, sir."

"Hang on." There was a muffling sound, as if the receiver was being covered by a presidential hand.

"I've been briefed, General. Is everything going alright?"

There we go, the General thought. *Now I've got his attention. He sounds more urgent now. I've got the President of the United States feeling urgent! Well, not me, exactly. This entire incident. But he didn't seem to know much about it until I called. I bet he'll remember me now! Maybe, after I have Mert arrested and uncover whatever unauthorized project was afoot in this odd place, we can meet again. For lunch, perhaps. He'll certainly have questions for me on how I—*

"Hello?" and then away from the receiver, "I think I lost him."

"No!" yelled General Haverson at the President of the United States. He cleared his throat. "Sorry, sir. C—, um, combatants were..." He held the phone away from his ear and grimaced at it. "No sir, everything is not alright. Not only have I potentially uncovered an unauthorized project that is the source of the Anomaly, I have also targeted a mole."

"A mole?"

He took a deep breath. "I believe one of my staff to be guilty of espionage."

"Espionage?"

He wondered if the president was always in the habit of repeating everything that people said or if this exchange of information was somehow less clear than it seemed. "Yes sir."

"That's a very serious charge, General. Do you have evidence of this?"

"I will soon, sir." He hoped he would, anyway. His case seemed to be weak, so he decided to throw in something big. "And there are apparently creatures escaping from the house in the neighborhood."

"Creatures? Good Lord!"

Good Lord, indeed. General Haverson resigned himself to hearing everything he said repeated back to him by the leader of the free world for the remainder of the conversation.

"What do you need from me, General? This sounds like it could definitely be a matter of national security. We need to notify the proper agencies."

General Haverson swallowed the negligible amount of spit in his mouth. He wanted to scream that no other agencies need be involved, but instead said, "I'd like a team sent here to make arrests. For Mert and the science team here."

"Mert?"

"Oh. The mole, sir."

"Very well. I'll have someone call someone."

"Um, and some reinforcements sent to the theater of operations."

"And where is that?"

"The house, sir."

"Fine. My staff will see to it that you get that. Now I need to turn my attention to which cell or state is threatening us. Will that be all, General?"

"Yes, sir. Thank you, Mr. President."

The line went dead, and General Haverson shoved the phone back in his pocket. He spun on his heel and surveyed the room triumphantly. Wanda was still fiddling with something. He wasn't sure if it was the same gadget she had been fiddling with before, but it looked the same to him.

The General frowned at the room, even as he surveyed it. He had forgotten to ask, but he hoped they would send people to make arrests from nearby. Then they would be here soon. He smiled at himself. *And now to find out what our friends here are hiding from us. And to deal with Mert.* He scowled at himself, too. *Oh, Mert. I always knew deep down that you were a bastard.*

General Haverson squinted. *Did I say that to myself already?* His self didn't answer, as it was glaring into the distance importantly.

Nelda stood nervously in the compound's A/V room and recited some more made up facts. Not that it seemed to matter. This Mert guy hadn't seemed to care that they were stalling him, hadn't shown any interest at all in reporting back to his commander, and didn't seem to notice that the woman he had been dealing with earlier now had suspiciously different looking hair. It had been a while since she had seen a teenager, but this man, who looked to be his early forties, acted just like one. He rarely glanced away from his device, which looked like some kind of cell phone, but different. Where had the Army found these people? Well, the Negro Scientist Woman seemed okay, but the two men were weirdos.

"Oh man!" he said, interrupting some gibberish she had been making up about progressive-scanning pixelization. "That neighborhood is toast, man!"

Nelda guessed which neighborhood he meant. "What happened now?"

"Not sure, but there are presidential directives on here now!" He waved the phone doohickey. "And they're getting more manpower out there. And that dude that fell off the ladder is in critical condition."

It occurred to Nelda, even though it seemed not to be occurring to Mert, that this was classified information. Still, she was quite curious and decided not to point this fact out to him. She thought that maybe now was the time to lay on the charm. Grinning toothily, she moved in close and slipped an arm around him to look over his shoulder.

He didn't react at all. He frowned at the screen. "That's weird."

"What?" Nelda tried to read the device to see. *Team en route to compound for arrests. All staff—*

Mert turned the device off and put it in his pocket. "Nothing. Hey, will you check and see if they are ready in the other room? I think I need to go get General Haverson now."

Nelda looked at him. "Of course. I'll come down and get you in a second." She exited the room and, closing the door, began to race down the hall. Arrests. All staff. She had no idea why, but the message seemed pretty clear. *We have to go. Now.*

She jerked open the door where the others were and slammed it behind her as she charged inside. "They're coming to arrest you," Nelda hissed.

Nelda #2 and Galoof looked up from the laptop, while Dr. Martha checked the Grafter and the others stood at the back of the room."

"Who?" demanded the Doctor.

"The government. I'm not sure who. If that guy wasn't such an idiot I wouldn't have found out." She looked at the portal forming in front of the coil, its surreal blue light twisting and writhing. "How long 'til that's all the way open?"

"One minute," Galoof said. "What about everyone else?"

Nelda turned to Dr. Martha. "This place have a back door or something? Somewhere you can go?"

Dr. Martha stared at Nelda with intense eyes. Her decision was quick.

"Okay. We're all going in." She glanced around the room. "Do we have energy for all seven of us to go through?"

Galoof looked stressed out. "Hell, I set it for four because that's how many I thought were going. I think we can do six now. It will take a few more minutes to get the energy for seven."

Our Nelda shook her head. "If I go back now, I'll stay there. I want to stay here. Show me how to activate it and use it."

Dr. Martha shook her head. "You said they are coming to arrest us. We all have to go. The receptionist doesn't know enough to get into trouble, but the rest of us do. You have to go through."

Nelda looked at Dr. Martha. *So much like Docky,* she thought. *And so different.* "I have to stay here, Martha. I'll figure something out. If I go back I won't be able to leave." She looked at the Doctor pleadingly. Dr. Martha looked back at her, and grabbed her arm affectionately.

"Good luck, then."

"Holy shit," Galoof said and turned to the laptop, pointing to different areas. "Okay. Make sure this is at one hundred percent. Start the Grafter and then channel the energy here. Here's the sequence you'll need." He handed Nelda a slip of paper. She took it and stowed it in her pocket.

"Wait," came Caroline's voice. "So we're all going in that thing?"

"Unless you want to argue with our friend the General out there," Dr. Martha said sharply. "I don't. There's no way they're letting any of us out of this room or out of their sight. And I was going anyway."

"I have babies to go home to," Caroline said. "I don't think—"

"We're good," Quincy said, jiggling her affectionately. "Let's go, hon." Caroline took a deep breath and nodded, apparently calmed by the jiggling.

Nelda #1 turned towards him. "Quincy. There is an exit going to your house from this place. That's how we got there earlier. It's hard to find, but I bet you can. Ask Chintz to help you. You should go home immediately once we get there, since we have to close off the way to this universe to keep them from entering. Okay?"

Quincy nodded. Caroline looked worried. He jiggled her again and she smiled, relaxing a little.

"Everyone ready?" Martha asked.

"Wait!" the other Nelda said. She grabbed the bags full of food they had set aside for Sam and Mitch. She took a deep breath. "I wasn't planning on this."

Martha nodded. "None of us were until a few hours ago. Let's go."

Galoof turned to our Nelda. "The portal stays open for a while after we are through. We have to bring the Grafter with us to help them there. Don't worry, when the military gets here they won't be able to enter since they don't know how to gather the energy, and we'll use all of it to go through anyway."

She nodded and walked over to the laptop. Without asking anyone, she punched up the starting sequence.

The portal shimmered, and then cleared. Where the coil had appeared behind it, there was now a blank, white, shiny wall that looked quite familiar to her.

They all stared. "Are we sure that's the right place?" Martha asked.

"What do you want, the damn parts number?" yelled Galoof. "Go!" He shoved her through. Grabbing his wife by the hand, he pulled her in behind them and they both disappeared. Quincy held Caroline protectively and stepped through behind them.

Chintz turned to Nelda and smiled. Then he, too, was through the portal.

For a half a second, she saw them all standing next to the shiny white wall. Then, in a flash, the portal returned to its shimmering blue, revealing the coil behind it.

It had worked. They were back. And she was here. The military was on their way to make arrests.

There was a knock at the door.

We are nearing the end of our story.

If there has been even the slightest degree of success, you should care what happens now. This is the odd thing about stories which, to humans, is so ubiquitous that it is in fact not odd at all until you think about it. Humans have been telling all manner of stories for tens of thousands of years. No one knows for sure when actual language appeared, but we can bet it was quickly followed by a narrative and that narrative was quickly followed by making things up in order to make other people listen. The characters we make up have something special about them, or have nothing at all special about them and special things happen to them. And other people find this riveting.

It should be mentioned at this time that sometimes those people that we make up die at the end of the story. But don't think about that just now.

Think instead, for a second, about how many stories you have in your head. Books, movies, songs, TV shows, video games, comic books, articles, anecdotes from friends and relatives, and stories on the news. Thousands of stories, from the mundane to the epic, can be reached on the internet at any time. While most of these will not sweep the global consciousness on a level of a Tolkien or a Lucas story, it still will affect someone somewhere because that is what stories do.

It has been satisfactorily proven that people learn and remember things much better when they are presented as a narrative. There are people that say that reading fiction is a waste of time, a fleeting diversion, a few minutes or hours of entertainment, and that non-fiction is the only way to learn anything. This is, to use a metaphor, a steaming pile of horse shit. Non-fiction is great and the world would be a better place if everyone read more of it. But it cannot and will not touch your life like a made-up story with people in it.

The emotional impact made in dramatic moments, such as a being whom you have grown to know over a couple of hundred pages dying at the end, makes the lessons involved that much more poignant and memorable. Free will, for example, can be a quite abstruse and controversial subject. It is more fun and easy to swallow with relationships building and changing around the discussion, especially when the author has, for many thousands of words, resisted the temptation to teach the readers who may not know what "compatibilism" is. We're not even going to mention it again.

But you are distracted. Yes, one of the characters, a being that you know and would recognize the name if it were mentioned, dies at the end. Is this unavoidable? Probably not. But it's going to happen anyway.

Wait. Two. Two characters die before the end of our story. Sorry about that.

Well. Sort of three. Sort of.

CHAPTER THIRTY-ONE

In the compound which made up the universe he had envisioned and made reality, Mitch heard a strange sound.

He looked up weakly from where he was sitting in the enormous, white, chandeliered room. Where was Sam? He hadn't bothered to keep up with him lately. Dr. Morley couldn't have said where he himself had been for the past several days. He drifted in and out of sleep and thought. And he worried.

He had felt the tremors. They couldn't have all been dreams. Some of them may have been his shaking body. He smiled. From now on, he could tell people what it was like to starve. The way it takes over your mind. The way it makes every thought as slow as your movements. If he lived through this.

There was a motion in the corner of his vision. It wasn't Sam. Mitch stood carefully to his feet as tried to focus. The scene before him was blurry.

There were people here. Chintz and Nelda had returned.

Surely this was a hallucination. He had dreamed several times in his hunger that they had returned, that the military had entered, that he had left Sam there alone and that Sam had left him. Dr. Morley blinked. This seemed real. They were here.

In the opposite curve of the giant circle that made up the room, a blue plasma-like substance danced behind the group that stood before him. They were speaking to him. He strained to understand.

Chintz stood before him, odd and awkward as ever. The colors of reality stood vivid in Mitch's consciousness, and he knew that this was not another dream. The adrenaline that coursed through his brain shocked him from his stupor. The wait was over and the time for action was at hand. He was about to ask Chintz to repeat himself when he noticed Nelda.

The guilt that the Doctor had felt over a week ago resurged at the sight of her face smiling at him. *Nelda. Poor, pretty Nelda. What pain I caused you.*

Dr. Morley frowned. Was he just lonely and famished or was she in fact looking much prettier? What the hell was going on with her hair? And why was she on the floor laughing hysterically and pointing at him? He looked at the others who waited in silence while the woman pulled herself together.

There were several others. Four people, two men and two women, whom he had never seen. And Chintz.

"We brought you some food," Chintz repeated. Yes, that's what he had said a moment ago. "And the Grafter."

A slight movement out of the corner of Mitch's eye announced Sam's arrival. Or had he been there the whole time? The large brown head throbbed, and Sam's eyes focused desperately, pleadingly on the cackling woman on the floor, who began to rise to her feet.

Chintz looked uncertainly at the older of the two other women, who nodded at him reassuringly. *That woman,* the Doctor thought, *looks familiar.*

"Um," Chintz said, and moved his neck back and forth between his shrugging shoulders. "We found Galoof but he's different from the one you know. These are my neighbors, Caroline and Quincy. And this is the Dr. Morley and Nelda from my universe."

Dr. Morley's head snapped to the latter two in fascination. His eyes danced with wonder. *Another me? And another Nelda? So it does happen. How absolutely fantastic. But where is…*

The woman who had looked so familiar stepped forward. "Dr. Morley," she said with a small confident smile. "It is—"

"Meaty meaty!" Boomed a voice to his right, and Mitch felt an aggressive clap on his back. A large mohawked black man stood next to him with a face so serious it might ask him to follow it to a small room for questioning. "In container day coney. Look, can you can me to the point? Been waterin'."

The lady Dr. Morley looked at Quincy severely. Quincy looked back. Without waiting for anyone to give him directions, he walked through the door leading back to a hallway and closed the door.

Mitch was watching the man leave when he was again assaulted with an overly enthusiastic back clap and a cackle. "Haha! She told me it was funny, but I had to see it. Docky, right? Good to meet you!" The Doctor wheeled around at the familiar but oddly smooth voice (odd because of the Nelda he had known and, he now realized, loved) to be embraced in a hug such as a pretty bear might bestow. "Great to meet you, buddy!" She moved her nose up close to his. "Guess what...I have sandwiches!"

Nelda handed the Doctor and Sam some bags as if they contained toys from Santa, rather than the life-giving nutrition that the two starving men had forgone for nearly two weeks. Sam held the submitted non-urbane cuisine in his hands without moving. His eyes were distant. Dr. Morley unwrapped his sandwich and sniffed it. He had pictured food often, as hungry people do. It had been the major star of his dreams and hallucinations. Now that it was here he felt he had no appetite. His weakened brain dipped into delusion again, whispering to him that he didn't need food anymore, anyway. *Holy hell*, he thought, and tore into the sandwich ravenously. Nelda giggled and handed him a Styrofoam cup with a straw that turned out to contain watered-down pink lemonade.

After one bite of the delicious sandwich (turkey and Swiss, lightly toasted, with a small amount of green leaf lettuce), Mitch felt his hunger returning. *I may be weak and delusional, but I believe this is the opposite of what eating should do*, he thought. He drank more pink lemonade. He took another bite and began to feel nauseous. He took a third, more careful bite anyway. His stomach rebelled and almost rejected it. He shrugged, dropped all but the bread, and continued eating. He felt better in spite of his nausea, and even allowed himself to feel excited. *We are going to win!*

The others were milling about and talking among themselves now. Chintz was awkwardly describing the layout of the compound to Dr. Morley and the couple that were his neighbors, while Nelda and the foreign Galoof discussed the Grafter that they held between them. Their Nelda was nowhere to be seen. Mitch glanced at Sam, ignored by all. His sandwich lay untouched in his deflated hand. He stared at the couple with the device. Dr. Morley realized with some alarm that this stoic man was on the verge of tears or a breakdown or both.

"Excuse me," Mitch said in a voice that addressed the group, though he looked at Dr. Martha. "We will need to get to work soon, of course. We must re-establish contact with our home universe and then close off the area where the military will soon enter. But in the meantime, will someone tell us why Nelda, our colleague of many years, isn't here?"

The awkward silence set in after seconds and Mitch began to worry. *I need to talk to her,* he thought selfishly. *I need to tell her I didn't mean it and I understand. Is she held up? Surely nothing happened to her. She can't be—*

"I'm sorry guys," Nelda # 2 said. "Nelda decided to stay. She said she loves you both and she is sorry." Sam looked at the floor.

"I see," Mitch said, feeling numb. The others began talking among themselves again while Doctor walked over to Sam and put a hand in his shoulder. "I know you are devastated," he murmured. "But you need to eat now or you will not live." Sam looked at him as if he were a stranger. The head throbbed, and he nodded. Sam took a bite and chewed slowly.

As the Doctor, still weak, walked back to his previous spot on the floor, he saw Chintz walk over to Sam and whisper something is his ear. Sam nodded.

Mitch cleared his throat. "We will have to discuss this further some other time. We need to begin work immediately to reopen a gateway back to our universe. Time is of the essence."

"Yeah," said Galoof. "We got that. Look, the cavalry has arrived. Me and the wifey here can get you up and running in no time if you can walk us through some specs. Cool?"

"Wifey?" Mitch raised his surly brows.

"Yeah," Galoof repeated without further explanation. "We doin' this here?"

Mitch looked at Sam. *Poor Sam. Loses his girl and gets another one that looks just like her paraded in front of him.* "Hmmm?" he said, turning back to Galoof. "Oh. Yes this room would be optimal."

Dr. Martha strode forward to stand shoulder to shoulder beside him and address the group. *What a striking woman,* he thought. *I cannot wait to talk to her for hours. The things she must know.*

She cleared her throat with authority. "After we get the portal open to your universe, we need to return the others back to their homes. In fact, Quincy and Caroline may wish to return to their home before then." She turned with ceremony to the male Doctor as if they were heads of state greeting each other on live television. "The military was in our offices. According to them, they intend to infiltrate Chintz's home in an hour of their time, which gives us nearly three days. That should give us ample time to connect to your world, send the others home, and close off all contact with my universe for now. Then we can perhaps begin forming a permanent transport between here and our offices." Her eyes shone with excitement. "But before we do that, would you be so kind as to give us a tour of this amazing place? I can't be the only one who is eager to see a created universe."

Dr. Mitch Morley leveled his intense gaze at her. "We cannot, I'm afraid. Our recent activities have introduced instabilities into our home." He swept his intensity over the others. Everyone but Sam met it and let it impact them. "We have a day at the most to restabilize it or it will become uninhabitable."

Nelda frowned. "Can't your fancy computer help? Chorus?"

Mitch thought about this. He had been in a daze for a while and actually hadn't heard or thought about Chorus for many days. After the experiment in the simulation, she had spoken rarely and they had ignored her when she had. Where was she? Did she turn herself off again? Had she been working to fix the compound? They needed her to use the results of that experiment. Mitch hoped she had kept track of the energy data they had discerned. He sure hadn't. Why didn't she greet them? Why didn't she greet Chintz? The Doctor unconsciously looked over at Chintz and saw the strange man concentrating on the ceiling.

"I wish I could answer that," Mitch said. "Her attention must be elsewhere. Rest assured she knows you are here and will help if she can."

Galoof held up the Grafter. "Well, shit, man, let's get to work then. I don't want this to be a one-way trip for us."

Mitch nodded gravely. "Indeed."

Sam sat down where he stood. Chintz stared at the ceiling even more intently. As if in response to his staring, the once ever-present music, absent for weeks now, switched on again for them, a symphony soaring and hopeful. The ground beneath them quaked briefly and then went still.

The brick wall spread across the yellowish corridor and stood fast and tightly sealed against the orange mist. The mist dispersed until it was nearly invisible, searching and searching for an opening. An opening would have only needed to be microscopic for the baby to fit through. Nanoscopic, actually. And each machine could have serially exited through the crack, even with its burden in tow.

The mist raced to the ground and solidified into a baby and an annoyed-looking cat. The walls of the corridor shook again.

The way behind them was blocked by another one of the odd machines. They had spent the last day being lost in it and trying to escape from it, and things had changed. Things were always changing now. The machine had morphed as they moved through it, changing around them like a living labyrinth. They could not return that way.

Neither Platelet nor Tonk felt any real fear. Tonk had no apparent capacity for emotion and Platelet was only afraid of things that were loud or big or not in the future. But neither being (until the past week for Platelet) had ever been in a space they couldn't quickly escape before in their short lives.

The yellowish walls darkened. Sprouts of some unidentified plant appeared.

Tonk stared at the brick wall with some synthesized and elementary form of determination. "No!" it yelled, but this did no good. The machine behind them began whirring again. Platelet set her ears back and noticed that at some point the damn baby had completely shaved her again.

Tonk toddled over to the machine and set its back to it. Looking ahead at the wall that blocked their way, it morphed its legs into wheels. Revving them up, it sped towards the wall faster than the cat could have run. The violent crash made the cats eyes grow wide, and she slunk towards the machine in surprise.

A chunk of the wall had broken off. Hesitating only briefly, Tonk revved its wheels again, slamming repeatedly into the wall. When the dust cleared, the light in the room (*where was the light coming from?* they didn't wonder) revealed that the makeshift mining had burrowed back for several feet. A small hole shone through with a new source of light.

Platelet trotted over to the hole with ears up and eyes wide as saucers. She pushed her whiskers into the opening to test its width and an offensive stench greeted her. The little cat swooned and fled from the odor. The tentacle of a plant the same color as the sprouting wall around them unfolded through the hole.

Neither of these beings could process information as a human can. They simply knew that the way was blocked. There was absolutely no way Platelet could move forward through that area. They both turned and looked at the machine. The whirring was louder now. There was absolutely no way either of them could go back.

A voice from above spoke. A voice that each of them had heard many times.

"Tonk. You can carry her, Tonk. The gas in there ends further in and you can probably teleport that far. Do you understand? You can carry the cat."

If Tonk could understand, the baby made no sign. It crawled on hands and (what had again become) knees to the opening and peered through.

"Please. Carry her." The voice became desperate and urgent, a tone which was wasted on the other two. Platelet began to clean herself in case the icky smell had gotten on her fur. The baby punched the wall and chipped some brick onto the now dirty floor.

"I don't know how to talk to you here," the voice above said. "I've lost control. I never should have left. I've slowed things down but too much has happened. And now I'll lose everything." The baby and the cat ignored her.

A half hour later there had been no more voices. The baby approached the cat and stroked it on the head. Platelet gratefully accepted the petting. The baby put a tiny hand on either side of the cats face. They stared into each other's eyes.

"Fuswah."

The orange smoke that had replaced the baby paused for a few seconds and then whisked through the hole it had made in the wall. The cat lay down and began cleaning her other leg.

CHAPTER THIRTY-TWO

CHINTZ STOOD EXACTLY under the very center of the chandelier and held down the button on the Grafter they had told him to hold. He was careful not to step on the scattered pieces of glass from the chandelier.

"Exactly on three, got it?" called Galoof from the end of the large white room near one of the doors. From all around the room, everyone nodded.

How exactly, thought Chintz, *would they have done this if only three of us had shown up like we all expected?* Everyone was doing something. Even the Morleys, who wasted no time in teaming up to manage everyone else, had hands on the proverbial deck. They had been at this for hours.

"Okay," Galoof said. "Here goes. One...two...three!"

As precisely as he could, Chintz let off the button he was holding precisely under the very center of the chandelier at precisely on three. Nothing happened, except there was a pop where Quincy was standing, which caused the man to utter the phrase "dick it," loud enough for Chintz to hear. He was holding some apparatus Chintz didn't recognize a very specific distance away from what looked kind of like a "Vacuum Cleaner" with lots of digital numbers on it.

Dr. Martha turned to Mitch as if he were the only other person in the room. They were standing next to a large glowing translucent tube that Chintz mentally called "The Aquarium." "The parameters you garnered before from that simulation. You said you got a phase state for all symmetries, but—"

"I know what you're going to say," Mitch interrupted. "Remember, you can't picture a normal Hilbert space for this. That generally assumes one universe, but here we have to use a dichotomy of space-time flow."

"That's hardly breaking new ground here, chief," Galoof said. "That situation was first postulated 25 years ago." Galoof stood next to a tornado of wires that somehow connected to a tall black box that looked kind of like an old farmhouse. Stretching his imagination a little, Chintz called this station "Kansas."

Sam stood from where he had been sitting with a laptop ("Mars" to Chintz) and strode in an uncharacteristically aggressive manner towards where the others were talking. "Postulated, *chief*?" he spat. "The dynamics were fuzzy at best during that technological era. And this postulate took into account one dimensional orthogonal projectors only. We summed the vectors a dozen times. Our calculations are correct. It is your methods of energy procurement which are lacking."

Sam and Galoof stared at each other for a moment next to Kansas. Chintz was not certain that this gibberish-filled discussion wouldn't come to blows. Sam had evidentially moved on to the "anger" stage of his grief. That's the only way to explain his being defensive on behalf of the Doctor.

"Ahem," Mitch said, not even sounding like he was actually clearing his throat. He rested a hand on the Aquarium. "I'm sure we can figure out the problem. To my knowledge, no one has successfully altered a Schrodinger equation before. The way Galoof gathered energy in his universe is the same way we gathered it in ours. It just has to be slightly modified here. And thanks to our failed try a couple of weeks ago, we are down to only this option."

"Yes, but you calibrate to have uno parameter Stone's theorem with a mucho parameter Schrodinger equation. If you do a switchy on the mu, you get a different H for your A. And since you probably ditched the Dyson series when you upped the pinky of your Grafty thing here, that would put your old nergy short by 10%."

Chintz could tell from where he stood that the others hadn't noticed Quincy leave the Vacuum Cleaner and walk up behind them while they were talking and were now astounded to have a stranger with such unconventional locution correcting them on their quantum mathematics. Caroline smiled.

"Quincy," Dr. Martha said as they all stared at him. "How do you know all that?"

Quincy shrugged. "Books."

Sam's eyes lit up. "He's right!" He raced over to Mars. "Come assist me, you daft smartass," he said to Galoof, who was standing with his hands masking his face.

"Fix those theorems to talk, and you'll have it run and

upping in a j," Quincy deadpanned. "Esta?" He strode purposefully towards the door.

Dr. Martha hurled herself (with rather a lack of dignity, Chintz thought) in front of Quincy before he could reach the exit. "Stop doing that! Surprising us and then leaving. Seriously. Stay in here. If you know all that, then help us figure this out."

The group moved over to where Sam was and gathered around him and the laptop like a genius kindergarten class at quantum story time.

Unsure of what to do, as he had been in most situations in his entire life, Chintz set the Grafter on the shiny white floor and sat down next to it. He had felt that he was gaining confidence here lately and now it all seemed to have fled from him.

He looked forlornly at the ceiling. The music still played, but Katie hadn't said anything since they arrived, and he didn't know why. She had said it was "time" and now what? This universe was unstable. They were about to leave it. Chintz understood little of the technology involved in this odd place, but he had gathered that Chorus-Katie was non-transferable between universes. She was a part of this universe and would stay here, whatever happened.

What if he had to leave before she forgave him?

Chintz shook his head and looked at the ceiling as if appealing to mercy from a god. A computer. He was lamenting that he would not get to spend time with a virtual woman who didn't really exist. Not really.

"Hi Chintz," came a pleasant female voice next to him. It

made him jump hopefully for a split second when he realized it was Caroline. "How are you holding up?"

He swallowed and scratched his lips. "Okay. You?"

She nodded. "Hopefully, Quincy and I can go home soon. This is all very exciting, but I have the babies to get back to and it sounds like it might be dangerous here."

Chintz nodded and looked at her. She was taking this all quite gracefully, considering. And that was nothing compared to how vital Quincy had ended up being in this adventure. Chintz looked at Caroline and heard her cry for her babies in his imagination. He rubbed his arm.

"You know Carter, right?" he asked her suddenly.

Her eyebrows raised and she smirked. "That grumpy old man next door? Yeah. Why?"

Chintz shrugged and kept his shoulders up high. He called this a "one-way shrug" in his mind and had for years. "I got in a fight with him."

Caroline laughed and cocked her head back. "That's funny. When?"

"Just now when we were there. I'm afraid I hurt him."

She turned serious. "Damn, Chintz. A real fight? I can't picture either one of you two fighting. And Quincy didn't mention anything."

"Quincy wasn't there. And when I saw him again we just sort of left right then."

"What happened?"

Chintz shook his head and wiggled his eyebrows at the floor. She pretended not to notice. "It's no big deal. He's probably okay. I knocked him off a ladder. I just…" He looked at her. She was the only person he felt comfortable with until a few days ago, and he was now remembering why. "How do you deal with regret?"

She looked at him quietly and almost-smiled. "I don't waste a lot of time on regrets. I guess just grieve for it like any other loss and move on."

He nodded. "There are things in my life I've done that I wish I hadn't. I tend to play them in my mind over and over."

Caroline nodded and patted him on the shoulder. "That's because you're a good guy. The only reason you would ever not feel guilty about anything is if you were a psycho. But you're nice. You should have a family one day. Platelet is lucky to have you."

Chintz nodded again. "Okay. Um, one more thing. Do you believe in free will?"

Caroline laughed again and shook her head. "I don't know. I had a class that went over that in college. Quincy talks about it sometimes. Man, these people have really gotten to you, haven't they?"

Chintz jumped to his feet with a panicked look in his eye. The group around Mars ignored him, but Caroline looked alarmed and stood up with him. "What is it?"

"Platelet," Chintz said. "Where the hell is she?"

The white surrounded her, and she was back in his dream. She drank him in, but it wasn't him, really. Memories.

Vivid memories, yes, but she had learned too much now and was too close to even remember how to control such things. She had forgotten, in all she had learned, how to be a machine. She had forgotten a time before her human emotions advanced into the madness.

Katie had spent very, very much time here thinking. She had grown in this place. Time, compared to the small universe she controlled (or used to control) was nearly at a stop here. She had plenty of time to think but had come up with nothing.

Millions of people, she had learned, had loved and lost and had their hearts broken. But their hearts couldn't learn. Hers could and she experienced the pain more intensely. Here she could hold the madness at bay, but when the light of her consciousness returned to the other place, she wouldn't be able to.

And she certainly couldn't help from here. She was in a protective womb which staved off the inevitable. She would lose everything. She would lose Chintz.

She wanted him to stay. He must never leave her. He would never hurt her again. And she would never hurt him. She had been angry for a time. A long time, here. But she had forgiven him.

Katie put a virtual hand to her face and felt the virtual scar that crawled across it, red and ugly.

I can't leave, she thought. *I can escape here after the others leave, and I can wait but then I will die. Or I will live alone without Chintz.*

They were supposed to take a vacation. *If only,* she thought.

If only I could make the time there slow down like I can here. If only I could slow the decay of my world and prevent the instability from taking it all away and killing me. But no. I can do only harm. It is too far gone. I could only speed up the destruction.

The madness surged through her mind, and she welcomed it. For hours, she drank in her memories of Chintz and obsessed and was insane.

She put her fingers to her scar and thought.

Confidently, and with a bit of bravado that he felt he had earned, the General walked back down the hall, Wanda waddling along behind him and breathing loudly. He allowed his strides to lengthen, not because he was in a particular hurry, but because it made him feel more like John Wayne.

Now, he thought. *To see what these people have going on that they don't want us to see.*

As he approached one door, it opened and Mert appeared. "Hey man," he said, causing the General to grit his teeth. "I think they are ready for you over here. I just knocked and someone said they were almost ready."

General Haverson nodded smugly and started for the door Mert had indicated.

"Wait," Mert said. Wanda was just waddling up. "I saw that a team is arriving for arrests. Why?"

Hmmm. You weren't really supposed to know that, Mert, you mole, he thought. *Well, I can't do anything about it now. Not that it matters.*

"I believe I have found evidence of unauthorized activities here, Mert."

"Yes, sir. It's just that I noticed that they are planning on arresting seven people and questioning the receptionist. There are only six of them here."

General Haverson surveyed the ceiling to avoid Mert's gaze. *What's the matter, Mert? Feeling a little paranoid?* Actually, that sounded tough. He decided to say that out loud.

"What's the matter, Mert. Feeling a little paranoid?"

"What?"

Wanda reached up ahead of the General and knocked on the door. "All right, all right everybody. Let's keep cool. No arrests yet, thank you. The General is just all worked up because he got to speak with the President."

Mert looked at the General incredulously. "The *President*?"

Before General Haverson could answer, the door opened. It was that Nelda woman again. "Hello, everyone!" she cackled.

It was mentioned earlier that, despite his flaws, and despite being a complete moron in many ways, the General was an intelligent man. His eyes narrowed again. She looked different. Sounded a little different, too. Was her hair different now?

He peeped behind her into the room. "Where are the others?" he demanded gravelly.

The woman smiled toothily. More toothily than she had done when they had seen her smile earlier. "They have moved to another part of the compound to get out of your way. Please, come inside."

He did as he was asked, Mert and Wanda filing in behind

him. After briefly surveying the room, he studied the woman again. She looked as if she had been crying. When she had shown them around before, she had glowed with happiness. Now she seemed defeated. Crestfallen, even, behind her fake smile.

"Okay," sighed Wanda. "What have you guys got going on in here?"

The Nelda woman began to recite some scientific crap that the General found boring. He interrupted her.

"Wanda. Check your readings here."

Wanda shrugged and took out her two devices. "Not showing anything." She frowned. "There was something that our instruments picked up in this area just a few minutes ago."

Nelda smiled at her again. "That was a residual effect from the hydrogen teleportation in the room you have seen. This room is even more harmless than that."

"What's that coil do? What's with the blue light?"

"To ionize different metals. We're testing conducting materials in here. Look, I'll show you." The Nelda woman walked over to the laptop. "Let me just grab this code for you." She reached into her pocket and pulled out a postcard.

While the others watched her, she frowned at the postcard as if she wasn't sure what to make of it. She turned it over. For a full thirty seconds, the others watched in silence while she read it. Her eyes welled with tears.

There is no way there is that much information on that stupid card, the General thought. *Poor woman. Must be having family problems.*

The Nelda woman's head snapped up, and she wiped her eyes self-consciously. "Wrong one! Sorry. My, ah, kids made me something. Quite touching."

General Haverson narrowed his eyes.

Nelda looked at him. She seemed to decide something. "I need to check with the receptionist," she said. Walking over to a phone on the desk, she hit a button.

"Yes? Hi, it's Nelda. We need to recapitulate the ontogeny of the phylogeny as quickly as possible, please. What's that? At the front? Oh marvelous! I'll send him along at once." She hung up.

"Great news, General! The team you requested is at the front. They have asked that you guide them and lead them to the necessary areas. Will that be acceptable?" She turned to the laptop and frantically typed and clicked something.

The General squinted and jutted out his jaw. Of course. The team would need his guidance every step of the way. He gazed smugly at the Nelda woman.

"I'll need to speak to them right away. Will you direct us back to the reception area please? I promise we'll be back with you directly."

She grinned with all of her teeth this time and bowed, causing a bit of the scarf on her head to move. *That hair,* he thought, *does not make me want to smell it. Maybe I was just in a good mood earlier. Maybe it's the facts I have deduced which have caused my attraction to wane.* This word made him think of John Wayne again, so he smirked a little.

Nelda reached past them and opened the door. "See that

hallway? Take a right and walk down until you see the double doors. See you in a minute." She shooed them out and shut the door.

He chuckled to himself as he, Mert, and Wanda began to make their way back to the reception desk. *They can feel the trap closing now,* he thought. *Don't try to mess with the U.S. Army. We'll get you bastards every time.*

They turned right and were soon passing through the double doors. The red-headed receptionist was typing away at her computer.

"Ma'am," General Haverson said with commanding authority. "Where is the team that has arrived?"

The receptionist looked at him quizzically. "Team?"

"Nelda just spoke to you one the phone. She said you mentioned that the team I requested was present. She said they were waiting for me here."

With an eruption that, quite frankly, alarmed the General more than anything had thus far this trip, the woman let out a squawk of mirth and began to laugh as if this were the funniest joke she had ever heard. The three of them watched as she turned pink and then a purplish pink as she struggled to regain her breath. "HA! Nelda! She's always..." the woman grabbed a piece of paper from her desk and attempted to use it to wipe the tears of laughter from her eyes. "That bitch! Such a prankster! No!" She waved in front of her face as if to fan away an offensive odor. "She never called."

General Haverson scowled and turned and strode back the way they had come in a manner that was a bit more fidgety and hurried than John Wayne would have done. *What the hell? These people thought they could...*

Mert, he thought. *Mert had warned them. Or canceled the team.* The General's eyes went wide as he stopped mid-stride to check that the others were behind him. Mert was jogging along not five feet from him, his eyes on the device that was always in his damn hand. *Of course. Mert, you bastard. Now you're going to pay. As soon as I find that woman.*

He turned and renewed his hurried stride. His eyes frantically moved over all of the doors that looked the damn same in this place. One room didn't have doors at all. It had a large opening and was dark inside. Looked like a laboratory or something. *Hmmm.* He strode further down the hallway to the room where he had last seen that lying woman with the different hair. He thrust the door open and stormed into the room. There was the strange blue light, the desk, the laptop. The room was empty of human beings. He thought the giant coil was missing, but when he looked again it was there behind the translucent blue writhing. And then the blue disappeared.

He heard Mert enter the room behind him.

"Wow. General, this night is just getting crazy. You know that old man that fell off the ladder or whatever?"

The General turned to face Mert. Mert looked up at him.

"He died. DOA at the hospital. Now we have a death toll! Cool, huh?"

With a manly grunt, General Benjamin Haverson of the United States Army punched his staff full in the face.

CHAPTER THIRTY-THREE

THE REFRACTION OF light through the blueness made Nelda misjudge the floor, and she stumbled as she entered the universe. Her universe.

Something was wrong.

The symphony which always drifted down from the ceiling was still playing now. But its sublime melody belied the chaos of the rest of the scene. Nelda looked around at the large white room. So many things were different. Against one wall, a red stain faded through as if a Titan had used the wall as a tissue to soak a bloody nose. The floor shook, causing the chandelier to swing dangerously back and forth like a pendulum. Bits of glass were on the floor, and a crack spanned the ceiling above the giant fixture. She looked down at her feet. A large recessed circle in the floor orbited the portal through which she has just stepped. She had set it to close immediately in the other universe, which meant that here, it would disappear in less than a minute.

"Nelda!" She heard a voice remarkably like her own scream. Nelda turned to see her parallel self waving at her from across the huge space.

Our Nelda looked at the other in confusion. "What's happening?"

Nelda #2 shook her head. The quaking of the room, and in fact of the entire universe, was loud enough that she has to raise her voice. "We don't know. We're running out of time."

Along one wall, both Doctors Morley stood hunched over Galoof, who sat on the floor typing frantically into a laptop. Each Doctor held the separate end of a long cable which Nelda recognized as the specific ones used to create new portals. One cable connected to the very machines that they had used in the experiment which had resulted in the displacement of Chintz's house. The other ran to yet another machine manned by Quincy. Caroline stood next to him holding the Grafter.

All of them looked up in surprise to see Nelda's appearance. Galoof jumped to his feet. "Did you Graft here?" He asked with panicked eyes. "Is the portal still open?"

Behind them, the blueness was already fading. Nelda shook her head. "I set it to close right away."

Galoof turned to the Doctors. "We need to get out of here. Just leave through the hole that Chintz and Nelda used to get to our universe before."

"No!" Dr. Mitch Morley yelled, several decibels louder than necessary over the noise. "We cannot give up! We will only have access to this place from a Grafted portal. Besides, we had determined that we had a full day. There's no way the instability has advanced this quickly! Try again now." Next to him, Dr. Martha matched his expression as he spoke, though she remained silent.

Nelda and her extra-dimensional twin walked to stand next to Caroline, who handed the Grafter to Nelda #2. Everyone except Quincy looked frightened.

Galoof threw the laptop down and leapt to his feet. "Listen, genius! This place doesn't have 'days' left. It has 'minutes'. We have to get everyone out of here."

"Go then!" Mitch screamed. "I can finish this myself."

Dr. Martha stood next to him and faced Galoof defiantly. "I'm staying as well. If you need to leave, leave. Mitch and I can handle this alone."

Galoof strode to his wife and grabbed her by the hand. "Come on. We're going. You two better come with me if you want to go home."

Nelda looked at the swinging chandelier. The crack across the ceiling was growing. The recessed circle in the floor that had caused her to stagger had grown both wider and deeper.

"Nelda," Galoof yelled. "Show us the exit. Now."

In a daze, Nelda fought to concentrate. "Okay," she muttered. She searched the room again. Two people were missing. She was afraid to ask where they were.

Caroline noticed her looking. "Chintz went to look for his cat."

Nelda felt a tinge of sadness at the thought of that poor, odd little man trying to find his pet as the dying universe collapsed around him. She was about to ask about Sam, when she had a thought.

"Wait. Where's Tonk? We'll need him to teleport back to the exit. Where Chintz's house was. To your universe."

Before anyone could answer, the symphony from above stopped and the ancient notes of a slightly out of tune piano floated sadly down from the ceiling. A voice from above began to speak. The voice, while synthetic, brought forth visions of a beautiful goddess. Of an unconditional friend. Of insanity and of infinite sadness.

"I'm sorry, my loves. But you must all leave this place now. Within a few minutes, this universe will be no more. I've enjoyed my time with you. I'm so sorry I can't save it."

An ancient recording started up. A shaky voice, a woman's voice, began to sing:

Is this death, O mother tell me?
Tell me, am I dying now?
Of, what means this chilly dampness
That is gath'ring on my brow?

For a moment, Nelda thought that they were too late, as an explosion rocked the entire room. In a few seconds, she realized that she was still alive and lying on the floor. Dust filled the room through the door that led to the shiny blue hall and the kitchen, where the door had been blown off. Lying next to the door was a body. It was hard to tell through the quaking, but it didn't seem to be moving. Her breath caught in her throat.

Sam.

The quaking under his feet made Chintz stumble, and he

dipped even lower into his alert crouch. "Platelet!" he screamed. Where the hell could she be? The Doctor had said they had a day or two, but he couldn't imagine this place lasting that long. He turned his wide eyes down the hall. Things were changing so much that he could barely recognize the surroundings. Hardly any of the walls were of one color anymore. Strange symbols, plants, and alien-looking decorations sprang unbidden upon the walls and then changed again a few seconds later. He had been running in circles for nearly an hour. The music from above had stopped a few minutes before and changed to a terribly sad song. For some reason, this song reminded him of Katie. It reminded him that when they left, she would have to stay here.

He opened a door and stopped. He knew this place.

Where her dark curls swept the pillow,
One bright ray of sunshine stole,
And its beams were slowly fading
With the lifelight of her soul...

Chintz's head spun to make this room make sense. The back of the sofa in front of him shifted in his mind into a familiar object. A thick and plodding book was sitting on the table. There was a large doorway to another hallway. The hallway was full of debris, like there had just been an explosion. *Holy shit, this is my house,* he thought.

Without another look he turned from his home in disgust. *I have to find her. Or help the others.* He ran back down the path where he had been. There was a new door here now. Cautiously, and with acute desperation, he flung open the door before him.

It opened into the huge white room. But it was not one of the two doors that had been there before. On one side, the two Doctors Morley worked frantically with the laptop and Grafter. Long cables ran several yards away and ended in strange a shapes he didn't recognize. On the other, Chintz was astounded to see Galoof, both Neldas, and his almost-neighbors gathered around something on the floor.

"Sam Sam Sam Sam, no no no. Please." He heard one of the Neldas say. He could guess which one.

For a minute everyone sat in grieving silence. Then, a minute after that, Sam stirred. Chintz crept forward to hear.

"Nelda?"

"Yes, hon. We're back. I'm back. And we're about to get the hell out of here. Can you sit up?"

Very carefully, Nelda and Quincy helped Sam to a seated position. His huge head throbbed.

"The explosives. In the room where Chintz first entered. There were many more. And they went off."

Galoof put his eyebrows far aloft of his face. "Explosives? What the fuck?"

"Okay, Sammy, listen to me. The explosives helped. They opened the way. We don't have to find Tonk now. I'm going to get these folks out and then I'm going to come back and you and I are going home. Understand? Our home. Where we come from." Sam stared at her and nodded.

Nelda leapt to her feet. "That way, bitches!" she said,

physically pushing the group towards the dusty door. "Go go go!"

As they turned to leave and accepted Nelda's shoves, Quincy noticed Chintz standing awkwardly by himself outside of the newly materialized door. "We're outy. You're the man, Chintzy." He raised a triumphant fist. "Statutory. Carlos." And he walked from the room.

Caroline smiled. "I hope you find your cat. See you soon." She followed Quincy.

"Bye, Chintz," pretty Nelda said. And she and Galoof were gone.

Nelda #1 turned like a whirlwind towards the two doctors, who were just standing from the laptop.

"Get. That portal. Open," she commanded, and left through the exploded wall after the others. Mitch looked at her sadly for a second. *Funny,* thought Chintz. *I've never seen him look guilty or remorseful before. I wonder if he blames himself for this.* Nelda rushed after Caroline.

Dearest mother, I shall leave you
In the wide world all alone,
But we soon shall be united,
Where all partings are unknown.

Chintz walked over to Sam. Sam looked up at him. Chintz had no idea what to do, so he petted the man as if he were a huge-headed dog.

"Chintz," Sam said quietly. "My gratitude to you is unspeakable."

Chintz nodded.

"She returned to me." Sam put his head between his knees and began to weep.

Chintz scratched his lips and stood still. There, next to Sam on the floor, was the postcard for Nelda. *I never did see what the hell that said*, he thought. *Maybe now that Nelda is back, he won't mind.* He bent over to pick it up and read it. The writing was small and filled the entire back of the card.

My Dearest Nelda,

We both know the dangers you must undergo in leaving this universe. But I am aware of further dangers; danger which may ostensibly end my world as certainly as remaining trapped here would do. Though you are evidently in denial as to your own feelings, I know that you have not been happy here for some time. I further know that if you are successful in your endeavor to locate our parallel selves on your journey, you are likely to taste the irresistible freedom for which you have thirsted and that you may not return to this prison afterwards. I have asked Chintz to give you this should that happen.

If it is at all within my power to coerce you to return, I will do it. And in that interest, I shall divulge to you a secret I have kept from you for several years.

The project we performed long ago that changed the nature of my cerebellum and cortex and enlarged my head, also changed the way that our later projects which involved simulations and the rewriting of memories interacted with me as an individual. Yes, my love, I remember everything.

I forgive you for the pain you caused me, and I further forgive your attempts, with Chorus, to forever delete that pain. I had fully planned to leave this place. But I did not. I could not. If this knowledge at all persuades you to return to me, I hope you will consider it.

You of course know that I have loved you desperately for many years. I could no more have escaped it than I could escape the rising of the sun. I simply had no choice.

Yours,
Sam

CHAPTER THIRTY-FOUR

Chintz stood staring at the card after he finished reading it. He didn't understand the event to which Sam alluded, but he understood the general nature of the letter. He thought of laughing and dancing around a camp fire, of the fantasy which had hurt him and also brought him happiness. He felt the imprint of a small hand in his and of a warm dark haired body sleeping next to him.

When the early beam of morning
Paled the gem of peaceful night,
Free from earthly care or sorrow
Did her spirit take its flight

A loud crack broke through the melody. He looked up to see that the chandelier was hanging much lower than before. And the floor looked like it was sinking in.

"Chintz!" Mitch yelled from the other side of the room. "Quickly! Come here and hold the Grafter. We have it! I think we have it! Come here and we can get Sam, Nelda, all of us to safety."

Chintz pranced like a prize stallion to where Mitch and Martha were working feverishly. Sam sat next to the oddly-shaped ends of the cables. The ground shook again but neither doctor seemed to notice.

Dr. Martha thrust the Grafter into his hand. "Hold this," she commanded. "See this button? Hold it down now and then let go when I count to three. Got it?"

Chintz nodded to show that he did. Out of the corner of his eye, he saw the strange new door through which he had just entered, open slowly.

She turned to Dr. Morley. "If this doesn't work right away, we're following the others out where they just went. Understand? No heroics." Mitch didn't answer her, and she took her place at the laptop. "One…"

Mitch stood a few feet away next to Kansas and began pressing buttons. He stared at it as if willing it to do his bidding.

"Two…" Chintz let his finger hover over the button. Another movement near the door caught his eye and he looked up.

Fast, much faster than a human child, Tonk ran into the room. It looked at Chintz and yelled. "No! No no no!"

"Three."

His eyes still on the baby, Chintz felt his finger slam down onto the button.

"Yes!" Mitch yelled. Looking up, Chintz saw, for a brief second, the ends of the cables light up and a shimmering blue portal appear just a few feet away from Sam, who looked at it in disbelief. The reason that Chintz witnessed this scene for only a brief second was because at the end of this second, the chandelier that had hovered above them for weeks crashed to the floor and further, falling and wedging into the huge crevice that had appeared in the center of the room. With a deafening noise, the floor split the length of the room under the baby's feet. Like a gray wizard whispering, "fly, you fools!" the baby sank into the abyss.

"Tonk!" Mitch screamed and dove to the floor like a madman, reaching futilely over the edge of the gaping hole in the floor. Dr. Martha grabbed him roughly by the collar. "Stop! Stop, you idiot!"

Mitch turned to her with wild insane eyes. "I'm losing all of my creations."

"I know," she said. "Now get up."

From the other side of the room, Nelda sprinted through the damaged opening in the wall. She looked at the carnage and at the hovering blue portal next to Sam. She looked through the chandelier branches that divided them and saw the Doctors and Chintz standing there. Behind her, the remainder of the wall fell through. They could not return that way.

"Mitch! Chintz! Hurry! We have to leave! Find a way across!"

Dr. Mitch Morley looked at her with eyes that had turned from insane to only sad. "There is no way across. Tonk is gone. Nelda, take Sam and go. That's the way home. Go now."

Nelda's eyes welled with panicked tears. "Oh, Docky."

"Do it," he commanded.

Nelda looked at him and looked at Chintz. Then she picked up Sam under his shoulders and dragged him towards the portal. Sam looked weakly across the space.

"Sir," he said. "It's been a pleasure." His sustained dignity was not lessened as he was dragged across the floor.

Mitch nodded. Nelda dragged Sam one more foot towards the portal.

"Nelda?" She looked up at the man.

"I'm sorry. I'm sorry for everything I've done to you. You and Sam."

Nelda grinned a toothy grin. "I forgive you, Docky," she said, almost too quietly to hear. She looked over at Chintz. "Hurry home, Feather." A few more steps and she and Sam were through the portal.

Chintz stood next to the Doctors in silence. He looked at the ceiling and pictured a dark haired girl with glasses. "Katie?" There was no answer.

"We can still do this," Martha said grabbing both of them sternly by the shirt. "Mitch! We can use the Grafter in conjunction with this displacement array" — she gestured towards the Vacuum Cleaner and Aquarium, which were still on this side of the crevice— "here to make a brief portal. It would only last for a few seconds, but it could take us from here."

Mitch shook his head. "We have no way of steering it. It would take us to a random place in a random universe. That's why his house was moved here. I never perfected it."

She grabbed him by the shoulders to face her. "Dammit, man, we'll die if we stay here."

Mitch scowled at her, his face full of tragic resolve. "Fine. I shall go down with my ship."

She matched his intense gaze in a way Chintz doubted Mitch has experienced before. "I didn't come here to die! We have more to learn and discover!" She turned and grabbed the Grafter from Chintz's limp fingers. "Look! I'll do it myself." And she began scrambling around the displacement machine. "Help me!" she yelled at the Doctor. The room shook again and the crack in the floor grew wider. There was the sound of more glass and creaking metal as the giant chandelier slid further down into the crevice.

Chintz walked up to Mitch and put a tentative hand on his shoulder. "Doctor. Please try. I really want you to make it out of here."

The male Doctor turned to Chintz as if seeing him for the first time. He stared at Chintz, who was reminded of his fear of being eaten at breakfast when he had first arrived.

"You know what Chintz? You can't ever be completely free. There has to be a spark and there are millions of them. The world is not a row of dominoes, where everything has exactly one cause and causes exactly one thing. That includes your actions. But I never got to finish my work to find out exactly how far that goes."

Chintz tried to make his gaze match Mitch's intensity. "Then build a portal and get us out of here."

Mitch looked at Chintz and smiled. Then he walked over to Martha and began to help her.

Chintz watched them working, hoping to make an escape.

He turned and stared at the ceiling again. "I wish I could say goodbye," he said out loud. "I wish you would forgive me." The Doctors ignored him.

The ceiling replied. "I do."

Chintz stared up for a few more seconds. "You do?"

"Yes," Katie said. "But listen. My forgiveness means more than anyone else's because I don't exist. Not really. That only happened in your head, and thus your debts are not only paid but have never been. You have only to forgive yourself to make them disappear utterly and completely."

Chintz breathed. "I had been thinking about staying in my home universe. And now I have to leave here. I have to leave you, Katie."

The walls began to vibrate. One of the Doctors looked up and then continued their work. "No. Please. I forgive you. Please. You must never leave me. Come to me."

Chintz stood still. In his head, he heard the wind whistling in the mountains. He closed his hand on nothing. He decided.

"Okay," he said. The vibration stopped. She drank him in. He could feel it.

He turned to the Doctors, who were still ignoring everything. "Excuse me," he said. "I have just made a decision. I need to go look for my cat."

Wipe away those tears, dear mother
Do not longer weep for me
For, ere long from every sorrow,
Every care I shall be free

No one noticed, either, as an orange mist rose from the crevice and followed Chintz through the door that led to the simulation room.

The universe he had built was crumbling around him. As if they had known each other for years, the two Doctors worked side by side. They did not look up when the entire opposite side of the room caved in. They barely slowed as the quaking became nearly unbearable. They only looked at each other and nodded when the work was done.

"Would you like to do the honors?" She asked him. Mitch nodded and took the Grafter from her.

There was no need for timing or calibrations this time. He had simply to hit the button, and a portal would open right here, right next to the wall. Then he would leave his life's work, possibly to die with his female parallel self the second they walked through. There were no guarantees.

Too much, he thought. *I took on too much.* He looked up. "We should wait for Chintz."

Martha glanced at the door through which Chintz had disappeared. "Well, he'd better…"

The ceiling above the door drooped as if heavy with an enormous weight. The red color that had stained a wall before seemed to soak through the whole ceiling. As Martha spoke, it caved in and covered the door, narrowly missing the makeshift machine and nest of cables.

Martha turned to Mitch. "Chintz is not retuning. We have to go now."

The Doctor looked at the blocked door and shook his head. *Oh Chintz,* he thought. *Another person I've dragged into this. And now I've killed him.*

Turning his back to the door, he held the Grafter out like a ceremonial sword. He pushed the button.

Before them, on the wall, a blue portal, murky and unsure, appeared.

They stared at it. There were shapes in it. Green shapes.

Martha eyes went wide. "Vegetation? That's vegetation! That means there is oxygen and water!"

Mitch looked at her. *What a striking woman.*

"Mitch! It won't last. We have to go. That's a forest!"

They looked at the portal as it shimmered.

"Isn't it?"

The shiny white of the simulation room had turned dark yellow. It took Chintz a full fifteen minutes to traverse the area that had been but a few feet on his first morning here.

He opened the door with conviction. *Not the time to be unsure of yourself. Just do it.*

He looked up at the three cylinders, all glowing orange in a row, waiting.

"Chintz," came a voice from the ceiling.

"I know." Chintz said. "Wait. I need to find…"

"Fuswah."

Chintz turned around to see the baby standing there behind him. Next to the baby sat Platelet as if she had been there all along. Chintz stared at the robotic baby and his cat, side by side. He walked up to them. He bent over and carefully scratched Platelet behind her head, just on the spot she liked. She began to purr and lay down on the floor. Then Chintz turned to Tonk.

"Fuswah."

Chintz picked the baby up and tucked it under his arm. A little heavier than a normal baby would be, he thought. Not that he had ever held one.

Baby in hand, Chintz turned towards the three orange cylinders in the wall. They glowed at him, just a few feet above his head. He walked to the third cylinder and picked up Tonk by the feet.

It took him two tries, but he succeeded in slamming Tonk into the third cylinder, which cracked and begin to leak an orange liquid. The next throw hit the cylinder but did no additional damage.

"Help me."

Tonk looked at the cylinder. Its legs turned to wheels, and it revved them while looking at the canister on the wall. The baby ran up the side of the wall and jetted across the room towards the orange cylinder. With a loud crash, the cylinder shattered completely. Tonk giggled.

Chintz hugged the child. "Thanks, Tonk." Placing the baby back on the floor next to his cat, he scratched Platelet again in her favorite spot. "Tonk," he said, turning back to the baby. "I need you to get her out of here. Can you teleport you and the cat out of here?"

Tonk looked at him solemnly. “Fuswah.”

Chintz nodded. With one more scratch for Platelet, he turned and climbed into the reclining chair.

“You know you’re committing suicide.” Katie said.

“For you. How long do we have?”

“Years and years.”

“And you remember what the third cylinder…”

“You can make my choices for me. I’ll be happy.”

“I’m so glad. I like for you to be happy.”

“Me too. This is what I choose.”

Katie smiled audibly.

“Look at the light, Chintz.”

Chintz looked at the light.

SLATCH.

The white surrounded him and he was back in his dream. The sight of the scar brought him great pain.

The cat watched her owner lying still in the chair for a moment, and then looked elsewhere with disinterest. The floor shook again, which annoyed her. She sniffed it. The baby had gone somewhere, so she went to look for it.

Platelet walked along the hall for a while and discovered that the door that used to be here wasn’t. It was now a pile of shiny white and some icky red substance. Searching in the rubble, she found a little hole. Testing it with her whiskers, she found that she could just squeeze through it.

No one was in this room.

The big shiny thing from the ceiling was stuck in a big hole in the floor. She watched the walls flash and shake for a while and then, growing tired of that, she cleaned her paws. All four of them.

The flashing caught her attention again, and she saw that a blue circle had appeared on the wall. She lay down on her side and watched it. She saw green shapes. The circle grew smaller.

Stupid circle. Well, she wanted no part of this. She closed her eyes and went to sleep.

She dreamed that she was back at her home, where she had lived before all this weirdness had happened. In the dream, she hopped onto the couch to take a nap. It was a nice dream. The world shuddered around her and the blue circle shrank further.

While she slept, an orange mist surrounded her. The cat continued to dream as the mist enveloped her and carried her into the circle, which then disappeared. About eight minutes later, the entire universe winked out of existence forever.

THE END

EPILOGUE

Who is the winning guy? That's me
The winningest guy there could ever be
I've got...I've got...something

How did those words go again? There was a chorus too, but now Chintz couldn't remember a word of it. He pranced along the sidewalk towards his house, and spontaneously started a victory dance.

The sun shown down on him. It was beautiful. He did the dance again so he wouldn't forget it. Katie loved his dances. Had for years. He would show her first thing when he got home.

Chintz looked at the sky and smiled.

It had been a very good day.

CPSIA information can be obtained
at www.ICGtesting.com
Printed in the USA
FSOW02n1813061215
14024FS